A DEADLY AFFECTION

CUYLER OVERHOLT

Copper Bottom Press

All rights reserved.
Copper Bottom Press
Printed in the United States of America.

ISBN 978-0-9848413-0-1

Library of Congress Control Number: 2011963294
Library of Congress Subject Headings:
1. Women Physicians—Fiction. 2. Psychotherapy—Fiction.
3. New York—History—1850-1950—Fiction.

Cover Design by Katie Francis

To Larry;
and to the memory of Ida Ruperti Marshall,
a.k.a. "SuperGran", 1900–2001

A DEADLY AFFECTION

CHAPTER ONE

The first Sunday of 1907 was so bitterly cold that icicles were hanging from the watering trough spouts in front of Mr. Fuller's house, and the sanitation men had resorted to chipping, rather than scooping, the manure from the street. I barely felt the chill, however, as I walked east across town, warmed by long-simmering anticipation. The months of preparation were finally over. Today, my experiment would begin.

I crossed Park Avenue and started down the hill toward the river, rehearsing my opening remarks. The thing was to appear confident but not aloof. My age and sex would be obstacles enough; I didn't want my subjects to think me unsympathetic. I realized that my shoulders had crept up under my ears, and pulled them back down. My research was sound, my subjects exactly as I had specified. The project would be a success.

I was rephrasing my introduction for what seemed the hundredth time, and had quite lost track of my surroundings, when the screech of a train announced I had crossed into the tenement district. I glanced up to see the Elevated tracks looming ahead of me over Third Avenue, and behind them the clock tower of the Hell Gate Brewery—looking just like an old Bavarian church steeple, except for the two intersecting beer barrels at its apex. As if on cue a wagon piled high with empty saloon kegs crashed down the hill behind me and sped past into the intersection, its uppermost barrels missing the Elevated girders by inches.

I followed it across and turned south on the opposite corner, inhaling the pungent aroma of malt and hops. As a child I'd overheard Nanny tell my brother's nursemaid that you could get drunk just by sniffing the air, when they were kegging the beer at the Yorkville breweries. I'd been quite struck by the notion—and although my earnest attempts to prove it never bore fruit, had been sure that with the right technique it could be accomplished; for I'd always believed that in the strange, polyglot neighborhoods that thrived just blocks from my home, all manner of magic was possible. And now, I thought with a hitch in my pulse, if everything went as I hoped, I just might work some magic here myself.

I was halfway down the block when I noticed the gang of street urchins huddled in front of Griesel's Market. My pace slowed as I found myself searching for the little blonde boy I'd seen before Christmas, when the local Tammany men had been handing out free turkeys and socks and tobacco on the corner. The shop door opened to spit out a customer, and the boys stepped into the warm draft. I saw him then, standing near the wall in a sleeveless coat and knickers a size too small. I felt the same catch in my breath, the same tug in my gut as before. With the uncanny perception of his kind he sensed me watching, and looked up. His expression shifted from alarmed, to wary, to calculating.

He trotted toward me and stretched out his cap. "Spare a penny, Miss?" he asked, limpid brown eyes gazing up at me under a fringe of dirty, oat-colored hair.

Brown eyes, not blue. Chin a little too pointed; mouth a shade too full. I fumbled in my purse for some change and dropped it in.

"Bless you, Miss." Scooping up the coins with red-tipped fingers, he bobbed his head and ran back to join the others.

I continued to the end of the block and across the street, stepping cautiously through the rutted ice in the intersection. On the other side I turned to look back. But the gang had already drifted up the street, and I could no longer see the little boy in their midst.

Forcing his gaunt face from my mind, I turned and continued east along 88th Street, passing row after row of drab brick tenements until at last the Holy Trinity church and mission bloomed into view on my right. I stopped and gazed up at the soaring, golden-hued bell tower. The complex was Serena Rhinelander's latest gift to the city's exploding ranks of immigrants, built on what had once been her grandfather's summer estate. Designed in the belief that beautiful architecture could raise both the spirits and the morals of its beholders, it was a startling oasis amid the desert of brick tenements, with its elegant facades, arched cloisters and park-like grounds set luxuriously back from the street. As I started down the path to the parish house I heard organ music wafting through the open outer doors of the church, where the second morning service was underway. I glanced up again at the bell tower, seeing in its exuberant design a symbol of hope and strength. Armed with the first, and praying for the second, I continued up the steps, under the arches and through the doors of St. Christopher House.

SPREADING MY NOTES on the pockmarked desk that Reverend Palmers had filched for me from an upstairs Sunday-school room, I cleared my throat and addressed the five women seated before me. "Good morning. I'm Dr. Genevieve Summerford." I smiled at the grim-faced woman directly opposite, but received only a ferocious blink in response. "I'm sure you're all curious to know why the Reverend sent you here," I went on, "so let me put your minds to rest. You're here because he believes I can help you."

Still no softening in the wary faces. I glanced around the room, wishing I could have offered them more inviting surroundings. The spot in the parish hall basement had sounded perfect when the Reverend described it; but it was in fact far too large for our little group, a cold and shadowy cavern rather than the intimate space I'd always imagined. The flimsy wood partition that separated us from the adjacent kitchen did little to mute the sound of settlement volunteers preparing lunch, and even less to staunch the scent of warming rolls and beef stew that had been slowly infiltrating the room. I knew the women were only here because they'd been told they had to come, if they wanted their free tonics and powders to continue. The mouthwatering smells from next door seemed just a taunting reminder of this price of admission, so grudgingly paid.

The next line of my notes read, 'things in common—terrible loss'. *Terrible loss.* The words suddenly seemed so inadequate. They suggested something measurable, something outside of oneself; when the losses these women had suffered seemed to have penetrated their very cells, keeping their pasts alive and contentment forever out of reach. Suddenly, an unbidden image broke into my own mind: a small boy lying nestled in white satin, holding a lily to his chest with a waxen hand. As if it were yesterday I saw the unnatural pink of his cheeks, and smelled the flower's reek, and felt again the desperate conviction that if I could just take that lily from his lifeless fingers and hold it in my own, I could make things right again. I could make Conrad whole.

I straightened my note pages, blinking the words back into focus. Looking up, I continued in what I believed was a reasonably steady voice, "You have been chosen for this program because you have two very important things in common. First, you have all suffered a terrible loss. Second, you are all experiencing physical symptoms that have no identifiable cause. I believe the two are related. I also believe that with the proper treatment, you can make your symptoms go away."

One of the women had raised her hand.

"Mrs. Miner?"

"There must be some mistake," she said. "I already have a doctor. I can't think why the Reverend asked me to come."

Four years ago Elizabeth Miner's infant son had suffocated in his crib sheets, while she was taking a bath. Her husband, a longshoreman, had deserted her soon after. Since the child's death Elizabeth had been attending church three or four times a week. According to the Reverend, she'd also become prey to headaches and stomach pains having no apparent cause. Customers at the family butcher shop where she worked reported that her moods had become increasingly unpredictable as well, veering between melancholia and an apparent oblivion to her son's death.

"I'm not an ordinary sort of doctor," I told her. "I don't bring down fevers or set broken bones. I treat a different kind of injury." I glanced across the row of taut faces. "Injuries to the mind."

The tension in the room was suddenly so thick I could have walked to the door without touching the floor. I might as well have said I was going to commit them all to Bellevue. I leaned toward them, determined to make them understand, eager to share the secrets that modern science had revealed. "You see, recently we've discovered that brain cell activity can be altered by painful life events. When a person has suffered a shocking loss, as each of you has, alterations in the brain can produce physical symptoms—things like dyspepsia or headache or rash. Just the sorts of things," I added pointedly, "that have been plaguing each of you."

Mrs. Miner's hands were twisting in her lap, while Florence Bruckner, who'd been having bouts of gastralgia ever since her husband swallowed a fatal dose of carbolic acid, had picked up her handbag and was glancing toward the door. "I'm not suggesting that your pains are imaginary," I hastened to add. "The fact that a stomach pain or a headache originates in the mind doesn't make it less real. But it does make it more difficult to treat. We can't do it with pills or surgery. The only way to cure it is through the power of the rational mind. It takes a combination of knowledge, and will."

Willpower from the patient—'persuasion' from the doctor. That was where I came in. I had only to convince them through the power of my doctoral authority that they could be healed, and those symptoms would disappear. As Dr. Cassell had put it, "Firm authority coupled with appeal to reason will effect the cure." I'd seen it work where baths and massage and electric shock had failed. And I hoped—no, I *knew* that I could make it work here. I leaned toward them over the desktop. "I know you believe your suffering must set you apart forever, but you're wrong. You can stop the pain, if you let me show you the way."

I thought I saw longing to believe blooming in their faces. Elizabeth Miner's hands had grown quiet in her lap. Florence was glancing cautiously, curiously at her neighbor. Only Anna Kruger remained as before, glaring at me under her low-slung eyelids. I turned my attention to her. Anna, the daughter of a wealthy industrialist, had snuck out of her house one night ten years before to elope with a penniless suitor. As she was leaving her civil ceremony she challenged her husband to a race across the street, then watched as he was struck and dragged to death by a streetcar. In the years that followed, according to the Reverend's report, she'd become an habitué of Chinatown's opium dens, fond of wearing Chinamen's silks and a long, flowered braid. She was arrested once during a Pell Street raid, and again for dancing naked in the East River Park, after which her parents washed their hands of her. Now, on her better days, when she wasn't confined to bed by a mysteriously recurring rash, she typed and filed at the church office in return for a room over the parish hall.

"The program is simple but effective," I said, speaking directly to her. "Each week I'll present a lecture explaining in greater detail how your thoughts and feelings are making you ill. After the lectures you'll learn exercises to help you suppress your self-defeating thinking and develop a more hopeful outlook."

Her black eyebrows rose in inverted Vs against her mottled skin. "Are you suggesting we can just will ourselves to feel better?"

"Well yes, that's the gist of it. I'm not saying it will be easy, but if you try there's every chance you'll succeed."

"What makes you so sure?"

"I've seen the program work for others," I told her. "I know what it can do."

She waved an impatient hand through the air. "But how do you know it will work for *us*?"

"I've read your clinic reports. What I've seen suggests that you're all suitable candidates."

"You've read our reports?" She snorted. "Do you really think you can know a person from some report?"

"Of course, it's only a start. But I believe I know enough, yes."

She leaned toward me, her dark eyes flashing. "Then I suppose you know I'd rather have my nails torn out one by one, than be told how to live by people like you."

I silently released my breath. Anna had been locked up twice in City Hospital on Blackwell's Island; knowing the facilities there, I doubted her treatment had been an enlightened one. I could understand why she would view all doctors as enemies. "I don't blame you for being skeptical," I said evenly. "But I would ask that you keep an open mind."

"Skeptical?" She barked out a laugh. "Is that what you call it? I thought the word was suicidal."

I sat back, noting the brilliance of her eyes and the upward thrust of her chin. She seemed determined to bring things to a head. "Would you call yourself suicidal?" I asked.

"You mean do I think about dying? A dozen times a day."

I acknowledged this with a nod. "It doesn't surprise me that you'd want to stop the pain."

"Doesn't it, really?" Her eyebrows snapped together. "Maybe you'd like to watch me do it, then." She reached into her skirt pocket and pulled out a thin, silver instrument. Her thumb pressed against the side and a narrow, two-edged blade sprang out of the tip. The women on either side of her gasped and pulled back, scraping their chair legs over the floorboards.

Anna turned her free arm over and raised it toward me. "I could do it right now," she taunted, holding the blade over the exposed wrist. "That would be a certain cure, wouldn't you say, Doctor?"

A brittle silence had fallen over the room, so complete I could hear the stew pots simmering next door. I held her gaze, searching for her real intent. I didn't see surrender in her eyes. I saw a woman who, if she was going down, would go fighting all the way; a proud woman in terrible pain, who didn't know how to ask for help. "If you'll give me a chance," I said slowly, "I can show you a better way."

"What could you possibly have to say that would be of any use to me?" she asked, with an angry toss of her head. "You don't know what it's like." She pounded a fist against her breastbone, eyes glittering now with tears. "You don't know how it *feels*. You don't know anything."

Murmurs of agreement fluttered through the room. Glancing at the others, I saw that if at first they had been frightened by Anna's behavior, now they appeared to be coalescing around her words. I could see doubt hardening their faces, their willingness to believe withering under Anna's scorn. My chance of helping them, of accomplishing what I'd worked so hard for, was vanishing before my eyes.

I gripped my stack of notes. I couldn't lose them now. I had to do something—anything—to gain their trust. I felt my mouth open, and heard myself say, "You're wrong. I do know what you're going through, because I've gone through it myself."

My words dangled in the air between us, causing me a prickle of anxiety. A psychotherapist wasn't supposed to reveal the details of his personal life; he was supposed to lead by word, not example. But it was too late now to take it back. "I've lost someone, too," I repeated. "Someone very dear to me. I know what it's like."

Anna studied me for a long, silent moment. At last her chin lifted in the barest of nods. With a little sniff, she snapped the blade shut and dropped back against her seat.

Their eyes all now turned to me. I shuffled my notes, spilling some pages over the side of the desk in my agitation. Margaret bent to pick them up and handed them to me with a shy smile. I laid them on top of the pile, feeling off-balance, aware of a shift in the room but unsure if it was for better or worse. "Well then, if there are no further questions, why don't I begin today's lecture . . ."

Before anyone could raise a hand I plunged into my prepared material, eager to be back on familiar ground. I'd worked long and hard on my first lecture, and it comforted me now like an old friend. My little slip couldn't be fatal, I decided as I made my way through the outline, explaining how Mr. Darwin's theory of species evolution applied to levels of complexity within the brain. The material spoke for itself. The women couldn't help but be impressed and encouraged by what they'd heard.

And yet, when the lunch bell rang and I finally laid down my notes, I could detect no visible signs of excitement among them; nor did a single hand go up when I opened the floor to questions. "No questions at all?" I asked, scanning their faces in concern. Where was the interest I'd seen earlier? I had barely brought the class to a close before they were rising from their chairs and heading for the open end of the partition.

I stood and trotted alongside them. "Thank you for coming," I called to their backs as they filed past. "I'll see you again next Sunday!" As they disappeared into the lunch crowd that was gathering in the adjoining room, however, I couldn't help wondering if I'd ever see any of them again.

I turned slowly back into the room, trying to fathom what had gone wrong. Was it my disclosure that I had suffered, too? By making myself one of them, had I compromised my position of authority? The possibility so consumed me that it was a moment before I realized I wasn't alone.

I pulled up short as I saw that Elizabeth Miner was still in her chair. Her head was bowed and her hands were pressed to her eyes. "Mrs. Miner?" I walked over and sat beside her. "Mrs. Miner, are you all right?"

She looked up with a sigh, wiping away a tear. "Please, call me Eliza."

"Of course, Eliza; but won't you tell me why you're crying?"

"It's just that I miss her so much."

"Miss who?"

"My daughter."

I glanced toward the patient folders on my desk; I could have sworn it was a son who'd suffocated in the crib sheets. "You had a daughter?"

"A beautiful baby girl," she said, with a quick sunburst of a smile. "I named her Joy."

I was certain the Reverend hadn't mentioned a daughter. I supposed the child must have died before he'd arrived in the neighborhood. Which meant that this poor woman had lost not one child, but two.

"I think about her all the time," she was saying. "Even though I know I shouldn't."

"I'm so sorry."

Her eyes welled with more tears. "They wouldn't even let me hold her," she said. "They just wrapped her in a blanket and took her away."

I shook my head in silent sympathy.

"They said it was for the best," she went on, "that she'd have a much better home than I could provide."

I stopped shaking my head, and stared at her. "You mean she didn't . . . she wasn't . . ."

She waited, eyebrows knit, for me to finish.

"Who said she'd have a better home?" I asked finally.

"Why, the doctor. And the nurse, who took her away."

"I see," I said slowly. "How old were you when this happened?"

She looked down at her lap. "Fifteen."

Fifteen, and they had taken the baby away. I thought the pieces were beginning to fall into place. "I gather you weren't married at the time."

She shook her head, staring at her knees, and mumbled something.

"Excuse me?" I said, leaning closer.

"The doctor said I was wicked to have had her," she said, forcing out the words, "and that she needed to be raised in a decent home."

"A woman isn't necessarily wicked because she becomes pregnant out of wedlock," I said, a bit more sharply than I'd intended. "It could just mean that she's young and naïve and trusting."

She said nothing, her face red with shame.

I thought of all the hours she'd been spending in church, hours the Reverend and I had assumed were spent repenting the death of her son. Perhaps it was actually this first guilt she'd been punishing herself for—or perhaps the two were, in her mind, inextricably linked, the sinful conception of the first child having somehow brought about the loss of the second. It was the same old story, I thought irritably: a woman taking the blame for a man's reckless satisfaction of his needs.

Professor Bogard's words echoed in my mind: *It is important for the therapist to be aware of his own attitudes and prejudices, to prevent them from intruding in his work with the patient.* Oh I was aware all right, I thought, reining my anger in. "Did you ever see your daughter again?" I asked.

"No." She looked up. "But I keep hoping that she'll come and find me."

"What would you say to her, if she did?"

Her tear-stained face took on a soft glow. "I'd tell her that I never wanted to let her go, that I wanted to be her mother more than anything in the world. I'd tell her that from the minute I felt her moving inside me, I knew she was a gift from God."

It seemed to me I could still see traces of that innocent fifteen-year-old in her shining face. From the Reverend's report I knew that she'd been an only child, whose father had died at a relatively young age and whose mother had been preoccupied with keeping the family store afloat. No wonder she had yearned for something of her own to love. I tried to imagine what it would be like to have a baby wrenched from you at birth—to be so filled with life one minute, and so empty the next. I knew how strong the craving could be for just one more look, one more touch of a person who was lost to you forever. And they hadn't even given Eliza a chance to say goodbye.

"I told Dr. Hauptfuhrer that God wanted me to have her," she went on, "but he said it was blasphemy to say so."

"Dr. Hauptfuhrer?" I repeated in surprise. He was a well-known physician in our part of town, attendant to some of the Upper East Side's most prosperous families. "He delivered your baby?"

She nodded.

"And he arranged to give it away?"

"Yes."

This struck me as very odd. Hauptfuhrer was a blood specialist of some renown. As far as I knew, he had no particular interest or training in obstetrics. "How did he come to be your physician?"

"Mother met him at the German Hospital, when she had her tonsils out."

I supposed he must have had staff privileges at the hospital, and met her while performing his obligatory ward rounds. "Did he give you any papers to sign when he took the baby?" I asked.

"I don't think so; I don't remember any."

"Well did he at least tell you where she was going? To one of the city foundling asylums, perhaps?"

"He said he couldn't tell me. He said everything about the baby had to be a secret."

"Perhaps he told your mother. Did you ever ask her?"

"I couldn't. She was very angry with me. She said I must never mention Joy again, to her or to anyone else."

So not only had Mrs. Miner suffered a devastating loss, I thought, but she had been forced to suffer it in silence, without comfort from family or friends.

"Do you think . . ." she began, but stopped.

"What?" I prompted.

"Do you think I should ask him?"

"I'm sorry; do I think you should ask who, what?"

"Should I ask Dr. Hauptfuhrer where Joy is, the next time I see him?"

I stared at her. "You don't mean to say you still use him?"

"Why yes, I have to, for my headaches; he gives me the prescription. Of course we never talk about what happened. But maybe this time . . . oh, Doctor, do you think I should ask?"

I knew what I ought to say. I ought to advise her to forget about the past. It was my job to help her suppress the guilty, unhappy thoughts that resided there and to imagine a brighter future. But I couldn't force the words to my lips. Because deep down I didn't believe that she should have to accept her loss. Surely no one had a right to take a mother's child against her will—even if that mother was young, even if she had behaved foolishly. Eliza had a chance, a small chance but a chance nonetheless, of righting that injustice. Her son was gone, forever. But her daughter was still alive, and conceivably living in the city. It might be possible for the two to establish relations.

Of course doing so would have repercussions; the sensibilities of the daughter and her adoptive family, if there was one, would have to be taken into account. But the idea of getting back someone you'd loved and lost—someone you blamed yourself for losing—held a powerful attraction for me. Part of me, the impulsive part, wanted to say, "Yes, Eliza, I think you should go to him straight away and demand that he tell you what's become of her. I believe you have every right to know."

But of course I didn't. Because I had learned not to listen to that part. It had taken me years, fighting against the grain, but I had at last reached the point where my rational intentions, and not my reckless impulses, were in charge. I asked instead, "Is that what you want to do?"

"I'm not sure." She frowned. "I do want to find her, more than anything, but . . ."

"But?"

"But what if I do and it turns out she hates me?" she blurted out. "I don't think I could bear it."

"Why would she hate you?"

Her eyes swam with fresh tears. "She might think I gave her away because I didn't want her."

"But that's not what happened, is it?"

"No, I did want her! I had it all planned; I was working nights at the bakery next door, earning extra money so I'd be able to have a girl come in and sit with the baby during the day while I helped Mother in the shop."

"You mean, you didn't know they weren't going to let you keep her?"

"Not until they took her away. I begged my mother to make them give her back, but she said we were lucky that Dr. Hauptfuhrer was willing to help, and must do exactly as he said."

"Was Dr. Hauptfuhrer aware of how you felt?"

"Yes! I told him I could be a good mother, but he wouldn't listen! He said he knew what was best."

In my mind's eye I imagined her, womb aching and half in shock, pleading to keep what every instinct told her was hers—and being roundly ignored. "And looking back on it now, do you agree?" I asked. "That he knew what was best?"

Her huge eyes fixed on mine. "No," she said slowly, with a trace of defiance in her voice. "I loved her. I would have taken good care of her, no matter how hard it was."

I said nothing, letting her savor this new perspective. "Perhaps he was the one who acted badly, then," I suggested after a moment.

I could see her turning this idea over in her mind. I didn't expect a reply; I had only wanted to plant the possibility. I glanced around the room, the same room that had seemed so barren just moments before, and felt the seeping warmth of accomplishment. Perhaps the morning hadn't been a complete disaster after all.

She continued gazing into the middle distance, apparently lost in thought.

I touched her arm. "Eliza?"

She swiveled toward me. "I'm going to do it. Tomorrow."

"Do what?"

"Ask Dr. Hauptfuhrer." She stood. "It's her birthday in two days, on January 8th. Wouldn't it be wonderful if this time I knew where she was?"

I rose beside her. "You realize he may not have kept track of her. And even if he has, he probably won't tell you."

"He might," she said, smoothing her hands over her skirt front. "If I insist."

The notion of this unassuming woman insisting on anything was so incongruous that I couldn't help smiling. "Eliza . . ."

"I have to try," she said, her cheeks flushing. "I owe her that."

I hesitated, wondering whether I should attempt to dissuade her. But before I could say anything more, she had picked up her coat and started for the door.

At the partition's splintering edge she stopped. "I'm going to telephone him as soon as I get home, to tell him that I'm coming. That way I won't lose my nerve." She smiled hesitantly. "Will you wish me luck?"

Again I was struck by how innocent—and how very vulnerable—she appeared. "Good luck, Eliza."

Her smile brightened, and then she turned and vanished around the corner.

She wasn't gone two seconds before the professor's words started circling in my head: *The therapist's extraordinary power within the therapeutic relationship must be carefully exercised; the impact of his wo* *and behavior on the patient cannot be overestimated* . . . .

I was of course aware that Eliza's story had affected me on a personal level, in more ways than one. But I didn't believe I had allowed this to influence my conduct. It was she, after all, not I who had suggested questioning the doctor. And looking at it objectively, I couldn't say that this was an inappropriate course of action. She'd been so riddled with guilt all these years that she'd never been able to speak up for herself, or even acknowledge her tremendous loss. Asserting herself with Dr. Hauptfuhrer had to be a move in the right direction. She needed to regain faith in herself, to learn to respect her own rights and to recognize the injury that had been done to her, before she could move on with her life.

I returned to my desk to gather my things. In all likelihood the doctor would be either unwilling or unable to disclose her daughter's current whereabouts, so there was little chance of complications on that score, whatever my feelings on the subject might be. Eliza would be disappointed, of course—but in the process of asking, she'd be taking her first step toward recovery. And that, I told myself as I pulled on my coat, was all her psychotherapist could ask for.

CHAPTER TWO

I emerged from the parish house to find that the sky had clouded over and a few light snowflakes were falling. Pulling up my collar, I retraced my steps north through the bustle of Yorkville and west across 92nd Street, toward home. By the time I reached my block the snow was coming down steadily, stirred by gusts off Central Park into little funnels that sifted up under my skirt and into my shoes. Already it had blanketed the tan and cream townhouses that lined my street, transforming them into a story-book gingerbread village. I spotted the glowing bay windows of Number 7 beckoning up ahead, and hurried toward them. Propelled by a final, bone-rattling shiver, I dashed up the steps and burst inside.

I stashed my hat and coat on the hallway rack and followed the sound of gasping bellows to the sitting room, where Mary, our parlor maid, was stoking the fire. I stood beside her on the hearth, holding my palms to the flames. "Are they back yet?"

She turned her flushed face up to me, her white cap askew. "Not yet, Miss. Katie says we probably shouldn't expect them until dinner."

I could feel the tension seep from my shoulders. Father had left early that morning to bring my mother back from a flower show in Philadelphia, and with road conditions so unpredictable I hadn't known when he might be back. It was a relief to think I might have a few more hours of peace before his return.

Grabbing an apple from the pantry I marched myself upstairs, determined to finish the journals Professor Bogard had lent me so I could return them at our meeting the following morning. I shut my bedroom door and sank into the armchair by the window with the first of the three journals opened on my lap. But while normally I might have found "The Appreciation of Time in Somnambules" a riveting bit of analysis, now I couldn't keep myself from glancing out the window at the street below, or listening for the sound of the front door. I adored my father but he was a stubborn man, unaccustomed to my disagreeing with him. We'd had quite a row over breakfast and I didn't expect our next encounter to be any less contentious.

When the dinner bell rang I was less than halfway through the second volume, and remembered very little of what I'd read. Laying the journals down in defeat, I descended the stairs to the dining room and took my usual place at the side of the table. Katie was standing by the sideboard, whacking Brussels sprouts around a chafing dish with the back of a spoon, looking more than usually severe in her black evening uniform and stiff white apron and cap. I took in the absence of other place settings with a mix of concern and relief. "I guess they're not going to make it," I concluded, as she carried a platter of roast chicken to my side.

She forked a chicken breast onto my plate. "No, Miss," she said, her Irish brogue thick with indignation, "I expect they're in a ditch somewhere, praying a farmer will come along to pull them out." She pushed some stray gray hairs back from her steam-dampened cheeks with her wrist. "A good dinner ruined, and for what?" she grumbled, returning to the sideboard. "I don't see why they couldn't have taken the train."

I took no offense; Katie had been with my parents since they were married, and her devotion was rather fierce. "Why don't you just leave it all on the warmer," I suggested as she returned with the sprouts, "and they can help themselves when they get back?"

"*If* they get back," she muttered, dumping a spoonful of limp sprouts beside my chicken. But she hoisted the chafing dishes from the sideboard and carried them into the pantry, where I heard them land with a resounding clang on the warmer.

I ate quickly, realizing that if I retired early I might be able to avoid another scene with my father until at least the following day. As soon as I finished I went upstairs to wash up, then climbed into bed with the journals. An article on the use of persuasion tactics to cure chronic melancholia caught my interest, as it appeared to support the program I'd designed for my class. By the time I'd finished reading it a second time, I was so reassured that I felt myself truly relaxing for the first time that day. Perhaps I would show the article to Father in the morning, I thought as I dropped the journals onto the floor. It might help him understand what I was trying to accomplish. Comforted by the thought, I settled lower on my pillow and gave in to the pull of gravity on my eyelids.

SOME TIME LATER I awoke to the sound of footsteps on the stairs. Though it was still dark outside, the furnace had burned low enough to let frost form inside the windowpanes, leading me to guess it was an hour or two before dawn. I pushed off my bedcovers and tread quietly to the door, pulling it open just in time to see my parents round the second floor landing and start up the next flight to their bedrooms. My father was behind Mamma, with one hand under her elbow and the other against the small of her back. In the dim light he appeared to be almost levitating her up the stairwell. I started to call out, but stopped, feeling like an intruder. I waited until they had disappeared around the newel post and then softly closed the door.

When next I awoke it was to the sound of the bread truck door slamming beneath my window. I quickly washed and brushed my teeth and ran shivering back to my room, where I hopped from foot to foot in front of the wardrobe as I decided what to wear for my meeting with Professor Bogard. I finally selected a warm green plaid suit with a fitted jacket and heavy flared skirt, and laid it on the bed. Stripping off my nightgown, I pulled on my corset, hose, drawers, corset cover and shirtwaist, shivering a little less with each layer. I stepped into the skirt, buttoned on my jacket and laced up my boots, then grabbed some pins from the dresser tray and piled my hair into a knot.

Turning to check the total effect in the standing mirror, I saw a large-eyed young woman who hardly looked old enough to be out of secondary school, let alone have a degree in medicine, gazing back at me. The long, straight nose that had been described as "patrician" on my mother, on me had grown only long enough to be called "pert", while the wide set of my mouth suggested more childish stubbornness, than the droll sophistication I would have preferred. If only I could grow out my unfashionable bangs I might look more my age, I thought for the umpteenth time, pushing the dark fringe aside. But then, of course, the scar would show. I turned away from my reflection and went to find Mamma.

She was sitting at the dressing table in her boudoir with her back turned partially toward me, sifting through her mail. I paused in the doorway, struck by the angle of her face, remembering how I used to watch her in just such a pose as she prepared to go out for the evening, years ago when she cared about such things. I would sit on the little tufted stool behind her, giddy with the smells of potpourri and cologne, watching her reflection in the amber mirror like a youthful apprentice witnessing the secrets of some ancient trade. As if it were a scene from one of the flickering moving pictures I'd watched on Broadway, I recalled the quick movement of her head as she slipped on a dangling earring, and the illicit dabs of rouge on her cheeks and the hollows of her shoulders—"just a dot," she'd whisper conspiratorially, her eyes shining at me in the mirror—and the sprinkling of white powder over her skin, as fine as fairy dust.

Inevitably, just after she'd applied the last spritz of gardenia-scented cologne behind her ears, we'd hear the knock. As Mamma swiveled on her chair the hallway door would open, and into this bastion of femininity would step the tall, dark, cherry tobacco-redolent figure of my father, his mustache freshly clipped and his high, starched collar pressing against the bath-pinkened skin of his throat. At this moment I always felt as if two worlds were colliding, sparking a strange, mysterious charge that made me long to dot rouge on *my* cheeks, and feel the swirl of satin around *my* legs. Father would pause for a moment on the threshold, his eyes glittering in the lamplight;

then he'd cross the room to stand behind Mamma, laying his hands on her shoulders and saying, "You'll be the belle of the ball."

At this point, unable to contain myself, I would invariably prompt, "Do you hope she'll save a dance for you, Papa?" And he would wink at me, and meet her eyes in the mirror, and say he most certainly did. It all seemed a terribly long time ago, I thought now, stepping into the boudoir.

My mother turned and smiled. Although she was still a beautiful woman, life had left its marks on her, like fingers on ripe fruit. Her once proud, high cheeks had softened and her temples thinned beneath the twin gray streaks that now ran through her sable hair. "I was just thinking of you," she said, resting a vellum card against her chest. "We need to arrange a time for Monsieur Henri to come fit your dress for the Fiskes' ball. He said he has a spot available tomorrow morning, if that will do."

"Next week would be better." I was planning to visit Reverend Palmers the following morning, to learn more about Eliza Miner's history.

"Oh, Genevieve," she said, her tone gently reproving, "the ball is this Saturday!" She handed me the card.

"Is it really?" I glanced at the invitation. "I'd lost track." Though the season was only a few weeks underway, I was already growing weary of dinner dances and cotillions and musicales. "I suppose I ought to go."

"Of course you'll go," she said mildly, turning back to the mail tray. "We've already ordered your dress. Besides, Bartie Mattheson will be expecting you."

Was I imagining it, I wondered, or had she been showing more interest in my social life lately? She must have noticed that I was getting awfully long in the tooth, and still showed no signs of landing a husband on my own. Poor Mamma; I think she'd half expected me to bring one home from medical school. My failure to do so must have stirred some latent sense of maternal duty.

I didn't put up a fuss, in any event, because this was one affair I was rather curious to attend. The courtship between nineteen-year-old Olivia Fiske and the forty-five-year-old Lord Branard was the talk of the town, and I was interested in observing how the two got on. I looked back down at the card. "I wouldn't mind getting a look at this Andrew Clearings Bernard Terrence Williams Hastings, 8th Earl of Branard," I mused, tapping my thumb over the guest of honor's name. "I wonder if he's as stuffy as people say he is."

"I'm sure Grant and Lucille wouldn't have encouraged the courtship if he was," my mother murmured, shuffling through her mail.

I frowned at the back of her head. Anyone who read the newspapers knew that the Fiskes had been in hot pursuit of the Earl for nearly two years, employing the services of multiple vendeuses to introduce themselves to titled society abroad, entertaining the Earl in Paris, London and Marianbad, and even building their own yacht to compete against the Earl's at Cowes. He was quite a catch—higher in rank than either Emily Donnelly's Baron or Clara Potter's Baronet. Not as impressive as May Goelet's Duke, it was true, but then impoverished Dukes were becoming scarcer than hens' teeth. I couldn't help wondering if, with such a prize at stake, a little thing like conjugal suitability would figure very largely in the elder Fiskes' minds.

But I wasn't about to vex Mamma by arguing. "What time did you get back?" I asked instead, dropping onto the tufted stool, which was now quite faded and frayed around the edges.

"It was nearly sunrise. We ran out of patching rubber, and poor Maurice had to walk miles to find some. I'm afraid Katie waited up for us; she was in a swivet. You'd think your father punctured his tires on purpose, just to upset her."

"Yes, I know. I thought she was going to set out after you on foot, if only to give Father a piece of her mind."

She smiled faintly and shook her head, dropping an advertisement into the waste basket. "How were things while I was gone?" she inquired, lifting another envelope. "Did you have a pleasant weekend?"

"I spent most of it preparing for my class."

She looked up. "Oh yes; your class! How did it go? Did the Reverend help you get settled?"

"He had a space set aside for us, just as he'd promised."

She slid the letter opener through the envelope. "Things got off to a good start, then," she murmured, scanning the envelope's contents.

"As good as could be expected, I'd say, considering the problems these women are dealing with." I had an impulse to tell her about Eliza Miner, but it quickly passed. "How was the 'Colors of Winter' show?" I asked instead. "Did you win a prize?"

She admitted to taking a first with her Miss Eloise hybrid, and then, elaborating typically little on her own success, launched into an account of the many other fascinating specimens she had seen at the show. Flowers were Mother's passion; the hours other women of her station spent shopping and visiting, she spent in her conservatory pinching, pruning, fertilizing and whatever else one did to cultivate new plants. I didn't resent this overriding interest—nor, I believe, did my father. Mostly, I would say we were relieved.

I smiled and nodded as she leafed through the show catalogue, stopping to enthuse at length over a rose called Bridget Amalie. I knew that she could go on for some time without any prompting from me. I had little affinity for things horticultural; but then, I didn't have to. My mother's passion was a private, complicated thing. It didn't require, or even enthusiastically admit, participation by others.

After a while my gaze wandered up from the catalogue, past her shoulder to the dressing table, settling on a silver-framed photograph that was nestled among the spray bottles and lacquered boxes beneath the lamp shade. The photograph was of a young boy, dressed in a square-collared sailor suit and stiff leather boots. He was looking directly at the camera, and frowning.

I remembered exactly when it was taken, because I'd been standing in the wings at the time in my red velvet firefly costume, waiting for my turn in front of the picture box. I had warned Conrad, just a moment earlier, not to blink when the photographer lit the flash. I always wondered if that was why he was frowning—because he was trying so hard not to blink, and ruin the picture.

The breakfast bell sounded downstairs.

"Better not keep Katie waiting," Mother said, laying the catalogue on the dressing table.

"Aren't you coming?" I asked, when she made no move to get up.

"Soon. I want to get through the rest of the mail first."

I rose reluctantly. "Is Father up and about?"

"I expect so," she replied, already back to her sorting. "You know your father."

I stifled a sigh. Running a hand over my hair, I returned a loose strand to its pin and went downstairs alone to face him.

CHAPTER THREE

He was seated at the head of the table, reading the morning paper.

"Good morning, Father," I said lightly, taking my usual seat on his left.

He glanced at me over the paper. "Genevieve," he responded with a nod.

I would never have guessed he'd been up most of the night; he looked fresh as the morning dew. But then, he always looked primed for action, as if underneath his ruddy skin he was all springs and rubber, rather than flesh and blood like ordinary mortals. "Mother tells me you had car trouble," I said, as Katie poured my tea.

"Mmph," he replied into his newspaper.

Katie muttered something behind him, which neither of us asked her to repeat. I stirred a spoonful of sugar into my tea. "Perhaps you should have taken Cleo and Anabel," I teased, referring to our carriage horses. "They've never been known, as far as I know, to break down in the middle of the road."

He lowered the newspaper as Katie landed a dollop of porridge into his bowl with a splat. "It wasn't the engine's fault," he retorted, eying her with misgiving. "It started right away, every time. It's the damned tires; they keep getting pinched between the cover and the wheel rim." He gazed out over the bowl of narcissus on the center of the table, his eyes growing pensive under his straight black brows. "There must be some way to protect them . . ."

I sipped my tea, wondering if this was going to become another of his projects. Father was, first and foremost, an improver: once a thing bothered him sufficiently, he set out to fix it. Thanks to an ample inheritance he had the time and money to do so, usually by finding and funding enterprising young minds. Tires, though, were outside his usual sphere of interest. Since my brother's death he had focused almost exclusively on medical implements: first an injectable heart stimulant, and more recently, an artificial breathing machine.

"I gather you had plenty of time to think about it last night," I said as Katie served me my porridge, hoping that if I kept up a light banter we might get through breakfast without a scene.

But it was not to be. As soon as Katie had cleared the porridge, served us our eggs and toast and bustled back to the pantry, he put down his paper and turned to me. "So, how was your 'therapy class?'" he asked, mouthing the last two words as if they'd been soaked in quinine.

I returned my cup to its saucer. "No one walked out," I answered with a smile.

He raised an eyebrow. "Is that cause for congratulations?"

"You have to understand that the concept of mental therapy is foreign to these women."

He snorted. "Now that, at least, I do understand."

"I believe I caught their interest, though," I continued, determined not to be provoked. "One patient was particularly responsive. I think I may be able to help her."

He stabbed a piece of butter with his knife tip. "Help her, in what way?" he asked with exaggerated politeness, lashing the butter against his toast.

"Why, to feel better, of course. As I believe I've explained to you before, these women are all suffering disorders that are linked to emotional shocks in their past. My goal is to return them to more normal functioning."

He mashed a bite of toast between his jaws. "Did it ever occur to you," he asked when he had swallowed, "that unhappiness may be a normal part of life? That it is, in fact, the natural state of man?"

Here we go again, I thought in dismay, lowering my fork to my plate. "There's a difference between unhappiness and a functional disorder, Father."

"Yes. The difference is that some of us get up and get on with our lives, while others wallow in self-pity."

"These women aren't weak; they're in terrible pain. It takes strength for them just to stay alive, day after day."

This only seemed to irritate him further. He bit off another chunk of toast, glaring at me while he chewed. "This is what they taught you in medical school?" he asked finally.

"Oh Father, don't you see? Accusing them of malingering is no better than blaming mental illness on evil spirits! This is the modern age; we know better! The key to curing mental disturbance lies in the principles of physics and chemistry, not in identifying moral defects. All we have to do is determine the underlying causes of psychic pain and we can master it."

"You don't think that's presumptuous? Believing we can master pain?"

"Presumptuous? Why? Look at all the advances we've made against physical disease—antiseptics, antitoxins, X-ray machines! Why shouldn't we do the same for emotional pain? Professor Bogard says it's the new frontier. He says that as we bring modern, scientific methods to bear on problems in abnormal psychology, we're bound to see extraordinary results."

"I suppose this professor of yours agrees that you can help these women?" Father asked, pushing a forkful of scrambled egg around his plate.

I hesitated, choosing my words with care. "He believes it's an exciting possibility . . ."

"A possibility!" he barked.

". . . that deserves to be explored."

He said nothing more, but his jaws were clamped as tightly as a clothes-wringer beneath his neat mustache.

"Look, Father, I know this isn't what you wanted me to do," I entreated, "but I really believe I could be good at it. Just think of all the people I could help! People who are truly suffering—"

His fist thudded on the table. "Why can't somebody else help them!" he thundered. "Why does it have to be you?"

Before I could answer, the fork dropped from his hand and he rose abruptly to his feet. I turned to see that my mother had entered the room.

"Good morning, Evelyn," said Father.

"Good morning, dear." She floated into her seat at the opposite end of the table and poured herself a cup of tea from the pot Katie had set out for her. "Were you able to get any sleep?"

"About an hour's worth, before Biggs arrived," he said, sitting down again. Mr. Biggs, our neighborhood barber, was more regular than Grandpapa's hall clock, arriving each morning at precisely 7:35 and departing exactly fifteen minutes later to reach Mr. Burden's house by 7:55. "What about you?"

"Too keyed up, I'm afraid. I'll just wait for my afternoon nap." She sipped her tea, her eyes moving from Father to me. "I didn't interrupt anything, I hope?"

Father began stabbing at his eggs again, while I stared down at my plate.

"She was just explaining to me how she's going to rid the world of unhappiness," Father muttered.

I lifted my chin. "What I said is that I'm hoping to lead my patients back to some semblance of normal functioning."

"And how long will that take?" Father asked, addressing me directly. "A month? A year?"

"What difference does it make!" I exclaimed, gesturing in frustration. "Why can't you be a little patient?"

"Genevieve," murmured my mother, nodding at my elbow.

Following her gaze, I saw that I had dragged my sleeve across my buttered toast. "Oh, damn," I said, swatting at it with my napkin.

"Genna!" gasped Mamma.

"Sorry," I mumbled. I had taken up swearing in medical school, and was finding it a difficult habit to break.

"It's not a matter of my patience," Father continued. "We have to think about the board of Mount Pleasant Hospital. They may not be as willing as I to wait."

"Listen to you—you're already assuming that I'll fail," I fumed, giving up on the sleeve, "and that I'll have to accept their offer, in the end."

"What other outcome can I possibly expect? You've given me no rational basis for believing that this project of yours will succeed."

I tried to swallow the lump that was growing in my throat. I had truly believed, when I conceived of my class therapy project, that it would make my father proud. "I don't understand why you're being so pessimistic. You, of all people! You've always been such an innovator; I should think you'd be all for it!"

He leaned toward me across the table. "What do you want me to say? That I think it's wonderful you're passing up the chance to do real healing so that you can waste your time on some untested nervous cure? That I think this is the best possible way for you to use your talents?"

Yes, I thought; it was exactly what I wanted him to say. "Persuasion therapy is not untested," I retorted. "Neither is the class treatment approach. You might at least keep an open mind. Better yet, you could just trust my judgment, and wish me luck."

"Well I'm sorry," he snapped, "but your judgment hasn't always been the best, now has it?"

My breath left me as completely and painfully as if I'd been kicked by a horse.

"Hugh," my mother murmured.

I struggled for air as the two Great Sins of my life loomed up before me: my brother's death, massive and overshadowing . . . and six years down the road its smaller, fainter shadow: the Incident with Simon Shaw.

My cheeks were stinging with hot blood. It wasn't fair; couldn't my father see that I had changed, that I was no longer that impulsive, self-centered girl? I thought of all the times in medical school when through sheer force of will I had controlled my natural inclinations, remaining silent when I felt like screaming, or smiling when I wanted to cry. Had I complained when my "gentlemen" classmates put cow eyes in my lunch pudding? No! I'd just spooned them out and polished it off. And when my professor asked me to describe the male ejaculatory function in front of the entire class, I hadn't run from the room—although the thought had certainly crossed my mind. I'd stayed and answered without protest or hesitation, even drawing an anatomically correct diagram on the board for good measure. I'd become so adept at disregarding my natural feelings and reactions and doing what was required that I'd graduated third in my class—and yet here he was, still treating me like an irresponsible child.

Father sat back with a sigh. "All I'm asking is that you reconsider. We fought for your medical degree together, you and I. You've achieved what few women dream of. It's no small honor for a female physician to be offered a position on a hospital in-patient ward. But if you don't take their offer now, there's no guarantee it will come again. You've seen what's happening; there's a backlash out there, and it's getting worse. You and I may know it's because the men don't like the competition, but that's not what the critics are saying."

I knew very well what they were saying: it was the same old nonsense, all over again. That the intimate workings of the human body were too graphic for the sensibilities of decent young women; that females were too intellectually limited, or too prone to hysteria, or just too plain sentimental to become competent physicians. One prominent author was even seriously contending that higher education enlarged the brains and stunted the bodies of female students.

I supposed we should have suspected that the prejudice against us had never really died. The only reason Johns Hopkins agreed to admit women in the first place was because a group of female donors promised to give it $500,000 toward the new medical school if it would do so. Once this prestigious institution opened its doors to women, other medical schools had felt forced to follow suit. And women had responded, filling a third or more of the available seats and garnering a lion's share of the honors. For a few years things had looked very rosy—so rosy that the handful of all-female medical colleges had all closed down, believing they were no longer needed in the new, co-educational age.

But since my matriculation in 1900, the supply of doctors had begun to exceed demand—and true to form, women were being blamed. Instead of handling the glut by letting the most talented physicians climb to the top, the predominantly male profession was closing ranks, kicking women off the bottom rungs. Female enrollments at Johns Hopkins and elsewhere had already been cut to less than five percent, while postgraduate training for women was becoming nearly impossible to find. I knew what Father was saying was true. But I wasn't interested in crusading for a cause; I had never wanted to fight, only to learn. "There's nothing I can do about what those idiots are saying."

"Of course there is," he retorted. "You can prove them wrong! You can take the job at Mount Pleasant and show them what a woman can do. Make a real contribution!"

No, I couldn't, I thought, staring at my plate. Not even for Father, not this time. And not just because I knew how unwelcome I'd be in a position I'd only been offered because of his influence. The truth was that I had no interest in general medicine, something I hadn't faced squarely until my last year of school. Conrad was the one who was supposed to be the doctor. I may have taken his place in the plan, but my heart had never been in it.

Traditional psychiatry had intrigued me at first, but I'd soon grown frustrated with its limited reach. I didn't want to spend my life as a custodian for the irreversibly insane, or testifying as to the mental capacity of criminal defendants. I wanted to improve people's lives. It was only during my practicum with Dr. Cassell that I'd discovered the fascinating new field of scientific psychotherapy. Dr. Cassell had observed that a number of his consumptive patients suffered from depression, which he believed hindered their ability to get well. He treated this depression not with shock treatment or medication, but by confronting his patients' mental attitude, urging them in weekly group meetings to develop a more positive outlook. And the patients got better. I'd seen it with my own two eyes.

Here, I was thrilled to discover, was something that looked beyond brain injuries and lesions and toxic reactions for explanations of mental illness, something that took life events and emotions into account. The idea that thoughts and feelings could influence body functions had been taken up by a handful of other psychiatrists and neurologists, I soon learned, who'd begun using the persuasion approach to treat a variety of physiological disturbances. By the time my practicum came to an end, I had decided that this was where my future lay. Using the tools of psychotherapy, I would identify what was broken, and fix it. I almost smiled now at the thought; perhaps Father and I weren't so very different, after all. "If I can show that psychotherapy works for symptoms caused by unresolved grief," I said evenly, "I'll be making an important contribution to an emerging field. Isn't that just as important as what you're proposing?"

He didn't answer immediately. His gaze roamed over my face, searching for something, I didn't know what. "Is it, Genna? Is it just as important?"

"I think so," I said, uncertain what to make of his change in tone.

His thumb slid absently over his fork stem. "You're sure about this, then."

I nodded.

He put the fork down. "Very well; we'll give it three months. I believe I can hold the hospital position open until then."

"Three months? For what?"

"To see if this project of yours is a viable one."

Three months—that was no time at all! It had taken Cassell that long just to wean his patients from their medications. "That's . . ." I stopped. He was trying so hard to be reasonable; I ought to at least meet him halfway. ". . . fine. Three months. Thank you, Father."

He grunted, and swigged the last of his coffee. "I'd better be off," he said a moment later, pushing himself up from the table. "Andre is meeting me at the lab; he's got a new valve he wants to show me, for the artificial lung." He strode to the other end of the table and pecked my mother on the cheek before starting for the door.

I swiveled in my seat to call after him. "Father?"

He turned.

"You won't be sorry. I promise."

Giving me the merest flicker of a smile, he tipped his head and continued out the door.

A FEW MINUTES later I was skimming over the icy Madison Avenue sidewalk, buffeted by yet another bitter wind that snaked under my muffler and pushed against the wide brim of my hat. Holding the hat down with one hand and clutching my book bag with the other, I tripped along through the maze of work-bound men with walking sticks that clogged the sidewalk at this hour, buoyed by my father's concession. I may not have entirely convinced him, but at least I'd opened his mind a crack to the validity of what I was attempting, which was more than I'd dared hope for.

I was halfway to Professor Bogard's house when the clang of an ambulance broke into my thoughts, growing louder as the vehicle raced up behind me and sped past. I watched the white-coated surgeon sway on the rear platform as the ambulance careened through the traffic and turned left at the end of the block, leaving a tangle of shying horses and honking motorcars in its wake. When I drew up to the intersection I saw that it had pulled over to the curb some twenty feet up the block, in front of a brick townhouse. I hesitated, wondering if my services might be required. A momentary lull in traffic decided me and I ran across the avenue.

Picking my way through the bystanders already congregating on the sidewalk, I followed the ambulance surgeon and his two stretcher-bearing attendants toward the townhouse entrance. A police officer stood watch at the door. As the ambulance crew hurried toward him, he spat out a stream of tobacco juice and advised, "Take your time, fellas. This one ain't goin' anywhere."

I stopped. Apparently, whatever had happened here was over. If I wasn't needed I really ought to be going, or I would be late for the professor. I turned, and had just begun to retrace my steps through the growing crowd, when an explosive backfire brought me around again. A dusty police car had pulled up to the curb behind the ambulance and sputtered to a stop. I watched as the door opened and a man in an ill-fitting sack coat stepped out. He had wispy red hair under a crumpled brown derby, and a long bony face that put me in mind of an underfed mule. He paused by the car for a moment, taking in the scene on the street, before starting toward the entrance. He came to a stop in front of the policeman. "Officer Mundy," he greeted him flatly, scanning the ground at his feet.

"Detective," the officer replied, inclining his head a fraction of an inch.

The detective gestured toward the ground. "What'd I tell you about spitting at a crime scene?"

I must say, I was surprised to hear him say it. The men of New York generally chewed, and spat, wherever they liked: in the streetcars, in the theaters, and in the finest restaurants. I knew there was some sort of law against it, but I would have expected a detective to have more important things on his mind.

"Jeez, I don't know," the officer replied with a surly smile. "What did you tell me?"

The detective's expression didn't change. "You're supposed to be protecting the crime scene, not contaminating it."

The officer shrugged. "None of the other detectives care if I chew."

The detective shook his head as if dealing with a dim-witted child. "What if the perpetrator liked to chew? Did you ever think of that? What if he was standing out here, thinking about whether to do the crime, and left a plug behind? We see that, we've learned something about our man. Maybe we even get lucky and find out what brand he uses. But what do we know now, eh Mundy? All we know is that you're a sloppy cop with a bad habit."

The officer's smile vanished. "Say, you're a regular Sherlock Holmes, ain't you."

"Yeah, that's me," the detective said sourly. "Sherlock Holmes." His hand shot out and grabbed the officer's wrist, twisting it palm up. "Now spit it out."

The cop's cheeks flamed red. His head swung toward the spectators, and back to the detective. For a moment I thought he was going to punch the detective with his free hand. But at last his gaze fell away, and he spat the tobacco noisily into his palm.

"Put it in your pocket," the detective commanded.

The officer shot him a look of pure malice, but closed his fist over the wet clump and thrust it into his pocket.

The detective nodded brusquely. "Now get these people to stand back. I want this area cleared—just in case there's anything left to find." Brushing past the officer, he pulled open the entrance door and disappeared inside.

"Yes, sir," muttered the officer, throwing a mock salute after him. He turned and raised his club in the air. "All right, everyone," he shouted, "stand back. Give us some room here."

Reluctantly the bystanders parted, creating a path between the door and a black patrol wagon that had joined the other vehicles at the curb. As the driver of the wagon strode up the path I was jostled further and further back on the sidewalk, until all I could see was a row of hats in front of me. When nothing happened for several more minutes, I turned once more to leave.

This time it was a murmur from the crowd that brought me back around. As the line shifted in front of me, I saw that two more policemen were emerging from the building, escorting a bareheaded woman whose face was turned toward the ground. The woman's coat was slung unevenly over her shoulders, and there were dark blotches on her pale green skirt. As the trio continued down the path toward the van, the woman lifted a bewildered gaze toward the staring bystanders.

My feet took root in the sidewalk. I recognized thosed slumped shoulders, and that thin, ashen face. Forcing my legs to move, I pushed to the front of the crowd. "Eliza!" I called. "Eliza, over here!"

She turned, and recognition swept across her face. "Dr. Summerford!" She lurched toward me, reaching out with both hands.

I made it only a step closer before one of the policemen blocked my path. "Stand back, there," he warned, nodding toward the other officer as he muscled Eliza back on course. He led her to the back of the wagon and lifted her in.

"Do you know the suspect?" asked a voice at my ear.

I turned to find the second policeman, a square-faced man with a crooked nose, standing beside me. "What?"

He pulled his domed hat lower as a gust of wind blew past us, slapping grit up against the wagon. "Do you know the suspect?" he repeated.

"You mean Mrs. Miner? Yes; can you tell me what's happened? Why are you taking her? She isn't hurt, is she?"

"What's your name?" he asked, opening the little black book in his hand.

"Genevieve Summerford."

He licked the tip of his pencil and entered this laboriously into the book. "Are you related to the suspect?"

"No."

"How do you know her?"

"She's a patient of mine."

He slowly wrote this down as well, as the electric wagon pulled away soundlessly from the curb.

"Officer," I begged, "could you *please* tell me what's happening?"

He closed his book and looked up. "You need to come with me," he said, taking hold of my elbow. "Detective Maloney's going to want to talk to you."

CHAPTER FOUR

He led me past the gawking bystanders to the building entrance. A brass wall plaque beside the door read, "Herman Hauptfuhrer, M.D. Hours 9-12". Hauptfuhrer: the doctor who'd delivered Eliza's baby. The one she'd told me she was going to visit this morning, to try to determine her daughter's whereabouts . . . .

The officer opened the door and gestured me through.

I took a hesitant step over the threshold, afraid of what I might find on the other side. But I saw nothing out of the ordinary in the entry vestibule. An empty hallway ran beyond it, down the length of the house, with a staircase along its right side. Two doors opened off the left side of the hallway. The officer led me through the first of these, into a small waiting room containing a row of black leather chairs. Embroidered pillows on the chairs proclaimed, "Health is the First Wealth", and "Patience is the Best Medicine", while a grandfather clock ticked placidly in one corner. A wall separated the waiting room from the back of the house. Two doors were set into it, both partially open. Through the one on the left I could make out the end of a metal examining table and a large standing scale; through the one on the right, a patch of golden Persian rug.

It looked like any other doctor's office, I thought, waiting for the daily parade of patients to begin. A moment later this illusion was shattered by a flash of light that suddenly spilled out of the room with the rug, followed by a sharp burning smell. A photographer's flash, I realized, as a ribbon of magnesium smoke curled out the door.

"This way," said the officer, leading me toward it. On the threshold he paused. Peering over his shoulder, I glimpsed what appeared to be the doctor's consultation room, with a heavy oak desk along the back wall, a bank of oak filing cabinets on the left and a fireplace on the right. The detective and the photographer were standing in front of the desk. A few feet away a uniformed man was brushing powder on the knob of a side door that led out to the hall.

The detective was looking down at something on the floor I couldn't see. "I want pictures from all four sides," he told the photographer.

"But I've only got one more box of plates," the photographer protested. "There won't be enough for the finger impressions."

"Then get more," the detective shot back, in the same disdainful tone he'd used with the officer on the street.

My police escort told me to wait and started toward them. As he moved away, the lower half of the room came into view. I shrank back against the door frame, repelled by the sudden onslaught of color. The vivid red of fresh blood was everywhere—staining the gold fibers of the rug, pooled on the parquet floor, splattered against an open filing drawer. It came from a man lying face down on the floor, and was most concentrated near his head, soaking his shirt and collar and matting his thin gray hair.

"Hold it, McKee," the detective barked at the approaching policeman.

The officer froze in his tracks.

"Who said you could come in here?"

"I found someone who knows the suspect," the officer explained, jerking his thumb over his shoulder.

The detective's pale eyes turned to me. He only held my gaze for a few moments; but in that time I had the sickening sensation that he was looking right through me, and could see every little guilty thing I'd ever done or thought of doing.

"Put her in the waiting room, and stay with her. Nobody comes in here unless I say so."

The officer led me back into the waiting room, muttering to himself as he deposited me in one of the chairs and took up position by the hallway door.

I slumped back in the chair. The man in there was dead, and much as my mind tried to refuse the implication, it appeared that Eliza was being charged with his murder. There had to be some mistake. She couldn't have killed someone . . . could she?

I felt a sudden constriction in my chest as I recalled our conversation at the clinic, seeing my words to her in a whole new light. With growing dread I remembered how I'd encouraged her to confront the doctor; how I'd as good as said that he was the guilty one, not she. My God, I thought, my stomach dropping like a stone; I might as well have put a weapon in her hand!

Here I'd thought that all she'd needed was a little shoring up, when all the time she'd been a powder keg waiting to explode. A wave of shame swept over me. I'd been so sure I understood her, so sure that I'd established a promising rapport. How could I have been so blind? I'd completely missed the signs: the deranged thinking, the destructive impulse that must have been there all along . . . .

I felt a powerful urge to get up and run, and might well have done so if another policeman hadn't come in from the hallway just then with a dazed-looking woman in tow. The woman had disheveled brown hair and eyes that were swollen from crying. The officer guided her into a chair at the other end of the row before continuing to the door of the inner office to announce, "I've got Miss Hauptfuhrer."

A minute later the detective appeared in the doorway. He crossed the waiting room and sat beside the young woman, opening his memorandum book on his lap. "I'm sorry for your loss," he muttered. Though he kept his voice low, his coarse Bowery accent ricocheted audibly off the paneled walls. "I know you already talked to the responding officer, but I've got a few more questions I need to ask."

She nodded, barely looking at him, clearly in a state of shock. I stared at her in morbid fascination. She was dressed in a tasteful wool suit, and her bearing, even under the weight of her grief, suggested the refinement that comes with travel and education. I noticed that, although she was a few years older than I, she wore no wedding band.

"Can you tell me what time your father came downstairs this morning?" the detective asked her.

"It was about half past eight," she told him in a trembling voice. "Right after breakfast. He always comes . . . came down early, to get his paperwork out of the way."

"Did he see patients here every day?"

She pressed a sodden handkerchief to her eyes. "He had hours every morning except Sunday. In the afternoons he made house calls, except on Tuesdays, when he volunteered at the German Hospital."

"Did he usually unlock the front door when he came downstairs?"

"Yes, he always opened it first thing, in case there were early arrivals."

"What about the service entrance?" the detective asked, scribbling in the book. "Did he unlock that too?"

She shook her head. "The maid opens the basement door when she goes down to the kitchen, around 6:30, so the furnace man can get in to tend to the fire."

"And at night?"

"She locks it up again at 11:00, after the fire's been banked for the evening."

"Where are the servants now?"

She drew a steadying breath. "Alice is our only boarder; she's a maid of all work. I take care of the upstairs rooms and the cooking, and a laundress comes in on Mondays to help with the wash."

"Did the laundress come this morning?"

"She hasn't come in yet; she isn't due until eleven."

"So Alice was the only servant on the premises at the time of the incident, is that right?"

"Yes."

"Did she see or hear anything?"

"Well I don't know; I haven't had a chance to speak with her. But she would have been in the basement, cleaning the breakfast dishes. I doubt she could have heard anything from there."

The detective nodded to the nearest officer. "Go find the maid and tell her to stay put." He turned back to Miss Hauptfuhrer. "What about the side door in your father's office, that leads out to the hall? Did he keep that locked, as a rule?"

"Oh, no, there was no need. His patients always came in through the waiting room or the examining room. The hall door was just for Father's use."

I glanced toward the inner office. Which room had Eliza come in from, I wondered, and how had she managed to overcome a man nearly twice her size? Had she snuck up on him, or hurled herself at him in a blind rage? I tried to picture both scenarios—but found I couldn't. I remembered too clearly her soft voice and gentle sorrow, and the glow on her face when she'd talked about Joy. All she'd wanted was to find out where her daughter was, and only Dr. Hauptfuhrer could tell her. What, then, could have prompted her to kill him?

Maybe she'd asked him where Joy was, and he had refused to tell her. In a person harboring sufficient rage, that might trigger a violent assault. But looking back over our conversation, I could find no evidence of such deep-seated anger in Eliza. She had no history of assault, nor had anything she'd said or done in our meeting suggested the presence of homicidal urges. As far as I could remember, I was the only one who'd been angry, when she'd told me her sad tale.

Perhaps that was it, I thought, my stomach lurching again toward the floor. Perhaps my own reaction had stirred up long-buried emotions within her. But if that's what had happened, I'd certainly had no inkling of it at the time. Indeed, if anyone had asked me how she'd appeared when she left my office, I would have said she was the picture of optimism. Which only went to show how wrong I could be.

"You told the arresting officer that you recognized the suspect," the detective was saying.

"Yes," Miss Hauptfuhrer said, "she's been a patient of my father for many years."

"Do you have any idea why she'd want to kill him?"

"I keep asking myself that," she said, her voice breaking, "but I can't come up with any answer."

"Maybe she had a beef about a medical treatment."

"No! My father was a wonderful doctor; he never received any complaints. Besides, I don't think her problems were very serious."

"What were they?"

"Well I couldn't tell you exactly; I'd have to go back through the records. But I'm familiar with my father's complicated cases, and I know that she wasn't one of them."

"Where would those records be?" the detective asked, jotting in his notebook. "We located her file in the office cabinet, but it doesn't go back very far."

"The rest are in the attic. We move the old ones up there, every few years."

"I'd like to see them, if I could."

"I doubt you could make much sense of them. Father used a personal shorthand to record patient visits—just a few words describing the complaint, and the treatment if there was any."

"Could you make sense of them?"

"Oh, yes; I had to learn to, early on, so I could help him with the billing."

"Do you think you could you go through Mrs. Miner's old records and let me know what you find?" the detective asked. "When you're feeling better, that is," he added reluctantly.

"If you think it could help," she answered, wiping her eyes.

The detective flipped to another page in his book. "You told the officer that your father had just been attacked when you came downstairs and found him. Did he say anything to you at that time?"

She shook her head. "No. He was already . . . he was already . . ." Whatever had been holding her together now apparently ran out, and she dissolved into helpless tears.

The detective grimaced. "All right, that's enough for now. Why don't you go back upstairs and we'll call you when the coroner gets here." He signaled to the crooked-nosed policeman to go with her.

Miss Hauptfuhrer rose unsteadily from her chair. As she did so her head turned, and our eyes met. Her brow furrowed, as if she was trying to place me. I could only hold her gaze for a moment before looking away.

The detective started toward me as she was led out of the room. "Miss . . . Summerford?" he said, glancing down at his book.

I sat up straighter. "Yes."

He tapped an index finger against his hat brim. "I'm Detective Sergeant Maloney."

"How do you do," I said hoarsely, wondering what, if anything, Eliza had told him about my provocative advice.

"I understand you know the suspect," he said, gazing down at me. His pale eyes were set deep in their sockets, underscored by purplish shadows.

"Yes, she's a patient."

"A patient? You mean you worked for Dr. Hauptfuhrer?"

He didn't know then, I thought with a surge of relief. Not yet, anyway. "No, I've never met the doctor. She's my patient. I'm a doctor, too."

He scratched the bony skull under his hat brim. "You're a doctor?"

"That's right."

"What, you deliver babies, that kind of thing?"

"I'm a psychotherapist."

He began jotting this in his book. "And that is what, exactly?"

"I treat mental and nervous disorders."

His hand paused over the book. "You were treating the suspect for a mental disorder?"

I shifted in my chair. Miss Hauptfuhrer apparently didn't know about her father's role in delivering Eliza's illegitimate child, or she would have told the detective. I was loath to be the one to reveal it. "Mrs. Miner lost a child a few years ago," I answered vaguely. "She's had some difficulty recovering."

"Was Dr. Hauptfuhrer aware that you were treating her?"

"I wouldn't know. I told you, I never met him."

"So you didn't tell him she had mental problems."

I frowned at him. Despite appearances, I didn't really know what had happened here. For Eliza's sake, I didn't want to jump to damning conclusions. The best I could do, I decided, was to tell him the truth about her mental state as I had believed it, until this morning. "I'm not sure what you mean by mental problems,

Detective," I replied. "Mrs. Miner suffers from an emotional disorder, which in her case takes the form of a relatively mild, recurring despondency."

He pursed his lips, not bothering to write this in his book. "Did you and she ever talk about the doctor?"

Whatever part I may or may not have played in the doctor's death, I wasn't going to improve things for myself by concealing information from the authorities. If I meant to align myself with the forces of law and order, now was the time to do it. And yet I hesitated. "Well, of course, I only met with her one time," I hedged.

"And she didn't mention him?"

I swallowed. My throat suddenly felt as parched as salt cod. "No," I said, "she never mentioned him." My God, I'd done it; I'd actually lied to him. Did that make me an accomplice to the crime?

He cocked his head, studying me with those unnerving eyes. "So tell me, Doctor, why do you think she did it?"

"I don't even know exactly what she's accused of, Detective. Perhaps you could tell me what happened here."

"Sure," he said with a shrug, "I could do that. What happened is that the woman you've identified as Elizabeth Miner entered the doctor's private office sometime between 8:30 and 9:00 a.m., approached the doctor from behind, and struck him fatally on the neck with a sword."

"A *sword?*" I repeated in astonishment.

He flipped back a few pages in his book. "A scimitar," he elaborated, exaggerating the pronunciation. "Like the Arabs use. In the desert."

"I know what it is; I just can't quite picture Eliza walking into the doctor's office carrying a sword."

"The weapon belonged to the doctor. According to his daughter, it was a present from Czar Nicholas, a leftover from—" he glanced back at the page "—the Caucasus War. It seems Hauptfuhrer and some other big-wigs were invited to Russia over the summer, to see if they could help the Czar's son. You know, the bleeder. The sword was kind of a 'thank you'. The doc must have been pretty proud of it, because he kept it on a stand on his desk. Which is where Mrs. Miner must have found it when she came in."

I was still digesting this information when I heard the street door open and shut, followed by the stamp of heavy feet.

"Damn!" exclaimed a burly, bearded man, as he came through the door into the waiting room; "it's colder than a witch's tit out there." He caught sight of me, and his chapped red cheeks turned even redder. "Beg pardon, Miss; I didn't realize there was a lady present."

"He's in there," the detective said, tilting his head toward the inner office.

"You finished with him?"

"He's all yours."

"Have you got an I.D.?" the bearded man asked.

"His daughter's upstairs." The detective instructed the crooked-nosed officer, who had returned to his post at the door, to go back up and fetch her.

The bearded man, who I deduced must be the coroner, lumbered past us into the inner office, pulling a draft of cool air behind him.

"Detective," I began tentatively when he was gone, "may I ask if anyone questioned Eliza about what happened, before they took her away?"

"The arresting officer talked to her."

"Could you tell me what she said?"

He looked me up and down, the pale eyes calculating. "Sure, why not?" he said finally, with a baring of teeth I supposed was meant as a smile. "We're both on the same side, right?"

I tried, not very successfully, to smile back.

"According to the suspect, she came to the doctor's office to ask for a prescription," he began in a sing-song voice, clearly intended to suggest incredulity. "The doctor answered the front door, told her to wait in the examining room and said he'd be right with her. He went into the adjoining office and closed the door. She doesn't know how long she waited but it seemed like a long time. After a while she knocked on the connecting door and called out his name, but he didn't answer. She opened the door and saw the doctor lying in a pool of blood. She went over to see if she could help and realized he was dead." He shrugged. "End of story."

I sat up, feeling a flutter of hope. I didn't know if the prescription part was true, but the rest seemed perfectly plausible. "Isn't it possible, then, that someone else came into the office while Mrs. Miner was waiting in the examining room? A common thief, perhaps? He could have—"

I stopped; Miss Hauptfuhrer had returned, accompanied by Officer McKee. I waited until she had crossed into her father's office, then lowered my voice and continued, "He could have come right in through the unlocked front door, and killed the doctor for his valuables."

But the detective was shaking his head. "Miss Hauptfuhrer found the suspect standing over the victim's body, with the sword at her feet and blood all over her skirt. Besides, the doctor was wearing a fancy fob watch and a very nice gold ring, neither of which were taken."

I sank back in my chair.

"There's no question she did it," he said flatly. "The only thing left to fill in is why." He waited, watching me expectantly.

A muffled cry reached us from the inner office. The next minute Miss Hauptfuhrer flew out with her hands over her face and ran sobbing into the hallway. She was followed more slowly by the ambulance crew, now bearing a loaded stretcher.

Maloney got up and approached the coroner, who was bringing up the rear. "So, is he dead?" he drawled.

"He's dead." The coroner handed Maloney the certificate over the draped body. "I understand you've got a suspect in custody?"

"One of his patients," Maloney confirmed. "It looks like an open and shut case."

The coroner nodded. "I don't think there's much doubt about the cause of death, but I should have the autopsy results by tomorrow afternoon."

"I'll keep the area sealed until then."

The coroner signaled to the ambulance crew to move out.

"Wait—" I pushed myself to my feet. "Could I see the wound?"

The coroner frowned. "It's not a pretty sight, Miss," he warned.

"It's all right," I told him, "I'm a doctor."

He glanced toward Maloney.

The detective eyed me with pursed lips, his gaze inscrutable. "She can't disturb anything, can she?"

"Not so long as she just looks," the coroner said with a shrug.

"Go on, then," the detective said to me. "Look away."

Crossing to the stretcher, I folded back the sheet and gazed down at the face of Dr. Herman Hauptfuhrer. It was a handsome face despite its bluish cast, past middle age but not yet jowly, with long, dark eyelashes and a silver-dusted mustache. It was his eyes, though, that seized my attention. Unlike the cloudy eyes of the nameless cadavers I was accustomed to, these stared up at me clearly—and, it seemed, accusingly—in their unblinking directness.

Drawing a deep breath, I pulled the cloth lower to reveal the wound. It was on the right side of his neck, as wide as my index finger and angled slightly downward. Once again I tried to reconcile my impressions of Eliza with this proof of vicious assault—and once again, I failed. I positioned my hands over the corpse's temples, glancing at the coroner. "May I?"

He bowed. "By all means," he replied, with an exaggerated sweep of his arm.

I grasped the head and started to tilt it for a better look—but let go reflexively as my fingertips registered the still-warm skin. I stared down at the white marks my fingers had left on the temples, where the lividity wasn't yet fixed, struck afresh by the enormity of what had occurred. Just an hour ago, this man had been eating breakfast; now, perhaps because of my careless words to Eliza, he would eat and breathe no more.

Struggling to regain a semblance of detachment, I took hold of the head once more and tipped it to the right to open the gash. Rigor mortis had not yet set in and it turned easily on its stem, revealing the full extent of the damage. The main blood vessels and trachea, I saw, had been completely severed, while the esophagus was sliced halfway through. It was a cruel wound, inflicted with clear and deadly intent. I released the head, and stepped back.

"Seems it only took one stroke," the detective mused, coming to stand beside me. "One clean stroke, coming down from above, while the doctor was squatting in front of the filing cabinets."

"How do you know he was squatting?" I asked dully.

"From the position of the body, and the fact that one of the bottom file drawers was open. We're guessing he was putting away the papers he'd come down to work on, when the suspect struck him from behind."

Yes, I could see it more clearly now. Eliza demanding to know where her daughter was. The doctor turning her down, refusing to discuss the matter any further as he went back to filing his papers. And then Eliza, aflame with the injustice I'd convinced her had been perpetrated against her, grabbing the sword from the desk and inflicting the fatal blow. I shook my head, trying to dislodge the disturbing images from my mind. It occurred to me that this must be why the detective had let me look: to shock me into accepting Eliza's guilt and ensure my full cooperation.

"Are we done here?" the coroner asked.

The detective nodded. "We're done."

The coroner pulled the sheet back up over the corpse and signaled to the stretcher bearers to move out.

Turning back to me, the detective asked briskly, "So what have we got?" Counting on his fingers, he summarized, "We've got the suspect standing over the victim's body, covered with the victim's blood; we've got the murder weapon on the floor two feet from where she's standing; and we've got some very nice finger impressions on the sword handle that I'm confident will match her prints." He spread his hands in the air. "In other words, it's a clear cut case, and that's what I intend to tell the boys from Headquarters when they arrive. I'm thinking this might even be the first New York case to win a homicide conviction based on fingerprint evidence." He peered at me. "So, Dr. Summerford, the only way you can help your patient now, the *only* way, is by telling me why she did it. Maybe she had a good reason. If there are any mitigatin' circumstances that could make things easier on her, you oughta let me know."

Maybe he was right, I thought frantically; maybe if her reasons were known the charges against her would be reduced, or a jury might at least be more sympathetic. But if I told him about our conversation, I'd not only be handing the prosecution a motive, I'd be revealing my own role in the murder, as well. So instead, I stalled for time. "You must understand, Detective Maloney, that anything my patient tells me, whether or not it has a bearing on this case, is strictly confidential. I would have to ask her permission before I could repeat it to anyone else."

His pale eyes narrowed, but he replied pleasantly enough, "Sure, you go ahead and get permission. Then we'll talk." He jotted something on a page of his book and ripped it out. "Give this to Officer Callahan, the arresting officer. He'll make sure you get a chance to see her."

I stared down at the paper. "But—where will I find her?"

"Harlem Police Court." He took the paper back and wrote down the address. "Callahan will take her there for her arraignment as soon as he's finished booking her. They ought to be there for a couple of hours."

I slid the paper numbly into my pocket and followed him out of the room. As we passed through the hallway I glanced up the staircase toward Miss Hauptfuhrer's living quarters, feeling a disturbing kinship. The doctor's daughter wasn't so very different from me, after all: an older unmarried woman, living a quietly productive life in the lee of her father's protection. Things like this weren't supposed to happen to people like her. To people like *us*. I couldn't help thinking how dreadfully quiet the house would seem to her in the days to come, with nothing to keep her company but the tick of the clock, and the endlessly repeating memory of discovering her father's brutalized body . . . .

"Detective," I mused aloud as we approached the front door, "you said that Miss Hauptfuhrer found Mrs. Miner standing over her father's body. Did she tell you why she happened to come down to his office when she did?"

I thought he hesitated slightly, before answering, "She heard screaming through the heating vent."

"You mean she actually heard her father being attacked?" I asked in horror.

"Nah, someone screaming for help."

I pulled up short. "Screaming for help? Who was it?"

"She says it was Mrs. Miner."

"Mrs. Miner was screaming for help?"

"So she says."

"But why would she scream for help if she'd just—"

"I've seen it before," he said with a shrug. "Something sets 'em off, they pull the trigger, then they get hysterical when they realize what they've done. It's as if for just that split second when they commit the crime, the devil is talking in their ear." He pulled the door open.

Yes, I supposed it could have happened like that, I thought as I stumbled on past him out to the street. A moment of unpremeditated violence, triggered by thoughts of blame and revenge; only in this case, the voice in the killer's ear may very well have been my own.

"Goodbye for now, Dr. Summerford," he called after me. "I'll be talking to you again, real soon."

CHAPTER FIVE

I broke through the handful of lingering gawkers and lurched blindly down the sidewalk, having no idea where I was going but desperate to get away. Images of the slain doctor seemed to be burned into the backs of my eyelids, while bits of my conversation with the detective kept repeating over and over in my mind, like an endless organ grinder's tune. Worse than the gore, though, worse than the memory of Eliza's dazed face or the detective's stony conviction, was the secret fear that I, once again, was at least partly responsible.

I didn't know what I was going to say to Eliza when I saw her at the police court. If only there was someone I could confide in beforehand, someone who could assure me that things weren't as bad as they seemed and tell me what I ought to do now. But who? Not my mother, of course, And certainly not Papa.

At the end of the street I turned left to avoid a baby carriage and, lacking any clear destination, continued walking south. A persistent wind lashed at my eyes, blurring the sidewalk under my feet as one block ran into another. It wasn't fair, I thought angrily, wiping the tears away. I wasn't the one who'd killed the doctor. I may have failed to recognize Eliza's state of mind—may even have provoked her, unintentionally—but I wasn't the one who'd raised the sword and struck a man dead. Why should my career, my professional reputation—and perhaps worst of all, my father's opinion of me—be wrecked because of someone I barely knew? Perhaps I ought to tell the detective about Eliza's lost baby, after all, without mentioning my advice to her, and let Eliza deal with the consequences of her actions. I could go back there right now, and be done with it.

But I knew that I wouldn't. I couldn't just abandon her. Because if I did, and she was sentenced to life in prison or worse, a piece of me would have to go with her.

I'd come to the end of another block. Looking up at the street sign, I discovered that I'd reached the intersection of Madison and 73rd Street. I squeezed my book bag against my chest in a spasm of relief; suddenly, I knew just where to go. I turned left and ran down the sidewalk, on legs still wobbly from shock. I was over an hour late, but with any luck he'd still be at home. The railed stoop of his brownstone reached out in welcome up ahead. Bounding toward it, I hopped up the steps and rapped sharply on the door.

The maid who answered my knock assured me that Professor Bogard was still in. I waited in the parlor while she went to inform him of my arrival, warming my hands in front of the fire, feeling a little steadier with each passing minute. If anyone could give me a fair assessment of my handling of Eliza, it was the professor. I glanced at the mementoes of his illustrious career, which covered the parlor walls: posters from his well-attended lectures; tinted daguerreotypes of distinguished colleagues; smaller tintypes featuring the professor in exotic locales. I spotted a recent photograph in the circular, box camera format, and drew closer. It was of my graduating class, taken the spring before the professor left Johns Hopkins to devote himself to lecturing full-time. The professor was standing at the end of the front row, smiling confidently at the camera, while I held pride of place on his right, with my blurry face turned in his direction.

I felt a small thrill, even now. I'd scarcely believed it when he'd asked me to continue as his research assistant after graduation. I'd known he'd been pleased with my prior work—the paper we co-wrote on Myer's theory of extra-marginal consciousness had been particularly well received—but I was sure there were many people more qualified than I who would have jumped at the opportunity to assist him. Now I thanked my lucky stars that we had remained in close contact, so that I could call on him for help.

The maid returned and led me down the hall to the professor's study, rapping twice on the door before she pushed it open.

"Genevieve!" cried the professor, rising behind his desk on sight of me. "I wondered what had become of you."

His plump torso was clothed in a canary-yellow waistcoat so bright it made his white beard glow. Despite the brilliance of his attire, however, my eyes were drawn immediately to the drab little man sitting across from him. "I . . . I'm sorry I'm late," I stammered, struggling to hide my dismay as the seated man rose more slowly to his feet.

"Never mind, there's still a little time," the professor assured me. "Dr. Mayhew and I have a luncheon appointment at Sherry's but we don't have to leave for another quarter of an hour." He gestured toward the other man. "You know Dr. Mayhew, I believe?"

I nodded. I knew him, all right; he was the professor who'd given me the drawing assignment on penile mechanics. "Professor."

"Dr. Summerford," he said, tipping his head.

"Mayhew's just arrived from Baltimore," Professor Bogard explained as we all sat down. "He's going to be teaching at the College of Physicians and Surgeons for the remainder of the year. Perhaps it's fortunate that you were delayed; now you can have the benefit of two minds, as it were."

I smiled with an effort. In contrast to Professor Bogard, Mayhew was a study in muted gray—gray suit, gray thinning hair, over-waxed gray mustache. His only compelling features were his bright little eyes, which were watching me now as a snake might watch a tethered mouse. "Perhaps I should come back later," I suggested, "when you have more time."

"No time like the present," the professor said breezily. "Besides, I'm leaving town tomorrow on a lecture tour, so I'll be spending the afternoon packing." To Mayhew he explained, "I've agreed to supervise Genevieve's clinical work here in the city, in return for her help with my research. She's developing a new therapy technique based on work she did with Herbert Cassell, applying the rational psychotherapy approach within a class format."

"Is that right?" Mayhew said, cocking an eyebrow.

"Yes, I'm employing Cassell's reeducation techniques to relieve my patient's physical symptoms," I explained, "by correcting the faulty thoughts and emotions that underlie them."

His other eyebrow rose to join the first. "How very . . . novel."

"It's fairly well established that emotional trauma can affect the nervous system on a physiological level," I countered. "In the same way that unhappy thoughts can decrease gastric secretions, leading to digestive disease, unhappy emotions elicited by trauma can negatively affect the nervous system, leading to physical symptoms. It follows that if you change the emotions that are linked to the trauma, you should be able to make those symptoms go away." I realized that, as so often happened in his presence, I was talking too fast and too much in an attempt to forestall his ridicule.

"And you expect to accomplish all that with several patients at once?" he drawled.

"It's been done before, in other contexts. With depressive consumptives, for instance. Cassell's class model is tailor-made for people who've shared similar traumas."

"Oh, I'm sure your precedents are sound. May I congratulate you, then, on a successful venture so far?"

I blinked at him, knowing he couldn't possibly have found out about Eliza, but feeling somehow exposed nonetheless. "Well it . . . it's really too early to say," I finally answered. "Yesterday was my first class."

"Yes, yes; your first class!" exclaimed Professor Bogard, glancing at the clock. "Tell us, Genevieve, how did it go?"

The ticking of the clock filled the silence as they waited for my response. I couldn't possibly tell the professor about Eliza's arrest in front of Mayhew. But I needed his advice, and I didn't know when I'd have another opportunity to get it. I decided I would have to try to present the core problem, without giving too much away.

I began with a brief description of the class members and their symptoms, before casually mentioning that one patient in particular had caught my interest. Trying my best to ignore Mayhew, who was now sprawling sideways in his chair with his chin propped skeptically on his palm, I sketched Eliza's history and her private revelations to me after class. I didn't mention the doctor's name, or that I had encouraged Eliza to confront him—or that he had been murdered just a few hours before.

"What did you make of her statements about the baby girl?" Professor Bogard asked when I was done.

"I suppose what concerned me most was her overwhelming guilt. I felt it was important to suggest that she wasn't the only one responsible for what happened."

"For what she says happened, you mean," Mayhew interjected. "You didn't accept it at face value, I hope."

So he was no longer content to belittle just me, I thought; now he sought to discredit my patients, as well. "Are you suggesting that there is no daughter?" I asked him. "That she's making it all up?"

"I'm suggesting that it may be a product of her unconscious, Dr. Summerford," he corrected. "You do remember the unconscious?"

I stared at him in surprise. When the unconscious motive theories had started trickling in from abroad during my first years at medical school, Mayhew had been their loudest detractor, pronouncing them "factually unsupported" and "prone to luridly sexual interpretation". Now that the great Stanley Hall had taken up the cause, however, calling for a grand symposium to formally introduce the theories to America, he seemed to have changed his tune. I turned to Professor Bogard, waiting for him to pooh-pooh Mayhew's farfetched assertion. But to my surprise, he was nodding in agreement.

"We'd certainly have to question the truth of her story," the professor said. "You say the Reverend never mentioned a daughter?"

"Well, no," I said, scrambling to follow this line of thinking, "but he only came to the parish a few years ago. I assume he arrived after the daughter was born."

"Or the whole birth story is an hysterical fantasy," Mayhew persisted. "You did consider the possibility?"

I felt a flush creeping up my temples. "I saw nothing in her file or in her interactions with me to suggest such a thing."

"That might indicate more a failure of observation, than a refutation of the fact, might it not?" he asked with a shrug.

"You say her son suffocated while she was taking a bath," Professor Bogard broke in, seemingly oblivious to Mayhew's needling.

"Yes," I told him, "that's in Reverend Palmer's records."

He drummed his fingers over his waistcoat. "From what the Reverend told you about the hours she spends in church, I think we can safely say she holds herself responsible for the death."

"I expect that's true," I agreed.

"One can only imagine the pain such a belief would cause," he went on. "It could, quite literally, become unbearable. In such a case, the fantasy of another, living child might provide some relief."

I sat slowly back in my seat.

"The doctor's involvement is a nice touch," Mayhew said. "She doesn't just give the baby up; it's taken from her forcibly, leaving her helpless and therefore, in this scenario, blameless."

I didn't know whether to be intrigued or horrified by their suggestion. If there really was no baby girl, then there was no reason for Eliza to have killed the doctor. At least, no rational reason. But then again, if she believed there was a baby, I supposed the result might have been the same. It would all depend on the power and persistence of the fantasy. "Surely, Professor, it would be difficult for her to maintain such a fantasy, if all those around her knew it to be untrue," I ventured. "She'd have to doubt its reality on some level, wouldn't she?"

"To the contrary," Mayhew answered, stroking his waxy mustache, "to her it would be very real indeed. The greater her guilt, the more energy she would have to invest in the defense against it. The mind, Dr. Summerford, is more complex than you give it credit for."

Still addressing Professor Bogard, I persisted, "But what if a key player in the fantasy were to repudiate it? What if she confronted the doctor, for example, and he insisted that none of it had ever happened? Might that be sufficient to pierce the hysterical belief?"

"Not necessarily," Bogard replied. "The fantasy would be protecting her from powerful feelings of guilt and incompetence— providing a relief valve, as it were. It wouldn't be easy to dispel. If one were to try, without defusing those emotions first . . ." he shook his head.

"What? What would happen then?"

He shrugged. "Who knows? Let's just say it would be best not to find out."

He must have sensed my distress, for he added in a not unkindly tone, "You must be patient, my dear. I know the desire to see immediate results when you're just starting out can be very strong, but overnight cures are rare in our line of work. You have to uncover the underlying complex before the symptoms will disappear. Take your time, and get to know the patient in your weekly sessions. That's where the cure will take place."

I don't think he could have made me feel worse if he had tried. It had never occurred to me that Eliza's story might all be an hysterical fantasy. If they were right, then Dr. Hauptfuhrer was completely blameless—and my own failure all the more glaring. "But what if she really did have another child?" I pleaded.

"Let's examine that possibility, shall we?" Bogard said brightly, as though we were in class, and this was all just some academic exercise. "We have before us an unmarried girl, carrying a bastard in her womb. On the one hand, she is deeply ashamed of her illicit sexual activity and the pregnancy it has initiated. On the other, she can't help but feel some natural affection for the infant growing within her."

"Producing," Mayhew chimed in, "an irreconcilable conflict: one part of her wants to love and protect the child, while another wants to destroy the symbol of her shame."

"And so," Bogard continued, slapping his palm against his blotter, "she projects her destructive urges onto the doctor who delivers it, bringing us right back where we were before: with this fantasy wherein the doctor forces her to give the child up against her wishes, allowing her to deny her own hatred for the baby at the same time she rids herself of it!" They beamed at each other over the desktop.

"But isn't it possible that her story is true?" I interjected. "After all, men do take sexual advantage of women every day. It seems quite plausible to me that she had this baby and wanted to keep it, but was forced to give it up."

"Of course it's possible, my dear," Professor Bogard said, "but in the absence of any corroborating evidence, it mustn't be assumed." Peering at me over his spectacles, he added, "Remember, it isn't only the patient's story that must be questioned. The psychotherapist must constantly examine his own objectivity, as well. It isn't unusual for a patient's experience to trigger memories and emotions in the therapist that could distort his understanding of the issues."

I shrank in my chair as the meaning of his words sank in. "I'm aware of that possibility," I said stiffly, hoping Mayhew didn't detect my discomfort.

"Being aware, and seeing it in ourselves, are often two different things," the professor said mildly, inspecting a fingernail.

My ears were so hot I thought they must be glowing like horseshoes on a forge. I hadn't suffered the same misfortune as Eliza, but as the professor knew, I had come close—so close that just thinking about it still made me blush to the roots of my hair. I'd told Professor Bogard about it one evening at school, while we were reviewing an article on control of the sexual impulse in male juveniles. I'd attempted a joke—a caustic allusion to the randy young seducer in Donne's "The Flea"—which the professor, typically, had refused to take at face value. After much teasing I'd finally confessed the whole story, striving for a tone of sophisticated nonchalance that was very different from what I'd felt.

I had told him about Simon Shaw. Just thinking the name, even now, was like stirring a bucket of muddy water. The first image to rise up was of the lock of dark hair that used to fall over one eye when he tilted his head, as he tended to do on sight of me. Next came his coat: a man-sized garment of shearling-lined suede, baggy on his young frame and stained around the cuffs from hard use. It had smelled of sweet leather and sweat and something bitter, like acorns; and when he wrapped it around me the night I snuck down to the stable, it was as cozy as a lap rug on a midwinter sleigh ride.

The mantel clock chimed the hour. "I'm afraid we're out of time," the professor said. "Much as I love Louis, I don't trust him to hold our table for very long. Is there anything else we need to discuss, my dear?"

I edged forward on my seat. He couldn't go yet; he hadn't told me what to do. "I'm still not sure how to proceed with my patient. I wouldn't want my inexperience to hamper her treatment."

"Don't worry, you know much more than you think you do," he cheerfully assured me, collecting his pipe and tobacco. "Besides, the best way to overcome a lack of experience is to simply throw yourself into the trenches. You never know what you're capable of, until you're pushed to it."

"But—couldn't we meet one more time before you go? So that I could fill you in on the details . . ."

He frowned down at his engagement book, shaking his head. "I'm afraid I'm going to be awfully busy, preparing for the trip." He looked up, his face brightening. "Just trust your instincts, my dear. Psychotherapy isn't as easy as knowing where to place the stitches or how to tie the knots. Sometimes you just have to feel your way."

I sat back in defeat, feeling as though the last lifeboat was floating away without me.

"With all due respect," Mayhew said to the professor, "if she wants to eliminate the fabrication, she could try removing the patient's uterus."

I barely suppressed a groan. The idea that hysterical fantasies could be triggered by nervous reflexes originating in the uterus had been almost universally discredited, the removal of the uterus having proved no more helpful than cauterization of the cervix, enlargement of the anus, or any of the other techniques that had been tried to stem the pathological flow of reflex from organs to the mind. Only a misogynist like Mayhew would cling to such an ineffectual solution. "I thought you believed the delusion grew out of her unconscious," I said.

He shrugged. "I do. But it's telling, is it not, that hysterical fantasies are seen almost exclusively in females? I don't believe we can rule out a physiological predisposition in the weaker sex."

Again I looked to Professor Bogard, waiting for him to refute this drivel; but he was busy rifling through some papers on his desk. I turned back to Mayhew. "A hysterectomy strikes me as extreme, especially when we haven't even established that we're dealing with a fantasy."

"Haven't we?" he said, his eyes widening in surprise. "Why, I didn't think any doubt remained."

I could feel myself succumbing to that state of mute humiliation I'd experienced so often in class, when he'd caught me with one of his barbs. But we weren't in the classroom now, and there was too much at stake to let him bully me. "I still have doubts," I said.

"Do you really?" He folded his hands delicately in his lap. "Then I'm afraid we must conclude that your tender feminine heart has caused you to mistake an hysterical woman's wishes for the truth."

The ratty tails of his mustache twitched with satisfaction, as I'd seen them twitch so many times before. This time, however, I couldn't hold back the anger the sight provoked. "Or we could conclude that she's telling the truth," I blurted out, "and that you, having so little regard for either women or the truth, are unable to recognize it."

For one exultant moment I reveled in the flush that mottled his face—before the realization of what I'd done came bearing down on me. The last thing I needed now was the enmity of my professional peers. We stared at each other, he in outrage, I in an agony of regret.

The professor unknowingly broke the silence. "Here it is!" he exclaimed, pulling a sheaf of papers from under his pipe rack and holding it out to me over the desk. "This is for you. It's my response to Pierre Janet's Harvard lectures on the major states of hystericals."

Another research assignment. I reached for it with a leaden arm.

"It's a bit rough, I know, but I was short on time. Most of the lecture material is reprinted in these." He passed me a heavy stack of Journal de Psychologie back issues. "I've jotted down the basic points, but you should of course feel free to add your own ideas."

I balanced the journals on my lap and flipped through his notes. A few handwritten lines were scrawled across each page, heavily punctuated with question marks and ellipses.

"Well, what do you say?" he asked jovially, as though offering me an irresistible treat. "Are you game?"

"Of course," I said mechanically, removing the journals I'd brought with me from my bag and replacing them with the new ones. "When do you need it?"

"Would the end of next week be too soon?"

"Next week!"

"I know, I know; but there's a publication deadline to meet."

"Well then," I sighed, "I suppose I can manage it."

"Marvelous!" He got to his feet. "I knew I could count on you." He stepped jauntily around his desk toward the door, the picture of confidence, a man clearly in charge of his affairs. My heart ached at the sight. It was all I could do not to grab hold of his sleeve and beg for his help.

"We'll see you out," he said, reaching for the doorknob.

I walked beside him down the hallway, as Mayhew trailed behind. I imagined I could feel Mayhew's eyes on my back, full of contempt for a woman who'd had the nerve to step outside the bounds of nature to assume a man's job. He had once said, in an anatomy lecture in which I was the only woman present, that the female brain was "rather too small for great intellect, but just large enough for conceit." As I stepped out the front door into a world newly fraught with uncertainty, I wondered for the first time if he might be right.

CHAPTER SIX

I rode the Third Avenue El up to 116th Street and walked the last five blocks to the Harlem Police Court. This was a fortress-like structure with a grim corner tower and thick bars over the windows of the attached jail. I followed two men carrying document cases past the jail's vehicular entrance and through a side door into the courthouse. An iron staircase spiraled upward from the entry hall. Following the signs, I climbed the polished terrazzo steps to the magistrate's courtroom.

Pushing through the heavy doors, I found myself inside a spacious room with a vaulted, coffered ceiling and carved wainscoting on the walls. A dozen wide benches in the back half of the room were filled end-to-end with all manner of humanity, from women holding squalling infants to elderly gentlemen in fastidious business attire. The magistrate sat across from them with his back to a two-story window. Between the benches and the magistrate's platform sat the lawyers and court personnel, boxed off by wooden railings.

I edged through the odiferous crowd at the door, craning my neck for a glimpse of Eliza. A long line of prisoners and their arresting officers stretched to the clerk's desk from a door at the side of the room, but I didn't see her among them. The steam pipes were going full tilt, spewing unchecked heat into the crammed courtroom. As more people pushed in behind me, I moved to a spot further up along the wall, fanning myself with a section of the professor's notes as I waited for her to arrive.

I still wasn't sure how I would feel or what I was going to say when I finally spoke with her—or for that matter, what she might be feeling or might say to me. For all I knew, she might be blaming me for whatever had transpired. I listened with half an ear as the parade of defendants took their turns before the magistrate: a grocer accused of selling skimmed milk; a shabbily dressed young woman charged with prostitution; a rotund man accused of stealing three pairs of trousers, by concealing them under his waistband. By the time the magistrate had appointed four reporters from the front row an "investigative committee" and charged them with determining whether the latter's waistband was capable of such a feat, sweat was trickling steadily down my ribs, and I was feeling faint from the heat. When the reporters rose to follow the man into the magistrate's private chamber, I scurried over to claim a spot on the vacated bench.

I had just sat down when the side door opened and Eliza stepped into the room, accompanied by the officer who'd driven her away in the van. She looked terrible—her face deathly pale, her hair falling from its pins, her skirt stiff with dried blood. She cowered behind the officer as they joined the line and shuffled toward the clerk's desk. I tried to observe her with a detached eye, searching for the unhinged woman I had failed to detect before. But no matter how hard I stared, I saw only a more frightened, confused version of the docile young woman I remembered.

As they approached the clerk's desk she glanced out toward the gallery, and drew up short. At first I thought she was looking at me— but then realized it was at something behind me. I turned to see a stoop-shouldered woman in a threadbare coat laboring up the center aisle, leaning heavily on a bamboo walking stick. She had thinning gray hair pulled back under a shapeless felt hat, and pale blue eyes that were trained on Eliza. She reached the gate and stopped, her shoulders drooping.

The Roundsman started toward her from the other side of the rail. Before he had taken two steps she crumpled forward, whacking the gate with her stick as she grabbed for it with both hands. I jumped up to catch her from behind at the same instant the Roundsman lunged for her over the rail.

"Whoa there, easy does it," he said, securing her in a beefy grip.

I wrapped my arm around the woman's shoulders to steady her while he came around through the gate, and together we lowered her onto the front bench.

"What are they going to do to her?" she whimpered, clutching her stick in both hands.

"To who?" the Roundsman asked.

She looked past him, toward Eliza. "My daughter."

My arm dropped reflexively from her shoulders. "You're Eliza's mother?"

She turned to me in a daze. "A man called me from the police station; he said I should get her a lawyer. But I don't have any money for a lawyer . . ."

"Are you going to be all right, ma'am?" asked the Roundsman, peering into her face.

"She's in shock," I told him. "I think she'll be all right if she just rests for a minute. You can leave her with me; I'll keep an eye on her." Looking relieved, he returned to his post on the other side of the rail.

I eased the woman's coat off her shoulders and fanned her with the professor's notes. At close range I realized she wasn't as old as I'd first supposed—not much older than my own mother, most likely. It was the heaviness of her movements, her air of long-suffering resignation, that had misled me. I could see now a clear resemblance to her daughter, in the long, oval shape of her face, and the pale blue of her eyes.

I looked back toward Eliza, who had reached the clerk's desk and was listening meekly as the arresting officer gave his statement. She turned her head at the same moment, and our eyes met. I felt a brief flash of anger toward her for putting us in this position, mixed with guilt over my own incompetence. Her own, soft eyes held no accusation, however. Again, I discerned only helpless fear and confusion. Sympathy rose up in me, uninvited. Of its own accord, my hand lifted in a small wave of encouragement.

Her mother turned and blinked at me, as if really seeing me for the first time. "You know my daughter?"

"Yes, I met her just yesterday, at the church." I held out my hand. "I'm Genevieve Summerford."

She frowned at me for a moment, as though trying to place my name. Suddenly her eyes widened, and her mouth fell open in recognition. "You!" she gasped, drawing back from me. "You're the one!"

I lowered my hand. "I beg your pardon?"

Her gnarled finger pointed at me from the top of her walking stick. "You're the woman doctor she told me about, who put all those crazy ideas in her head!"

I licked my suddenly dry lips. "Mrs. Braun, I'm not sure what Eliza told you, but all I did was—"

"I know exactly what you did!" she interrupted. "You got her all excited and talking foolishness! You should have known better; you're a doctor! Couldn't you see she isn't right in the head?"

The courtroom seemed to have suddenly tilted and slid off center. "What do you mean, she isn't right in the head?" I asked faintly.

She pushed herself to her feet. "It's all your fault," she fumed, leaning over me with her eyes ablaze. "Everything that's happened; it's all your fault!" She backed into the aisle, her cane bumping against the bench legs as she dragged it after her. I turned and watched her stagger to an empty spot three rows back and sit down, her concave chest heaving and her face livid with indignation.

I swiveled back toward the front of the room. My heart was racing and my eyes refused to focus. Eliza, the clerk, and the magistrate all merged into a blur, until I could see nothing but accusing eyes glaring down at me. Not Mrs. Braun's eyes—Papa's eyes, cold and empty as the darkest reaches of space. I gripped the edge of the bench, helpless to resist, as I was swept back to that day long ago . . . .

I LAY ON my stomach on the cool parquet floor, at eye level with the huge blue porcelain urns that had been magically transported from the distant Orient to house the giant palms in each corner of our drawing room. The fronds of one of these palms curved luxuriously over my head, creating a perfect hideaway. In the summer, when the rug was rolled up and the blinds were half-drawn to keep out the heat, this was my favorite place to draw.

My brother Conrad lay propped on his elbows beside me, watching the horse on my drawing tablet come slowly to life. His own drawing lay beside him—large messy strokes of blue broken by stepped, horizontal lines that I knew from experience were rooftops.

"Can I help?" he asked me.

"No. It's a present, for Mamma. It has to be just from me."

Feet scurried around our heads as the maids rushed about setting tall vases and crystal decanters and shining brass spittoons in place. From time to time I glanced up at the commotion through the fingers of the palm frond. I'd never seen the chandelier glow so brightly, or the piano reflect it with such a perfect shine. The entire household had been put to work preparing for Mamma's 35th birthday party. Even Eleanor, our new governess, had been pressed into service repairing a tear in one of the pillow covers. I could see her sitting in the tete-a-tete across the room, her small brown head bent over the velvet cover as her inexperienced fingers fumbled with the needle.

In the hallway I heard Mamma ask for the hundredth time, "Have the flowers arrived?" For weeks we'd been hearing about the special flowers that she'd ordered for the event, the mere mention of which brought a sparkle to her eye. They were coming all the way from France, or Italy, or some other such inconceivable place, raced over land and water to arrive fresh and dewy at our door on this, her special day. Except that the deliverymen seemed to be cutting it awfully close, and as the time before the main event ran short, so did Mamma's temper.

Conrad leaned over to watch me draw the horse's rear leg. "Yikes," he exclaimed, yikes being his word of the week, "that's a good horse."

I bumped over so he could see the whole thing. "This is the hardest part," I explained. He watched in respectful silence as I drew the knee, hock and splaying hoof, so close to me I could smell the Pears' soap that Eleanor used to wash his hair. I paused to examine the hoof and, deciding it was too small, drew a second line wider than the first. I pushed myself up on my hands to judge the result, and heard Conrad's soft grunt of approval.

"All right," I relented, "you can fill in some of the sky. But only this part, right here."

He scuttled on elbows and knees to the box of wax coloring sticks Mamma had brought back from France, and returned with a blunted blue. We set to work, and were just applying the finishing touches when a flurry of gasps and cries from the hallway informed us that the flowers had finally arrived. A moment later Mamma burst into the drawing room, trailed by Katie and two of the maids, each carrying an enormous arrangement. I pulled my drawing from beneath Conrad's hand and flipped it over as she bustled past, her hair flying in untidy wisps around her shirtwaist collar.

She turned and scanned the room like a general surveying his battlefield. "Let's see . . . that one right there, I think," she directed the parlor maid, pointing to the round table; "and that one on the piano. No, wait: that one should go in front of the window. This one," she said to Katie, who was straining under the weight of an enormous jardinière, "should go on the piano." She watched, fists on hips, as Katie slid the urn-shaped vase on top of the case. "Yes; perfect!"

I eyed this last arrangement with interest. It was nearly as tall as my brother, an elaborate construction of twining greens and extraordinarily long-stemmed roses that curved languidly over the edge of the vase. So these were the flowers that had put my mother in such a dither of anticipation. My blood quickened, as an idea began to take shape in my mind.

"Where do you want these little ones, ma'am?" asked the chambermaid from the doorway, holding three vases in her arms.

Mamma strode over to relieve her of one of the vases. "One on the hall console, I think, and two on the dining room sideboard. Here, I'll show you. Eleanor, could you give us a hand?"

Eleanor put down her needle with relief and followed them out.

Conrad and I were alone in the drawing room. I got up and walked over to the piano for a closer inspection of the roses. They were as soft as velvet and perfectly shaped, as evenly formed as the special rosette trim in Mrs. Cunningham's hat shop. I lifted one of the plump heads to my nose and breathed its intoxicating perfume, as my idea burst into full form.

I released the rose and dashed out the door. Returning a few moments later with a pair of scissors, I approached the piano and examined the roses with a critical, artist's eye. The differences were slight but some of the blossoms seemed a bit fatter to me, and slightly more symmetrical. I snipped one of these off with several inches of stem and set it aside. Working slowly to avoid the thorns, I continued to cut one after another of the best heads, until there was a good-sized pile on the piano top. I carried these back to my drawing place and set to work.

I was lost in the requirements of color and proportion when, some time later, my concentration was broken by my mother's startled cry. "Genna! What have you done?"

I looked up to see her standing beside the piano, staring at a trail of petals that led from the bench to my little hideaway. I was vexed that I'd been found out before my masterwork was complete; but disappointment quickly gave way to delicious anticipation. I jumped to my feet, holding up my drawing with both hands. I had punched the rose stems through the heavy paper and twisted them together underneath, so that the precious flowers now formed a nearly full wreath around the horse's neck. "Happy Birthday, Mamma!"

"Oh, Genna." Her eyes were dark with disappointment.

I lowered the drawing uncertainly to my side. "It's not finished yet. It will look better when it's done . . ."

"What is it?" Father stood in the doorway, having chosen this moment to look in on the preparations. "What's happened?" he asked, striding to my mother's side.

"It's all right," my mother said quickly; "she was just trying to make me a present."

Father's gaze moved from Mother's face, to the rose garland. "No, it is not all right," he fumed. "Not all right at all! Genevieve, how many times have we told you that you must think before you act?"

I stared down at my shoes.

"What on earth possessed you? You know how much your mother has been looking forward to receiving those roses! Why would you want to destroy them?"

I looked up in surprise. "I didn't destroy them! They're right here, see? On the horse's neck."

His cheeks bulged the way they had when Mrs. Wall asked me how I liked her fruit cake and I said it tasted moldy. "That was a thoughtless and foolhardy thing to do."

I didn't yet have a full grasp of the fatal flaw which would soon so radically change my life. But I was already well acquainted with words like "rash" and "thoughtless" and "foolhardy"—and most familiar of all, "selfish". I truly didn't mean to be selfish. For some reason I couldn't explain I just didn't stop to think, when I tried to tunnel through the lawn to China, that I would need a new dress to replace my hopelessly soiled one; or to consider, when I stopped to spin tops in the vacant corner lot after school, the distress my absence would cause my governess. Each time I promised myself to do better—but no matter how often I promised, I always seemed to end up here, staring at my shoes.

Mother laid her hand on Father's arm. "Genna," she said, "why don't you take Conrad out into the yard. I'll have Eleanor call you when it's time for your supper."

"Yes, Mamma."

"And please see that he doesn't get dirty. Eleanor has enough to do without giving him another bath."

"All right, Mamma."

She stooped in front of me, taking hold of the picture. "Why don't I put this somewhere safe for now? Then later we can dry the flowers and put them in our keepsake box."

I handed it over without a word. I didn't want to remember it now; it looked clumsy and stupid in her hands.

I took Conrad by the wrist and dragged him out into the hall, through the pantry to the little stone terrace behind our house. He immediately ran off across the patch of lawn beyond it, toward the trickling fountain in the back wall that separated our property from Aunt Margaret's. Yesterday the lawn had been bustling with men raking up chestnut burs and cutting the grass, but today all was quiet save for the splash and gurgle of the fountain.

At least I didn't have to worry about Conrad disturbing father's project, I thought, starting after him. Two weeks before, Father had decided to make a string of electric lights to decorate the chestnut tree for the party. Since electric service hadn't yet reached our neighborhood, and we didn't have enough space in the cellar for a private dynamo, he'd set to work building an "earth battery" which, he'd explained, would draw electricity right from the earth, costing nothing but the price of a few metal plates and magnets and the wire to connect them. Unfortunately, as he was constantly adjusting the depth and alignment of the plates in an effort to improve results, we children could never be quite sure where danger lay, and had been scolded more than once for tripping over the wires. When by the week of the party he'd only captured enough current to light two small bulbs, he finally gave in and bought an Edison battery for the job, to our private but great relief.

Now the plates were gone, the holes were filled in, and the lawn was level again. I cut across the smooth grass toward the back wall, resisting the urge to take off my shoes so as not to soil my stockings. Instead of continuing toward the fountain, however, Conrad suddenly veered to the right, making a beeline toward a wheelbarrow that was standing under the chestnut tree. "Conrad, wait!" I cried after him, mindful of my mother's instruction to keep him clean. "Let's see if there are any more raspberries in the hedge!"

He paused in mid-stride, glancing at me over his shoulder, then changed his course toward the patch of raspberry canes that arced over the far side of the lawn. Belatedly it occurred to me that raspberries posed even more of a threat to his shirtfront than did the dirty wheelbarrow. I hurried after him as resentful thoughts rustled through my head. Why did I always have to look after Conrad? Why should I get in trouble just because he did something wrong? I caught up to him just as he was reaching for a shriveled berry on one of the lower canes. "I'll get it," I said, pushing his hand away.

I plucked off the few remaining fruits that hadn't gone all pruney or been pecked hollow by the birds, and we sat on the grass to divvy them up. I had just popped the last, seedy berry into his mouth when a shrill chirp erupted from the grass at our feet, making both of us jump.

"It's a cricket!" Conrad said, dropping onto his hands and knees to grab at the leaping black blur. He came up empty, and grabbed again. "Got him!"

"Careful you don't squish it," I said, crouching beside him.

He made a peephole in his fist and squinted through it.

A shiny black antenna poked out of the hole. "Let me see," I ordered, leaning closer.

He cracked open his fingers to give me a better view. Unfortunately he miscalculated, and the cricket jumped out to safety. The creature's leap, however, was now lopsided, his arc of flight too low to clear the grass.

"He's hurt," I said, crawling after it as it lurched unevenly through the dense blades.

The cricket paused a moment beneath a half-shorn dandelion head, and we bent for a closer look. One of its rear legs was indeed sticking out from the top joint in a most unnatural way.

"Leg's broke," Conrad announced matter-of-factly.

"Maybe it's just bent a little," I said, feeling a spasm of remorse.

He pursed his lips, studying the leg. "It's aw' right. I can fix it."

Even at this young age, Conrad was always trying to fix things. He took after Father that way. I, on the other hand, was consumed by unanswerable questions: what was the cricket feeling? Was it aware that its life had just taken a terrible turn for the worse, or oblivious to its plight?

I grabbed Conrad's arm as he reached for it. "Don't. You'll only make it worse."

He blinked at me. "No I won't. I'm going to put a stick on it, like when Uncle Travy broke his leg."

"A splint, you mean." I peered at the whisker-thin leg. "I suppose a matchstick might do it. Or a sliver of popsicle stick."

"I'll go ask Katie," he said, getting to his feet.

"No," I said, pushing him back down. "I'll go." If we were going to nurse the cricket back to health, we'd need something to keep it in, and I had just the thing in mind: an orchid box that had arrived that very morning, with tiny air holes already cut through. I could make a lovely little house out of it, with a bed of shredded cotton and an empty balm tin for water. "I'll be right back," I said, jumping to my feet. "Keep your eye on him, but don't pick him up."

At the door I glanced back, remembering that I was never supposed to leave Conrad outdoors by himself. He was sitting with his chin propped on one knee, watching the cricket as his fingers absently flicked a blade of grass. In my mind, there were two kinds of rules: Big Rules, like never telling a lie or taking candy from the jar without paying; and numerous, peskier Little Rules which could, when circumstances required, be safely ignored. Not leaving Conrad alone in the rear yard felt like a Little Rule to me. Besides, I would only be gone for a minute.

I dashed through the empty pantry, down the hall and up the two flights of stairs to Mamma's boudoir. The orchid box was still on the dressing table where I'd last seen it. A balm tin took a little longer, but I finally found a half-empty one in the back of the medicine closet. I wiped it clean and dropped it into the orchid box, tossing in a toothpick, some silk floss, and a tube of liniment for good measure.

Altogether I couldn't have been gone more than six or seven minutes. When I ran back outside, however, Conrad was no longer sitting in the grass, or anywhere in sight. He must be hiding in the wheelbarrow, I thought in exasperation, stalking toward the tree. Within a few strides, however, I could see that the wheelbarrow was empty. I was wondering whether he might have climbed the turnstile into Aunt Margaret's yard, when a movement in the chestnut tree's branches caught my attention.

I looked up, shading my eyes. He couldn't have climbed up there, I reasoned; he was too small to reach the bottom branch. But then my gaze dropped down the gnarled trunk, and despite the sun on my face, I felt a sudden chill.

A weathered wooden ladder was propped against the side of the tree, barely visible against the trunk's mottled bark. Moving closer I saw the coil of electric lights that hung from a nail near its top rung.

The workmen must have been planning to use the ladder when they returned, to string the lights on the tree.

Covering the remaining distance at a trot, I grabbed the sides of the ladder and peered up into the leafy canopy. "Conrad?"

Leaves rustled high above me, and a small voice answered, "I'm up here."

Directly above my head, so high that it made me dizzy to look, I made out the bottom of a boot, and a pale leg encircled by dark short pants. Tilting my head farther back and to the side, I made out the rest of my brother's diminutive form. He was standing on a branch some two feet out from the trunk, holding the limb above him with both hands.

"Genna?" he said in the same small voice, bending forward to search for me through the leaves.

The branch swayed with his movement. I tried to shout a warning, but it wouldn't come out. "Don't move!" I finally managed to croak. "Conrad, stay right where you are!"

"I want to get down," he said, in the whiny voice that always came before tears.

"No! Just stay there, and I'll come get you." I pulled myself up the ladder, kicking my skirt out of the way. Things always looked higher from the ground, I reassured myself, trying not to feel afraid. I'd just shimmy up there and guide him down, and no one would ever be the wiser.

But when I leaned back to check on him from the top of the ladder, I discovered that one of his feet was now dangling in open air. I held my breath as he stretched it slowly, tentatively toward a lower branch that was at a slight angle to the one he was standing on. I wanted to shout to him to stop, but he'd already let go with one hand to lower himself onto the limb. My breath dragged like taffy through my lungs as his foot moved closer, closer . . . and landed safely on the lower branch.

I was so thankful he hadn't slipped that I didn't even yell at him for disobeying. No sooner had the flood of relief washed through me, however, than it became apparent that his new perch was much flimsier than the one he'd been standing on. When he shifted his weight it gave too easily beneath him, jiggling him up and down and nearly costing him his footing.

He froze, spread-eagled between two branches, one hand clinging to the limb above him and the other reaching for a nonexistent support. I was suddenly reminded of Aunt Margaret's cat, the time she got stuck in the chestnut tree—so completely still you'd have thought she was enjoying the view, if it wasn't for her pitiful mewing.

I heard a soft, hiccoughing sound, and realized he'd started to cry. "Hold on, Connie," I implored him. "Just keep holding on!" I stood in an agony of indecision, not sure whether I should try to reach him myself, or run get Papa.

The flimsy branch bobbed again as he scrabbled for a better foothold, making my mind up for me. Grabbing the lowest branch, I planted one foot on the tree trunk and started to hoist myself up. My leather sole slid over the rough bark, dumping me back onto the ladder. I was about to try again when I heard the fresh rustling of leaves overhead, followed by a soft gasp of surprise.

When I looked up I saw Conrad falling freely through the branches, his short-pants billowing around his knees. I heard his arms thwack against leafy twiglets, and then a crack as his head hit a branch square-on. For a moment he seemed to hang in thin air, suspended over the obstructing branch, before he rolled off and plummeted downward once more.

Flinging my arms out in front of me, I half jumped, half fell off the ladder. I felt something sharp dig into my forehead as my foot caught in my skirt, pulling me short of my intended trajectory. I dropped onto the grass on my hands and knees a split second before Conrad landed with a thud a few feet away.

I waited for the crying to start, but he didn't make a sound. I crawled closer, close enough to touch him, and stopped. He was lying on his stomach with one arm beneath him and his head twisted to one side. A few white dandelion seeds swirled around him, landing on his cheek and parted lips. I reached out and gingerly shook his shoulder. "Connie?"

He didn't respond.

I'd never seen him so utterly still, not even when he was sleeping. I climbed slowly to my feet as my ears filled with a painful thudding. Turning, I raced back to the pantry door and yanked it open. "Conrad fell! Conrad fell out of the tree!" I shouted over and over from the threshold, until my parents appeared, breathless and pale-faced, and followed me outside.

He was lying exactly as I had left him. My father knelt beside him and turned him over, pressing his face between his hands and calling his name, while Mamma hovered behind the two of them, clutching her chest with spastic fingers. I stood a little way off, waiting for my father to fix things, as he always did. But no matter how hard Papa breathed into the small lips, or how many times he stroked the pale round face, my brother wouldn't stir.

I was feeling a deep ache in my own chest, as if it was I who had fallen from the tree. I wanted to run to my mother and bury myself in her arms—but she had dropped to her knees and was pulling at the grass, making strange, whimpering noises in her throat. I stared at my father's stricken profile, wishing he would turn to me, wanting him to make my pain go away.

At last, he did turn and look at me. I started toward him. "Papa–" I stopped as he staggered to his feet and lurched toward me, his face contorted almost beyond recognition.

"What was he doing in the tree?" he rasped.

I opened my mouth to respond, but nothing came out.

He lunged forward and grabbed me by the shoulders. "What was he doing in the tree?" he asked again, shaking me, staring at me with wild eyes.

"I . . . I . . ." I pulled back, trying to break free of his grasp.

Suddenly his fingers went slack on my shoulders. His arms dropped to his sides as he turned and walked back to the silent form on the ground.

I couldn't move for several long moments. Then, as if they had detached themselves from my spinning brain, my feet started forward, one stiffly following the other, slowly gaining speed until I was running full out across the lawn, over the terrace, and into the dim house. I raced down the hall and up the stairs to the second floor landing. There I stopped, unsure where to go. Everything looked different, somehow; the carved bench on the landing, the pattern in the carpet, the paintings along the wall all oddly unfamiliar, as if I'd run into the wrong house by mistake. Filled with a terror unlike anything I'd ever known, I spun around and raced back down the steps, around the newel post and into the coat closet under the staircase. I pulled the door shut and groped forward in the dark, pushing through the hedge of cedar-scented coats, burrowing deeper and deeper until I struck the wall and could go no farther.

My father didn't come looking for me. Not then, or anytime that night. But the memory of his eyes stayed with me in the darkness. I couldn't forget—had never forgotten—those eyes. They were the eyes of a stranger, looking at the person who has killed his son.

CHAPTER SEVEN

"Guilty."

I returned to the present with a start, half-expecting to see my father standing before me, pointing an accusing finger. But the declaration had come from a lad some twelve or thirteen years of age who was now standing before the magistrate, flanked by two smaller boys.

"What about you?" the magistrate asked one of the young confederates.

"Guilty, yer honor."

"Me too," piped up the third.

The magistrate turned to the first boy. "Tell me, Mr. Smeallie, how many times have you been in here for shooting craps?"

"Once or twice, I guess," the boy answered, hanging his head and twisting his cap in his hands.

"And how many times have I let you go?"

The boy's head dropped lower still, until it was nearly level with those of his mates.

The magistrate drummed his fingers on the papers in front of him. He glanced toward a table in the boxed-off area where assorted lawyers and policeman and court officials had been coming and going all morning. "You want 'em?" he asked.

The man he addressed was seated at one end of the table with his chair pushed back and his legs stretched out in front of him. This was not the first time the two had communicated; on several previous occasions I'd noticed the magistrate glance in his direction, and seen the man nod or shake his head in response. Now, for the first time, the seated man spoke. "I hear they're shorthanded at Fleischmann's bakery," he told the magistrate. "I think I can persuade Raoul to take them on."

The voice had a faintly Irish lilt that sounded familiar. I leaned to the side to get a better look, but the man's back was almost directly to me. Although his clothes were well-cut, he had the broad shoulders and sturdy neck of a laborer, or perhaps an athlete, with thick dark hair that spilled over the back of his collar.

"That all right with you, Mike?" the magistrate asked the arresting officer.

"Why sure," the officer said, "if it's all right with Mr. Shaw."

My breath stopped in my throat.

"All right, boys," the magistrate said, "I'm giving you one last chance. Mr. Shaw here is going to take you to the bakery and see that they keep you busy. You're to do exactly as you're told and keep your noses clean. Do you understand?

Three heads bobbed in the affirmative.

"They're all yours," the magistrate said.

The dark-haired man got to his feet. Walking over to the boys, he turned two of them by their shoulders and shepparded them all toward the gate.

I nearly gasped out loud. It was him—broader now in the shoulders and chest, and with his hair trained back from his face—but unquestionably our old stable hand, Simon Shaw. As he passed through the gate he said something to the Roundsman that prompted a low guffaw, making his own lips twitch in return. I knew I should have felt anger and disgust at the sight of him, or ought at least to have managed a cool indifference; but instead I could only stare and marvel at what he had become. Of course he'd always been good-looking, in a sharp-boned, disheveled sort of way—a city-streets version of the defiant-eyed Lakota warrior, Crazy Horse, I used to imagine in my more besotted moments. But maturity had filled out his face and hardened his body, even as it veiled the intensity of his eyes, creating an impression of strength and self-possession that, for a moment at least, made me forget the malignant core I knew lay inside.

As the foursome came through the gate, he glanced across the front bench. I thought he paused—but with the boys bumping along just ahead of him, it was hard to tell. When he continued down the aisle without a second look I realized I'd been mistaken. He hadn't recognized me at all. My cheeks burned at the thought.

I had no opportunity to indulge this humiliation, however, because Eliza had just stepped up to the magistrate's bench. "Is this the defendant Elizabeth Miner?" the magistrate asked, scanning the information sheet.

"It is," the arresting officer confirmed.

"Officer Callahan, do you swear that the statements contained herein are the truth, the whole truth and nothing but the truth, so help you God?"

"I do."

The magistrate eyed Eliza over the sheet of paper. "I see you plead not guilty. Do you wish to have counsel represent you?"

She stared dumbly up at him.

"Do you want a lawyer," Callahan prompted.

"I . . . I don't know," she replied, in hardly more than a whisper.

"You're charged with a very serious crime," the magistrate said. "I'd strongly suggest that you obtain the services of counsel before we proceed. I can send an officer to fetch someone, if you'll give me a name."

"I don't know any lawyers."

One of the moth-eaten attorneys who'd been lounging behind the rail since I arrived sprang to life at these words, approaching Eliza with his card outstretched. He leaned toward her and whispered urgently into her ear. She shook her head once, twice, and then nodded, looking dazed.

The lawyer turned toward the magistrate. "I represent the accused, your honor."

"So noted," the magistrate said, as the clerk entered this in the record. "Officer Callahan, will you recount the facts of the case in your own words for the court?"

Callahan proceeded to describe the scene at Dr. Hauptfuhrer's in a matter-of-fact tone that, to my ears, made it sound even more gruesome than it had been, if that was possible. I saw with dismay that the four reporters at the other end of the bench, who'd appeared to be dozing since their return from the judge's chamber, were now fully awake and snapping back the pages of their writing tablets in their zeal to record every detail.

"Do you have the murder weapon?" the magistrate asked Callahan.

"Yes, sir." He opened a bag at his feet and lifted out the doctor's sword with a flourish, holding it aloft for all to see.

I stared at it in morbid fascination. It was some two feet in length, with an exotic, single-edged blade that curved up and broadened toward the tip. The hilt was actually rather lovely, set with red and yellow stones and wrapped with a golden cord. It was the blade that seized my attention, however, for it was encrusted with dark, dried blood.

There was a collective gasp from the courtroom. As Callahan carried the sword to the magistrate the reporters rose en masse and charged the rail, clamoring for a closer look and pitching questions at Eliza. To my annoyance, Eliza's new lawyer seemed as mesmerized by the sword as the rest of them, staring at the weapon in frank amazement and doing nothing at all to protect his client from the verbal barrage.

"Order in the court," the magistrate growled.

When this didn't produce results, the Roundsman strode to the rail and dragged his club along the top of it, clipping all slow-moving fingers and elbows. The reporters reluctantly backed up and took their seats.

The magistrate turned back to Eliza. "Mrs. Miner, you've heard the charges against you. What if anything do you have to say to them?"

"They're not true," she said, only slightly louder than before.

"Do you disagree with the facts as they're set forth in the complaint?"

"Well, no . . . but I didn't kill him. It wasn't me who did it."

He studied her a moment, lips pursed. "What about finger impressions?" he asked Callahan, glancing at the information. "Did you find any on the weapon?"

"We got a couple, but they're probably not hers. She was wearing gloves when we found her, with blood all over 'em. We figure the prints belong to the doctor or his maid. We ought to know more by tomorrow."

This was astonishing news. Detective Maloney hadn't mentioned to me that Eliza was wearing gloves; in fact, he'd made it sound as though her conviction was just a finger-print match away.

"Mrs. Miner," the magistrate asked, frowning down at her, "can you tell me why there was blood on your gloves?"

"I—I don't know," she said.

"Isn't that the sort of thing a lady would notice? Getting blood on her gloves?"

"It must have happened when I went over to see if I could help . . ." She trailed off, glancing over her shoulder into the gallery as she did so. I supposed she was seeking reassurance from her mother or me, but the gesture had the unfortunate effect of making her look furtive.

One of the reporters shouted from his seat, "What did you have against Dr. Hauptfuhrer?"

"Were you and the doctor lovers?" called out another.

"Did he say anything before he died?" yelled a third.

"All right, boys," the magistrate growled, "keep it down or I'll have to throw you out." He scanned the information again. "What's this about a 'mental problem'?" he asked Callahan.

"Detective Maloney called the station house just before we left to say he'd uncovered evidence suggesting the prisoner ain't right in the head. He told me to add it to the report."

I sat bolt upright on the bench. The detective must have been referring to his conversation with *me*. He was taking what I'd told him out of context, calling it evidence and using it to incriminate Eliza!

"What kind of mental problem?" the magistrate asked.

Callahan shrugged. "The kind that would make someone take a swing at someone else with a sword, I guess," he answered with a smirk.

"Could you be any more specific?"

"That's all I know. You want me to find out more?"

"No, that won't be necessary," the magistrate said, sitting back. "This isn't a trial; the issue of mental status can wait for later." He laid down the information sheet. "Based on the evidence presented, I'm holding the prisoner over for examination. Mrs. Miner, because you are charged with a crime punishable by death you will be held without bail until the grand jury hears your case. Your attorney will instruct you on how to proceed."

"But I didn't do it!" Eliza gasped, clutching Officer Callahan's sleeve.

"All we've established today is that there are reasonable grounds to believe you committed the crime," the magistrate explained. "The grand jury will decide whether or not to indict."

Eliza's lawyer pulled what appeared to be a contract for services out of his pocket and pressed it into her hand, as the Roundsman took her other arm and half led, half-dragged her toward the door to the jail, followed by Callahan. The reporters pursued them along the opposite side of the rail, pelting Eliza with questions.

I stood and hurried after them, digging Detective Maloney's note out of my bag. "Officer Callahan," I shouted, "wait!"

Eliza stopped and turned at the sound of my voice, forcing the Roundsman and Callahan to pause as well.

"I have a message from Detective Maloney," I said, handing Callahan the note. To the Roundsman I explained, "I'm the prisoner's physician. Detective Maloney has asked me to speak with her, concerning a confidential matter. He feels it could be important to the case."

The Roundsman and Callahan looked at each other. Callahan shrugged.

"All right, you can talk to her in the detaining cell," the Roundsman said, "while she's waiting for the wagon to the Tombs. Stay here and I'll arrange it with the matron."

The three of them continued out the side door. I started back toward the bench to wait but was intercepted by the reporters, who now turned their sights on me. I put up my hands and shook my head, looking desperately for a way through. As I did so I caught sight of Eliza's mother exiting from the other side of the courtroom. I broke away from the reporters and bolted after her, catching up at the top of the stairs. "Mrs. Braun!"

She turned, and stiffened on sight of me.

"You have to get Eliza a better lawyer," I said breathlessly. "She's going to need someone really first rate."

"How am I supposed to afford someone like that?" she snapped. "We barely have enough to pay our bills as it is."

"I could help. I have a little money put away."

She took a halting step toward me. "Can a lawyer turn back the clock?" she asked, leaning on her walking stick with both hands. "Can he put Eliza back safe and sound in the shop with me, instead of alone in that office with the doctor?" She grimaced, shaking her head. "Save your charity, Dr. Summerford. You've done enough to 'help' already." She turned and started down the stairs.

I stood rooted in place, hearing her earlier words to me with each strike of her stick on the terrazzo steps: ". . . all your fault . . . everything that happened . . . all your fault . . ." I reached blindly for the wall as a wave of panic washed over me. I couldn't be responsible, not again. I knew, deep down, it would be the end of me.

I forced myself to take a deep breath. Only Eliza knew the truth. Not Detective Maloney, not Professor Mayhew, not even Mrs. Braun. I lifted my head and wiped my damp palms on my skirt. I had to speak with Eliza before I could draw any reliable conclusions—about her guilt, or my own.

WHEN I RETURNED to the courtroom the Roundsman was back in front of the rail, where another arraignment was in progress. He gestured to me to come through the gate, then led me through a side door into the hallway. "Matron Gilbert will take you down," he said, pointing to a stout woman by a steel-bar door, halfway down the hall.

I followed the matron out the door, down a staircase, and through another, armored door into the jail. Several twists and turns later we arrived at a chain link gate, where Officer Callahan was having a smoke with the man on guard. After the matron had searched my bag and pockets the guard opened the gate to let us through.

I hesitated, looking at Officer Callahan.

"I'll be right here if you need me," he said, with a wave of his cigar.

I followed the matron onto the ground floor of the jail. Five cell doors were recessed into a thick brick wall on my left, facing a narrow courtyard. Looking up, I saw several more tiers of cells cantilevered out above me. Each had a security post in one corner, separated from the cells by chain link fencing.

Jangling her key ring, the matron led me to a cell with the number 2 inscribed in its arched lintel. The brick enclosure was so narrow she had to stand partially sideways as she turned the key in the lock. "You've got ten minutes until the wagon gets here," she advised me, pulling open the door.

I peered past her into a dim cell lit by a single incandescent globe. Two wirestrung bunks were attached to the wall on the left. The top one was folded up flush against the bricks, the bottom one suspended over the concrete floor by chains at its corners. Eliza sat on the edge of the lower bunk, staring up at me. The matron's hand pressed me forward and the door slammed shut. I heard the key grate in the lock, and then the matron's footsteps receded down the courtyard.

Eliza rose from the bunk, her eyes huge and her arms clasped around her trembling body. A hundred uneasy questions had been circling in my mind, awaiting her explication; but as she stood there shivering before me, the first thing that rose to my lips was, "Are you cold?"

"Oh, Doctor..." she wailed, rushing toward me with outstretched arms.

I held her as she started to cry, deep sobs that welled up one after another, and seemed as though they might go on forever. Finally, she raised her head and wiped her face with her hands. "I was afraid you'd think I'd done it," she said, between stuttering intakes of breath.

"I didn't know what to think, Eliza," I replied, stepping back from her. "I still don't."

"I didn't kill him, I swear! If you'd seen what he looked like . . ." She stopped as a shudder rocked through her. "I could never do that to anyone."

If this was an act, it was a bravura performance. I scrutinized her face for tell-tale signs of dissembling, but for the life of me couldn't find any. "Why don't we sit down, and you can tell me exactly what happened." I stepped around a puddle that was snaking across the floor from the toilet in the corner, guiding her back to the open bunk. "We don't have much time," I said as we sat down, "so you need to tell me as quickly and clearly as you can everything that you remember."

"All right, I'll try." She paused to collect her thoughts, then began, "I got there early, before office hours, so that I could talk to the doctor without being disturbed. He answered the door when I knocked. He said he'd be with me in just a few minutes, and asked me to wait in the examining room. So I waited, and the minute he came in, I asked him."

"Asked him what?"

"Where Joy was. I wanted to ask him right away so I wouldn't lose my nerve."

"You mean you actually talked with him in the examining room?" I asked. "That wasn't in the detective's notes."

She colored slightly. "I didn't think I should tell the police about Joy. I had promised Dr. Hauptfuhrer never to tell, and there didn't seem any reason for them to know."

"So instead," I said, recalling my conversation with Detective Maloney, "you told them you went to ask the doctor for a prescription."

"I really did need a new prescription, for my headache powders. I was going to ask him for it when we were done."

She was clearly eager for me to believe that she was telling the truth. So far, I saw no reason to think that she wasn't. As Professor Mayhew had pointed out, however, what Eliza considered the truth wasn't necessarily rooted in reality. "How did the doctor react when you asked him where Joy was? Did he seem . . . surprised?"

"No, not surprised. I had telephoned him the day before to tell him I wanted to talk about her, so he was expecting it. But I can't say he was very pleased."

"What did he say, exactly?"

She frowned. "He said it would be best for everyone concerned, especially Joy, if we left what happened in the past."

That didn't sound like someone confronting a fantasy, I thought. "And how did you respond?"

"Well, I didn't want to do anything to hurt Joy. But I couldn't see any harm in just knowing where she was. So I promised that if he told me where she lived, I wouldn't try to talk to her—I'd only look at her, without her even knowing. But he said . . ." she hesitated, color rising in her cheeks. ". . . he said he couldn't be sure I'd keep my word."

So Joy wasn't just some hysterical concoction, I concluded. But that meant that Eliza had a real reason for resenting the doctor. Had that resentment kindled a violent assault, when Hauptfuhrer refused her request? "And how did that make you feel?" I asked, watching her closely.

"I felt . . . ashamed, I suppose, the way he said it. Embarrassed for even asking. But then I remembered what you'd said, about how I had a right to know; and that made me feel stronger, somehow. So I looked him right in the eye and told him that she was my daughter and that if he didn't tell me where she was, and give me some sort of proof that what he told me was true, I'd go to the police and let them know he'd taken her without my say-so." She smiled crookedly. "I don't think I would have dared to, really, but I suppose it must have frightened him, because after a minute, he agreed."

I sat back, making the bunk bed creak. "He agreed?"

She nodded.

I'd considered half a dozen other scenarios, but this one had never occurred to me. I stared at her, wanting it to be true, while she gazed steadily back at me. "And then?"

She shrugged. "And then he went to get me proof."

"What kind of proof?"

"Well I don't know, because he never returned."

"All right, let's back up a bit," I said, racing to put these new pieces into place. "Where exactly did he say he was going, to get this proof?"

"He didn't say. He just told me to wait while he went to get it. Then he went through the connecting door into his office and closed it behind him."

"You didn't go after him?"

"No! Although I was so excited I could hardly sit still. I kept thinking how wonderful it was going to be to see Joy again, even if I could only watch her from a distance. But then I heard the doctor shout . . ."

"He shouted? You mean he called something out?"

"It was more of a noise, really, like . . ." She imitated a startled yelp. "And then there were bumping noises, and a minute later a door slammed."

"Which door?"

"I'm not sure, but I think it must have been the one that led from his office into the hallway. The noise came from that direction."

For the first time since her arrest, I felt hope stirring inside me. "What did you do then?"

"Well, at first, I was too frightened to move. When it was quiet again, I called out his name, but he didn't answer. So finally, after another minute or two, I got up and opened the door, and that's . . . that's when I saw him."

"What did you see, Eliza?"

She swallowed. "He was lying on his back on the floor, all covered in blood. There was an awful gurgling noise coming from his throat, and the blood was just . . . spurting up, out of his neck." Her hand rose unconsciously to her own neck. "I didn't want to go any closer, but I thought there might be something I could do to help, so I made myself walk over to him. At first I thought he was trying to say something, but when I bent down to listen I realized it was just . . . dying noise, I suppose. Finally it stopped, and he was still." She drew a breath. "Then his daughter came in—the one who answers the door during office hours. I tried to talk to her, but she just backed up and ran out of the room. I wasn't sure what to do then, so I waited, thinking she'd return. And then a few minutes later, the patrolman arrived."

I listened with mounting excitement. If she could be believed, then the facts of the case as presented by Detective Maloney took on a very different light. The open file drawer, for instance; Detective Maloney had assumed the doctor was filing unrelated paperwork when he was attacked, but he might just as well have been retrieving Eliza's proof from that drawer, while she waited innocently in the adjoining room. And then there was the blood on Eliza's gloves and skirt. A severed carotid artery could spurt blood a distance of several feet; if the doctor's artery was still pumping when Eliza stooped beside him, as she had suggested, she most certainly would have been splattered. The fact that she had remained at the crime scene instead of running away, moreover, suggested not culpability, but only a desire to help. "Is it true that you screamed when you saw the doctor?" I asked her. "The detective on the case told me Miss Hauptfuhrer came downstairs because she heard you through the air vents."

"Why, yes, I suppose I did," she said, a bit sheepishly. "It was just such a shock, seeing him there on the floor."

"You needn't apologize. It was a perfectly natural thing to do." Surely, I thought, if Detective Maloney heard the full account that Eliza had just given me, he would realize that they'd arrested the wrong person. "You have to tell the police what you heard," I told her. "Once they know that there was someone else in there with the doctor, they'll have to let you go and start looking for the real murderer.

"But I already did," she said in surprise.

"You told them about the shout? And the door slamming?"

"I told the patrolman as soon as he arrived."

I gritted my teeth. Detective Maloney had not bothered to convey this critical information, to me or to the magistrate. It was beginning to seem as though he'd closed his mind to the possibility of Eliza's innocence, long before all the evidence was in. What evidence he had considered, he seemed ready to distort in the interest of wrapping up his case. I'd seen what he did with the little I revealed about Eliza's emotional state. He had also suggested, to me at least, that her fingerprints were on the sword, which was apparently untrue. I remembered too his hesitation, when I asked him what had brought Miss Hauptfuhrer downstairs. He clearly hadn't wanted to tell me, no doubt because it didn't mesh with his version of events.

"Do you think I should have told them about Joy, too?" Eliza asked.

It was a good question. If the police knew that Eliza was trying to discover her daughter's whereabouts, they might conclude she had no reason to harm Hauptfuhrer, who was the only person who could tell her. But they might just as well spin out a sensational scenario featuring Eliza as a vengeful mother righting a long-ago wrong. In light of Maloney's conduct thus far, I had little reason to expect the former. Nor, in light of his deception, was I inclined to fulfill my promise to obtain Eliza's permission to tell him all that I knew. "What I think," I told her, "is that you need a good lawyer. Not that dreadful man who foisted himself on you in the courtroom. I mean a really good attorney, who's had some experience with . . . cases like this." There was no reason, I had decided, to let Mrs. Braun keep me from doing what I was sure was in Eliza's interest, no matter how much she might blame me for what had happened. "I could ask around and get some names, if you like."

"All right, if you think that's best."

I smiled, touched but also daunted by her trust in me.

The matron reappeared at the door, jangling her keys. "The wagon's here," she announced.

Eliza shrank back on the bunk as the key grated in the lock.

I took her cold hand in mine. "Try not to be afraid," I said, giving it a squeeze.

The door swung open and I rose to go. Eliza, however, remained seated, clinging to my hand.

"It's going to be all right," I said hoarsely. "We'll get to the bottom of this, somehow."

I cringed as the matron shackled her wrists, then followed helplessly as she was handed over to Officer Callahan at the gate and led to the front of the jail, where the wagon that would take her to the city prison was backing through the vehicle entrance. I watched Callahan load her into the wagon with four other women, feeling the weight of her trust on my shoulders. Though I would do everything in my power to help, I feared it wouldn't be enough. I was out of my element, my medical school honors and advanced training of no use in navigating the city's criminal justice machinery. Finding her a better lawyer would be a good first step, but I didn't know how much he'd be able to accomplish, without evidence corroborating Eliza's story.

What we needed, I thought as the van drove off, was someone with influence. Someone who could use his connections to stall Maloney's steamroller tactics, and give us time to uncover the truth. Unfortunately, the only person I knew who might fit that description was the last person I'd choose to ask for help. He'd gotten those boys off, however, and the young prostitute. Maybe he could help Eliza too. I was going to have to swallow my pride and ask him, for her sake.

I followed the wagon out to the street, then went back in the side door and up the staircase to the police court. At the first break in the proceedings, I leaned over the rail and hailed the Roundsman. "Can you tell me where I might find Simon Shaw?" I asked him.

"This time of day?" He scratched his head. "I'd say your best bet would be at his saloon, on 84th and Second."

"He owns a saloon?"

"Well, sure, and more than one," he said, as if this were common knowledge. "But the Isle of Plenty is where you're most likely to find him. That's where he takes care of business."

I would have liked to ask what kind of business; but before I could do so he had turned away to call the next case. And so I left the police court behind, and set out to discover the answer for myself.

CHAPTER EIGHT

I gazed across the street at the Isle of Plenty's curtained windows, shifting from foot to foot in the slush. So Simon had become a saloonkeeper. I wouldn't have expected it of him; but then, I supposed I'd never known the real Simon Shaw. I caught a glimpse of the saloon's warmly lit interior as the door opened and a customer walked out, followed by strains of piano music. It looked like a decent enough place. Still, although my stockings were soaked through and my feet were numb from the cold, I was hesitant to cross.

I'd been nine years old when Katie brought young Simon back from the boat with his mother, our new parlor maid, and installed them both in the loft over the stable. Of course Conrad and I weren't allowed to play with the hired help, but I was aware of the boy, as children are, and on the rare occasions when his mother brought him to the house I found him to be an interesting, if reserved, young lad.

It was perhaps inevitable that when adolescence struck, Simon became the target of my youthful longings. My parents hadn't seemed to notice that I was becoming a woman. They'd provided me with tutors in French and astronomy, with dance lessons at Dodsworth's and tennis lessons in the park; but they had done nothing at all to prepare me for the internal roilings of new womanhood, waiting for my debut year to launch me into society and its attendant, time-tested mating rituals. And so in the lonely evening hours when father locked himself in his study and mother tended her flowers in the conservatory, I spent far too many hours staring vacantly over my needlepoint while fantasizing about a perfect beau. In time, with this paragon's hazy image fixed in my mind, I began to search for a flesh and blood counterpart among the boys of my acquaintance. The man of my dreams was made of more substantial stuff than the tongue-tied, sweaty-palmed boys at school or at Dodsworth's, however. I had almost despaired of finding him when, shortly after my sixteenth birthday, Simon was assigned to escort me on my morning rides, so that the coachman could drive Mamma on her errands.

I had a chance then to study the nearly-grown Simon up close, and what I saw set my heart to pattering. I found that he was courteous, but never self-effacing. He didn't wear a hat but if he had, I'm sure he would never have doffed it to me. Though he was unfailingly gentle with the horses, the maid told me he had once beaten an older boy to within an inch of his life, for calling his mother a pretty piece of baggage. He had stopped school after the sixth grade to help earn his keep, but I knew he liked to read, and his opinions always seemed well-reasoned. There was some mystery about his father, but I deduced that Mr. Shaw had abandoned the family shortly after Simon's birth, which perhaps explained his son's barely veiled—and to my mind, rather thrilling—disdain for authority.

His humble origins didn't deter me, for I was convinced that he would do great things. Once, after watching him brush Mamma's mare to a sheen worthy of Madison Square Garden, I'd asked if he didn't mind taking care of other people's horses. He'd smiled and said, "I couldn't be sure they'd be properly cared for if I left it to someone else, now could I?" Thinking this a noble but somewhat backward way of looking at it, I'd asked him bluntly if he wouldn't rather be doing more important things. "I will, someday," he'd explained, "But this is practice, see? You've got to take things one step at a time."

I thought I understood him. And as I lay restlessly in my bed at night I dreamed, absurdly, of some vague but contented future together. And I waited: for I didn't know what. An unidentified something, to resolve the unfamiliar tension building inside of me.

Thus came about the night of my disgrace. I remembered it with the clarity memory was wont to impose on things one would rather forget. I had gone down to the basement kitchen for something to eat before bed; it was Katie's night off and Margaret, our cross-eyed new kitchen maid, was washing the servants' dishes. I had just sat down to the remains of a strawberry jam sponge cake when Margaret pulled on her coat and hat, hoisted a bucket of spotty apples from under the table and announced she was taking the apples to the stable on her way home.

Immediately I saw my opportunity. Jumping up from the table, I grabbed Katie's old coat from its peg and offered to take the apples myself. Of course Margaret had been quite shocked, protesting that it was her job to bring them on Katie's night off, and that I'd catch my death going out in my thin chemise and robe, and asking what my mother would say; but I was not to be deterred. Stepping into the pair of old work boots that stood by the door, I pulled on the coat, snatched the bucket from Margaret's reluctant hand and clumped past her into the hall and out the service door.

I could still remember how the nubby boot lining felt against my bare feet as I half-ran, half-shuffled around the corner and up one block to our stable. I shut the door behind me and paused in the lantern light, breathing in the scent of lamp oil and sweet hay. Kellogg neighed in greeting, and I hurried over to shush her with one of the apples. She had just chomped down on it with her big yellow teeth, spraying drops of juice through my open coat onto my chemise, when I heard footsteps on the loft stairs behind me.

Holding my breath, I counted the steady footfalls on the treads: six, seven, eight. The footsteps stopped, and I turned.

He was standing at the bottom of the stairs, cloaked in shadow. "Did they send you for the carriage?" he asked, his eyes gleaming like polished jet in the lamplight.

"No."

He tilted his head, studying me in that unhurried way of his. "Well, you're not going for a ride. Not in that."

"No," I agreed, dizzy with excitement. "I'm not going for a ride."

He waited, his dark eyes questioning.

Unable to explain even to myself why I'd come or what I expected, I simply smiled—an open, offering smile that I suppose anyone but a fool would have recognized. And Simon was no fool. He must have known, then, what I was feeling for him. And I, silly creature, seeing him smile in return, had been certain that he felt the same way.

BUT THAT HAD all been a long time ago, I reminded myself, shaking the memory off. I was no longer a dreamy, ignorant little girl. I could handle the likes of Simon Shaw. Pushing off the curb I strode across the street, under the green canopy, and into the Isle of Plenty.

I stood inside the door for a moment as my eyes adjusted to the dim light. Through the warm haze of tobacco smoke I saw with relief that the saloon was indeed of the respectable sort, with rows of glassware stacked neatly on handsome wood shelving, and wall decorations limited to a simple gilt mirror, some boxing magazine covers, and an assortment of news clippings on the rear wall. A piano in the corner tinkled out "The Mansion of Aching Hearts", just loud enough to be heard over the chatter of patrons two-deep at the bar, while a few families enjoyed an early supper of chowder and biscuits at the tables by the windows.

The bartender glanced up at my entrance with a welcoming smile. I started toward him, edging through two burly men at the counter. "I'm looking for Mr. Simon Shaw," I said. "I was told I might find him here."

"He's in the back," he said, jerking his thumb toward a door in the wall behind the piano.

I made my way across the room to the door he had indicated. I straightened my coat collar, adjusted my hat, and raised my hand to knock—then paused, as I heard the sound of laughter and male voices on the other side. It would be hard enough talking to Simon alone. I didn't think I could manage it in front of an audience. I decided to wait for his visitors to leave.

While I waited I scanned the newspaper clippings that covered the rear wall. Simon, I discovered, was in most of them. There was one with a sketch of "Alderman Simon Shaw" receiving a certificate of appreciation from the East Side Ladies' Guild, for prohibiting horse-cars from a residential side street; and another showing "District

Captain Simon Shaw" presenting a check to a newsboy shelter. In the bottom row there was even a piece about "friend of the arts, Simon Shaw" introducing William Butler Yeats at a YMCA poetry reading.

So saloon keeping was just a side business, I concluded. Simon, it seemed, had become a politician. A Tammany district captain, to be precise. That would explain why he'd been in court that morning; as district captain he'd be responsible for keeping potential voters and their families out of jail. Of course Eliza, being a woman, couldn't vote—but she did live in his district, and was part of a larger immigrant community whose support was vital to Tammany. Simon, as a member of that entrenched political machine, might be able to help her in ways that I couldn't even imagine.

I jumped upright as the door suddenly flew open. A fresh burst of laughter rolled out on a cloud of smoke, followed by a barrel-chested man with an expensive-looking coat slung over his arm. The man stopped short, looking me up and down. "Well now, if this isn't the loveliest thing I've seen all day," he exclaimed in a rolling Irish brogue. "Join me for a drink, dear lady, and I promise to take that frown off your pretty face."

"I'm here to see Mr. Shaw," I told him, keeping my frown firmly in place.

"I should have known," he said with a sigh, managing to look both jolly and crestfallen at the same time. "Simon!" he shouted over his shoulder, "what do you mean by keeping this sweet young thing waiting?" He winked at me and stepped aside, gesturing me into the room.

I had little choice but to enter. Gripping the handles of my book bag, I stepped over the threshold into a windowless room that was hardly larger than a coat closet, thick with smoke and illuminated by a single overhead globe. A half-dozen men in shirtsleeves sat at a round table that took up most of the space, nursing mugs of beer and smoldering cigars. Their conversation came to a halt as I walked in. From the way they were all staring, I gathered women didn't come in here very often.

Simon was at the opposite side of the table, facing me. He was coatless and collarless like the others, and wore his shirtsleeves rolled up to his elbows. He sat with his chair tipped back and one foot propped up on the table, holding a sweating mug on one thigh.

"Mr. Shaw," I said, tipping my head.

He nodded back, but made no move to get up.

"I'm sorry to intrude, but I have something rather urgent to discuss with you."

Still he said nothing, but waited for me to go on.

"Perhaps you don't remember me," I said. "I'm Genevieve Summerford. You used to . . ."

"I know who you are."

The other men stirred, glancing from me to Simon. One of them pushed back his chair and started to his feet.

"It's all right, Joe, you can stay," said Simon. "This shouldn't take long."

I felt a blush creeping up my cheeks. "I was hoping we might speak in private."

"Whatever you've got to say, you can say in front of my friends here."

I took a deep breath. "Very well. I'm here on behalf of a woman in your district, who's been accused of a murder she didn't commit."

"The one in court this morning."

"Why, yes," I said in surprise. He had left before Eliza's hearing, and I hadn't expected him to be aware of her case. "I saw how you helped all those other people. I was hoping you could do something for her."

His thumb tapped the rim of his beer glass. "They say she killed a doctor."

"She didn't do it."

"They never do, do they?"

I hadn't expected sarcasm. Whatever his other flaws, Simon had always been quick to defend an underdog. I remembered one time in particular when he'd stuffed a boy down a coal chute for dangling a helpless kitten from a sewer grate. "I have good reason to believe she's innocent," I told him. "But the detective in charge—a man named Maloney—won't even consider other suspects. He's convinced he already has the case wrapped up."

"Sounds like Maloney," snickered one of the men, lifting his mug to his lips. A brass-buttoned blue coat was hanging from the back of his chair. He was a policeman, I realized—and if the shield pinned to his coat was any clue, a policeman of some rank. I glanced around the table at the other men, wondering who they were and why they were drinking beer in Simon's private parlor.

"Why do you care what happens to her?" Simon asked me. "She's not fancy enough to be a friend of yours. What's it to you?"

The scorn in his voice made my cheeks burn even hotter. I told myself to let it pass, to focus on what I'd come for. But the anger and humiliation I'd thought I'd conquered long ago were bubbling up again inside me—and try as I might, I couldn't stop the memories from bubbling up with them. Suddenly I was sixteen again, cowering in the armchair in my bedroom, listening in stricken silence as my father revealed the bitter truth.

"It's all through the servants' quarters!" he had shouted; "he's boasting that you let him fondle you! Couldn't you see that he was taking advantage of you?"

I, innocent still, had refused to believe it, insisting that Simon loved me and would never demean me in such a way—to which my father, who had never before spoken a bigoted word in my presence, retorted that the boy was arrogant Irish trash, unfit to utter my name. I'd known he must be convinced of what he was saying to be so upset—but I still couldn't believe that it was true.

With Simon I had felt . . . lovable. I couldn't bear to think it had all been a deception. And yet, I had never doubted my father before. He'd told me I must never speak to Simon again and I, frightened and confused, had finally agreed. He'd calmed down then, saying he held himself partly responsible for failing to educate me properly, and saying that that could be fixed—provided I hadn't "compromised" myself more seriously than he knew. It was a moment before his meaning sank in—but when it did, the shame was excruciating. Although I assured him quite truthfully that I hadn't, by now the kisses and touches I'd shared with Simon seemed quite wicked enough in themselves. Father let out his breath then, and said that everything would be all right, but of course I knew it wouldn't be. I had failed him, once again.

What came next was almost worse than my father's anger. He left the room for a moment and returned with a little green book, handing it to me with instructions to pay particular attention to pages 72 and beyond, before he beat a hasty retreat. Over the next several hours I received my first formal instruction on the subject of the sexual function—or more accurately, of its abuse—from Professor F. C. Fowler, certified doctor of physiognomy and anthropology. I read the book in my armchair with the door closed, growing smaller and smaller by the page, returning repeatedly to the most damning parts in hopes of finding some absolving exception—but there was none.

I could still remember whole passages by heart: "Animal love, as opposed to platonic love, is the kind of love we see in brute beasts, and in man often descends even lower than among the cattle. It is a blind, unreasoning impulse that urges its possessor to its gratification, regardless of the consequences." When the sexual function was made an instrument of passion and pleasure, the professor warned, "the penalty is sure to follow in all its revolting forms"—including leprosy, weakened bones, depletion of the vital forces, and a marked tendency toward criminal behavior.

While I had been guilty largely of ignorance, the young male mind, it seemed, was riddled with lecherous thoughts and images. Right-minded young men resisted these thoughts, Dr. Fowler explained, by reading about noble folk, or praying, or joining crusades; only the most debased would ever act upon them. "A pure minded man or boy," he asserted, "would no more defile the woman or girl he loves than he would his mother. As her natural protector he allows himself toward her only the purest, most chivalrous of feelings."

I recalled then the sharp intake of Simon's breath when we kissed, and the urgent pressure of his body against mine, and with sickening hindsight I understood: if he had really loved me, he would not have debased me so. And he most certainly wouldn't have boasted about it to others, in the crudest and most impersonal terms. It was just as my father had said; I was the master's daughter, the toy on the highest shelf, desirable precisely and only because I was unattainable. And I had let him kiss me, and press against me, and run his fingers over my breasts. It made me want to scrape myself with something sharp and inflexible.

I was sent off to Europe with my Aunt Margaret on a three-month tour. The only way to ease my humiliation, I found, was to banish Simon from my mind and affections, and I did so with surgical precision. On the steamer to England his hands grew hairy and grasping in my imagination, while his smile became a drooling leer. My interest in him, I came to see, had not stemmed from an understanding of his true character, but was in fact a misdirected yearning for the "pure love" that Professor Fowler had so radiantly described. By the time we reached Liverpool, I was able to view what had happened as an unfortunate but educational experience, for which I need not hold myself too harshly to account.

There followed dozens of pre-arranged visits to acquaintances abroad, along with numerous receptions and dances where I saw how properly attentive a well-bred young man could be. By the time I sailed back past Lady Liberty into New York Harbor three months later, I could honestly say that Simon Shaw was no more than an unpleasant memory. When I discovered upon my return that his mother had left our employment for more gainful work elsewhere, taking Simon with her, my only feeling was one of relief.

Simon Shaw had no more power to affect me now than a fading old photograph—or so I had believed until today. And yet here I was, blushing in front of these strangers as Simon tried to prove once again, this time through his belittling, that he was as good as or better than I was. It was only the thought of what I had come for that held my temper in check. He was nothing to me, I reminded myself—but he could be critically important to Eliza. And so, when he asked why I cared about what happened to her, I answered simply, "I'm a doctor now. She's a patient of mine."

"A doctor." His eyebrow rose. "Your father must be very proud."

"Yes, I believe he is."

He looked around the table. "What do you think, boys?"

"Wouldn't hurt to ask a few questions," said one tentatively.

"Sure," shrugged another. "What harm could it do?"

Simon looked back at me, pursing his lips. "Give me one hard fact," he said, "that says she didn't kill him."

"She isn't constitutionally capable of murder."

"I said fact. That's your opinion."

"It's my professional opinion. I'm a psychotherapist, and she's my patient."

"It's still just an opinion. You'll have to do better than that."

"There was someone else in the room with the doctor, while Eliza was waiting to speak with him. She heard signs of a struggle."

"Did anyone else hear it?" he asked.

"Not that I know of—but isn't that what the detective ought to be investigating?"

He shrugged. "Not if it's obvious she's lying. What else have you got?"

I mentally rummaged through the jumble of information I'd accumulated over the past few hours, but found I was longer on theory than on hard fact. "Her fingerprints aren't on the murder weapon," I ventured.

"That doesn't mean anything. She was wearing gloves."

I blinked at him in surprise. "How did you know that?"

"It's in the police report."

"But you'd already left the court when Officer Callahan testif . . ."

"It's my job to know what's going on in my district," he said, cutting me off.

Maybe he had recognized me in court, after all, I thought, and made it his business to find out why I was there—not out of concern, but out of a festering malice . . . .

"Is that all?" he asked impatiently. "Because if it is, it's not enough."

"She has no one else to ask!" I cried. "You helped those other people. Why won't you help her?"

"I've got no interest in putting murderers back on the street."

"But she isn't a murderer!"

"So you say."

"And you don't believe me?"

The front legs of his chair struck the ground with a crack. "Let's just say that if I have to choose between believing you or Maloney, I'll take Maloney any day."

I glared at him, as the other men gazed down at the table or fidgeted with their mugs. It seemed there was no end to Simon's desire to publicly humiliate me. But at least this time, I didn't have to let him get away with it. He'd made it clear he wasn't going to help Eliza, and I had nothing else to lose.

"Well, it seems you can take the man out of the stable," I said tartly, pulling up my gloves, "but you can't take the stable out of the man." I strode to the door, turned, and looked back. "Detective Maloney's opinion is horseshit. No wonder you prefer it." Standing as tall as my corset supporters would allow, I stalked out of the room.

CHAPTER NINE

The ripple of laughter that followed me out provided cold comfort. It didn't soften the fact that my only hope for help was gone. I left the saloon and started for home without bothering to button up my collar, glad of the wind's bite. I hated that Simon had so easily rekindled my old feelings of shame and humiliation. I hated that I had let him. Most of all, I hated that his refusal to help had left me feeling even more frightened and alone than before.

Perhaps I should just tell my father what had happened, and pass my awful burden over to him. He had a wide circle of acquaintances; he might know someone who could help. But just the thought of telling him made me quake. I could predict his reaction with knee-knocking certainty: first bewilderment, as he confronted the unacceptable fact that I was involved with a suspected murderer; then shock, as the truth bore through his reflexive denial; and finally the cold, flat disappointment that would fill his eyes whenever he looked at me.

No, I couldn't tell him what I'd gotten myself mixed up in. At least not until Eliza was proved innocent. But how was that going to happen, if no one would take up her case? There seemed only one answer. I was going to have to prove her innocence myself.

I was an intelligent, capable person, I thought, kicking an empty Knickerbocker bottle out of my path. There was no reason to feel so overwhelmed by the prospect. Hard evidence, that's what it boiled down to. All I had to do was find credible evidence that someone else had killed the doctor, and the police could take it from there. But where in the world should I begin?

Where the police generally began, I answered myself, as I cut across Park Avenue. At the crime scene. Of course Maloney and his men had already gone over it, but they'd only been looking for evidence to support their foregone conclusions. If I were to examine it with a fresh eye, I might find something they'd missed. I knew it was a long shot, but no other ideas were coming to mind. At the end of the next block I stopped. To the right was home, to the left Dr. Hauptfuhrer's office. I stood for several moments by the lamppost, reviewing all the reasons I should not attempt an unauthorized entry into a crime scene. But I could see no other way.

And so a few minutes later I found myself walking along the north side of 83rd Street with my hat angled low over my face, trying to look inconspicuous as I peered across the street at Dr. Hauptfuhrer's house. The first floor window shades were fully drawn, making it impossible to see inside. There was a handwritten sign on the door which I couldn't read, but which I presumed gave notice to patients that the doctor was no longer available.

I circled the block to gather my nerve and made a second pass, along the building side of the street. I was betting that Miss Hauptfuhrer was somewhere up on the private floors, quite possibly sedated, and not wandering around the downstairs rooms. The laundress should have finished hours ago, if she'd come at all, while the furnace man wouldn't be back until late. That left only the maid-of-all-work to worry about.

According to my pendant watch it was nearly five o'clock. By now the maid should have finished lighting the lamps and drawing the shades and building up the fires. Normally at this hour she'd be in the basement kitchen, helping to prepare the family's dinner, or setting the dining room table on the private floors. With the household routine in disarray, however, it was hard to predict where she might be.

My hastily composed plan was to sneak in through the servants' entrance in the basement and make my way upstairs from there. I took a quick glance around. Except for two other pedestrians farther up the block with their backs to me, the sidewalks were empty. It was now or never. Pulling up my skirt, I ducked down the areaway steps, turned the knob on the servants' entrance door and eased silently inside.

I stood stock-still in the hallway, deafened by the sound of my own breathing, not quite believing that I'd actually done it. I could still turn around, I told myself, as a flurry of doubts assailed me. But I was rooted by a sense of inevitability—as when once having breached the golden perfection of Katie's crust as a child, I felt obliged to finish the whole pie. And so, straining to hear over the rattle of the steam pipes, I proceeded cautiously down the dim hallway.

As I had anticipated, the basement level mirrored the floor above, with a hallway along the right side giving access to rooms on the left. The first room was dark, and presumably empty. But a dim light and sounds of running water warned me that the kitchen beyond it was occupied. I crept up to the door frame and peered around it. A young woman in black and white evening uniform was standing in front of the dumbwaiter with her back to me, placing a tea tray on the lift. Before she could turn, I hurried past on tiptoe and bolted up the staircase at the end of the hall.

The first floor landing was almost directly across from the side door into the doctor's office. I eyed the rope that had been strung in front of the door, knowing that I could be in a whole new world of trouble once I crossed it. I hadn't come this far to turn back, however. Easing the door open, I ducked under the rope and into the room.

It looked almost exactly as it had that morning, except that the doctor's body had been replaced by a chalk outline on the bloodied rug. I closed the door softly behind me and slowly surveyed the scene. Nothing helpful leaped out immediately. There was nothing obviously out of place: no torn button lying in plain sight on the floor, or papers in disarray. The desk was bare except for a blotter, a pen, and the sword stand, while the shallow wastebasket appeared to be empty.

There was, however, that bottom file drawer, which had been left in the open position. As far as I knew, the police hadn't even bothered to check its contents, assuming that whatever the doctor had been filing when he was attacked had no bearing on the case. But if, as I suspected, the doctor had been looking for Eliza's "proof" and had been interrupted before he could retrieve it, whatever he'd been looking for would still be inside. And that could be of value to Eliza's defense down the road. If I could show that Hauptfuhrer had been about to give her what she'd come for, then even if her accusers found out about her baby, they couldn't convincingly argue that she'd killed him in a frustrated rage.

Dropping my book bag on the floor, I started toward the drawer. I had only taken three steps, however, when the sound of male voices stopped me cold. They were coming through the open door that led to the adjacent waiting room. From the snippets of conversation I could make out—something about a prize fight raid the night before, and the arrest of someone named "Rubber Jack"—I deduced that they belonged to policemen who'd been left to protect the crime scene.

Every instinct told me to turn and run. Just a few yards away, however, on the other side of the narrow room, the open file drawer beckoned seductively. My fingers itched to run through it. But if I cut across the middle of the floor, the policemen might see me through the open door.

So instead, I dropped to my hands and knees and crawled along the wall to the back of the room, and then across the floor to the desk—a surprisingly difficult maneuver, it turned out, thanks to my bulky skirt and floppy, wide-brimmed hat. Stopping from time to time to pull the folds of my skirt from beneath my knees, I continued on all fours from the desk, to the potted fern, to the opposite side of the room. There I paused, waiting for whistles to blow and the sky to fall in. But it seemed I had not been detected.

Rising carefully to my feet, I sidled down the wall to the bank of file cabinets. So far, so good; but if I moved out on the floor to inspect the bottom drawer's contents, I would be directly in the officers' line of sight, sure to be seen if I lingered for more than a moment or two. If I wanted a thorough look, I was going to have to at least partially close the connecting door.

I waited until the men were engaged again in conversation, then darted out around the bulging drawer and back to the wall on the other side. From there it was only a few more steps to the door. I put my eye to the crack between the hinges. Two uniformed officers were sitting directly opposite, with their chairs angled toward each other and a spittoon positioned in between. I laid my trembling hands on the back of the door and waited for a good time to push.

And waited. And waited some more. I heard the distant whistle of the tea kettle, and then the thud of the dumbwaiter door, but still couldn't summon my nerve, worried that the movement of the door would draw their attention. I was beginning to think I'd have to abandon my search, when one of the men suddenly got to his feet.

"I'm going out for a hot dog," he said. "You want one?"

"Make it two," the second officer said, digging into his pocket. "With sauerkraut."

As the money was being exchanged I eased the door forward inch by excruciating inch, until it was nearly three-quarters of the way shut. I waited with my heart in my throat for some reaction from the other side, but heard only the thud of the front door closing. I tiptoed back to the open drawer and crouched before it. It was less than half-full, divided into alphabetized sections labeled "V" through "Z" that appeared, upon a cursory search, to contain only current patient files. In the very back was a divider labeled "Miscellaneous". I pulled this forward to discover two handwritten pages, each divided into three neat columns. The first column on each page appeared to be a list of dates, in chronological order. In the middle column, next to each date, were pairs of capital letters followed by either a "bg" or "bb". Treatment notations had been scribbled under some of the entries. I recognized treatments typically prescribed for newborns: "potassium bromide, 15 grn." for abdominal cramps; "silver nitrate, 3x" for infantile conjunctivitis; "nitro. wrap" for jaundice. I sat back on my heels. Bb, bg. Could the letters stand for "baby boy" and "baby girl"?

Lifting the pages out, I crept back to the door to take another look through the hinges. The remaining officer appeared to be dozing in his chair, lulled by the hiss of the steam pipes. I returned my attention to the list, scanning it for additional clues. Halfway down the first page, in the second column, I saw the capital letters, "E. B.", followed by a "bg". Eliza's maiden name was Braun, I remembered with excitement. Might these letters stand for 'Elizabeth Braun—baby girl'? I looked at the date to their left. January 8, 1887. Eliza had told me that her daughter's birthday was two days away—on January 8th. She'd also told me that she was fifteen when her baby was born. I did the math. In 1887, Eliza would have been about fifteen years old.

The third column contained yet more paired letters, or initials. Next to the "E. B.—bg" entry, the doctor had inscribed the letters, "L. F." I could come up with no immediate connection. Remembering that Dr. Hauptfuhrer had spoken of giving Eliza's baby a better home, however, I wondered if these might be the recipient's initials. If so, it would mean that Joy had not been placed with an orphan asylum, as I'd originally surmised, but directly with an adoptive parent.

What about the other entries on the list, then? Could each be the record of an illegitimate birth and adoption? I counted thirty-one entries in all, the last one made just a month earlier in December of 1906. Thirty-one babies, born over a period of twenty-three years. Taken from their birth mothers, if my guess was correct, and given in secrecy to someone else. The transaction recorded in code, and filed under "miscellaneous". The only conclusion I could draw was that the esteemed blood specialist Dr. Hermann Hauptfuhrer had been providing some sort of illegal adoption service, on the side.

I stared down at the list, my excitement building as I pulled the threads together. Eliza had mentioned that her mother met the doctor at the German Hospital, where he was a regular volunteer. I imagined the doctor would have encountered many indigent women in his work there, including the occasional unwed mother. Perhaps he had been asked to find a home for an illegitimate baby, and had consented. Word might have spread, with one unofficial placement leading to the next. It could have happened almost by accident, with the doctor feeling justified, perhaps, in bending the law for what he considered a humanitarian purpose.

My mind reeled at the implications. If my guess was correct, I had uncovered a whole new slew of potential murder suspects. Other young women like Eliza, who'd never wanted to give up their babies in the first place—or mothers who'd changed their minds and asked for their babies back, and been told they couldn't have them. Indeed, any one of the women in the left-hand column could have attacked the doctor, either out of revenge, or in a failed attempt to discover her child's whereabouts.

All that remained was to find the key that matched the initials to actual names. Returning to the drawer, I thumbed through the rest of the "miscellaneous" material in hopes of locating it. I found some old bills, a certificate of Union Club membership, and maps of London and St. Petersburg—but nothing that looked like a key. I couldn't imagine Hauptfuhrer leaving such vital information to memory. I glanced around the room. It could be anywhere: in one of the other file drawers, or his desk, or some other room entirely . . . .

The sound of footsteps interrupted my thoughts. They were moving quickly, in my direction. I scurried back behind the door, barely concealing myself before it was pushed open. I caught the knob and pulled the door against me so it wouldn't bounce off my toes, waiting sickly for it to be jerked back out of my hand and my presence exposed. But the footsteps walked on past, into the office. I heard the desk drawer open, followed by a sharp, rasping sound and the pungent scents of sulfur and tobacco. I nearly collapsed with relief. The officer had only been looking for a match for his cigar. So much for Detective Maloney's "sealed" crime scene, I thought bitterly. I pressed back against the wall, making myself as insubstantial as possible as the footsteps clumped back out the door.

Thank you Lord and I'll never ask for another favor, I swore, stuffing the doctor's list under my waistband. Key or no key, I'd had enough. While the officer was still walking back to his chair I ran straight across the room, grabbed my bag and ducked out the side door. My luck held and I encountered no one in the basement, the maid having apparently gone upstairs to deliver the tea tray to Miss Hauptfuhrer. I continued out the service door and up the steps to the sidewalk, welcoming the smack of cold air on my face. I looked to my left; all was clear. I looked to my right—and saw the second officer walking up the block with a stack of hot dogs cradled in his arms.

He paused on sight of me, then started accelerating over the sidewalk.

I turned off the top step and walked briskly in the opposite direction.

"Hey, hold up there!" he called.

I lengthened my stride, praying he'd lose interest. But my luck seemed to have run out. As I approached the corner, I heard his whistle blow. I broke into a run, cutting diagonally through the intersection as drivers honked and shouted all around me. On the far corner I turned to look back. The officer had just started through the intersection after me, crushing the hot dogs against his chest as he blasted repeatedly on his whistle to summon help.

I didn't wait for assistance to arrive. Holding onto my hat I ran full-out down the next block and careened around the corner onto Fifth Avenue. Stately homes fronted by wrought iron gates lined the right side of the block. I ran a few more yards and turned in at number 1027, taking the steps two at a time. As there was no time to wait for someone to answer the bell, I did the unthinkable; I pushed the heavy door open and let myself in.

It closed with a solid thud behind me. I stood stock-still in the silent marble vestibule, catching my breath as I listened for sounds of pursuit outside. I heard two more muted whistle blasts, but they seemed to be moving up the Avenue. When no one pounded on the door after several more moments, I concluded that my escape had gone unobserved.

But I had no intention of venturing out again anytime soon. I was deciding whether to try to hide in the vestibule, or to continue inside and announce myself, when the parlor maid appeared in the hallway. "I beg your pardon, Miss!" she exclaimed, pulling up short, her eyes darting around the vestibule in confusion. "I didn't hear the bell . . ."

"Well I rang and rang," I said, trying hard not to pant. "I suppose the bell must be broken. It's so dreadfully cold out, I thought I'd better just let myself in." I took off my hat and coat and handed them to her with a smile. "Is Miss Emily at home?"

"Miss Emily?" she repeated, still gazing distractedly around the vestibule.

"Could you tell her Genevieve Summerford is here?"

Her eyes snapped into focus. "Miss Summerford? Oh my goodness; I didn't recognize you, it's been so long! Please, make yourself at home and I'll let her know you're here."

It had in fact been two years, I calculated, since I'd last paid a visit to Emily Clark. Though we'd never been fast friends, we'd commiserated through years of dancing classes, and there was a time when we'd visited regularly. I thought I should be able to muster sufficient conversation to outlast whatever search party might be organizing outside.

Emily seemed genuinely glad to see me when she joined me in the drawing room a few minutes later, and as we sat arm to arm on a deeply cushioned ottoman before the fire, catching up on each other's lives, I could almost relax enough to pretend it was an ordinary social call. We spoke of simple things: the new roof garden at the Colony Club; the figure-enhancing merits of Hoffman's tonic; whether the North Pole would most likely be breached by ship or balloon. Though normally I shared Father's distaste for Moorish décor, tonight the Clarks' heavily furnished drawing room—with its deep green shades and hanging rugs and layer upon layer of pillows and shawls—provided welcome insulation from the outside world.

Eventually our talk turned to recent social events, and inevitably, to the Fiskes' upcoming ball. "I suppose you're going?" Emily asked me.

"I suppose."

"You don't sound very enthusiastic."

"Well, you know how it is. The same old faces, talking about the same old things."

"Now you mustn't go all cynical on me," she said, folding her arms over her chest. "Promise me you'll be there. We spinsters have to stick together, to spread the pity around."

I laughed, shaking my head. "I don't think anyone's putting you in the spinster category just yet. From what I've heard, you're more likely to be included in a Bowery 'Believe It or Not' for all the offers of marriage you rejected last year. Speaking of which, whatever happened to that golden-haired fellow from London you were so keen on last time I saw you—the one with the fabulous library?" Emily, one of the few women in our set who actually liked to read, had a tendency to measure a man by the size of his library.

"The books were fakes," she said with a sigh. "Every last one of them. Nothing but false covers with gilt trim."

"Oh, Em . . ."

"It's a sign of the times, I'm afraid," she said, sipping her tea. "Men today are all form and no substance." She eyed me speculatively over the rim of her cup. "Speaking of golden boys, how's Bartie Mattheson? He must be glad you're back in town."

"That's the second time today someone has put me and Bartie in the same sentence," I told her with a frown.

She shrugged. "There are worse places to be. I know plenty of girls who'd like to share a sentence with Bartie Mattheson."

"Oh for heaven's sake; I've known him since he was in short pants!"

"Yes, and he's always had a soft spot for you."

I waved this aside. "Only because I never joined in when Billy Eastman called him Farting Bartie."

We both laughed. I wished things could go on like this forever; just the two of us before the fire, making small talk, untouched by the world outside. But when the maid returned to ask if she should put on an extra plate for dinner, I reluctantly rose to go.

"Are you sure you won't stay?" Emily asked. "There's still so much to catch up on."

"I'm afraid I can't. My parents will be expecting me. But I'll see you again on Saturday, at the ball."

"I'll take that as a promise." She walked me to the vestibule and helped me into my coat, giving me a parting hug before she let me out into the night. I cautiously descended the steps, relieved to see that the only policeman in sight was directing traffic two blocks up the Avenue. My relief couldn't keep a pall from settling over me, however, as I watched the tide of humanity returning uptown. A side-whiskered man was climbing the steps to the building next door, jangling keys in his pocket, while two little girls with dancing frocks peeking out beneath their coat hems skipped past him on the sidewalk, holding their governess's hands. It was a familiar neighborhood scene, the wearily peaceful end to a busy day. Tonight, however, the well-ordered universe it suggested seemed to belong only to others, as out of my reach as a stroll in the park was now out of Eliza's. I'd spent years trying to ensure that I'd never be uprooted from that safe, predictable world again; and yet somehow, in just a few short hours, everything I'd thought was solid had been thrown into flux. And whatever I did to try to fix it only seemed to make things worse. Not only were my professional credentials now in jeopardy, but I was a fugitive from the law as well. And for what? What had my latest little adventure gained me? Nothing but a list of dates and initials—hardly the compelling evidence I'd been searching for.

I passed through the gate and fell in behind a trio of young ladies bearing armfuls of Bergdorf Goodman boxes, staying close enough that I'd appear to be part of their group if anyone was still looking for me. Their lighthearted chatter made me feel even more alone. An elegant carriage spun past us on rubber wheels, carrying men in gleaming opera hats and women in flashing tiaras. I felt a pang as it rolled by, remembering what it was like to have nothing more pressing on my mind than what Broadway show to see, or which dress to wear for dinner. By the time I reached home my spirits had reached an all-day low.

Glancing into the dining room, I saw that the table had already been set for breakfast. Dinner was served promptly at six o'clock at our house and waited for no one. I proceeded to the sitting room, where I found Father reading the evening paper in front of a crackling fire.

He looked up as I entered. "There you are. We missed you at dinner."

I sank onto the floor in front of his armchair and pulled off my damp shoes, stretching my feet toward the flames. "I'm sorry," I said, flexing my icy toes. "The time just got away from me."

"I don't know why we bothered to install a telephone, if no one is going to use it," he grumbled, snapping his newspaper straight.

I dropped my head against the arm of his chair, too tired to respond. The day's toll seemed to have caught up with me all at once;

I could have sworn there were little people hanging from my eyelids. I gazed up at the back of his newspaper, struggling to keep my eyes open—and for the second time that day found myself staring into the face of Dr. Herman Hauptfuhrer. "EAST SIDE DOCTOR MURDERED;" read the caption under the artist's sketch; "GUEST OF TSAR MEETS GRISLY END."

"What was it that kept you, if I'm not prying?" asked my father.

"I was visiting Emily," I mumbled, twisting my head to try to read the article.

He folded the paper against his chest and looked down at me. "Emily Clark?"

"Yes."

"I always liked Emily," he said.

I pointed to the article. "Father, did you see this, about the doctor who was murdered?"

"Yes, I was sorry to learn of it. He struck me as a decent enough fellow."

"You mean you knew him?" I asked in surprise.

"We ran into each other occasionally. He was friendly with members of the hospital board. His mother's a Maidlaw, if I'm not mistaken. I believe he was an expert on diseases of the blood."

"Why do you suppose someone would want to kill him?" I asked, pulling my knees up under my chin.

"They say it was one of his patients."

"I don't see how they could know that, so soon," I said, a bit too forcefully. "They don't seem to have any motive."

"Here," he said, peeling off the front section and handing it to me. "I see that your morbid curiosity has been aroused. Gorge to your heart's content." He went on reading where he'd left off.

I spread the page on my lap and scanned the article. It was essentially a recap of Officer Callahan's story, with allusions to "a blood-smeared blade" and a suspect who "appeared confused". District Attorney Jerome was quoted promising a quick conviction, based on the evidence in hand. There was some biographical information concerning the victim as well: the doctor was indeed a Maidlaw, although not from the family's most illustrious branch.

He'd attended Columbia and Harvard, was associated with two prestigious laboratories, and had practiced medicine in the city since 1878. He had special expertise in blood disorders and had been consulted regarding the health of several important personages, including, as Detective Maloney had informed me, Czar Alexander's hemophiliac son, Prince Alexei.

"You don't suppose he could have been involved in something sinister, do you?" I asked.

"Hmm? Like what?"

"Oh, I don't know. White slavery? Opium smuggling? Or . . . illegal adoptions, perhaps?"

He snorted and turned the page. "It's too bad we can't think of a more constructive outlet for that imagination of yours."

I watched the firelight flit over his face, softening the lines of his mouth and chin. How bad would it really be, I wondered, if I were to tell him what had happened? He'd be angry, disappointed, alarmed— but he wouldn't refuse to help. And help was what I needed now, more than anything. I hugged my knees against my chest, feeling a confession rise to my lips.

A log fell in the fireplace, loosing a shower of sparks. "Well," Father said, folding the newspaper, "it's getting late, and I have some correspondence to attend to." He stood. "I'll leave you this." He handed me the rest of the paper as I rose clumsily to my feet.

"Katie left some dinner on the warmer, if you're hungry," he went on. "Don't forget to say good night to your mother before you go up."

"No, I won't. Good night, Father."

He walked to the door, and turned. "By the way, I've given some thought to our discussion this morning, and I'm willing to admit that I've been pigheaded. You're a grown woman after all, capable of making your own decisions. It was wrong of me to doubt you."

"Oh no, Father, you needn't apologize; you were just—"

"I haven't finished. You'll be pleased to know that I spoke with the hospital board today, and told them that you're no longer interested in the position."

"You did?"

"Yes. I wouldn't count them out altogether, though; it seems to me that once you've established a record of success, we ought to be able to interest them in this 'class treatment' of yours. If it's as effective as you say, I should think there'd be a place for it at the hospital."

"Why, that's . . . that's . . ." I gripped the back of the armchair. "I hardly know what to say."

"You needn't say anything," he said, sounding pleased with himself. "I'm just glad we finally see eye to eye. Now, do try to get some sleep. You look exhausted."

I listened to his footsteps move down the hall and up the stairs, shivering in the cooling air. I sank into his vacated armchair, burrowing into the cushions in a vain attempt to extract what little warmth remained. Except for the whine of the dying embers, the house was silent: the staff in their rooms upstairs or gone home for the night, Mother ensconced in the conservatory, and Father partaking of his nightly palliative in the study—three shots of whiskey, no more and no less, the same dose he'd downed every evening for the past fourteen years. I was alone once more.

But perhaps not completely alone, I thought; no doubt Eliza was holding me close in her thoughts, praying that I'd produce a miracle. I looked down at the newspaper as tears of fatigue and frustration blurred my eyes. Maybe if I read the article again, I'd discover something I'd overlooked. Pulling myself erect, I started from the beginning, focusing on one sentence at a time. But the information remained the same. Hauptfuhrer appeared to have led an exemplary life. He had had a conventional upbringing, a successful career, a wealthy clientele . . . .

A wealthy clientele. I looked back up at the doctor's sketch. Hauptfuhrer's well-to-do patients could afford to pay for whatever their hearts desired—including, it occurred to me now, a newborn child. I remembered the gossip years ago, when a close friend of my mother's announced after a decade of barren marriage that she was pregnant. People had hinted at an extramarital affair—but while I was drawing on the floor one night behind the sitting room sofa, I'd heard my mother confide to my father that the woman wasn't pregnant at all; that she was only pretending to be, intending to take her maid's unborn child as her own. Four months later the friend departed to Europe for the remainder of her "confinement", taking her lady's maid with her. In the fall she returned with the babe in her arms, and a wet nurse in place of the maid.

There were undoubtedly other women of means who were unable to conceive. Women who would pay handsomely for a discrete adoption. Perhaps the doctor hadn't been so selfless after all. Perhaps he'd been using his connections to supply illegitimate babies to those who wanted and could afford them, earning himself a substantial income on the side. In which case, I thought with excitement, the list of potential murder suspects would include not only the women on the left side of the doctor's list, but on the right side as well.

Dr. Hauptfuhrer's rich clients would have expected absolute secrecy for their money; if he threatened to disclose their children's identities for any reason—whether at the request of a remorseful birth mother, or for a medical intervention, or even in an attempt to extort more money—one of them might have taken steps to silence him. Since Hauptfuhrer's baby transfers had presumably never been approved in court at a public hearing, they would have no legal force, and likely would not hold up should a birth mother seek to reclaim her child—meaning that disclosure might even cause an adoptive family to lose a beloved son or daughter. Surely, that was motivation enough to commit murder.

It seemed a real enough possibility. But again, without a key to the names, I didn't know how to test it. I was staring down at the newspaper, agonizing over how to unlock the mystery of the list, when the simple answer occurred to me: the newspaper society pages. If Hauptfuhrer's adoption clients were the sort of people I thought they were, they would almost certainly have published birth announcements. In which case determining the identity of the adopting families—including the one who had taken Eliza's baby— might be as simple as checking back issues of the New York Times.

I pulled the crumpled list from my waistband. All I had to do was compare the initials in the third column with those of parents who'd announced a birth around the same dates. If I could find enough matches to defeat an assertion of coincidence, I'd have something solid to show Maloney. I was wide awake now, vibrating with excitement. I couldn't wait to test my hypothesis; but unfortunately, the library didn't open for another eleven hours. I threw a log on the fire, returned to the chair, then bounced back up again. Crossing to the bookshelves, I ran my finger along the titles, looking for something to distract me. I finally selected a book on Robert Scott's Discovery Expedition into Antarctica and carried it back to the chair.

The minutiae of polar expedition preparation proved to be a powerful soporific, and a half hour later I had closed the book and laid my head back against the armchair. As disjointed images flitted through my mind, dredged up by the events of the day, I found myself reliving the old Simon fiasco. It had taken me years to fully overcome the shame that it caused me. It wasn't until I was in medical school that I'd come to fully accept my physical stirrings as normal, and to understand that I'd done nothing perverse. My only real error, I'd realized then, was in thinking that any man had the power to make me feel happy and complete, and I'd resolved never to make that mistake again. I had no intellectual quarrel with romantic love; I just didn't see it in my own future. Experience had left too bitter a taste in my mouth. It would be enough, I had decided, to find a man with compatible interests and values, with whom I might peacefully coexist.

As time went on, however, the sexual question had continued to haunt me. The act itself, the stuff of poetry and peepshows—what was it really like? How did it feel to have another person enter your body; to share, as it were, your very tissue? The question hung over me like the proverbial albatross, too awkward to discuss but too large to ignore, until finally, I could bear it no longer.

I decided to undertake a scientific study of the matter. After much consideration I selected a studious young man in the class ahead of me, with whom I shared a mutual regard. He was shy, fit, pleasantly deferential and open to progressive ideas. The weekend before his graduation I obtained some sheaths from a local midwife and engaged a room at an inn two towns away, under a false name. On the appointed evening we shared a light dinner at the inn before retiring to our room upstairs. At my direction we undressed beneath the light of a sputtering gas lamp, then turned out the light and lay side by side on the bed. I waited for indescribable excitement to overtake me—but nothing like it ever arrived. I had little desire to touch him; I was, in truth, somewhat repelled by the bumpy pallor of his skin, which looked fish-belly white in the filtered streetlight. Having come this far, however, I felt obliged to carry through. It was a good thing that he couldn't see my face when I touched his engorged penis; for I'll admit that I experienced then a moment of extreme indecision. I pushed through it, however, and after some struggle with the sheath, the deed was carried out.

I had expected the pain of penetration. What I had not anticipated was that it would come as a welcome distraction from the feelings that threatened to swamp me as his damp, alien body pumped furtively, apologetically above me. A few silent thrusts, a stifled groan, and it was over.

Later, as I braced myself under the scalding shower in the women's dormitory, I felt both disappointment and relief: disappointment that the experience had been so unfulfilling, relief that the act had been stripped of its festering allure. My experiment had simply proved that forbidden fruit was sweeter in the imagination than on the tongue. The sexual act itself, I saw now, was emotionally and morally neutral: it was like a baseball bat which, when used for its intended purpose, was a highly effective tool, but if taken up by the wrong hands with the wrong intent, could inflict serious harm. I felt freed at last from its pull—and from any need to experience it again, until my time for child-bearing had come.

The last log fell with a hiss in the fireplace. I opened my eyes and stared into the fire's remains. It was the not-knowing, I decided now, that had pushed me into Simon's arms those many years ago. That, and the loneliness. I had thought to achieve with him some magical union that would take all my pain and emptiness away. But it could never happen again. I didn't believe in that kind of magic any more.

CHAPTER TEN

I'm off to the library," I announced the following morning at breakfast, bolting the rest of my tea.

"More research?" asked my father, cocking an eyebrow.

I walked around the table to kiss my mother's cheek. "Yes, the professor's asked me to help him with a new project."

"That man takes advantage of you."

"Getting published would be good for my career, too," I reminded him.

"So he's going to put your name on it this time?"

"Well, he might."

"Good God," he groaned; "not that same old carrot."

"Just be sure you're back by 11:00," my mother said.

"Why, what's at eleven?" I asked her.

"Oh Genna, you haven't forgotten? Monsieur Henri is coming to fit your dress!"

I had forgotten completely. "Oh, bother; why can't I just wear the damask and lace I wore for New Year's?"

"Yes, why can't she?" my father echoed, slicing himself a piece of ham. "Just think of all the starving children we could feed with the money we'd save."

"She can't wear the same dress twice in one season," Mother said placidly.

"No, of course not," Father said; "I'm sure the earth would stop spinning if she did."

"I'll be back by eleven," I told my mother, "but do you think we could skip the tea and cookies, just this once? I'm going to be awfully pressed for time."

"Now Genna, you don't want to offend Henri," said Mamma. "You know how he likes his madeleines."

Clearly the day's priorities had already been set. "Well I won't be eating them," I retorted. "Not if I hope to fit into that torture chamber he calls a dress." Monsieur had chosen pale blue net over darker blue satin for my gown, insisting that I was too young for the heavy brocades currently in vogue with the older unmarried set. Although I rather liked the décolleté bodice and short puffed sleeves of his final design, I acceded reluctantly to the tiny, breath-defying waist—and drew the line at a hem of heavy black jet. It would be hard enough dancing with a corset strung tight as a bow; I didn't intend to kick chain mail around all night, as well.

Dresses were the last thing on my mind, however, as I hopped off the streetcar thirty minutes later and trotted across 78th Street toward the Webster Public Library. This was my favorite of all the branch libraries springing up over town. Smack in the middle of the Bohemian neighborhood, it was like a school, Czech street fair and natural history museum rolled into one. With its self-service stacks, extensive hours and liberal borrowing policies it was a far more inviting place than the stuffy subscription libraries of my youth—but more importantly, for my current purposes, it had a special department for helping teachers pursue individualized courses of study. Retrospective periodicals being considered essential to scholarly pursuit, this department contained an abundance of back issues of the daily and illustrated newspapers, which I hoped would contain the answers I was seeking.

As I turned the corner onto Avenue A I spotted the prominent steps and oversized lanterns that characterized the new Carnegie libraries, symbolizing the users' ascent toward enlightenment. A long line of children was snaking toward the entrance from the school across the street. I hurried to get there ahead of them and pushed through the door. As usual, the reading tables were filled to capacity under the hanging lamps, generating a noise level more commonly associated with playgrounds than libraries. A lecture was taking place around one of the display cases, while a few feet away two tots were rolling what appeared to be a cocoanut across the floor. I'd read that Mr. Carnegie's decision to donate 65 libraries to the City was based on his calculation that a great metropolis needed one library for every 70,000 residents. When I visited the Webster branch, I often wondered if this ratio hadn't undershot the mark.

Skirting an exhibit of preserved reptiles mounted just inside the door, I climbed the stairs to the periodical room. Although it was quieter up here, none of the tables were empty. I claimed a seat between two bearded gentlemen reading foreign newspapers, then carried the doctor's purloined list to the desk and enlisted the librarian's aid in locating the issues I needed. I brought these back to the table and placed the list of initials beside them. I intended to begin with the January and February issues from 1887, searching for the mysterious "L. F." who, if my theory was correct, had adopted Eliza's baby.

This task proved more difficult than I had expected. The older papers didn't have a well organized society section, and birth announcements were sprinkled haphazardly through the end pages. A half hour of searching yielded only three announcements, none of which was posted by a woman with the initials "L. F." I found a Patricia Fallon who announced the birth of a baby girl on January 19th , and eagerly scoured the paragraph for her husband's name in the hope that he might be the "L." in question—but it was a disappointing "Frank". I was about to give up on "L. F." and switch to another pair of initials, when I flipped the page of the second February issue and gasped so loudly that every head at my table turned.

In the center of the page, set off by an elaborate floral border with a beatific infant at one corner, was a birth announcement containing the initials I'd been looking for. Not *that* L. F., I thought; it couldn't be. I read the paragraph two more times before I could even allow myself to entertain it—and still had to check the next two issues to be sure there was no other, less fantastic candidate. There wasn't. I returned to the announcement and stared down at it in disbelief. I couldn't have been more astonished if the subject in question had reached up and socked me in the eye.

If my theory was correct—and the congruence of dates and initials seemed too striking for it not to be—Eliza's baby had been adopted by Mrs. Lucille Fiske, wife of the traction king Charles Fiske, whose fortune from his rapidly growing streetcar company was said to rival that of the Schwabs and Vanderbilts. As I and all of society knew, the Fiske baby had been named Olivia, after her paternal grandmother. I didn't need a newspaper to tell me that she had been raised like a princess; that she was, in fact, the closest thing to royalty we had in America. I knew that she was tall, and slender and 20 years old—and that she was currently being courted by Andrew Clearings Bernard Terrence Williams Hastings, 8th Earl of Branard.

I needed corroboration. Counting back from the date of birth, I hurried back to the librarian's desk and requested more issues from the autumn of 1886. In the second October issue, I found it. A single, innocent sentence among the hodge-podge of society notes: "Mrs. Lucille Fiske sets sail on the Steamer Deutschland today with her sister, Mrs. Adriana Monroe, for an extended visit to Egypt."

Egypt. A place where she would be unlikely to see anyone she knew. A place where she could wait out her "term" in solitude until Dr. Hauptfuhrer wired to say that the baby was about to arrive. My whole body was tingling with excitement as I carried the newspapers into the washroom, ripped out the two notes and slipped them into my bag. I returned the issues to the nice librarian, trying not to look guilty, and asked for another batch.

AN HOUR LATER I was pondering the results of my search as I jolted home in a hansom cab. I'd found three more matches for the initials on the list, enough to convince even Detective Maloney, I thought, that my theory was worth investigating. I planned to look for more at the next opportunity, but already my head was swimming with possibilities. I was acquainted with three of the four adoptive families

I'd uncovered that morning, and knew that one of them, the Backhouses, had recently suffered financial reversals. I wondered if a cash-strapped Thomas Backhouse could have been blackmailing Dr. Hauptfuhrer, threatening to reveal his activities to the authorities. Perhaps it was he who'd entered the doctor's office yesterday morning, intending to collect but becoming embroiled in a life-or-death struggle instead.

Or I supposed it could have been Hauptfuhrer who was doing the blackmailing. His clients' desire for secrecy would, of course, have given him considerable leverage. Perhaps, finding himself in need of funds, he had threatened to expose one of them unless she handed over more money, forcing a peremptory strike. I looked down at the doctor's list, now covered with my penciled notations. Suddenly, it seemed I had more suspects than I knew what to do with.

At least I had discovered where Joy was. I knew the Fiskes; I'd danced at their cotillions and enjoyed their extravagant feasts. Though some of the old-timers disapproved of Charles, considering his business manipulations ungentlemanly and his oversized mansion pretentious, my father and he had always gotten along. I knew they went to breakfasts together with the mayor around election time, and shared stock tips in the sauna at the Metropolitan Club. Father admired the man's directness—not to mention his extensive gardens, and the good sense he'd shown in setting his house back from the street. And I believed that Mr. Fiske, on his part, was grateful for my father's support among established society.

Whatever one thought of Charles Fiske's iron-handed business practices, it was hard to imagine a more advantageous situation for Eliza's daughter. The Fiskes had power, wealth and connections; they could give—had given—Olivia everything a mother could want for her child, and more. I thought Eliza would be happy if she knew. I was not as sure, however, that it would be wise to tell her, considering everything that had occurred.

The cab had turned onto my street. Glancing at my pendant watch, I saw that I had only five minutes before Monsieur Henri was scheduled to arrive. I lifted the speaker tube from the armrest and instructed the driver to pull up at Number 7, then hopped out and handed up the dollar fare. It was Wednesday, baking day, and the scent of ginger cookies greeted me in the entry. Perhaps an almond cake as well, I thought, sniffing the air with interest. There was no time now to eat, however—and besides, I still had to squeeze into that dress. I threw my hat and bag on the side table and continued down the hall to the staircase, where Mary was brushing off the steps. "Mary, have you seen my mother?" I asked her.

"Yes Miss, she's in the conservatory. She said you're to pick out the jewelry for your gown and bring it to her boudoir, for your fitting. She said she'll meet you there."

I thanked her and started up the stairs, eager to get the newsprint off my hands and to fix my hat-tousled hair; but before I'd even reached the top, the doorbell rang. I turned back down with a sigh. "I'll get it, Mary; you'd better go tell Mamma that Monsieur Henri has arrived." Smoothing my hair with my fingers, I descended to the front door and pulled it open, bracing myself for Henri's effusive greeting.

But it wasn't Henri standing on the threshold. It was Simon Shaw. Or rather, Simon Shaw transformed. I stared in mute amazement. He was dressed in impeccable morning attire—his coat a fine blue wool, his collar faultlessly pressed, and his tie in a perfect Windsor knot.

"Well, can I come in," he asked after several seconds had ticked by, "or did you want me to use the servants' entrance?"

"I'm sorry," I said quickly, stepping back; "you took me by surprise. I was expecting someone else."

He walked past me into the hall, removing his scarf and gloves. I laid these on the console and led him into the drawing room.

He stopped inside the door, glancing around the room. "I always wondered what it looked like in here," he mused. He made a frame with his fingers and squinted through it. "All I could ever see from the street was a patch of ceiling, and a bit of that chandelier."

"Won't you sit down?" I asked stiffly, indicating one of the two matched chairs by the piano.

He lowered himself onto it. His muscular frame looked out of place in the fringe-skirted armchair, despite his well-tailored clothing.

"So you really did become a doctor," he said, nodding at my graduation picture on the piano. "Just like your father always wanted."

"Just as I always wanted," I corrected, perching on the chair beside him.

"That's not how I remember it."

I clasped my hands in my lap. "Mr. Shaw, as I said, I'm expecting another visitor at any moment, so perhaps you ought to tell me why you've come."

He leaned back, stretching his legs over the flowered carpet. "You were seen leaving the doctor's office."

I swallowed a gasp, willing my face to remain impassive. "I beg your pardon?"

"They put out a pretty good description. Joe Brady had seen you at the Isle of Plenty, and made the match. It occurred to him you might have been tampering with evidence. He came to me before he went to Maloney; for some reason, he seemed to think I'd care if they threw you in jail."

"I have no idea what you're talking about."

He shrugged. "You can tell me what you were doing there, or not. It's up to you."

I shifted in my seat, studying his face, trying to figure out what he was up to. "If I had been tampering with evidence, which of course I haven't, why on earth would I tell you? You'd only pass it along to your good friend Detective Maloney."

"I'm not interested in doing Maloney's job for him."

"Then why are you here?"

"Let's just say I don't see you as the evidence-tampering type. I'm curious to know what would make you act so out of character."

"Well, if I ever were to break the law," I cautiously replied, "I'm sure it would only be because I felt I had no other options."

"I'm not talking about breaking the law. I'm talking about sticking your neck out for somebody else. That isn't like you."

There was my answer, I thought, feeling my face flush; he had come here to pay me back for ridiculing him in front of his peers— and to prove to himself that he could still lord it over me, if he chose.

I jumped to my feet. "I'm afraid I'm going to have to ask you to leave."

"Sit down."

I didn't move.

"Sit down, Genna," he said more firmly.

The sound of my name on his lips was more startling—and effective—than a yank on my arm. I sank slowly back onto the chair.

"I don't think you realize the trouble you're in."

He was enjoying himself, I thought with disgust, enjoying making me squirm. "If you're so sure I've done something wrong you ought to just turn me in."

"I could. But that wouldn't help Mrs. Miner, now would it?"

"You don't care what happens to Mrs. Miner," I scoffed. "You've made that abundantly clear."

"I do if she's innocent. I'm still waiting to hear some reason to believe that she is."

"We both know that her guilt or innocence has nothing to do with you helping her," I said, quite certain by now that his only interest in Eliza was as a means of getting at me.

"To the contrary, I don't like seeing people unjustly accused."

"You're going to help her, then? Is that what you're saying?"

His fingers tap-tap-tapped on the chair arm. "I'm willing to listen."

I couldn't quash a small surge of hope. Insulting or not, self-serving cad or not, he could still be a most useful ally. I hesitated, deciding what I might safely reveal. "What if I told you that for several years before his death, Dr. Hauptfuhrer was running an illegal adoption service?"

"I'd say that's an unusual sideline for an uptown doctor," he said slowly.

"And potentially a very lucrative one."

He nodded. "Go on."

I related in detail what Eliza had told me about hearing an intruder in the doctor's inner office, then articulated my theory about a frightened or vengeful adoption client taking the doctor's life.

"It makes a good story, I'll give you that," he said. "But what reason do you have to think the doctor was arranging adoptions?"

I supposed I couldn't expect him to take my assertion on faith. But I wasn't about to tell him that Eliza had first-hand knowledge of the doctor's dealings, and the only other way to prove it was to show him the stolen list.

"If I was planning to turn you in, I would have done it already," he prompted, watching my face.

Still I hesitated, remembering what had happened the last time I'd trusted him. "Will you promise to help Mrs. Miner, if I tell you?"

"I can't do that. Not until I've heard what you've got to say. But I can promise that whatever you tell me will go no further."

I decided it wouldn't do any harm to tell him what I'd found in the doctor's office, so long as I didn't reveal that Eliza was on the list. I stood up. "I'll be right back," I said, and went to retrieve the list from my bag in the hallway. "I found this in Dr. Hauptfuhrer's files," I said, handing it to him. "It's a list of women who gave up their babies, the babies' medical conditions, and their adopting families. There are over thirty entries in all."

"Initials?" he said, looking it over. "All you've got is initials?"

I moved around behind him. "It's enough." I pointed over his shoulder. "See here? The 'H. R.' stands for Helena Rivington, and the 'bb' stands for baby boy. Mrs. Rivington announced the birth of a son in the papers four days later." I moved my finger down the list. "That's Christiana Willard there . . . and the 'M. B.' is Margaret Backhouse. Each of them announced the birth of a child within days of the dates listed here."

"Crimus," he murmured, "it's like a page out of the bloody social register."

I was leaning so close to him I could feel the warmth of his skin through my shirtsleeve. I straightened and dropped my arm. "It makes sense when you think about it."

"They want a baby, they just buy one."

"Yes, and then everyone's supposed to live happily ever after. Except that it doesn't always work out that way, as the doctor unfortunately found out."

He was silent, studying the list. "What about this one here?" he asked after a moment.

"Which one?" I asked, bending down again.

"This 'E. B.'"

My breath caught in my throat. He couldn't know Mrs. Miner's maiden name; he had to be guessing. I looked up, right into his probing gaze. "What about it?"

"You don't suppose that could be Elizabeth Braun, do you?"

"Elizabeth . . . Braun?"

"Braun's her maiden name. Didn't you know?"

I stared at him. Of course I knew, but how in God's name did he?

"Her family owns Braun's Meats, around the corner from the Isle of Plenty," he said, as if reading my mind. "I recognized her in court." He glanced back at the left side of the list. "If she's in her mid-thirties now, in 1887 she would have been what, fifteen or so?" His dark eyes lifted back to mine. "Did the doctor by any chance deliver Mrs. Miner of a baby, when she was a girl?"

I didn't answer, wondering frantically if there was any way to force the cat back into the bag.

"I'll take that as a yes," he said with a grimace. "Which, if we accept your theory, means that she had as good a reason as the rest of them to want the doctor dead."

"It wasn't her," I blurted out.

"How do you know?"

I dropped back down onto my chair. "Because all she wants is to find out where her child is. If she killed Hauptfuhrer, she'd be destroying all chance of finding out."

"Maybe she asked him, but he wouldn't tell her," he suggested, grasping the situation with daunting alacrity. "In that case, she'd have nothing to lose by settling an old score."

"He didn't refuse! Eliza told me he was in his inner office, getting her proof of the child's whereabouts, when the intruder came in and killed him."

He frowned, shaking his head. "She could have been making that up."

"I'm telling you, she had no desire to kill him. She's always held herself responsible for losing the baby. Besides, it all happened twenty years ago. If she'd wanted to kill the doctor, why would she wait until now?" A guilty voice inside me whispered a possible answer, but I shut it out. "There are plenty of other people on that list who might have had a reason to kill him," I insisted. I leaned over and jabbed my finger at the "M. B." near the bottom of the page. "Margaret Backhouse's husband lost his shirt in the copper market. The family is keeping up appearances, but it's rumored they can't pay their bills. I think Mr. Backhouse may have been blackmailing the doctor, threatening to expose his adoption business."

"But if you're right about the list, Backhouse was a client. If he exposed the doctor he'd be exposing himself and his child, too."

"If he was facing financial ruin, the risk of exposure might have seemed the lesser of two evils."

He was looking skeptical.

"Or it could have been one of the adoptive parents," I said, changing tack. "If the doctor was planning to reveal a child's adoptive status, for whatever reason, the family might have felt compelled to kill him to keep their secret safe."

He looked back at the list. "Who's the 'L. F.' next to Mrs. Miner's entry?"

"Lucille Fiske," I said, feeling a bit smug, waiting for his reaction.

His head snapped up. "As in the Fifth Avenue Fiskes?"

I nodded. "It seems that Olivia Fiske is actually Eliza Miner's long-lost daughter."

He let out a low whistle. "Did Mrs. Miner know?"

"No, I told you, she never knew what became of her daughter. That's why she went to see Dr. Hauptfuhrer yesterday. To ask him where she was, nothing more."

He stared down at the papers for another moment or two, before lowering them to his lap.

"All right, I've told you everything," I said. "Now will you help her?"

He slowly shook his head. "I don't see how any of this changes the facts of the case. There might be others who *could* have wanted to kill him, but she's the one who was there. She's the one they found with blood on her hands.

"You can't tell me this list doesn't mean anything," I said angrily, snatching it out of his hand.

"Not by itself, it doesn't. You've got nothing solid to refute Maloney's version of events."

"And he has nothing solid to prove it! No witnesses, no finger impressions; all he can show is that she was nearby when the doctor was killed. I don't know why you're so quick to assume he's right. As far as I can tell, he's a close-minded bully with little or no interest in determining the truth."

"Eddy Maloney may be a stubborn son of a bitch, but he happens to be one of the best detectives on the force."

"I suppose that's why the other policemen can't stand him," I scoffed.

"He isn't popular because he can't be bought. His old man was a cop too, one of a handful who wouldn't take part in the graft. He was murdered one night by a couple of armed thugs who were never apprehended. Eddy's always believed the cops were behind it. So maybe you can understand why he is the way he is. He does things by the book, and he doesn't care what anybody else thinks."

"That's all very well and good," I fumed, refusing to feel sympathy for Eliza's persecutor, "but he's still rushing to unfounded conclusions. There's simply no reason to believe that Eliza would attack the doctor in an unprovoked fit of rage."

His eyebrows rose. "No reason? What about the fact that she's mentally deranged?"

"Oh for heaven's sake, she's not mentally deranged! Maloney made that up."

"There's no use lying about it," he said shortly. "It's right there, in the doctor's file."

"No it isn't; Maloney got the idea from some remarks I made— remarks he didn't understand, and used completely out of context. He was just shooting in the dark, trying to make his case stronger for the magistrate."

He was watching me with an odd expression. "You really don't know, do you?"

"What?"

He sat back. "Elizabeth Miner is in the early stages of dementia."

I shook my head in exasperation, "Maloney will say anything to build his case, don't you understand? He is not however, as far as I know, a physician!"

"Dr. Hauptfuhrer was, though. And he believed she was showing signs of mental degeneration. He said so."

"Hauptfuhrer said that?" I stared at him. "When? To whom?"

He reached into his waistcoat pocket and extracted a sheet of folded paper. "Here. See for yourself."

CHAPTER ELEVEN

Brady brought it back with him," he went on, holding the paper out to me. "They found it in Mrs. Miner's file, in the doctor's office."

I made no move to take it. "It's not possible. I would have known . . ."

He thrust it into my hand. "Go on, read it."

I slowly unfolded the sheet. It was a handwritten letter dated December 18, 1906, addressed to Dr. George Huntington of Hopewell Junction, New York:

Dear Dr. Huntington,

I recently had the pleasure of reading your monograph on chorea in the Medical and Surgical Reporter. I am writing concerning a female patient of mine who appears to exhibit many of the symptoms you describe. I refer in particular to the spasmodic action of the muscles, together with a failure of sustained attention manifesting in lapses of memory, and bouts of melancholia alternating with irritability, which I fear may be the first signs of the mental degeneration you identify as characteristic of this disease.

For reasons I am not free to disclose it is imperative that I confirm the diagnosis as quickly as possible. I am therefore requesting that you do me the great favor of examining the patient upon your earliest convenience, so that we might have the benefit of your expertise. In light of the unfavorable outcome of the affliction I would prefer not to inform the patient of the true purpose of the consultation until the diagnosis is confirmed. Your cooperation in this matter is greatly appreciated.

Yours respectfully,

Herman Hauptfuhrer, M.D.

I lowered the letter, feeling as if a sack of oats had just been dropped on my head, trying to remember what I knew about chorea. Professor Osler had taken an interest in the subject, devoting a section to it in his "Principles and Practice of Medicine," one of our primary texts at Johns Hopkins. That section, however, had dealt mainly with the simple, or "Sydenham's" form of chorea, a short-term illness that was thought to be caused by an infectious agent and affected chiefly children. It was characterized by involuntary muscle contractions, speech problems and minor psychical disturbance—such as a formerly docile child becoming cross and willful, or prone to crying spells.

Huntington's Chorea was, however, an entirely different form. Although it was mentioned only briefly in Osler's book, I remembered that it was distinct from the childhood version on several important counts: it was inherited; it came on relatively late in life; and it could not be cured. It was also, if I recalled correctly, characterized by some degree of dementia.

"Do you know what he's talking about?" Simon asked.

"I've heard of Huntington's Chorea." Mrs. Braun's comment that Eliza "wasn't right in the head" now came hurtling back to me. I'd chosen to believe she was referring to a simple emotional lability in her daughter, caused by unhappy events in her past; but now I had to confront the possibility that she'd meant something much worse. I looked back at the mention of "spasmodic action of the muscles" in the letter, remembering the hand-wringing and lip-twitching I'd observed in Eliza at the start of class. And what about the comments in her clinic report, about her forgetfulness and changes of mood? Could these be indicators of dementia, as well?

"You still think she's innocent?" Simon asked.

I handed him back the letter. Many neuro-degenerative diseases were accompanied by mental enfeeblement; but while this enfeeblement impeded a person's ability to function, by narrowing the scope of his mental faculties, it didn't generally lead to vicious behavior. Besides, if Eliza had Huntington's Chorea, she must still be in the very early stages. I didn't see how her mental faculties could already be so compromised as to affect her moral judgment. "I haven't seen anything to support Hauptfuhrer's suspicions," I told him. "Granted, she's experienced some melancholia over the past few years, but melancholia is hardly exclusive to chorea. Where's Dr. Huntington's response?"

"There isn't one."

I blinked at him. "He didn't reply?"

"There was nothing in the file."

"Why then, it's entirely possible that Hauptfuhrer was wrong!" I said, as the air started moving freely again through my lungs.

"It's entirely possible that he was right, too," he answered with a frown.

"That letter was only written three weeks ago," I pointed out. "If there's nothing else in the file, the most likely explanation is that Huntington never had a chance to examine her, meaning that Hauptfuhrer's suspicions were never confirmed."

"Hauptfuhrer sounded pretty convinced."

"But he was no expert on chorea. He could easily have been misinterpreting what he saw, or even misunderstanding the nature of the disease. As he himself was clearly aware."

"Are you saying his opinion doesn't count?"

"It's certainly not conclusive."

"Fine," he said, returning the letter to his inner pocket. "You're a doctor, what's your opinion?"

I hesitated. I couldn't be absolutely sure, at this point, that Hauptfuhrer's suspicions were unfounded. But as Eliza's only defender, I didn't feel I could afford to convey the slightest doubt. "Eliza has lost two children under difficult circumstances," I said finally. "I should think a little melancholia, or even irritability, would be in order. I personally have seen nothing to indicate dementia."

"Maybe you don't want to see it."

"What's that supposed to mean?"

He shook his head. "There's something cock-eyed about this whole thing. The way you're putting yourself out, breaking the law even, to try and clear her name. Why do you care so much? What's Mrs. Miner to you?"

"Isn't it possible that I just want to see justice done?"

"You don't give a tinker's damn about justice," he said flatly.

I jumped to my feet, glad for the anger his words provoked, grabbing onto it like a life line. "I think I've had just about enough insults for one day, Mr. Shaw. If you don't intend to help Eliza then there's nothing more to talk about. If you'll excuse me . . ."

He was on his own feet before I could finish. "I'm sorry if I've offended," he said, not sounding sorry at all. "But I can only speak from past experience."

I gaped at him, unable to believe my ears. "Past experience? You have the nerve to speak to me about past experience? When you're the one who—" The sound of the front door closing interrupted me. Monsieur Henri, I thought, struggling to collect myself; I'd forgotten all about him.

"I'm the one who what?" Simon growled.

A dozen stinging replies leaped to the tip of my tongue. It would have felt good to let them fly; so good after all these years. But I was better than that. Better than him. "I'm trying very hard to forget our past," I said, biting off the words. "I suggest that you do the same. There are more important things at stake here than our sordid little history."

"Sordid little history?" he repeated. "My God, you do have a way with words! I couldn't have put it better myself!" He suddenly stiffened, staring at something over my shoulder.

I turned to see my father standing in the doorway. "Father!" I cried with barely concealed dismay. "What are you doing home?"

"My meeting broke up early, so I thought I'd come home to have lunch with your mother, and see if the new disk for the lung had arrived." He smiled at Simon. "But I see we have a visitor." He walked toward him, extending his hand. "I'm Genevieve's father, Hugh Summerford."

"We've met," Simon said, without moving.

My father stopped, as the smile died on his lips. "Shaw," he muttered, dropping his hand. "The stable boy."

They glared at each other, tense as two pit dogs straining at the leash.

"Mr. Shaw is in politics now," I said, locking my arm around my father's elbow. "He's a district captain, in fact."

"A Tammany man," Father said, nodding with distaste. "So you finally found a place among your own. I'm glad to hear it."

I could see Simon's hand flexing at his side. "He's here for a wonderful cause," I interjected, racking my brain for something worthy. My eyes fell on a pair of Mother's gloves on the corner table. "It's a . . . a mitten drive! For the children of all those tunnel workers dying of caisson disease." I risked a glance at Simon's face, and saw that he was staring at me as though I'd gone completely mad. "He's asking everyone in the area to pitch in," I blathered on, quickly averting my gaze. "I told him I was sure we had some spares in the mitten basket." The purple vein in Papa's neck, I noticed, had receded slightly. "Why don't we go check the basket right now, Mr. Shaw," I said, gesturing toward the hallway, "and see what we can find?"

"I don't want your mittens," he said in disgust.

"Well of course not," I said with a shrill little laugh; "what could I have been thinking? You can't very well carry them all back with you, now can you? I'll just go through them myself, then, and send them on later with Mary . . ." I petered to a halt. The expression on his face could have made a corpse blush.

"Mittens," repeated my father, apparently recovered from his shock. "So Tammany's handing out something more useful than beer and tobacco these days."

"Father, that's not fair," I chided, gripping his arm. "Tammany Hall helps the poor in all sorts of ways, you know that."

"Your father wouldn't know anything about helping the poor," Simon said.

Father drew himself to his full height, thrusting out his chest. "As a matter of fact, I happen to be on the board of several local charities. I believe I know a thing or two about what the poor of this city need."

"Charities." Simon grimaced. "People don't want to be taken care of like little children. They want to take care of themselves."

"And you help them do that by plying them with beer, and looking the other way when they break the law?" Father asked.

"I don't tell my constituents what they need. They tell me."

"Your 'constituents'?" Father repeated, as the vein popped back out over his collar. "I take it you consider yourself their chosen representative?"

He shrugged. "I'm one of the few people they can turn to, until they get their citizenship, and the right to vote."

"Yes, that's the whole point, isn't it? To buy the immigrant vote with Tammany favors?"

"Father!" I cried.

"I'm sorry, Genevieve, but I don't put much stock in self-serving political machines. I happen to believe in organized charities, accountable to the public and governed by law."

I was never gladder to hear the thud of the knocker on the front door. "That must be Monsieur Henri!" I cried in relief, releasing my father's arm. I heard the door open, and Mary's murmured greeting. A moment later a short, round-faced man in pince-nez strutted into the room.

"Mademoiselle!" he cried, throwing his arms wide to embrace me, "I am late! A thousand apologies—but that is the price of perfection." He kissed me on each cheek before turning to address the two male attendants who were trailing behind him, staggering under their load. "Carefully, carefully!" he barked at the one carrying my dress. "It is not a sack of potatoes!" He turned back. "I am truly sorry, mademoiselle, but I could not leave Madame DeWitt before I had transformed her from a moth—" he squeezed his thumb and fingers together and then flung them apart "—into a butterfly!"

Knowing the dour-faced Mrs. Dewitt in question, I understood why this might take some time. "That's quite all right, Monsieur; as you can see, we've had an unexpected visitor. Will you excuse me while I show him out?" I gazed beseechingly at Simon, lifting my hand toward the doorway.

For a moment I thought he wasn't going to budge. Finally, with a curt nod to Henri, he turned on his heel and strode wordlessly from the room. I hurried after him, leaving Father to entertain Henri. "Simon, wait," I hissed, catching up to him in the entry.

He swung around to face me. "He's still calling the shots, isn't he?" he said, jerking his head toward the drawing room. "You're just as afraid of him as you ever were."

"Afraid of my father?" I said, stepping back. "I certainly am not."

"Have you told him about this patient of yours?" His eyes scoured my face. "I didn't think so. Why not? Why don't you want him to know?"

"I just . . . don't want him to worry."

"Why would he worry? She's the one in jail."

"It's complicated," I said, looking away.

"So instead of telling him the truth, you expect me to lie. To him, of all people."

"I'm sorry," I mumbled, irked that I had put myself in this position. "I just said the first thing that came into my mind."

He nodded. "Right. Just looking out for Number 1, as always." He grabbed his muffler and gloves from the console and pulled open the door.

I had an urge to lift the letter opener from the mail tray and hurl it between his shoulder blades. But even as I imagined the satisfaction this would bring, another image thrust itself into my mind—of Eliza, cowering on a dirty cot, waiting anxiously for the help I had promised to deliver. The help that was about to walk out the door. "Wait."

He turned, one hand still on the knob.

"Forget about me for a minute. This isn't about me. It's Mrs. Miner's life we're talking about. If you don't help her, she could very well go to the electric chair." It was impossible to read his face. "Won't you at least meet with her? To judge her story for yourself?"

He looked out the door, over the street, his back muscles visibly bunched beneath his coat. An endless moment passed. "All right," he said finally. "I'll talk to her."

I stifled a sigh of relief. "When?"

"I'm leaving town tomorrow, but I'll be back Thursday morning. I'll talk to her then."

"Fine. I'll meet you there. What time?"

His face swung back to me. "I'll talk to her alone."

"Oh, I don't know if that would be wise . . . she's been through a terrible ordeal. It would be better if I were there."

"I don't intend to harass her."

"I know, but she's never even met you. She trusts me; if I urge her to speak openly with you, she will."

He frowned. "All right," he said grudgingly. "Be at the Centre Street entrance at 10:00 a.m."

I nodded. "Centre Street."

"And don't be late." He looped his muffler around his neck.

"Just one more thing," I said, hoping I wasn't pushing my luck. "Could you recommend a good lawyer with experience in these sorts of cases? Eliza's going to need one."

He considered a moment. "Abe Hummel would have been her best bet. But unfortunately he's no longer available."

"Hummel? Isn't that the lawyer who was just convicted for paying a witness to lie?"

"You disapprove?"

"I'd prefer to engage someone reputable."

"There are two kinds of lawyers in this town," he said curtly. "Those who know the law, and those who know the judges. From what I've heard so far, your patient's going to need the second kind."

Although I supposed he knew what he was talking about, I didn't like the idea of putting Eliza's fate in the hands of some shifty pettifogger. "But can a person like that be trusted?"

"Trusted to get the job done," he shot back. "Before Hummel was disbarred he and his partner managed to get more accused murderers released from the Tombs than all the other lawyers combined."

"All right, you've convinced me," I said hastily. "But since Attorney Hummel has in fact been disbarred, is there someone else you could suggest?"

"Try Bernie Harlan," he said. "He's more discreet, but just as friendly with the criminal court judges. I know Hoffman and Cardozo have both been eating at his trough. His office is on Broadway, near Leonard. You can tell him I sent you."

"Thank you. I'll contact him immediately."

"Save your thanks. I'm not doing this for you." With a malevolent glance toward the drawing room, he pulled out a calling card from a fine leather case and tossed it on the console tray. "Something for your father to remember me by," he said, and stalked out the door.

"Ow." THOUGH I was already corseted so tightly I could hardly breathe, I tried to suck in my belly another fraction of an inch to avoid the pin Henri's assistant had just lodged in my spangled stomacher.

Henri slapped the back of the man's head, muttering something I'd never heard in French class.

"Genna, do stop fidgeting," said my mother. "You're only making things more difficult."

The fitting had not being going well. My racing thoughts seemed to be connected by invisible strings to my limbs, making it impossible to stand still. I was desperate to have it over with so I could get to the medical library and read up on Huntington's Chorea, and assure myself that Eliza's mind was not impaired by disease. But the more I shifted and slumped, the more repinning and adjusting I had to endure.

Henri pinched in the seams on either side of the diamond-shaped stomacher. "Just a little more here, I think, to show off your natural waist."

A muffled groan escaped me.

"Why don't we break for tea," said Mamma, shooting me a warning glance. "Henri, you must be famished."

Allowing that he was, Henri dabbed his shining forehead with a handkerchief and sank gratefully into the chair beside mother's dressing table. Mamma crossed to the annunciator box to call down to the kitchen, while Henri's assistants lifted my unhemmed skirts so that I could shuffle over to the settee. I perched stiff as a bisque doll on the settee's edge, afraid to lean forward for fear I'd either be stabbed by a pin or black out from lack of oxygen.

I forced myself to relax. Maybe I couldn't make time move any faster, but I could at least try to wring from it some useful information, to narrow the search for Dr. Hauptfuhrer's real killer. Monsieur Henri, dressmaker to society, was after all a mother lode of gossip, and for the moment, he was all mine.

Mary arrived with cookies and tea and Mamma commenced to pour. She was passing a cup to Monsieur Henri when her gaze was arrested by something at the door. "Hugh, dear, will you be joining us for tea?"

"No, thank you," my father said from the doorway. "I was just looking in." He nodded awkwardly to Henri, and disappeared.

"Well Monsieur," Mamma continued smoothly, offering a cookie to our guest, "I imagine you've been very busy this week."

He shrugged. "It is the season, Madame, is it not? And unfortunately, there are only so many hours in the day." He selected a jam-brushed cake, took a bite, and nodded in approval.

"Such is the price of perfection," I reminded him.

"So true," he said, taking a sip of his tea.

"After all, you could hardly expect Olivia Fiske or Tessie Spencer or any one with a speck of pride to commission someone else for such an important event," I added, hoping I wasn't laying it on too thickly.

His eyes narrowed, regarding me with new appreciation. "Exactly as you say, Mademoiselle."

Taking a cup of tea, I continued wistfully, "I still remember that extraordinary gown you made for Emily Backhouse, for the Vanderbilt's costume ball. The Russian peasant dress with the lovely ruby belt. It quite outshone anything from Worth or Pacquin."

"A triumph," he recollected, growing misty-eyed.

"I can hardly wait to see what you've done for her this time," I added, lifting my cup to my lips.

His cheeks drooped. "Unfortunately I was not given the opportunity to repeat that success for Mademoiselle Backhouse."

"No!" I dropped my cup back onto its saucer with a dainty clatter. "I can't believe it; she hasn't abandoned you! But—wherever would she go?" I raised my fingertips to my mouth. "Not to Mrs. Moorehouse! Her dresses are superb, I'll admit—so very up-to-the-minute; I just loved that blue Liberty silk she did for Caroline Pease—but still, one would expect Emily to show more loyalty!"

Poor Henri had turned such an awful purplish color that if I hadn't known better, I'd have thought he was choking on his madeleine. "I can assure you that Mademoiselle Backhouse would never go elsewhere," he said, "given a choice."

"Ah, I see! You meant you were too busy to take her on. Poor thing, she must have been crestfallen. One knows it can happen, but somehow, one is never quite prepared. To be let down by the one person you trust to show you to your best advantage . . ." I shook my head.

"Mademoiselle misconstrues," he interrupted. "I would never turn away a loyal customer. The family of the lady in question is . . . indisposed to purchase a gown at this time."

I leaned forward, ignoring the pressure my bodice's bone stays exerted on my ribs. "It's true, then, about their financial reversals?"

He tipped his head. "So it would seem, Mademoiselle. Something I would not have believed myself—and would never have repeated— were it not for the matter of a rather large, outstanding bill . . ."

So it was as bad as people said, I thought. Thomas Backhouse couldn't even afford to buy his daughter a new dress.

"Of course, as loyal past clients, I would normally be happy to extend them credit; but with Mrs. Backhouse in such ill health, I must presume that as funds become available, they will be diverted to her care."

"Mrs. Backhouse is ill?" I asked in surprise.

"Oh yes, the family is quite distraught. The financial pressures, I fear, have taken their toll."

Well this was something, I thought; if Mrs. Backhouse had needed costly medical treatments that her husband couldn't afford, the likelihood that he might resort to blackmailing Dr. Hauptfuhrer seemed even greater.

"I'm sure they'll be back on their feet in no time," my mother murmured with her characteristic disregard for reality, putting an end to what I'm sure she considered an unseemly topic.

I sat back, effectively cut off at the pass. I decided to try another front. "But you did design Olivia's dress," I comforted Henri. "I can't wait to see what you came up with. Of course I wouldn't dream of asking for details—but could you, perhaps, give us just a hint?"

"You mustn't tease Monsieur," said my mother. "You know he can't tell you."

The dressmaker smiled coyly. "I can say only this: Mademoiselle Fiske will shine as brightly as the North Star among a firmament of heavenly bodies."

"How lovely," I said with a sigh. "And will the Earl fall helplessly in love with her, do you think?"

He glanced at my mother, pursing his lips, and studiously stirred his tea.

"I'm sure he'll be enchanted," my mother answered for him.

Henri sniffed, and continued to stir his tea.

I eyed him uneasily. A rash of the so-called "dollar princesses" had been leaving their storybook marriages in recent years, citing cruel treatment, spendthrift spouses, or just the excruciating boredom of titled life as their reason. Although I knew Olivia's match was a calculated one, I had hoped it would offer something better—a chance, at least, for companionship and affection. "He does care for her, doesn't he?" I persisted.

He shrugged. "I couldn't say, Mademoiselle. I am only a dressmaker."

My foot tapped involuntarily on the floorboards; I didn't have all day. "But Monsieur, that isn't true!" I coaxed. "You know the Fiskes as well as anyone; I would trust your opinion absolutely."

I watched the struggle play over his face. A certain amount of gossip was to be tolerated, even expected, of a society dressmaker. But one had to tread carefully; if one stepped on the hand that fed one, one might find oneself on the next steamer back to France. "No doubt the Earl appreciates the advantages the match will afford," he said at last.

"I understand he's quite reliable," added Mamma. "Not one of those gadabouts you hear of so often. And if any of our girls would make him a capable Countess, it's Olivia. I'm sure he'll come to love her in time."

Henri hesitated, weak in the face of an opportunity to display inside knowledge. "Perhaps," he said, placing his cup and saucer delicately on his knee, "that would be too much to expect."

"Too much to expect?" I repeated, wondering at his choice of words. "You don't mean he's a homosexual?"

"No, no—quite the opposite."

"There isn't another woman?"

His eyebrows rose as he took a sip of his tea.

"The Earl is in love with someone else?"

One shoulder rose in a delicate shrug.

"Then why doesn't he marry her?"

"Apparently," said Henri, putting down his spoon, "the lady in question is already married. But she has been his mistress for years."

"What does he want with Olivia, then?" I protested.

Henri glanced at my mother, who answered, "I expect he wants a child, dear. An heir."

I stared from one to the other in disgust, wondering if Olivia knew she was being delivered to the Earl as a breeder. It was one thing to trade prestige for money; at least such an arrangement did not preclude the possibility of respect and affection. But to enter into a marriage while publicly flaunting a mistress, for the sole purpose of carrying on the family name . . . . "Why couldn't the old goat at least pick a European girl, who'd understand such things?"

"Because he needs American money to rebuild his castle walls," Henri patiently explained.

"And Olivia's parents are content with this arrangement?"

Again he shrugged. "The Earl needs money to maintain his estates, and Madame Fiske needs the Earl to give her daughter a title. Apparently, the arrangement suits."

"Hugh," said my mother, "do either come or go."

Turning toward the door, I saw that my father was hovering again on the threshold.

"I just wanted a word with Genevieve," he said. "When she's done."

"That may be a while," said Mamma. "Would you like to speak with her now?"

"No, no, it can wait. Carry on." He bobbed his head once more to Henri and vanished from sight.

It didn't take an Edison to guess what he wanted to talk about. In the last several hours I had become a fugitive from the law, been told that Eliza might be suffering dementia, and learned that Joy/Olivia was about to marry a man who didn't, and probably never would, love her. I didn't think I was up to hearing my father's thoughts on my renewed relations with Simon Shaw, as well.

As the fitting resumed my mind returned uneasily to the letter Simon had shown me. Dr. Hauptfuhrer's suspicions had to be wrong. If Eliza was in even the earliest stages of dementia, the prosecution was sure to argue that it had caused her to kill the doctor. And they didn't even know what I did: that she'd had a real reason for hating him, a reason that had festered for years and could have provided the spark to ignite an increasingly agitated mind. The thought made my knees sag, prompting a "tut-tut" from Henri, who was laboring over my hem.

I straightened, forcing myself to face the possibility that it was true. But what if it was? What if Eliza's judgment had been weakened by disease, leaving her vulnerable to emotional impulses? What if she had in fact killed the doctor in a moment of unpremeditated violence, triggered by a desperate craving to be united with her daughter? Wasn't there still some argument to be made on her behalf?

I thought of the millionaire Harry Thaw, currently on trial for the murder of his wife's old lover, Stanford White. I'd read that Thaw's lawyers were expecting to win his acquittal by arguing that he'd been in the grip of a "natural" rage when he shot White dead, induced by the violation of his "sacred" spousal relationship. This, even though Thaw had known about the lover for years before he pulled the trigger. Other men had been acquitted on similar grounds. I remembered in particular a U. S. Congressman from New York, who was not only absolved of murdering his wife's lover, but widely praised for ensuring the man couldn't seduce other Washington wives. His spousal relationship was deemed so sacred that its breach justified murder—despite the fact that the Congressman had traveled to England with a prostitute during his wife's pregnancy, and even presented his whore to the Queen.

Wasn't a mother-daughter relationship at least as sacred as the spousal one? Why was killing someone who had taken away your child any different than killing a man who had seduced your wife? Shouldn't Eliza's "natural" feelings and "sacred" maternal bond also be taken into consideration, when determining what punishment to apply?

But of course I didn't expect a jury to be sympathetic to such an argument. And not just because Eliza didn't have the influence and lawyers that Harry Thaw's $40 million dollars could buy; but because she was a woman, accused of murdering a man. An all-male jury was unlikely to sympathize with a mother's pain, especially where it had resulted in the murder of one of their own. It might be different if women were allowed to serve on juries—but of course, wishing couldn't make it so.

Which made it all the more imperative to prove that Eliza was innocent. With a renewed sense of urgency, I tried again to glean some useful tidbit from Henri, but elicited nothing of value. As the last stitches were being basted into my hem, I asked him outright what he'd heard along the Avenue concerning the doctor's murder. His response suggested that the dominant reaction, along with the expected shock and incredulity, was a sort of vague disapproval that the perpetrator had committed the deed so close to the most important ball of the season, followed by relief that she'd been apprehended so quickly and that life could go on as before. "For which I am sure," Henri concluded, "even the poor doctor would be grateful."

As soon as we had finished I retired to my mother's bedroom and changed into my street clothes in record time, anxious to get away before Father returned. Before I could leave for the medical library, however, I needed to contact Attorney Harlan and recruit him on Eliza's behalf. As Mamma was returning my dress to Henri, I snuck out the hallway door and down the stairs to the telephone closet, where I found Harlan & Bidwell in the subscribers' pages and put a call through to their Broadway office. I was disappointed to learn that Attorney Harlan would be in court for the rest of the day, but made an appointment to meet with him the following afternoon. As I stepped out of the phone closet I heard rustling to my right, and turned to see Katie dusting off the candlesticks on the hall console table.

"Everything all right?" she asked.

"Everything's fine," I whispered. "Where's Father, do you know?"

"In his study, I think," she whispered back. "Do you want me to go look?"

"Oh no, you needn't bother. If he asks for me, could you tell him I had to go out, but will be back soon?" The medical library of the College of Physicians and Surgeons, where Professor Bogard had secured research privileges for me, was over forty blocks away; even if I took cabs both ways, I'd be lucky if I was back by dinnertime. Father would be angry—but I could see no way around it.

Katie raised her feather duster in the affirmative, then watched with a worried frown as I donned my hat and coat and slipped quietly out the front door.

CHAPTER TWELVE

The malady known as chorea, I discovered over the next few hours, had a long and bizarre history. The first report of the disease was recorded shortly after the Black Death swept through France, involving a mysterious band of Germans who wandered into the town of Aix-la-Chapelle and broke into a frenzied "dance" on the village square, jerking about like puppets on a string until they collapsed, exhausted, to the ground. This so-called "dancing mania", which the Renaissance physician Paracelsus would later attribute to "ideas of the imagination" as opposed to any physical cause, gradually spread to other locales—most famously to the city of Strasbourg, where priests counseled its victims to pray to the city's patron saint, St. Vitus, for help. The terms "St. Vitus' Dance" and "chorea"—from the Greek word for dance—had both been used ever since to describe a wide range of afflictions involving uncontrollable, writhing movements of the limbs.

Although the hysterical form of the disease eventually burned itself out, other types of chorea were identified over the centuries which seemed more driven, in the words of Paracelsus, by a physical impulse to "allay an internal sense of disquietude". The most common of these was Sydenham's Chorea, the form highlighted in Professor Osler's book. According to Sydenham, a person affected with this disease "can by no means keep in the same posture for one moment. If a cup of drink be put into his hand, he represents a thousand gestures like a juggler before he brings it to his mouth." This type, as I had correctly recalled, was caused by a germ infection, was self-limiting, and did not progress to death. It also almost always struck during childhood, effectively ruling out Eliza as a potential victim.

Huntington's Chorea, however, was an entirely different form. It took me some time, but I finally managed to locate the monograph that Dr. Hauptfuhrer had referred to in his letter. It was in the "Communications" section of the April 13, 1872 issue of the Medical and Surgical Reporter, entitled simply, "On Chorea". It began with a discussion of the common type of chorea, noting that this condition, although distressing to the one who contracted it, was not a dangerous or serious affection, and providing a more detailed description of the dancing motions it entailed:

> The hands are kept rolling—first the palms upward, and then the backs. The shoulders are shrugged, and the feet and legs kept in perpetual motion; the toes are turned in, and then everted; one foot is thrown across the other, and then suddenly withdrawn, and, in short, every conceivable attitude and expression is assumed . . .

I skipped to the discussion of the more troubling type of chorea, which occupied only a single page at the end:

> And now I wish to draw your attention more particularly to a form of the disease I have observed in my practice in Long Island, which is peculiar in itself and seems to obey fixed laws. The hereditary chorea, as I shall call it, is confined to certain families and has been transmitted to them, an heirloom from generations away back in the dim past. It is spoken of by those in whose veins the seeds of the disease are known to exist, with a kind of horror, and not at all alluded to except through dire necessity, when it is mentioned as 'that disorder'. It is attended generally by all the symptoms of common chorea, only in an aggravated degree hardly ever manifesting itself until adult or middle life, and then coming on gradually but surely, increasing by degrees, and often occupying years in its development, until the hapless sufferer is but a quivering wreck of his former self.

It was a chilling description. I dreaded to think Eliza might be so afflicted. But at least there was no mention of an aberrant mental component. If the symptoms of Huntington's Chorea differed from those of common chorea only in degree, as this paragraph suggested, then there was no reason to doubt Eliza's sanity, even if she had the disease. I scanned the rest of the page, hoping I'd seen the worst—and landed on the following paragraph:

> The tendency to insanity, and sometimes that form of insanity which leads to suicide, is marked. I know of several instances of suicide of people suffering from this form of chorea, or who belonged to families in which the disease existed. As the disease progresses the mind becomes more or less impaired, in many amounting to insanity, while in others mind and body both gradually fail until death relieves them of their sufferings. At present I know of two married men, whose wives are living, and who are constantly making advances to some young lady, not seeming to be aware that there is any impropriety in it. They are suffering from chorea to such an extent that they can hardly walk, and would be thought, by a stranger, to be intoxicated...yet they never let an opportunity to flirt with a girl go past unimproved. The effect is ridiculous in the extreme.

I rocked back in my seat. This went much further than mere changes in temperament; Dr. Huntington seemed to be describing a slide into full-scale dementia—a type of insanity which, if the lecherous men in his example were any indication, impaired not only one's intellectual processes but one's moral judgment as well. This must have been what Dr. Hauptfuhrer was referring to in his letter. Apparently, after reading this monograph, he had concluded that Eliza was beginning to show the symptoms it described.

I couldn't dismiss his conclusion out of hand, however much they conflicted with my own impressions. The doctor had attended Eliza for years, and been in a position to detect subtle changes that I could not. The monograph's explicit reference to sexually inappropriate behavior, moreover, was disturbing. I couldn't help wondering if the promiscuity that led to Eliza's illicit pregnancy in her youth might have been an early indicator of the disease.

But there was a hereditary aspect to this illness, I reminded myself. It couldn't be acquired; it had to be present in your genes at birth. I backtracked to the discussion of its hereditary transmission, searching hungrily for some reprieve:

> When either or both of the parents have shown manifestations of the disease, and more especially when these manifestations have been of a serious nature, one or more of the offspring almost invariably suffer from the disease, if they live to adult age. But if by any chance these children go through life without it, the thread is broken and the grandchildren and great-grandchildren of the original shakers may rest assured that they are free from the disease. This you will perceive differs from the general laws of so-called hereditary diseases, as for instance in phthisis, or syphilis, when one generation may enjoy entire immunity from their dread ravages, and yet in another you find them cropping out in all their hideousness. Unstable and whimsical as the disease may be in other respects, in this it is firm, it never skips a generation to again manifest itself in another; once having yielded its claims, it never regains them.

This was the exception I'd been hoping for. I grabbed my pen and ink and started copying the section onto my writing tablet. The only way Eliza could be affected, according to Dr. Huntington, was if one of her parents had the disease, which did not appear to have been the case. Mrs. Braun, although not in the most robust of health, displayed none of the incoordination or writhing movements that Dr. Huntington described. Nor was there any mention of paternal illness in Eliza's clinic file. I finished copying the last sentence, underlining it for emphasis, and then turned to the final paragraph:

> Its third peculiarity is its coming on, at least as a grave disease, only in adult life. I do not know of a single case that has shown any marked signs of chorea before the age of thirty or forty years, while those who pass the fortieth year without symptoms of the disease, are seldom attacked. It begins as an ordinary chorea might begin, by the irregular and spasmodic action of certain muscles, as of the face, arms, etc. These movements gradually increase, when muscles hitherto unaffected take on the spasmodic action, until every muscle in the body becomes affected (excepting the involuntary ones), and the poor patient

presents a spectacle which is anything but pleasing to witness. I have never known a recovery or even amelioration of symptoms in this form of chorea; when once it begins it clings to the bitter end. No treatment seems to be of any avail, and indeed nowadays its end is so well-known to the sufferer and his friends, that medical advice is seldom sought. It seems at least to be one of the incurables.

I frowned down at the monograph as uncertainty returned. The late onset of the disease posed a potential problem. Since Mrs. Braun was well into her fifties, and exhibiting no symptoms, I could be fairly confident that she was not afflicted. But Eliza's father was a different story. Although Eliza's file didn't indicate he'd ever been diagnosed with a disease, it did mention he'd died at a relatively young age. It was therefore possible he'd carried the disease but died too early to manifest it.

Or perhaps he had exhibited choreic movements toward the end of his life, but no one—including Dr. Hauptfuhrer—had recognized them at the time. Years later, after his death, when Hauptfuhrer happened across the monograph introducing the disease, he might have recognized the father's symptoms in retrospect, prompting him to view Eliza's current behavior in a suspicious light.

I squeezed the bridge of my nose. Even if Mr. Braun did have the disease, and passed it to Eliza, that didn't necessarily mean that her mind was already affected. If it had manifested at all, it had to still be in its early stages, since she was exhibiting few or no physical symptoms. I didn't see how her mental and moral faculties could already be so impaired as to drive her to murder. Indeed, nothing in the monograph suggested that the impairment brought on by the disease was of a kind apt to lead to criminal conduct. Inappropriately flirtatious behavior was, after all, a far cry from murder—while suicide, for someone cursed with this disease, might well be viewed as a rational act. I pulled another journal from the stack in front of me, anxious to put the possibility to rest.

The next three reports, by Elliotson, Waters and Lyon, revealed that choreic movements ceased during sleep, and appeared to be more severe when the disease was inherited from the father. It was unclear whether the affliction was caused by lesions in the cerebrospinal system, or a malformation of the motor cortex, or an overgrowth of neuroglia—but everyone agreed that the only cure was death. All described the same relentless progression of symptoms: the initial grimacing and twitches, followed by larger movements of the torso and limbs, with increasing difficulty speaking and swallowing. But there was no suggestion of a propensity toward criminal behavior, the only psychical changes noted being gaps in attention and memory, deepening depression, and what were described simply as "emotional outbursts".

I reached for another handful of journals and told myself to relax. This turned out to be a mistake. The next report, by R. M. Phelps, compiled a long list of mental disorders that had been observed in patients with Huntington's Chorea, including melancholia, delusion, suicide, irritability, loss of emotional control, and an inability to foresee consequences. Even worse, according to Sinkler, as quoted by Mitchell, victims of the disease had been known to exhibit paranoia, irrational jealousy and aggression relatively early in the disease's progression, while they were still active and ambulatory. A report from the 1905 meeting of the American Medico-Psychological Association, which followed several generations of a family with Huntington's Chorea, similarly found that "in every member in whom the disease appeared, the mental breakdown was clearly manifested before the onset of the choreic symptoms." One of these victims terrified his family for years with "outbreaks of cruelty and brutality" before being committed to the Taunton Insane Ayslum, where he died nine years later "much demented."

I scribbled automatically on my tablet, enlisting the familiar routine of research to keep rising panic at bay as I summarized other cases where patients had thrown things during fits of rage, or shouted obscenities, or attacked those who tried to restrain them. Finally, when there was nothing left to read, I put down my pen and sat back.

I'd studied many deadly affections over the years, but never had I seen anything so greedy. If Eliza had this disease, she was surely one of the unluckiest people alive. She was also almost certain to be convicted of Hauptfuhrer's murder. The prosecution would have a field day, claiming that the disease had ravaged her mind and caused her to attack the doctor in a fit of dementia-induced rage.

But I was getting ahead of myself. I wasn't nearly ready to concede that Eliza was so afflicted. Pulling my tablet toward me, I started jotting out a rough strategy. Our first defense must be to argue that neither of her parents had had the disease. I could help Attorney Harlan establish this, by contacting people who'd known Eliza's father before he died. Mrs. Braun was the logical place to begin; but as I wasn't sure she'd be willing to speak with me, given her hostility in the courtroom, I decided to start with Reverend Palmers instead. He had known the family for years, and hopefully seen enough of the father to confirm the absence of symptoms.

Even if it turned out that the father was afflicted, all was not lost. Huntington's monograph specifically stated that "one or more" children in each generation might inherit, meaning it was possible that Eliza had been spared. I could arrange to have her examined by a physician familiar with this type of chorea, preferably Dr. Huntington himself, to try to prove that this was the case.

My stomach growled, reminding me that I'd eaten nothing since breakfast. Indeed, I could hardly remember when the long day had begun. I decided to call it a night. As I was returning my pen and inkwell to my book bag my fingers brushed against something I didn't immediately recognize. Peering into the bag, I saw Professor Bogard's notes sticking out between two journals. Dear God: the research paper. I'd forgotten all about it. And I'd promised to have it done by the end of next week.

It was just too much, I thought, feeling tears spring to my eyes. I couldn't write the paper on top of everything else. The professor would just have to find someone else. Then I remembered he was out of town, giving lectures. If the paper wasn't substantially completed by the time he returned, he would miss his publication date. "Damn," I muttered. "Damn, damn and triple damn." I didn't even realize I'd spoken out loud until I heard the man at the next table clear his throat, and turned to see him frowning at me over his spectacles. Shielding my face with one hand, I pulled out the notes and slapped them on the table. I'd give it one hour. It wasn't nearly enough but it was all I could manage for now.

It was well past the dinner hour by the time my hansom cab rolled to a stop in front of my house. A soft light shone through the window shades, promising a warm plate of leftovers and the sweet oblivion of my bed. But I knew that father would be waiting for me as well, upset over Simon's reappearance and angry that I'd left without speaking to him. The horse shifted restlessly in the harness but I made no move to get out. Poor Father; he'd been trying so hard to treat me like an adult, disregarding his doubts to support me and my class experiment. And look what had happened. It terrified me to think I might have failed to see a mental defect in Eliza where others would have. If it turned out she was guilty, I didn't know how I could ever stand confidently in front of a class again, let alone hope for my father's respect. The specter of such an outcome flushed me with new resolve. Grabbing the speaker tube, I told the cabbie to continue on, to 88th Street.

I ARRIVED AT the Holy Trinity Church rectory to learn that Reverend Palmers had left just moments before, to visit a family in the cigar tenements on 73rd Street. I hurried back to the cab, which I'd left waiting at the curb, and instructed the driver to follow him down. As I was unsure precisely where the cigar tenements were located, I told him to let me out at the corner, intending to ask for directions. The moment my feet hit the ground, however, I was struck by a dank, woodsy odor that made any inquiry unnecessary. I followed the smell toward a row of shabby tenements that squatted along the middle of the block, fronted by the longest line of ash cans I'd ever seen. Continuing apprehensively down the unlit street, I was rewarded by the sight of the Reverend's spry form alighting from his buggy at the curb.

As I was hurrying toward him he looked up and waved to a dark-haired young girl who was leaning out of a tenement window. The girl waved back, then drew inside and pulled the window shut. The Reverend secured the reins and started toward the building's entrance.

"Reverend Palmers!" I called.

He turned. "Dr. Summerford!" His eyes blazed with their usual intensity at my approach, tempered only slightly by surprise. "What brings you this way?"

"Your wife told me you'd be here. Have you heard about Eliza Miner?"

"Why, no," he said with a frown. "Not bad news, I hope?"

Before I could respond the tenement door opened and the girl from the window ran out onto the sidewalk.

"Good evening, Father," she said breathlessly, dropping an awkward curtsy. She was about ten years old, with large dark eyes and wavy brown hair that hung loosely to her shoulders. She had a deep crease between her eyebrows, and stains on her wide collar that matched her sallow complexion.

"Good evening, Fiala," the Reverend replied. To me he explained, "Fiala is a member of the mission's sewing club. Her mother is ill—I suspect with consumption, from the tobacco dust—but refuses to go to the hospital. Fiala has asked me to try to convince her."

"Hello, Fiala," I said. "It's a pleasure to meet you."

"Good evening, Miss," she answered, with another little curtsy.

"This is my friend, Dr. Summerford," the Reverend told her.

The crease softened on her forehead. "You're a doctor?" She turned excitedly toward the Reverend. "You've brought a doctor to see Mamma?"

The Reverend cocked an eyebrow at me. "Would you mind? If Mrs. Petrikova doesn't go to the hospital, you may be the only physician she'll have a chance to see. We could ride back together afterward, and you can tell me about Mrs. Miner. Unless you feel it can't wait . . ."

"No, I'd be glad to take a look," I said, mindful of the little girl's hopeful eyes upon me.

As we walked toward the entrance I peered into one of the ubiquitous ash cans. It was filled with a brown material resembling wet straw—the source, my nose immediately informed me, of the pungent smell that was permeating the street.

"Tobacco stems," the Reverend explained over my shoulder. "That's all that's left when they're done."

We followed Fiala up the narrow, dark stairs to her living quarters, where the odor of fermented tobacco was so intense it took an act of will not to cover my nose. Two people were sitting at a workbench in front of the dark windows: a very young girl, perhaps three years younger than Fiala, and a sickly looking woman of indeterminate age. The woman rose slowly to her feet as we came forward, erupting into a dry, hacking cough. She was frail as a twig, with stooped shoulders and yellowish-gray skin drawn tightly around her protruding eyes.

"This is my mother, Kamila Petrikova," Fiala told us, "and my sister, Milka."

I smiled in greeting as the Reverend bowed and said, "Very pleased to make your acquaintance."

"Neh Anglitsky," wheezed Mrs. Petrikova, waving her hand.

"She doesn't speak English," Fiala translated for us.

"Please tell her that we're sorry to hear she's ill," the Reverend said, "and that we're here to see if we can help."

Mrs. Petrikova received this information without comment, eyeing us warily.

"Tell her that Dr. Summerford here is a highly trained physician, and would like to perform a brief examination to determine the nature of her condition."

Fiala did so, in the tongue-twisting Czech language of her family's homeland.

Mrs. Petrikova shook her head, breaking into an agitated reply that ended with, "Neh nemosnitza! Neh nemosnitza!"

Fiala glared at her, her lips clamped shut.

"Oznamit yeh!" her mother commanded, waving toward us.

The girl turned to us, her lips quivering. "She says she knows you are here to take her to the hospital, but that she won't go," she translated. "She says thank you but no, she is needed here."

For a moment I thought the girl was going to break into tears; but instead she turned back to her mother, stamped her foot, and launched into what even I could tell was a frustrated entreaty—although "doktora" was the only word I recognized.

Mrs. Petrikova's expression gradually softened as she listened to her daughter's plea. As Fiala sputtered to a close, she leaned forward and ruffled her hair, speaking to her in a teasing tone. Gesturing to me to come closer, she stuck out her tongue with an exaggerated "ahhh", making Milka giggle.

I stepped forward and peered into her throat, willing to play along. But Fiala's concerns were clearly well-founded. Continuing with my examination, I found that her pulse was far too fast, and her forehead abnormally warm and moist. The nails on her hands were thick and cupped, as well. When I tapped my chest, pantomiming a palpitating heart, she nodded in response.

Though she didn't have the phlegmy cough of the typical consumptive, her shallow breathing and clubbed nails indicated an advanced stage of lung disease, most likely brought on by exposure to tobacco dust as the Reverend had surmised. Her heart palpitations, sallow skin and sweating suggested she was suffering from chronic nicotine poisoning, as well. "If you won't go to a hospital," I urged her when I was done, "you ought to at least get away from the tobacco."

Fiala anxiously translated.

Mrs. Petrikova's labored breathing stilled for a moment. Her gaze slid to the girls, lingering on their sallow faces; then she turned and looked me straight in the eye. I knew what she was thinking without her uttering a word: she would never get away from the tobacco. She would end her life as she had spent it, here in this reeking, dust-filled room.

Despite the Reverend's protests she insisted on serving us tea, shuffling over to the tiny kitchen area to brew it while Fiala brought out two more stools and set another kerosene lamp on the workbench. I set my stool next to little Milka, who hadn't stopped working since our arrival, watching as she lifted an enormous, fan-shaped leaf from a pile at her feet and cut out the center vein with the thimble blade on her finger. Fiala took a seat beside her and started rolling bunches of smaller leaves into thin cylinders, binding each in one of Milka's large leaves before placing it on a slotted tray.

"You're awfully good at that," Reverend Palmers said, positioning his stool at her side.

Fiala smiled at him. "We used to make 4,000 cigars a week, before Tata died, and I had to go to school." Her face clouded. "But now we can only make 3,000. And next year, Milka must go to school, too . . ."

Under the Reverend's gentle probing we learned that their employer/landlord paid the family $6 for every thousand cigars they rolled, providing just enough money each month to pay his exorbitant rent, plus the grocer and butcher bills. To meet their quota the girls had to work from six o'clock in the morning until nine or ten o'clock each night, with Fiala taking hours off for school.

Mrs. Petrikova returned with a box lid holding five mismatched cups, passing them around before she took her seat again at the workbench. With Fiala interpreting, we commenced a halting conversation, discussing the classes at the mission and the possibility of borrowing a book for Milka from the circulating library. When I asked Fiala what she was going to do when she finished school, she told me she was planning to marry a boy who lived in the tenements as soon as she came of age, an arrangement that had apparently been worked out by the parents. And so the cycle would be repeated, I thought, with Fiala living out her days in another room much like this one.

Mrs. Petrikova was trying hard to be a good hostess, but her tobacco-stained hands were shaking as she wrapped each of Fiala's bound cylinders into yet another, more finely-textured leaf and secured the ends with a dab of clear paste. It was obvious that our visit was tiring her, and as soon as we'd finished our tea we rose to go.

"Please, don't get up," the Reverend insisted, as Mrs. Petrikova started pushing herself to her feet. "We can show ourselves out. Fiala, if you'll stop by the library after sewing class, I'll have some books waiting for your sister."

"You have two wonderful daughters, Mrs. Petrikova," I added after I'd said my goodbyes. "You must be very proud."

Fiala translated for her mother, who glanced at the girls with affection. As her head swung back toward the worktable, I saw her catch sight of her own reflection in the dark window. She stared at her shrunken face for a still moment, her expression unreadable in the glass. Then she picked up the next cylinder, and a large leaf, and started wrapping another cigar.

"WHY DOESN'T SHE join a union?" I asked the Reverend as we were descending the tenement stairs a few moments later, for I'd heard that the unions provided financial support for ill members.

"The unions don't like the tenement factory workers, because they undermine their bargaining leverage. They resent the women, especially, since they're more apt to accept slave wages from the factory employers."

"But—if the unions would accept the women, they wouldn't have to accept slave wages, and that would solve the problem, wouldn't it?"

He sighed. "You're right, of course. And there's nothing in the union charter to exclude them. But the local shops just won't take them in. Which is especially ironic when you consider that in Mrs. Petrikova's home country, only the women are employed in the trade, and are therefore the ones with the greatest skill."

I was familiar with such antipathy, having had to wheedle my way into what was once exclusively male domain. But I had had my father's help. What was someone like Mrs. Petrikova supposed to do, without a man's money or influence to aid her? Her real curse, it struck me, was not that of poverty, but of gender. A woman born poor, stayed poor, but for a man's good graces. For perhaps the first time, I sensed how thin was the line that separated me from women like Mrs. Petrikova—a line drawn by men, that could change any moment at their whim.

"I hope that wasn't too much for you," Reverend Palmers said, as we climbed into the buggy.

"Of course not," I replied. "I'm just sorry I couldn't have been more help." In truth, however, the visit had left me badly shaken. In the past, my small successes had led me to believe that if I just tried hard enough, or thought long enough, I could find a solution to most any problem that came my way. But with every passing hour the world was proving to be a far darker, less responsive place than I'd ever imagined, and my own effectiveness far less certain. I couldn't think now what had possessed me to believe I could help Eliza; clearly, I was no more capable of overcoming the forces against her than I was of healing Mrs. Petrikova's withered body. It terrified me to think that her life was in my hands.

And yet, it was. And so, remembering my original purpose for tracking the Reverend down, I drew a deep breath and focused on eliciting what information I could from him. As he started the buggy down the street with a snap of the reins, I told him about Eliza's arrest and the claims of her mental impairment, keeping back only Eliza's revelations about Joy. He asked a number of questions, mainly concerning her current condition and whereabouts, which I was able to answer, and whether he might be allowed to visit her, which I was not. He was clearly sympathetic to her predicament. And yet, he did seem not as shocked by her arrest as I would have expected.

"Forgive me, Reverend, but you don't seem very surprised," I remarked.

"When you've seen as much as I have, my dear, surprise is a rare commodity."

I couldn't help wondering if it was life in general, or Eliza Miner in particular, that had failed to surprise him in this instance. "You don't mean that you would have expected something like this of her?"

"No, no; not at all. I only meant that I have come to expect the unexpected." Muttering what sounded suspiciously like an oath, he swerved the buggy to the left to avoid a clanging streetcar. "But tell me, Doctor, what can I do to help?"

After explaining that I was trying to bolster her defense in light of what I considered a biased investigation, I asked if he would share with me his impressions of Mrs. Miner and her family.

"Certainly," he replied. "Of course, we haven't had a great deal of contact, but I have known Elizabeth for several years. We first met when she started volunteering at the Sunday school, right after it opened ten years ago. She was a very reliable worker, always willing to fill in when the other teachers were indisposed. She stayed on until she gave birth to her baby boy, about three years ago. Then, as you know, the boy died in his crib, and she took it very hard."

"Did you visit her after his death?"

"Yes, although there was little I could do but pray for her. She didn't speak for several days, just lay in bed sleeping or staring at the wall. It was weeks before she regained any semblance of her former self. As you might expect of a mother who's just lost a child."

"Have you noticed anything odd since then, in either her behavior or her physical movements?"

"I'm afraid our paths haven't crossed as much, these last few years. I do see her in church, of course, but she's never sought me out, and we rarely exchange more than a greeting after the service. That said, I can't recall ever noticing anything wrong with her physically."

"Have you seen anything that might suggest the beginnings of dementia?"

He frowned. "What sorts of things do you mean, exactly?"

"Lashing out in anger, perhaps, or using obscenities, or engaging in wild flights of fancy. Or any kind of unlawful or socially inappropriate behavior, for that matter."

"Good heavens, no. Nothing like that. She's always struck me as a decent, rather ordinary young woman. Not one to complain. Certainly not one to cause trouble. I've never heard of any brushes with the law."

When I asked him about the comments from other parishioners he'd entered in her clinic file, he explained, "Those were made after her son died. The couple who used to own the bakery next to the butcher shop came to speak to me, after church. The wife had been friendly with Mrs. Miner, and was worried that she wasn't recovering from her loss. She had noticed that Mrs. Miner would have several good days, but then become depressed and withdrawn again. One morning, Mrs. Miner was wearing a bandage on her wrist in the shop, and became agitated when her friend asked her about it. The friend was concerned that she might have attempted to take her own life, by cutting her wrist. I called on Mrs. Miner that same afternoon, but it turned out that she had only burned herself on the iron. She was happy enough to remove the bandage, to show me."

"So her friend was mistaken."

"That was my conclusion at the time, yes."

"And yet, the neighbor must have had some reason to be so concerned."

"I had that thought, as well," he said. "And though she did seem to get much better over time, I never entirely stopped worrying about her. Which is why I thought of her, for your class."

I reminded myself that depression caused by grief, even suicidal depression, wasn't necessarily an indication of insanity. "What about her family members?" I asked him. "Did they ever speak to you about any problems she was having?"

"There's only her mother, as far as I know; the father died before I came to the mission."

"You mean you never knew Mr. Braun?"

"Why, no; as I say, he had already passed away when I arrived." He glanced at me. "You're disappointed."

"I was hoping you might be able to give me a picture of her father's health before he died. Apparently, if neither of Eliza's parents had this illness, she can't be affected."

"I don't remember hearing anything about the father being in ill health. All I really know about him is that he died of an accident of some sort, while still in his prime. I did spend some time with Mrs. Braun, though, during my visits after the baby's death. She would sit with me while Mrs. Miner slept, and we chatted to pass the time."

"Did she ever confide any concerns about Eliza to you?"

"Not beyond the effects of the immediate tragedy. Mostly she reminisced about her own life. It seems she has quite a head for numbers. She worked as an accountant before her marriage, in a wallpaper factory I believe, where she rose to a position of some responsibility. Of course once she was in the family way, they had to let her go, and that's when she joined her husband in the butcher shop."

"Did she ever say anything to suggest her husband had been impaired in any way?"

"No, I can't say that she did. But then, I don't remember her mentioning him much at all."

By the time the buggy pulled up in front of my house, the feeling of doom that had followed me out of the cigar tenements was beginning to recede. The Reverend had confirmed my own impressions of Eliza, which did not support Dr. Hauptfuhrer's diagnosis. Nor had he had any damning information to impart about her father.

Of course I would have to dig deeper before I could say with any certainty that the father was disease-free. Which meant that tomorrow, like it or not, I was going to have to try to persuade Mrs. Braun to put aside her resentment and speak with me. I put this unpleasant duty from my mind for now, determined to wrest a few hours of rest and recuperation for myself before the night was over. I'd have to deal with Father before I could finally retire, but I had excuses for my absence ready; and if he proved particularly difficult I was not beyond claiming, truthfully, that I had a headache, and escaping to my room.

CHAPTER THIRTEEN

G iven my life of late, I should have known that the remainder of the evening would not go as I had hoped. The minute I walked through the door Mary pounced on me, taking my coat before I had a chance to do it myself and then hovering behind me with the coat dangling over her arm as I deposited my book bag on the side table. "Did you need something, Mary?" I asked her.

"No, Miss," she said with a start, turning belatedly toward the coat closet.

I was sifting through the mail when from the corner of my eye I noticed Katie standing halfway down the hall, dusting the same candlesticks she'd been dusting earlier that afternoon and casting furtive glances my way.

I looked from her to Mary, who was now lingering in front of the closet door. "What? What is it?"

"Is that her, Mary?" I heard my father call from the drawing room.

"Yes sir," Mary replied, staring at me as if I was Christ on his way to the cross. "It's Miss Genevieve."

"Send her in, please."

Mary grimaced at me, biting her lip.

I put down the mail and crossed the hallway into the drawing room. My father was standing in front of the piano. Seated beside him, still wearing his coat and hat, was Detective Maloney.

I stared at the detective in horror, as he got to his feet.

"That will be all," my father said to Katie and Mary, who had followed me to the door. He waited until their footsteps had faded down the hall, then said, "Genevieve, this is Detective Edward Maloney, of the New York City Police." The vein in his neck was pulsing ominously against his collar. "He's come to talk to you about a case he's working on, which he seems to think you know something about."

I licked my dry lips, wondering how long the detective had been there and how much he had revealed. "Good evening, Detective."

Maloney touched a finger to his hat. "Doctor."

"Apparently the case involves one of your patients, from the church clinic," Father continued. "She's been accused of committing a murder. A *murder*, Genevieve!"

"I see," I said, taking a few more steps into the room. "Well thank you, Father. I'm sorry to have kept you waiting, but I can take it from here."

He flushed. "I'm not going anywhere; not until I hear what this is all about."

"But Father," I said, "if it involves one of my patients, I'll need to speak to the detective alone, to protect her confidence." I gestured toward the hallway. "I'm sure you understand."

He stared at me, his jaws flapping, while I gazed innocently back and hoped that my knees wouldn't buckle beneath me. "Very well," he said at last. "But I want to speak to you the moment you're done." He stalked out of the room.

I closed the pocket doors behind him, listening for a few seconds to be sure he wasn't still on the other side. I wouldn't put it past him to eavesdrop—although I hoped the prospect of being caught by Katie or Mary would deter him. Only after I'd heard his footsteps recede down the hall, did I turn to face the detective.

"Kind of wound up, ain't he," he said.

"Naturally, he's concerned."

"I guess you didn't tell him about your patient being arrested for murder."

"I try not to worry him unnecessarily."

He grimaced. "I can see why." He glanced around the drawing room. "Nice place."

"Thank you." I thought of the last time I'd seen the detective, when I'd been half in shock and ready to believe the worst. He had taken advantage of my distraught state to try to convince me that the case against Eliza was clear-cut, and persuade me to supply evidence against her. I was determined that this time, he wouldn't find me so malleable.

He bent to look at a photograph of Conrad and me on the piano, lifting it by its leather frame. I didn't like him touching it; I didn't like him being here at all, upsetting the household, invading my private life.

"Who's this?" he asked.

I stepped forward and snatched the picture from his hand. "My brother Conrad," I said, replacing it on the piano. "But you're here to discuss Mrs. Miner."

He straightened. "All right," he said with a grimace, "I'll get straight to the point. You had your chance to talk to her. It's time to fill me in."

"Actually, I was hoping you might fill me in on something, Detective. Eliza told you she heard someone struggling with the doctor in his office, while she was waiting in the examining room. For some reason, that wasn't mentioned at her arraignment hearing. I'd like to know why you're ignoring critical evidence."

"Come on, Doc; it's late, and I haven't eaten yet. I'm not in a joking mood."

"Neither am I, Detective, I assure you. Why didn't you tell the judge about the intruder? For that matter, why aren't you and your men out there looking for him right now?"

He shook his head. "It may surprise you to learn that statements made by people trying to avoid conviction are sometimes looked upon with suspicion."

"In other words, all suspects are considered guilty until proven innocent?"

He shrugged. "As far as I'm concerned they are."

"But how can they be proven innocent, if you won't investigate?"

"I don't get paid to go on wild goose chases."

"There's evidence to support her story! The fingerprints on the sword, for instance; those don't belong to Eliza. Although you led me to believe they did."

"Just because her fingerprints aren't on the weapon don't mean she didn't kill him. All it means is that she was smart enough to keep her gloves on when she did it. The doctor probably showed that sword to a lot of people; the fingerprints we found could have been on there for weeks, or months."

"Or they could belong to the real murderer! Can't you at least admit that it's possible?"

"We caught her red-handed, standing over the doctor's body."

For all the man's supposed devotion to detail, he seemed incapable of diverging from his preconceived version of events. Knowing what Simon had told me about his alienation from the rest of the police force, I wondered if this rigidity really reflected an indifference to outside opinion, or was a bullheaded reaction to it. In either case, now that his mind was made up I feared it would be impossible to change. "She entered the room after the murderer left," I said, determined to try nonetheless, "and went over to see if she could help."

"Then why was there blood all over her?"

"The sword cut through the doctor's carotid artery. A severed carotid artery will keep spurting blood—up to a distance of several feet—until the heart ceases to pump, which can take five minutes or more. If Mrs. Miner knelt beside the doctor while he was in his death throes to see if she could help, she most certainly would have been splattered." My face was hot, my words spilling out with increasing urgency. There were valid arguments to be made on Eliza's behalf. If the detective wasn't willing to explore them, we might never know what really happened that morning in the doctor's office. "Besides," I continued, "if she had killed him, why wouldn't she have just run away? The doctor was the only one who'd seen her there that morning. No one would have been the wiser if she'd fled. Instead, she not only stayed by the doctor's side, but actually screamed for help!"

"Well now, Doc, you know the answer to that as well as I do." He tapped the side of his head. "Because there's something off with her up here."

It was like trying to plant a seed in a bed of granite, I thought in dismay. But why, if he was so convinced he already had a case, did he need me to say there was something wrong with Eliza's mind? Perhaps, it suddenly occurred to me, because he'd been unable to get confirmation from Dr. Huntington. Surely after reading Hauptfuhrer's letter, he would have tried to track Dr. Huntington down to confirm the damning diagnosis. The fact that he'd come back to question me suggested he'd been unsuccessful in this attempt.

I decided to put this hypothesis to the test. "You can't prove there's anything wrong with Eliza's mind."

"As a matter of fact, I can. We found a copy of a letter written by Dr. Hauptfuhrer in her medical file. It says straight out that Mrs. Miner has a disease that causes 'mental degeneration'."

"Rubbish," I said. "She has no such thing."

His eyes narrowed. "Those were the victim's own words."

"Do you mean to say that Dr. Hauptfuhrer made a definite diagnosis? Even though he is no expert in such matters himself?" I challenged.

He hesitated, then said, "definite enough."

"Well, I most certainly don't agree."

"Look," he snapped, "you told me yourself you were treating her for mental problems."

"I never suggested she was losing control of her faculties."

"So what exactly were you treating her for?"

I was afraid that if I tried playing the doctor-patient confidentiality card again, I'd only confirm his suspicion that I had something to hide. But I could no more tell this close-minded man about Joy than I could personally strap Eliza into an electric chair and throw the switch. "As I told you before," I said finally, "Mrs. Miner's son died in his crib three years ago, and she blames herself for the death. Her husband left her soon after the child died. She's picked up her life as best she can, but she still experiences periods of melancholia."

"You're right, you already told me that. What else?"

"That's all there is."

He shook his head. "You know, I'm starting to think there's more to your relationship with Elizabeth Miner than meets the eye."

"What do you mean?" I asked quickly.

He shrugged. "You're a nice, decent lady, brought up in a respectable home. Seems to me you oughta be bending over backwards to help bring a criminal to justice. Not withholding evidence from the police."

"I'm not withholding evidence."

"No? Then why did you go back to the crime scene, after you talked to the prisoner?"

I stared at him in mute horror.

"Usually," he went on, "it's either to plant evidence or to hide it. I'm guessing in your case it was to hide it."

"I don't know what you're talking about," I wheezed.

"We got a good description of a woman leaving the doctor's house on the afternoon of the arrest."

"Well it wasn't me! It was probably just the maid."

"Nah, I've seen the maid. It wasn't her. The description matches you exactly."

Drops of perspiration trickled down my ribs as I contemplated being charged with obstruction of justice, or worse. Maybe if I confessed now, and told him what I'd been after, he'd be lenient with me. But if I showed him the list, he was sure to identify Eliza's initials on it, just as Simon had done, and jump to the wrong conclusion.

The detective reached over the piano top and picked up the glass snow globe Father had bought for my mother during their honeymoon in France. "You've got a pretty nice deal here, Doc." He gave the ball a shake, making the artificial snow swirl around the miniature couple and cozy little cottage inside. "It ain't so nice where I could put you, if you don't cooperate."

"Please, be careful with that."

He looked up at me. "All I'm asking for is the truth. So let's try this again: have you seen any indications of 'mental degeneration' in your patient?"

"No, I haven't."

"No 'episodes of forgetfulness or unusual irritability'?" he persisted, echoing the phrases from Hauptfuhrer's letter.

"No."

He bounced the globe lightly in his hand. "Would you swear to that in court?"

"Yes," I answered truthfully, "I would."

He nodded slowly, lips pursed. Suddenly, he launched the glass ball into the air. I gasped as it spun around, catching the light from the chandelier at the top of its arc, making the metallic flakes sparkle; then held my breath as it started its descent, feeling the detective's eyes on me as I waited helplessly for the smash of glass against wood. At the very last second, he reached out and grabbed it from the air.

"OK, Doc, we'll leave it there for now," he said, returning the ball to its stand. "But I'd suggest you give some thought as to who you ought to be protecting. Mrs. Miner is a very dangerous woman. You wouldn't want to be responsible for letting her back out on the street, where she could hurt someone else." He tapped his bony finger against his hat brim. "I'll see myself out."

As soon as he was out the door I collapsed into the fireside chair. My previous experience with lying had not prepared me for the job of protecting Eliza. I doubted I'd persuaded the detective that I hadn't returned to the crime scene; indeed, I was afraid that by denying it, I'd only managed to convince him that everything else I'd said was also a lie, including my belief in Eliza's innocence. I was still pondering the possible ramifications when I heard footsteps coming toward the drawing room. I barely had time to square my shoulders and lift my head before my father strode into the room.

"Well, Genevieve," he said, closing the door behind him, "you have some explaining to do. Your poor mother is in a state!"

I considered getting to my feet, but wasn't sure my wobbly legs were up to it. "There's nothing for her to worry about," I said, as confidently as I could manage.

"Nothing to worry about? When one of your patients is involved in a homicide?"

"She's only been arrested, Father. They haven't proven that she did it yet."

A strangled sound escaped him. "This is why you turned down an opportunity to work at one of this City's finest hospitals? To mingle with lunatics and murderers?"

"Father, please. You're overreacting."

"Overreacting? My daughter's safety is at sake, and I'm overreacting?"

"Whatever this woman has or hasn't done, she's in custody now. She can't do me any harm."

"What about the rest of them? These other women whom you've told me can't function normally in society?"

"I don't suppose the odds of having two murderers in one class are very high, do you?" I said with a smile, hoping to defuse the situation.

This, however, only caused the vein in his neck to pulse more violently. "I don't play the odds, especially when it comes to my daughter!" He straightened, making a visible effort to control himself. "I tried to support you in this venture, Genevieve, although it went against my better judgment, and here's what's come of it. I can't allow it to continue any longer. I want you to terminate this project immediately."

"That's impossible. I can't just—"

"I insist! You may meet with these women one more time, to tell them it's over. In the meantime, I'd suggest you start thinking about what you're going to do to salvage your career."

I thought of the promises I'd made to the women in my class, and how I'd practically begged them for their trust. "I can't just turn my back on them."

He stepped toward me, his eyes ablaze. "As long as you are living under my roof and in my care you will do as I say. And I say that you will stop immediately!"

"But I made a commitment—"

"You made a mistake! I tried to warn you, but as usual you just barged right ahead."

I opened my mouth, but suddenly there seemed no reply I could make.

"Do we understand one another?"

I nodded.

"Good."

I started getting to my feet.

"Just a minute; there's something else we need to discuss."

Dear God, I thought, sinking down again, would this day never end?

"I've made some inquiries about Simon Shaw. I thought you might be interested to hear what he's been up to."

"Why should I be interested in Mr. Shaw's affairs?"

"Your comments this morning led me to think that you believe he's changed—that he is, perhaps, an honorable man."

"I don't have an opinion one way or another," I said wearily. "I just don't think he should be disparaged for becoming a politician. After all, he hasn't had the advantages others have had. He shouldn't be blamed for taking one of the few paths open to him."

"What about prospering from illegal activities? Should he be blamed for that?"

"What do you mean?"

He clasped his hands behind his back. "According to my sources, Shaw is negotiating with the District Attorney to acquire one of Richard Canfield's gambling operations, in Saratoga. The State shut it down last year and confiscated the assets."

I waited, but there was nothing more. "Is that all?" I had of course heard of Richard Canfield, whose gambling house on East 44th Street had been a favorite target of our previous reform mayor, Seth Low. Though Canfield's gambling operations were illegal, they were frequented by some of the most prominent residents of the city. "I thought you were going to tell me he'd been dipping into the public coffers, or worse."

"I fail to see a distinction," he bristled. "Gambling is an addiction. Taking the bread money from an addicted man's pocket is no better than taking it by theft or threat of force."

"Yes, I suppose you're right," I said, having no strength left for debate. "But I don't understand; if the State shut the Saratoga property down, how can the District Attorney allow Simon to take it over?"

"My sources aren't privy to the details, but I expect Shaw intends to operate it under the guise of a social club. He wouldn't be the first."

"I thought the District Attorney was supposed to be a pillar of virtue. Isn't he the one who's always pictured in the papers breaking into policy shops with a hatchet?"

"Jerome's as ambitious as the next man," he replied. "I've heard he's considering running for Senate. It may be that Shaw is holding something over him from his past; or perhaps he's offering a carrot, instead—Tammany support in the election, or some such. The point is, you shouldn't assume that just because Shaw dresses like a gentleman, he is one. A gentleman doesn't profit from the misery of others."

It was disappointing, though hardly shocking, to learn that Simon had taken the low road to prosperity. It did not, however, make me any less inclined to seek his help. At this point, I didn't care if he was in league with the Devil himself, so long as he was willing to help Eliza. "All right, I won't assume he's a gentleman. But perhaps you shouldn't be so quick to assume the worst, either. For all we know, he's planning to turn the place into an orphanage."

"You're joking, of course."

I sighed. "Look, Father, whatever Mr. Shaw is or isn't, it has no bearing on me. There's no need to concern yourself on my behalf."

"How do you know?" he fumed. "Can you see inside his mind? Can you be sure he doesn't have some ulterior motive for showing back up on our doorstep?"

"What do you mean? What motive could he possibly have?"

"I don't know," he said darkly. "I just hope to God we don't find out." The clock on the mantelpiece chimed the hour. "Well that's all I have to say on the matter," Father declared when the last chime had faded. "Will you be joining your mother and me for coffee?"

"I think I'll go straight up to bed, if you don't mind. It's been a long day."

"You do look pale," he said with a frown. "Get some rest, then, and we'll see you in the morning."

I retrieved my bag from the hallway and trudged upstairs to my room, where I fell into the chair by the window feeling sick at heart. My father may have doubted my judgment in the past, but he'd never doubted my honesty. I had never given him reason to. Tonight, however, I had lied to his face. I had no intention of abandoning Eliza or my class. I couldn't, not if I hoped to maintain the smallest shred of self-respect. But I'd been too much of a coward to tell him so.

I'd had to lie to Maloney, to ensure that he didn't misuse what I had learned from Eliza. But where Father was concerned my motivation wasn't nearly as selfless. I was afraid, pure and simple, to tell him how intimately involved I was with Eliza and her decision to confront the doctor. I would have to go on lying, about all of it, or suffer his additional disappointment. How many times could I let him down, before he'd stop caring altogether? I thought of Anna Kruger, living under the eaves of the Holy Trinity mission, cast out by her family because she'd failed to live up to their expectations. And she hadn't been responsible for her own brother's death.

The only way out of this mess was for me to prove Eliza's innocence, and prove it soon, before the web of lies fell apart and I was found out. I feared it wouldn't be enough to establish that she didn't have a degenerative disease; I was going to have to put my finger on the real murderer, or at least come up with a viable suspect. I pulled Dr. Hauptfuhrer's crumpled list from my book bag. The answer lay here in my hands, I felt sure of it. I just hoped to God I could find it in time.

CHAPTER FOURTEEN

I endured a strained breakfast with my parents the next morning, during which no one said a word about either my class or the detective's visit. My father instead delivered a running commentary on the death of the Shah of Persia and the other front page stories in the newspaper, seeming to believe that if he didn't mention the unpleasantness of the evening before, it would simply go away. As usual my mother followed his lead, acting as though nothing had happened to upset our delicate familial harmony, although her eyes flit constantly between my father and me over her teacup.

As soon as I reasonably could I pushed back my chair and announced I was going to the library, to work on my paper for Professor Bogard. This was not a complete lie. Dressing warmly for what promised to be another nose-numbing day, I hoisted my book bag over my shoulder and set out for the library, by way of Mrs. Braun's shop.

I found Number 230 on the south side of 83rd Street, midway between Third and Second Avenues. It took up half the ground floor of a five-story brick tenement, squeezed between a tailor shop on the left, and a bakery in the adjacent building. "Braun's Quality Meats" was painted in gold letters on the window. Except for a box of cured sausages and a placard advertising the weekly specials, the display area was bare. Peering through the glass, I saw that the interior was equally Spartan: a narrow room with plain white walls and a service counter running across the back. Mrs. Braun was standing at the register in a striped apron, making change for a customer. I waited for the customer to leave, and then slipped in the door.

"What are you doing here?" she asked the moment she saw me.

"I need to ask you some questions."

"I have nothing to say to you. I thought I made that clear."

Her eyes were puffy and rimmed with violet, leading me to guess she hadn't slept much since I'd last seen her. "Mrs. Braun, please," I said, stepping up to the counter. "The police found a letter in Dr. Hauptfuhrer's files that could be detrimental to Eliza's case. I need you to help me determine if what it says is true."

"What letter? What are you talking about?"

Before I could reply the door bells jingled and a woman in a maid's cap entered the shop. "I'll wait," I said quickly, stepping out of the customer's way.

Lips pursed in displeasure, Mrs. Braun turned to the customer and took her order. I watched her closely as she selected some chops from the tray beneath the counter and dropped them onto the scale, looking for the choreic-type movements I'd read about. She worked with a slow, deliberate air—rather like an old horse that, knowing there's no escape from the harness, has set its pace for the long haul; but there was nothing jerky or uncoordinated in her movements as she wrapped the meat, marked its weight with a thick red pencil and secured it with loops of twine.

As soon as the customer was out the door she turned to me and asked again, "What letter?"

'Have you ever heard of Huntington's Chorea?"

"No, I haven't," she answered, wiping her hands on her apron.

"Dr. Hauptfuhrer never mentioned it to you?"

"I told you, I've never heard of it."

Since I didn't know how much time I had before she threw me out, I decided I'd have to get straight to the point. "It's a progressive disease that affects both the mind and the body. According to a letter in his files, Dr. Hauptfuhrer believed that Eliza had it."

She stared at me, uncomprehending.

"But it's not at all clear that he was right," I went on. "The disease has to be passed directly from a parent. I can see that you're not affected. If we can establish that your husband was free of it as well, we can prove that Dr. Hauptfuhrer's suspicions were unfounded, and keep the prosecution from using them against Eliza."

The door bell jingled again, and another customer walked in. Once again I stood aside and waited for Mrs. Braun to serve her. This time when she was done she locked the shop door and turned out a sign that said *"BE BACK SOON!"*

"You'd better come with me," she said grudgingly, folding back a hatch in the counter.

I followed her behind the counter and through a narrow door into the back room. A square table covered by a pea-green oilcloth occupied the center of the space, surrounded by four plain chairs. There was a walk-in meat locker on the left, a chopping block on the right, and a double-sink hanging on the far wall beneath the windows. The bare wood floor was scrubbed clean and scattered with fresh sawdust around the chopping block, while the block itself, although pitted, had been scoured down to new wood. Except for an assortment of mops and brooms hanging from pegs near the door, and a shelf holding twine and brown paper above the chopping block, the walls were bare.

Mrs. Braun took off her apron and hung it on the back of the door, replacing it with a moth-eaten sweater. She lowered herself into one of the chairs and gestured for me to take the one across from her. "What is it you want to know?" she asked wearily.

"Why don't we start with your husband's age at the time of his death."

"My husband was forty years old when he died."

"What was the cause of his death?"

"He broke his neck."

"Oh, I'm sorry; I didn't realize . . ."

"His passing was a blessing," she said curtly.

I sat back. "Why is that?"

"He was a drunk. He couldn't stay away from the bottle, no matter how foolish it made him. I tried to make him stop, but he wouldn't listen. It did him in at the end."

"Do you mean he was drunk at the time he died?"

She snorted. "He was drunk nearly all the time, by then. That night was no different."

"Could you tell me how it happened?"

She pulled her sweater more tightly around her. "He'd just come home from the saloon. It was very late, past midnight, but he didn't care; he started bellowing from the bottom of the stairs for his dinner like he always did, making a ruckus for the whole neighborhood to hear." She paused, her eyes clouding with the memory. "I heard him start up the stairs, cursing like a fiend on fire and bumping off the walls. And I—I just couldn't bear it any more. I got up and locked the door, locking him out, praying to God with all my heart to end my misery. And that's when it happened. He lost his balance, and fell back to the bottom. They said he landed on his head."

"Oh my God, how dreadful . . ."

"He brought it on himself, with his infernal drinking."

Remembering Dr. Huntington's reference to the appearance of intoxication in his choreic patients, I felt compelled to ask, "Are you sure that he'd been drinking?"

She laughed bitterly. "As if I wouldn't know! There was hardly a time when he hadn't been. Of course he'd say he'd only had a drink or two, but anyone could see. The man could hardly walk on his own two feet without falling. And the language that came out of him!" She pressed her hand to her chest. "It got so the only time I had any peace was when he was asleep."

Uneven gait, bursts of temper, uninhibited speech: all could be signs of Huntington's Chorea. "Had he always been that way?" I asked uneasily.

"Lord, no, do you think I would have married him if he had? He was a good provider, in the beginning." She gestured around the room. "He built this business from nothing. Bought the building outright after two years, and the one next door just a few years later, and filled them both with good tenants." She frowned. "God gave him a good mind, but he ruined it with the drink."

"When did the trouble start, can you recall?"

She thought a moment. "It was a year or so before Eliza started working in the store. I remember I was worried the customers would notice he was slurring his words, so I put her on the register as soon as she was done with school."

"He was slurring his words?" I repeated, adding this reluctantly to the list of suspect symptoms.

"Oh yes, he'd try to hide it but if he said anything more than hello or goodbye you could tell."

"And how old was he, at that point?"

"I suppose he would have been thirty-three or thirty-four."

According to Dr. Huntington's monograph, symptoms of Huntington's Chorea typically appeared in the third or fourth decade of life and progressed gradually over the next several years. "Mrs. Braun," I said slowly, "in light of what you've just told me, I think we have to at least consider the possibility that your husband did have the disease I was telling you about, and was showing symptoms before his death. What you thought was drunken behavior could have been caused in part by the illness. The staggering walk, for instance—that's a classic symptom."

She crossed her arms over her chest. "I saw the beer go down."

"I'm not saying alcohol wasn't a factor. But the drinking might only have been making his symptoms worse. Did Dr. Hauptfuhrer ever examine him?"

"My husband hated doctors. He used to say, 'God heals and doctors take the fee'. The only time he went to Dr. Hauptfuhrer that I know of was when he broke his arm, and then only because he couldn't cut the meat without a cast. Not that he was much help with the meat, by then."

"When was that, do you remember?"

"Oh, about a year before he died. It was in the spring, just after the new lamb arrived."

By which time his symptoms, if he had the disease, would have been relatively pronounced. But *were* they symptoms of chorea? I sagged back against my seat. I had hoped this interview would put an end to my uncertainties, but instead it had only added new ones. Chorea might have produced Mr. Braun's symptoms. Or he might simply have been an alcoholic, as his wife believed.

It was time to ask the question I'd been dreading. "Mrs. Braun, when we were talking at the magistrate's court, you told me Eliza wasn't 'right in the head.' What exactly did you mean by that?"

Her gaze dropped to the tabletop. "It was nothing," she muttered. "I was upset."

"Please," I urged, "you know I only want to help."

"She's my daughter. My only child. I don't want to say anything against her."

"I would never use anything you told me against Eliza, I swear to you. I'm just trying to make sense of everthing that's happened, for her sake."

She sighed, and raised her eyes to mine. "I thought it must have been because I dropped her, when she was a baby," she said dully. "I suppose I should have known better than to try to carry her; I was so sick after I gave birth I could hardly walk. But she was crying loud enough to bring down the house, and when I took her out of the basket, she just . . . squirmed out of my hands. I always thought that must be why she turned out so strange."

"But—what do you mean by 'strange'? I haven't seen anything unusual."

"Well you're not around her all the time, are you?" she snapped.

I sat back, clasping my hands tightly in my lap. "Please, tell me what you mean."

She shook her head in frustration. "It's just . . . the way she goes from hot to cold, with no reason at all. And says she doesn't remember things. I don't know how many times she's told me straight to my face she didn't say something when I heard it with my own two ears. And all that fidgeting with her hands! I tell her it will make the customers nervous, but she pays no attention."

I had noticed Eliza's hand wringing, of course, but concluded it bore no resemblance to the palms-up, rolling motion described in the literature. As for the not remembering, "forgetfulness" was a fairly common weapon in the childhood arsenal. I imagined that Mrs. Braun, forced to run the store and raise a child largely by herself, had not always been the most patient of mothers. As an only child, Eliza might have needed to resort to subterfuge at times to escape her firm hand—a habit that could easily have persisted into adulthood. The key, of course was in the timing. "When did you start noticing these things?" I asked her. "Has it only been in the last few years?"

"Lord, no. She's been like that ever since she was old enough to have a mind of her own."

I was very glad to hear it. "What about the hand wringing you mentioned; does it remind you of her father? For that matter, do any of her physical movements ever remind you of Mr. Braun?"

"I told you, he was a drunk. Elizabeth may be a trial, but she can't abide even the smell of beer."

"You haven't noticed that she's more prone to stumbling or falling, then, in the last few years?"

"No, I certainly haven't."

"Does she ever have emotional outbursts?"

She frowned. "Now, that's a different story. She can have a temper when things don't go her way."

"Could you give me an example?"

"Just the other day, I told her to clean out the things under her bed so I could store some orange crates the grocer gave me. She nearly snapped my head off, telling me it was her room and I had no right to tell her how to use it."

This didn't strike me as completely unwarranted. "There's usually a reason for her outbursts, then, would you say?"

"Well I suppose so," she sniffed, "but not necessarily a good one."

I sat back, digesting everything she'd told me.

"So what does it mean?" she asked. "Is Elizabeth sick, like the doctor said?"

"I don't know," I admitted. "I still can't be sure. We need to have her examined by an expert."

"But if she is? You said they could use it against her."

Someone was knocking on the door out front. "As I mentioned before, Huntington's Chorea affects the mind as well as the body.

There are reports of it causing people to act impulsively. Even . . . aggressively."

Her eyes widened. "You mean it could have made her do what she did?"

Once again, I was struck by her apparent willingness to accept Eliza's guilt. "Mrs. Braun, do you really believe that Eliza murdered the doctor?"

Her mouth worked silently, as she pulled at the misshapen sweater. I sensed the one thing we hadn't talked about, the most important thing of all, hovering in the air between us. Mrs. Braun may have kept Joy's birth and adoption a secret from others all these years, but I guessed it was affecting her own perceptions of what had transpired in the doctor's office. "Mrs. Braun," I said, "I know about Eliza's baby. The one Dr. Hauptfuhrer took away. Eliza told me."

Fear flared in her eyes. She shrank back in her chair, reminding me of a sow bug scurrying from the light.

"Just because the doctor took her baby against her will twenty years ago, doesn't mean she killed him," I said firmly.

"They found her there, with that sword," she said, her voice shaking, "and the doctor dead at her feet."

"Someone else could have attacked him, while she was waiting."

She shook her head. "I saw how agitated she was that morning; I could feel it in her. And now you say she might have this disease . . ."

"You mustn't give up on her!" I drew a deep breath, trying to calm myself. "We haven't even established for certain that her father was a carrier. I want to contact your husband's family next, to find out if there's any history of the disease among his relatives."

"His family lives in Germany, I don't know where. I've never met them." She started pushing herself up from the table as the knocking at the front door grew louder.

This was undeniably a setback. But I wouldn't let her see my disappointment, determined to try to force her out of her apathy. "We can still have her examined by an authority on the disease," I insisted.

She drew herself erect. "And if he says that she's sick? What will you do then?"

"I don't know," I conceded. "I'll just have to cross that bridge when I come to it."

She frowned down at me. "I know you think you can help, Doctor. But what's done is done. There's nothing anyone can do now." She started for the door.

"We have to try!" I said, following after her. "We can't just sit back and do nothing—"

She abruptly stopped and turned, silencing me with an upraised palm. "There is a time to fight," she said sharply, "and a time to accept. It's in God's hands now. Just—let it be."

I TRUDGED DOWN Second Avenue feeling as though I were towing a sack of bricks behind me. I seemed to be the only one, with the possible exception of Reverend Palmers, who was inclined to believe that Eliza was innocent. Was Mrs. Braun right when she said there was nothing more I could do to help? Was I, as Simon had suggested, allowing my guilt to blind me to the truth?

Unfortunately, obsessing over the question didn't bring me any clarity. Turning my mind to more concrete matters, I turned in at the 77th Street Pharmacy to pick up some medications I'd ordered for Mrs. Petrikova. I'd read about a new consumption treatment showing promise in Berlin, a mixture of eucalyptus, sulphur and charcoal that I was hoping might offer the ailing woman some relief. Arriving at the tenement flat a few minutes later, I showed Mrs. Petrikova how to warm the Sanosin mixture in a dish over a spirit lamp and breathe in the fumes, to ease her pain and coughing. With the assistance of Fiala, who'd stayed home from school to help meet the family's weekly production quota, I also instructed her on the safe use of digitalin for her palpitations, writing down the proper dosage and showing her how to check her pulse to be sure she didn't take too much. When we were done they all saw me to the door, thanking me warmly, Fiala most profusely of all. I promised to return with more supplies in a few weeks; for although I didn't expect to cure Mrs. Petrikova, I did think I might at least stave off the inevitable, and make her a little more comfortable in the interim.

Leaving the building feeling slightly better than when I'd arrived, I continued by streetcar to the medical library. Since there was nothing more I could do for Eliza before her meeting with Simon the following morning, I was planning to use the rest of the day to put a dent in Professor Bogard's paper. I found it difficult to concentrate, but forced myself to stay with it, stopping only for a quick lunch at a nearby tearoom. When the street lights came on outside the library windows, I'd managed to cobble together the professor's outline with sufficient supporting research to call the thing a first draft.

By the time I crawled into bed that evening, I was nearly dead with fatigue. I must have fallen into a very deep sleep, for the next thing I was aware of was a tapping on my bedroom door, and Mary's voice asking if I wanted Katie to save me some breakfast. When I asked her the time, she informed me that it was nearly half-past nine o'clock.

I bolted upright in bed. I was supposed to meet Simon at the Tombs in thirty minutes. The last thing I wanted was to give him a reason to renege on his promise. And so just a few moments later, with my belly empty, my skirt askew and my hair in a lopsided pile under my hat, I found myself rushing headlong back out the door.

CHAPTER FIFTEEN

The stone façade of the New York City Prison loomed up ahead on my right, behind a thick two-story perimeter wall that separated it from the bustling streets of the municipal district. Although still referred to as "The Tombs" because of an earlier incarnation's resemblance to an Egyptian mausoleum, the current prison more closely resembled a medieval French chateau, with curving walls, picturesque cones and spires on the roof, and an aerial bridge that connected it to the Criminal Courts building. I hurried through the massive columns that framed the entrance, praying that Simon would still be there.

To my intense relief I saw him immediately, chatting with a guard at the gate. I paused inside the door to catch my breath, taking the opportunity to observe him unawares. I was struck again at how comfortably he wore his adult body. It didn't surprise me that the Tammany machine had found a place for him. He was the kind of man that people wanted to be around—to give their loyalty to, even— because his self-assurance made them feel safe. But I knew, as others might not, that he would always put his own interests first. I had to keep that knowledge foremost in my mind, as I navigated our uneasy truce on Eliza's behalf.

He looked up, and saw me at the door. "You're late," he said, sauntering over.

"I know. I'm sorry." I held up the abandoned newspaper I'd found on the El as a sop. "Look at this."

He scanned the front page with a frown.

Pointing to one of the headlines, I recited, "Prominent Financier Found Dead in Fifth Avenue Home."

He looked up, his face blank.

"It's Thomas Backhouse!" I said. "Remember? His wife's initials were on Dr. Hauptfuhrer's list. They're saying he killed himself because of financial reversals."

"So?"

"Well, don't you see? Thomas was obviously desperate for money—desperate enough, I should think, to try to blackmail Hauptfuhrer. Perhaps he tried to collect, but Hauptfuhrer wouldn't pay, and he killed him in a fit of rage. Afterwards, he was so distraught that he took his own life."

He shook his head. "That's an awfully big 'perhaps'".

"It's entirely plausible," I insisted.

"Not as plausible as Mrs. Miner killing Hauptfuhrer in a demented rage."

I was stung to hear him say it. I looked down at the newspaper, trying to hide my disappointment. The hope that Simon would help Eliza, I realized now, had been the one thing sustaining me in recent days. "I don't understand," I said, looking back up at him. "I thought you were going to keep an open mind. If you've already decided she's guilty, why are you here?"

"I don't think the woman should be punished for doing something she couldn't control. If she's mentally unhinged, I can try to see that she goes to an asylum, instead of to prison."

"Are you saying that's the best she can hope for? To be locked away in an insane asylum for the rest of her life?"

"I can't change her condition," he said with a shrug.

"Well I've been reading up on her supposed 'condition'," I retorted. "You might be interested to hear what I've learned." Pulling him over to a bench near the wall, I related everything I'd learned about Huntington's Chorea, explaining that it was an inherited disease and exactly what this meant. Briefly I recounted how Gregor Mendel's experiments, conducted forty years earlier but only recently unearthed, had revealed that individual factors could be transmitted from generation to generation through the reproductive process. "Apparently that mechanism is responsible for the transmission of certain diseases," I finished, "including Huntington's Chorea."

"So Mrs. Miner can't have this disease unless she got it from one of her parents. Is that what you're saying?"

"Correct. And although Mrs. Braun is certainly frail, she's not exhibiting any of the symptoms described in the literature."

"What about the father?"

Choosing my words with care, I replied, "He died years ago. In an accident. He was never diagnosed with any disease."

"Is there any reason to think he might have had it?"

I hesitated. So far, I'd only shared my concerns about Mr. Braun with the Reverend and Mrs. Braun. I was sorely tempted to keep those concerns between the three of us. With Simon watching me so closely, however, I found this impossible to do. Reluctantly I related what Mrs. Braun had told me about her husband's "drunken" walk, angry outbursts and increasingly slurred speech. "So it is theoretically possible that he had it," I conceded, "without anybody realizing."

"Poor bugger," he muttered, sounding all too ready to believe the worst.

"But it's also entirely possible that Mrs. Braun was correct, and his problems were brought on solely by the drinking. Or that he did have the disease, but didn't pass it on to Eliza."

He said nothing for a moment, gazing out over the room. "So the thing keeps getting passed from one generation to the next," he mused aloud, "with no possibility of a cure. . ."

I could almost see little wheels turning in his head. "What?" I asked when I could stand it no longer. "What are you thinking?"

"I'm just wondering if you might have put your finger on the real murderer, after all."

"Thomas Backhouse, you mean?" I asked eagerly.

He shook his head, apparently still working something out.

"Who, then?"

He turned to face me squarely. "Let's say, for a minute, that you're the son of a sharecropper," he said, his voice suddenly edgy with excitement. "Imagine you go out in the world, and through luck and cunning and a bit of head-knocking, you manage to build yourself a nice fortune. You find yourself a fancy wife, get yourself a fancy house, buy yourself whatever your heart desires. There's nothing you can't have—except the child your barren wife can't give you."

He paused to be sure I was with him, then continued, "Now let's say that through more luck and your growing connections, you manage to adopt said child—a daughter—in secret. You give her everything money can buy: clothes, tutors, travel abroad; turning her into someone better than yourself, who can take her place at the top of the heap with apologies to no one. And then, when she's finally ready, you play your trump card. You find a titled bachelor willing, for a price, to make her his wife. An earl, no less, to give your darling the crown she deserves and show the world how far you've come.

"And now further suppose," he went on, lowering his voice ominously, "that just weeks before the marriage agreement is signed and sealed, the doctor who procured your child comes to inform you that this flower on which you've lavished so much care, this bearer of your grandest dreams, could have a hideous and incurable disease."

I leaned slowly back against the wall. Of course; if Hauptfuhrer believed that Eliza had inherited the disease, he would have worried that her daughter had inherited it, as well.

"A disease which," Simon continued, "should she have little Earlets, could very well be passed on to them. Suppose this doctor insists he has a duty to tell not only the daughter, but also her prospective bridegroom, of this unspeakable possibility. What do you suppose you would do?"

I stared at him. "Are you accusing Charles Fiske of murder? You might as well accuse . . . the President!"

"You said it yourself—the people on that list are just the kind who'd expect to get away with murder. And Fiske's the most powerful of the lot. I don't see him standing idly by while someone trumpets it about that his daughter is damaged goods."

"You just don't like him, because he's rich," I scoffed.

"I don't like him because he's a heartless bastard who'd as soon run a working man over as drive around him."

"I agree his treatment of the unions has been far too harsh—but you can't assume he's capable of cold-blooded murder just because of that."

"And you can't assume that just because he throws a few of his millions at charities every year, and has drinks with your dear old da at the club, he isn't."

I supposed he was right. I had no reason to assume Fiske was any less capable of murder than the others on the list.

"It would explain why the doctor was so eager to confirm that Mrs. Miner was sick," he insisted. "He'd want to know before there was an official engagement, to give the Earl a chance to bail out without embarrassing himself."

Though I would have preferred to come up with a less prominent and intimidating suspect than Charles Fiske, what Simon said was making sense. And it was a relief to hear him considering someone other than Eliza, for a change.

"There's another thing," he said. "I had a look at Dr. Hauptfuhrer's appointment book. They collected it for evidence."

"How did you—" I stopped, realizing it was pointless to ask. "And you discovered something?"

"The initials 'L.F.' were written in, on the Friday before the murder."

"Lucille Fiske," I breathed, feeling a tingle run down my spine.

"I didn't make much of it before, but if the scenario I described happens to be true, it could be significant."

"You think the doctor met with her to discuss his suspicions?"

"It would fit. Let's say, for argument's sake, that Huntington responded immediately to Hauptfuhrer's letter, and examined Mrs. Miner over the next week or two. Assume he confirmed that she was sick, and told Hauptfuhrer so. Or maybe he didn't examine her, but Hauptfuhrer was so worried about the Earl proposing to Olivia he decided not to wait for confirmation. Either way, Hauptfuhrer might have passed on his suspicions to Lucille Fiske that Friday, insisting that they had an obligation to inform the Earl. She would have told

Charles, who had the weekend to decide what he was going to do about it. On Monday morning, Charles could have gone to the doctor's office and killed him."

"But wouldn't he have tried to talk to Dr. Hauptfuhrer first, and persuade him to change his mind?"

"Maybe he did, but was unsuccessful."

"Or maybe," I said slowly, "Hauptfuhrer contacted him on Sunday with even more bad news."

"What do you mean?"

"Eliza telephoned Dr. Hauptfuhrer on Sunday evening to say she was coming to his office the next day, to ask about her daughter's location. He might have called the Fiskes, to find out how they wanted him to handle it."

"Even better," he said with a nod. "So now the Fiskes not only have to worry about the doctor spoiling their daughter's marriage prospects, they also have to worry about the natural mother showing up on their doorstep, if he tells her where her child is."

We stared at each other, both taken aback, I think, by the way the pieces were fitting together. "How do we determine if there's anything to it?" I asked.

"Well, you could start by finding out where Charles Fiske was supposed to be, on the morning of the murder."

"Me? How on earth am I going to do that?" I asked, aghast at the thought of snooping in Mr. Fiske's private affairs. What if our suspicions were somehow found out, and we were wrong? It made me dizzy just thinking about it.

"I thought you were friendly with the Fiskes."

"I see them on occasion."

"Will you be seeing them anytime soon?"

"Well, I'm going to their ball on Saturday."

He shrugged. "There's your chance."

"For what?"

"To ask around. If I were you, I'd start with the servants. They can be very informative, if you put it to them right."

"Good Lord, I can't possibly go around questioning the servants! What would people think—" I stopped, conscious of his scowl.

"Ask or not, it makes no difference to me," he said shortly. "You're the one who's convinced that Mrs. Miner is innocent."

I thought of Eliza's terrified face in the detention cell, and the promise I had made her that things would be all right. "Supposing I did ask around," I said, "and discovered something suspicious. What would happen then?"

"Well, then I might be able to persuade the D.A. to postpone Mrs. Miner's grand jury hearing, pending further investigation. Jerome's stubborn, but he won't want to waste his time on a worthless indictment. I'd bet he'd be willing to wait a little longer while the boys at the detective bureau took a closer look at Fiske's involvement."

"Maloney won't like it. He's convinced he's already got the killer."

"If Jerome wants him to follow it up, he won't have any choice."

It was an enticing possibility. I supposed no harm would come from asking a few questions at the ball, so long as I was discreet. "All right, I'll do it," I said, getting to my feet. "And now I think it's time you met Eliza."

WE PRESENTED THE passes that Simon had procured for us to the guard at the gate and were waved through into the crowded inspection area. Morning visiting hours were in full swing and the room was crammed with people speaking a babble of languages. Leaving Simon at the end of the men's queue, I joined a long line of women and proceeded slowly toward the females' room. Once inside I was patted down by an assistant matron, told to turn out my pockets, and directed to a table where my bag was thoroughly searched.

Simon was waiting for me when I emerged, accompanied by a club-footed keeper. We followed the keeper out of the main building into a brick courtyard, where a group of male prisoners were playing medicine ball despite a reading of 10 degrees on the giant wall thermometer. To our right, I could see the covered stairway leading to the "Bridge of Sighs" that brought convicted prisoners over from the adjacent courthouse, named in an era when hangings still took place in the prison yard. Shivering in my thick woolen coat, I hurried across the courtyard behind the others, into a low building in the rear that a sign identified as the Female Prison Annex.

A matron in a heavy blue shawl sat at the front desk, registering two new prisoners who were still wearing street clothes. The keeper gestured toward some empty chairs against the wall, told us to wait, and clumped back out into the yard. The blast of cold air that blew past me as the door swung shut behind him did nothing to diminish the institutional odor of coffee, urine and tobacco that permeated the air, making me close my mouth and contract my nostrils in a vain attempt not to breathe it in.

As the new arrivals were led away, Simon crossed to the matron's desk and handed her our passes. "We're here to see Elizabeth Miner."

"Are you family?" she asked.

"In a manner of speaking."

"And what manner is that?" she asked him drily. She had kind eyes, beneath her no-nonsense exterior, and a tone that suggested nothing could surprise her.

"Well now, we're all God's children, aren't we?" he said with a smile, sliding an official-looking piece of paper across her desk.

She glanced down at the paper, and shrugged. "If that's good enough for the warden, it's good enough for me." She pushed the visitor's log toward us. "Sign in here."

An assistant arrived to bring us to Eliza's cell. I trailed a few feet behind her and Simon, looking about me in morbid fascination. The original Tombs had been built on a marshy site inside the old Collect Pond, causing it to eventually sink and crack and allow water into the building. This newer facility, built only five years earlier, seemed destined for the same fate. Already I could see fine cracks along the walls, and damp spots on the floor. It seemed that more thought had been paid to the prison's facade than to its functioning, for the lighting inside the annex was uneven, and the heating system clearly not up to its job. On the garbage trolleys parked against the walls I could see the remains of the morning meal: a pasty blend of potato chunks and shredded meat that was of questionable vintage and, judging by the abundant leftovers, even more questionable taste.

A sense of propriety kept me from staring into the prisoners' cells as we passed, but the little I saw made it clear that these living quarters, though less dilapidated than the cells at the magistrate's court, were just as stark and forbidding. I'd heard stories about the Tomb's more privileged male residents, said to warm their feet on Kidderminster carpets and to sleep under down-stuffed quilts. Just a few weeks before I'd read an article in Munsey's about a wealthy embezzler who left his cell each night to dine with his family at home. More recently, the papers had been flush with descriptions of Harry Thaw's custom mattress and silk pajamas and imported, hemstitched sheets. Indeed, it was said that the only time Thaw's cell door was locked was when he requested it, to preserve his privacy. I saw no evidence of such freedom or luxury here, however, in the dim cubicles of the women's annex.

As we continued toward Eliza's cell I debated how much I should tell her. Although I knew she'd be happy to learn that Joy had been well cared for, I doubted she'd be willing to leave it at that, and this hardly seemed a good time for a mother-daughter reunion. Informing her that she might have Huntington's Chorea, moreover, on top of everything else she was going through, seemed just plain cruel. My decision made, I drew abreast of Simon to advise him, "I don't want to tell her about the disease. Or the Fiskes. Not until we're sure. She has enough to deal with already."

"You're the doctor," he said with a shrug.

A few moments later we pulled up alongside Eliza's cell. She was hunched on the far end of the iron bed, dressed in coarse prison issue. She lifted her head on sight of me but made no move to get up.

The assistant retrieved a small stool from further down the hall and set it in front of the cell door. "There's only the one, so you'll have to take turns."

"Couldn't we go in inside?" I asked. "I'm her doctor. I'd like to examine her while I'm here.

"Sorry, Miss, but thems the rules."

Simon slipped a dollar bill into the young woman's hand. "And the best part of rules is breaking them, don't you think?"

She glanced down the hall, as her hand folded over the bill. "You've got fifteen minutes," she said, inserting her key into the lock. Simon picked up the stool and ushered me into the cell.

I hurried in and knelt before Eliza. She did not look well. Her eyes were glazed and her face dreadfully pale. "Eliza, how are you feeling? You look exhausted."

"I can't sleep," she said, massaging her temple with a trembling hand. "I hear things moving at night. I think it must be rats."

"Try throwing some coffee grounds around your bed," Simon suggested, drawing up beside me. "Mothballs are even better, if you can get them."

She frowned up at him uncertainly.

"This is Mr. Shaw," I said, getting to my feet. "He's the Tammany election captain for your district. He's here to see if he can help."

She sat up a little straighter, smoothing a loose strand of hair behind her ear.

"I had to tell him, Eliza," I told her. "About Joy, and the doctor. He needed to know if he was going to help."

"Don't worry," Simon said, "I'm not going to repeat anything to the police. But I would like to hear your story first hand."

Her large eyes were fixed on his face. Whatever she saw there seemed to reassure her, for she nodded solemnly and said, "All right."

"Good!" I said, relieved that everyone was getting along. "Then let's get started." I positioned the stool in front of her and sat down, so that Simon had to stand behind me. Though I couldn't very well object to his asking questions, I intended to remain firmly in charge. "We don't have much time, Eliza, so why don't you begin by telling Mr. Shaw what you heard while you were waiting for Dr. Hauptfuhrer, in the examining room."

She did as I asked, repeating everything she'd told me in the detaining cell at the magistrate's court. I listened with half an ear to make sure nothing had changed in the retelling, watching at the same time for any signs of chorea I might have missed earlier. This, however, proved to be a frustrating exercise. According to the literature, early symptoms could be as subtle as an exaggerated gesture, or a moment of unexplained clumsiness, or even just excessive restlessness. I didn't know how I was supposed to distinguish the normal from the early-symptomatic with any certainty. That slow rotation of her shoulder, for instance; was that an involuntary muscle contraction, or was she just stretching her neck? And what about the slight tremble in her arm, when she wiped the back of her wrist across her forehead? Did that indicate an early loss of muscular control, or was it merely a product of shock and fatigue? Only in hindsight, it seemed to me, could the existence of disease at this early stage be absolutely confirmed or denied.

There was no question, however, that she wasn't well. She kept rubbing her temples as she labored through her narrative, squinting up over my shoulder at Simon as if through a haze of pain. I could hear the intake of her every breath, and see her teeth clench with the effort of continuing. "Eliza," I finally broke in, as she swayed on the thin cot, "are you all right?"

"I feel a little dizzy."

"Have you had anything to eat?" I asked, beginning with the simplest explanation.

"Some soup, last night."

"What about breakfast?"

"I couldn't."

"You need to eat, to keep up your strength."

"I just couldn't," she repeated, her eyes welling with tears.

Remembering the congealed substance I'd seen on the trays in the hallway, I could understand why she might find the thought of breakfast upsetting; although I guessed her teary response was a product of underlying exhaustion, as well. "I'll talk to the warden before we leave about bringing you some proper food on my next visit." I smiled encouragingly. "And some mothballs."

She nodded, but her expression was so distant I couldn't be sure she was even listening.

Twisting around on the stool, I murmured to Simon, "We've got to do something. She's sick, and this place isn't helping."

"What do you think is wrong with her?"

I shook my head. "I don't know; it could be the grippe, or something she ate. But whatever it is, if we don't do something soon I'm afraid it will only get worse."

"There's an infirmary downstairs. We could ask them to bring her down."

Prison infirmaries weren't known for a high standard of care under the best of circumstances; with the prison currently overcrowded, the likelihood that she would get even cursory attention seemed slim. "I doubt they could do much for her here. Is there any way we could have her moved to a private facility?"

He looked at Eliza for a long moment, his lips pursed, then back at me. "I'd like to ask her a few questions."

I supposed I couldn't very well refuse. "Fine, but try to keep it short," I said, as I reluctantly gave up the stool. "We don't want to overtax her."

"Don't worry. This won't take long." He settled himself onto the stool, propping his elbows on his splayed knees, looking utterly at ease on the awkward little seat as I hovered anxiously behind him. "Mrs. Miner, if you don't mind, I'd like to get straight to the point."

"All right," she said evenly.

"Did you kill Dr. Hauptfuhrer?"

I clucked in dismay, trying to step around him. "What kind of a quest—"

"No," Eliza replied. "I didn't."

"I wouldn't blame you for hating him," he said. "He took your child from you."

"I don't hate him. I never did. I just didn't want him to take her."

He studied her for a long moment, saying nothing, while she steadily returned his gaze. "You told the police you arrived at the doctor's before office hours. Why so early?"

"I'd waited for so long," she said softly. "Once I made up my mind to ask him, I just couldn't bear to wait any longer."

"For your prescription, you mean?" he asked with a frown. "Were you in pain?"

"No, I mean I couldn't wait to ask him where Joy was."

Simon scratched his head. "So . . . you're saying that the reason you went to the doctor's office that morning was actually to ask him about your daughter?"

I shifted uneasily on my feet. I hadn't told Simon that part, fearing he'd distort its importance.

Eliza glanced at me over his shoulder. "Why, yes, didn't Dr. Summerford tell you? She was the one who gave me the idea, after class. She said I had a right to know what happened to my baby. I'd always felt too ashamed to ask, but Dr. Summerford made me see it differently. I don't think I'd ever have found the courage without her."

"Is that right," he said slowly. "And what exactly did Dr. Summerford say, if you recall?"

"Oh, I remember it very clearly," she answered, her face luminous in its pallor. "She said that Dr. Hauptfuhrer should have let me keep her, and that he was the one who'd acted badly, not I."

"Actually," I broke in from behind Simon's shoulder, "I believe what I said was—"

Simon threw a hand up into the air to silence me. "So when you went to see the doctor," he continued, "you were of the mind that what happened was his fault, and that you had a right to know your daughter's whereabouts. Is that about right?"

"Yes, that's right."

"It must have been quite a letdown when he wouldn't tell you."

"Oh, but he was going to."

"Really? You mean he agreed?"

"Well, not at first. But then I told him that if he didn't, I'd let everyone know what he'd done."

"And that did the trick."

"Yes. I suppose he believed I'd do it, although I wasn't really sure at the time."

"So there was no more need to argue."

"That's right."

He leaned back on the stool. "You must have been very convincing."

She hesitated, apparently confused by his tone. "Yes. I suppose."

"And did he tell you where your daughter was?"

"Well no, he went into his office first, to get her records. I'd told him I wanted proof, so that I could be sure he was telling me the truth. And that's—that's when somebody killed him."

"That's when somebody killed him," Simon repeated. "Somebody who'd been waiting inside his office, all along."

She nodded.

He squinted up at the ceiling. "But . . . didn't you say the doctor went into his office earlier to finish up some business, after he let you into the examination room?"

"Yes, that's right."

"And there was no one with him then."

"I don't think so. At least, I didn't see anyone through the connecting door, when he went in."

"We believe the murderer came in later, through the side door," I said. "While the doctor was in the examining room with Eliza."

"I didn't see anything about that in the police report," Simon said.

"That's because Maloney left it out."

"Why would he do that?"

"I don't know," I shot back. "Why don't you ask him?" I saw his shoulder muscles stiffen.

"Mrs. Miner," he continued, "you said you heard a shout. Is there any other evidence you know of—besides the dead body, I mean—that suggests another person was in that room with the doctor?"

"She told you, she heard the door slam," I answered.

His hand shot back up into the air. "Mrs. Miner?"

She looked uncertainly from Simon to me. "I heard the door slam," she repeated faintly.

Simon turned then, and looked at me. I didn't like the expression on his face.

"Time's up," said the matron's assistant, appearing at the door.

"We're not finished," I told her.

Simon stood. "I've heard enough."

"Wait." I dug a dollar out of my purse and pushed it through the bars to the assistant. "Just five more minutes; please."

She pocketed the money with a nod. "Just five, then. I'll wait at the end of the hall."

Dropping back onto the vacated stool, I asked Eliza, "Did you ever feel the slightest desire to harm the doctor, at any time? Tell us the truth."

"No, never."

"Did you take the sword off his desk?"

"No."

"Not even just to threaten him?"

"I never touched it, I swear! I never even knew he had a sword, until I saw it lying there on the floor."

"And you had no other way to find out Joy's whereabouts, isn't that true? If you killed the doctor, you would destroy your only chance of finding her."

She nodded, biting her lip.

I shot a defiant look at Simon over my shoulder.

"Ask her about Dr. Huntington," he said.

I turned slowly back to Eliza. "Did Dr. Hauptfuhrer ever ask you to be examined by another physician?"

"No," she answered with a frown. "Why would he?"

I hesitated, choosing my words with care. "He seemed to think you might have inherited a . . . a certain condition from your father, that might make you more prone to violence. Apparently he'd been planning to have an expert examine you."

"He never said anything about it to me," she muttered, rubbing her stomach with the heel of her hand. She seemed distracted, as though attending to some internal discomfort.

"Eliza," I asked, peering into her face, "are you all right?"

She winced, then bent bent forward with a stifled moan.

"What is it?" I exclaimed, as she started rocking back and forth on the cot.

She groaned again, bending lower over her knees.

"Is it stomach cramps?" I asked, remembering the putrid food on the breakfast trays. "Eliza, please, talk to me."

Suddenly the rocking stopped, and her head rose. Her eyes were wide and staring in her chalk white face.

The matron's assistant had appeared at the door. "What's the matter with her?"

"I don't know." I started rising from the stool as her eyes fluttered shut and her head dropped toward her chest. Before I could reach her, she had keeled to one side and slid off the bed, landing in a heap on the floor.

"Eliza!" I cried, kneeling beside her.

"I'll get Matron," the assistant said, and dashed off down the hall.

I grasped Eliza's wrist, trying to determine whether she had fainted or had had some kind of seizure. There was none of the loss of muscle tone I would have expected with an atonic seizure; nor did she have an elevated pulse. In fact, it seemed abnormally slow. "Eliza," I said, patting her cheek. "Eliza, wake up . . ."

She was still unconscious when the matron arrived a few minutes later, followed by two men with a stretcher. The men picked her up by the armpits and dragged her into the corridor, where they dumped her onto the waiting stretcher.

"I'm coming with her," I said, as they started down the hall.

"Visitors aren't allowed in the infirmary," the Matron said, waving me off.

"But I'm her doctor."

"Dr. Orly will see to her," the Matron said firmly, blocking my path.

I didn't know who Dr. Orly was, but I had no intention of leaving Eliza in his hands. I swiveled around to ask Simon if he could get the warden to assign her to my care—but to my astonishment, the corridor behind me was empty. Simon had disappeared.

CHAPTER SIXTEEN

He wasn't anywhere in the annex. Nor did I see him in the courtyard, or in the main building when I was escorted back inside. As I emerged from the Centre Street entrance I looked up and down the street—and just caught a glimpse of him disappearing around the corner.

I started after him, zig-zagging through the clusters of reporters and lawyers and bondsmen's runners loitering outside the prison wall. He was walking quickly, with his head bent forward and his hands jammed into his pockets. I broke into a run, and caught up to him under the connecting bridge. "Simon, wait!"

He turned. I stopped short at the look of cold fury on his face.

"Why didn't you tell me?" he spat out.

"If you're referring to my conversation with Eliza at the clinic," I said, trying not to cringe, "I didn't believe it was relevant."

He shook his head. "Here I was thinking that you might have changed, that you might actually care what happens to this woman. When all the time, you were just trying to save your own arse."

"That's not true! I do care what happens to Eliza!"

He thrust his face into mine. "All you care about is what people would say if they thought you'd provoked a patient to commit a murder."

"That's absurd."

"Is it? You convinced an unstable woman that her doctor had betrayed her, and the next day that doctor was dead."

"Eliza isn't a murderer."

He straightened. "I suppose you're going to tell me she doesn't have the disease, either."

"That's right, I am."

"People don't drop into a dead faint for no reason."

"They don't do it because they have Huntington's Chorea, either! It's not a symptom of the disease."

"If you're so sure she's innocent, why were you afraid to tell me her real reason for seeing the doctor?"

"I was concerned that you might draw the wrong conclusion, just as you have done."

"Right. So you've never entertained the possibility that she might have actually killed him."

"Of course I have; I've been asking myself whether she could have done it from the moment I found out she was arrested. And I still say, the answer is no."

"What a load of malarkey," he said with disgust. "You can't even be honest with yourself, can you? You're too much of a coward to admit you made a mistake—a mistake that may have cost a man his life. Well I've had enough of you and your lies. Good bye to you, and good riddance." He wheeled around and started across the street.

I watched him go for the space of several pounding heart beats, before ten years of pent-up anger let loose inside of me. I started after him, reaching him just as he was climbing the opposite curb and pulling him around by his coat sleeve. "Who do you think you are to speak to me like that? You, of all people! What right do you have to question my honesty?"

A horn blared behind me. I turned to see an electric motorcar bouncing toward me over the rough pavement, and leaped up on the sidewalk.

"What right?" Simon asked, landing beside me. "Can your memory possibly be that short? I suppose you thought it was very amusing, putting ridiculous ideas in the stable boy's head, bringing his blood to a boil before you tossed him out like so much dirty dishwater to go off on your Grand Tour."

I stared at him in disbelief. "Are you suggesting that I owed you something? What, it wasn't enough that you bragged about me to the other stable hands? Was I supposed to remain at your beck and call? Oh—I know! You encouraged the other boys to have a go at me, is that it? Told them how stupid and gullible I was, how willing to let you touch me?"

"What are you saying," he muttered, his eyes very dark in his suddenly ashen face.

"Ahh . . . so you didn't know I'd found out! That would explain how you'd have the gall to stand there and call me dishonest!"

"I never said a word to anyone about what happened between us."

He looked so sincere that if I hadn't known better, I would have believed him. "You only discredit yourself further by denying it. The kitchen maid overheard you, while she was feeding apples to the horses. She told father all about the boasts you made to the other boys."

"The kitchen maid? You mean cross-eyed little Margaret O'Leary? Why, she had her sights on me from the minute she arrived at the house."

I slapped my palm to my forehead. "Thank you so much for sharing that with me!" I cried, unable to keep the hysteria from my voice. "I'm sure I couldn't have rested easy until my list of your conquests was complete!"

He moved a rigid step closer. "I wouldn't have anything to do with her. She was peeved with me for it, but I paid her no mind."

"I'm not interested in what happened between you and the kitchen maid," I told him between gritted teeth.

"Well maybe you should be, if she's the one who accused me."

I didn't take his point at first; but when it finally hit me, it hit me right between the eyes. Details I'd long forgotten started trickling into my mind: how badly Margaret had wanted to take the apples to the stable herself that night, and how I'd practically had to pry the bucket from her hand. I hadn't wondered about it at the time. Nor had I bothered to hide my own nervous excitement from her.

She was a cunning girl—when she left our employ a year later, she took a silver teapot with her—and must have realized what was happening between Simon and me. Perhaps she had followed me to the stable that night, or perhaps she'd only guessed. Either way, in her jealousy she might very well have made up the story about Simon's boasting, just to spite us both.

"Sweet Mother of Jesus," Simon said, raking his hand through his hair. "So that's why your father threw us out. All because of silly Margaret O'Leary."

"Threw you out?" I gaped at him. "What are you talking about? My father didn't throw you out."

This time his expression was one of such absolute, uncontrived astonishment that I couldn't doubt its veracity. I felt a terrible sinking sensation, as if the solid pavement I'd been standing on had just developed a sizeable crack. "You left," I said, "because your mother found a better position."

He had grown very still. "Is that what he told you?"

I didn't answer, paralyzed by the cold brilliance of his eyes.

"And you believed it."

"My father has never lied to me," I said, pulling my coat more tightly around me.

"He did if he told you it was our idea. He ordered us out the day after you left, without giving any reason. He wouldn't even write my mother a reference. She couldn't find decent work without one. She worked in a factory on Orchard Street until her eyes gave out, and then she scrubbed floors in the public baths until I could make enough to make ends meet."

I hadn't asked, when I returned from Europe, what had happened to the stable boy who'd caused me such disgrace; indeed, I don't believe the question could have been dragged out of me by a team of Percherons. My father had informed me nonetheless, in the clipped tone he used for dealing with necessary unpleasantness, that Simon had gone to Boston with his mother, who'd found a more lucrative position there than the one she held with us.

I believed my father was a fundamentally honest man. But he was also a devoted father, who'd thought his daughter had been sullied by an arrogant stable boy. If he'd been angry enough to send me off to Europe, I realized now, it was possible—even likely—that he'd sent the Shaws packing as well. I didn't know why it hadn't occurred to me before, except that one didn't dismiss a servant lightly, especially a single woman with a half-grown son in tow. Mrs. Shaw had done nothing wrong; I wouldn't have believed my father could treat her so harshly. But the timing, I saw now, was too coincidental. I knew in my heart that what Simon had said must be true. "I didn't know."

He shook his head in disgust. "Maybe you should have asked."

Yes, I thought, I should have. Instead, I'd avoided Simon like one of the debased sex fiends in Professor Fowler's book. Given a choice between acute humiliation and the purposeful obliteration of all tender feeling, I'd chosen the latter. The obliteration must have been incomplete, however; for as I looked now at his agitated face, memories of our night in the stable raced through me like a rogue freight train. With a violent uprising of my senses, I remembered the rivers he'd traced along my back and breasts, and the intoxicating sweetness of his kisses, and the way his heart had pounded when I pushed up his coarse shirt to press my ear against it. I remembered, too, how he'd sounded when he spoke my name. Certain. Determined. As if making a promise no one could ever make him break.

It had all been very novel and exciting for an inexperienced young girl like me—but also, I saw now, rather innocent. Certainly he could have gone much further than he had; could easily have pushed my willing body past whatever puny resistance my mind might have tried to impose. But it was he who had finally buttoned me up and stood me on quivering legs; he who had brushed off the strands of hay and urged me to return to the house before I was missed.

I was swamped by regret. Margaret had lied; Father had lied; but Simon had done nothing wrong. Because of my willingness to believe the worst, something good had been turned into something ugly and hurtful. I wished I could ask for his forgiveness; to explain that my distress at thinking myself deceived by the one person I'd believed cared for me had blinded me to the truth. I wished I could just wave a magic wand that would make the last ten years disappear. But of course, the past could never be undone.

So I asked for the only thing I felt I had a right to. "Will you help Eliza anyway?"

He slowly let out his breath.

"It's not her fault. She shouldn't pay the price for my mistakes."

"You really believe she's innocent?"

"Yes. I do."

"You've known her less than a week. How can you be so sure?"

I considered reiterating the arguments I had made to Detective Maloney, marshaling logic and fact in Eliza's defense. But in the end, it was neither of these that had persuaded me. "I can't give you any absolute proof," I said. "It's just . . . what I feel."

"What you feel," he repeated.

I nodded.

He looked out over the street. Though he had changed over the years, I could still see the boy I had known in his profile—in the strong, flushed cheekbones, and the determined set of his chin. For a moment, the years fell away. I felt a rush of longing, followed by a painful twist in my gut. Simon Shaw: in one fell swoop, found and lost again.

"All right," he said flatly, turning back to me. "I'll get her out."

"You'll what?" I said, thinking I hadn't heard properly.

"I'll get her released into house arrest, on medical grounds. That's what you wanted, isn't it? To get her out of there?"

I stared at him. "Is that possible?"

"Judge Hoffman's son is running for state assembly. He needs Tammany support, and he has to go through me to get it." He consulted his pocket watch. "He'll be in session all day; I'll have to wait for him to break. Is there someone willing to take responsibility for Mrs. Miner after she's released?"

"There's her mother; they live together, over the store."

"Tell her to be at the prison by 3:00. I should have the papers for the warden by then. I'll send a man to transport her."

I nodded in a daze, not quite able to believe what was happening. "Do you really think the judge will agree?"

"He'll agree." He closed his watch. "But he's going to want to keep it as quiet as possible. I'll do what I can on this end to make sure no reporters get wind of it. I'll have to promise to post a man in front of her building, too, to make sure she doesn't try to leave. I assume you're willing to take charge of her medical treatment?"

"Yes, of course."

"You'll want to be there when they release her, to make sure she's in good enough shape to get home."

"I'll be there." I hesitated, searching his closed face, brimming with emotions I didn't know how to express. "Simon, I—"

"I'll go talk to Hoffman's clerk, then," he said, cutting me off, "and find out when the judge will be free." Pulling up the collar of his coat, he turned his back on me and started for the courthouse.

I CONTINUED ON toward Attorney Harlan's office, which was just a few blocks south on Broadway. I was now more determined than ever to engage the lawyer's services, even if I had to sell some of the stock grandfather had left me to pay for them. Imagining Eliza out of jail, and Attorney Harlan working on her defense, I could feel something almost like optimism stir inside me.

When I arrived at Harlan & Bidwell's bustling office, however, I was advised that Attorney Harlan had been detained in court. The receptionist invited me to wait; but as he had no idea what time the attorney would be back, I arranged instead to return at 4:00, after Eliza's release.

On my way to the Italian restaurant the receptionist had suggested for lunch, I stopped at a Western Union office to send a telegraph to Dr. Huntington in Hopewell Junction. In blunt telegraphic phrasing I informed him that Dr. Hauptfuhrer had been murdered; that his former patient Elizabeth Miner had been charged with the crime and was being held under house arrest; and that as Elizabeth's current physician I urgently needed to know if she was suffering from Huntington's Chorea. I provided my home telephone number and address for his reply. My next stop was a corner telephone booth, where I called Mrs. Braun at the shop to tell her that Eliza was going to be temporarily released. She fretted with characteristic gloom that the release would only falsely raise her daughter's hopes, but agreed to close up early so that she could be at the prison by 3:00.

Only when I was seated by the window in the restaurant on Mulberry Street, waiting for my mysterious "stufato del vitello" to arrive, did I allow myself to fully face what Simon had revealed. If what he'd said was true, I had done him a terrible injustice. Instead of trusting him—or at least giving him a chance to defend himself—I'd turned my back on him, leaving him and his mother to suffer the consequences. The thought made me almost physically ill. Why was it that I always managed to hurt the people I cared most about? Conrad, my parents, Simon; they'd all have been better off if I'd never been born.

A funeral procession marched slowly past the restaurant window, led by red-coated trumpeters with icicles hanging from the bells of their instruments. Their sorrowful dirge echoed inside me as I thought of what Simon and his mother had lost because of me. Except for a hefty dose of embarrassment, my trip to the stable had cost me nothing but a trip abroad. But Mrs. Shaw had apparently been sent into a downward spiral of poverty and ill health, while Simon had been forced to grow up before his time, doing whatever low work he could find to support them both. He'd always believed the future was his, if he was only willing to work for it. What might he have achieved if I hadn't come crashing into the stable that night, hell-bent on romance? I had set the trap, albeit unwittingly—and when it snared him, I'd sailed away and left him dangling. It was no use reminding myself that I'd been young and confused at the time, or of the kitchen maid's perfidy. Simon and his mother had been made to pay for something that was entirely my fault, and I hadn't lifted a finger to help them.

I couldn't imagine how much he must hate me. Well, yes I could; he'd made it pretty clear. But was it only his anger speaking, or had he been right when he'd said that I was afraid to face the possibility that my advice had caused Eliza to kill the doctor? Was I only convincing myself that she was innocent, because I wanted her to be?

The waiter lowered a plate in front of me, containing a creamy stew scented with an herb I couldn't identify. "Buon appetito, signorina. I hope you like it."

"I'm sure I will," I automatically replied. But in truth, I wasn't sure of anything anymore.

IT WAS SNOWING when the prison door swung open at 3:27 and the matron stepped out into the twilight, followed by Eliza and Mrs. Braun. So he'd actually done it, I thought in amazement, watching from a newsstand across the street. It was the first time I'd seen Eliza and her mother together and I was struck by their physical resemblance. Indeed, Eliza's ordeal seemed to have partially obscured the difference in their ages, stealing the brightness from her face and the bounce from her walk, so that I hardly recognized her in the gray half-light. I started across the street, glad at least that she was on her feet and walking without assistance.

Mrs. Braun noticed me first. "You needn't have come," she said, as I stepped up onto the curb. "I told you I'd be here."

Eliza bent toward her mother's ear. "Reverend Palmers must have sent her," I heard her say.

"Why, no," I said in surprise, "I haven't spoken to the Reverend; Mr. Shaw told me he was arranging your release. Of course I wanted to be here, to be sure you were strong enough to make it home. How are you feeling?"

"I'm fine," she said tersely, as if she hadn't been lying unconscious just a few hours before.

A closed carriage had rolled up alongside us. "I'm here for the prisoner Elizabeth Miner," the driver called down to the matron in a thick Irish accent.

"That's her," the Matron said, gesturing toward Eliza. "Can I see your papers?

The driver jumped off the box. He was a big, square-shouldered man with big square hands to match, and swollen red knuckles that looked as though they were put to frequent use. He pulled a folded document from his coat pocket and handed it to the Matron.

"I'll come by your flat once you're settled in," I told Eliza as the matron perused it. "I want to give you a thorough examination."

"That won't be necessary," Mrs. Braun said. "I'll see that she gets everything she needs."

"I'm afraid it is necessary," I told her firmly. "I've been asked to tend to her medical care. It's a condition of her release."

"Really, you needn't bother," Eliza said uncomfortably. "I told you, I'm feeling fine."

I was perplexed—and a bit hurt—by her resistance. "Just because you're feeling better doesn't mean you're out of the woods," I told her. "I'll need to keep a close eye on you over the next few days."

The Matron pocketed the paper and nodded to the driver, who pulled open the carriage door. I reached for Eliza's elbow to help her in—but to my distress she recoiled from my hand, climbing into the carriage unaided.

Where, I wondered, was the sweet-eyed young woman who'd so recently clung to me, entrusting me with her future? She was acting as though she couldn't get away from me fast enough. Had her mother soured things? Had she been disparaging me to Eliza, blaming me for what had happened? I could think of no other reason for the painful rebuff. "You should put her straight to bed when you get home," I told Mrs. Braun as she started into the carriage after her, trying not to show my distress. "You can try giving her a little quinine if the stomach pains return. I'll come by right after I've met with her new lawyer."

Mrs. Braun paused with one foot on the footplate. "What new lawyer?"

"Eliza has authorized me to retain Attorney Harlan on her behalf." So put that in your pipe and smoke it, I silently added.

She peered into the carriage. "Elizabeth?"

"I never said any such thing," Eliza replied from the shadows.

"Well of course you did," I said in astonishment, drawing closer to look into the vehicle. "In the cell at the magistrate's court; don't you remember?"

"I'm sorry," she mumbled, "you must be mistaken."

Her face was obscured by the collar of her coat, and I couldn't see her features clearly. Was she afraid to admit it, I wondered? Afraid of going against her mother's wishes?

Mrs. Braun hoisted herself into the carriage and sat down. "I told you before," she said sternly, reaching for the door handle, "we don't have the money for a fancy lawyer. Now move aside, please, and let me take my daughter home."

I remained where I was, willing Eliza to look at me, needing some sign to reassure me. But she continued looking straight ahead, rigid as a post except for her hands, which were twisting and turning in her lap. I jerked back as Mrs. Braun pulled the door shut, nearly closing it on my fingers. The carriage rolled off down the street and the matron went back inside.

I stared after the carriage, remembering what Mrs. Braun had said about Eliza going "hot and cold". Is that what I had just experienced? And if so, what did it mean? Did Eliza's sudden coolness reflect a purposeful change in attitude, or the sort of uncontrollable mood swing that characterized Huntington's Chorea? I thought it felt more like the former, but I couldn't be sure. I decided to chalk it up to exhaustion and her mother's influence for now, until I'd had a chance to talk with her in private.

Checking my watch, I saw that it was now 3:40. I'd have to get moving if I didn't want to miss Attorney Harlan. I walked to the intersection, and was about to cross Center Street, when I glanced to my right and saw Simon coming out of a building on the opposite corner, which the canopy identified as Tom Foley's Saloon. With a warm flush of recognition, I changed course and started toward him across Franklin Street, wanting to thank him for the near-miracle he had achieved. I was nearly at the opposite curb before I realized that another man had followed him out of the saloon. I stopped, recognizing the battered hat and slump-shouldered carriage of Detective Maloney.

The two men spoke for a moment on the sidewalk. I watched their faces, trying to gauge the tenor of their conversation, asking myself why Simon would be having a private meeting with the detective. "Big Tom Foley", as even I knew, was a prominent

Tammany assembly district leader; any saloon of his, especially down here in the government district, would be the sort of place where people went to trade favors and cut deals. Is that what Simon and Maloney had been doing there? Cutting some sort of deal?

I felt a dull pain in my chest, as I belatedly wondered why, after all the harm I'd caused Simon and his mother, he had agreed to help me. Was it possible he had only pretended to be persuaded by my entreaties? That he was actually working for Maloney, hoping to pass on information useful to the prosecution, as a way to exact revenge? But no, that didn't make sense. It was Simon who had suggested Charles Fiske as an alternate suspect. Unless that had only been a ruse, to make me believe he was on our side . . . .

The men parted, Maloney walking east along Franklin Street while Simon continued toward the intersection—and me. My first impulse was to hide. I turned on my heel and started blindly back across the street, and was nearly run over by a truck. I leaped back to the curb as the driver honked, drawing Simon's attention. He spotted me, and paused.

I pulled myself upright. What on earth was I doing? Hadn't I learned anything about jumping to premature conclusions? There was probably a perfectly good explanation for what I'd just seen. All I had to do was ask. Planting a smile on my lips, I straightened my hat and approached him. "Hello again."

He looked over my shoulder, toward the prison. "She should have been out by now," he said with a frown. "I brought the order over an hour ago."

"Oh yes, she's already come and gone. Your man drove off with her a few minutes ago. I just wanted to thank you for getting her out. I still can't believe you managed it."

He shrugged. "It won't do anyone any good if she's too sick to stand trial."

Several seconds ticked by, as I waited for him to volunteer the fact that he'd just been meeting with Detective Maloney. "Was that the detective I saw you with?" I asked finally.

Surprise flickered across his face. "Yeah, that was him."

"What were you talking about?"

He hesitated, perhaps only because he detected an edge in my tone. "Mrs. Miner's release."

"I don't suppose he was very happy about it," I said, although I didn't think the detective had looked particularly upset. I reminded myself that he was not a man given to showing his emotions.

He shrugged. "That's why I wanted to tell him. I knew he wasn't going to like it. I thought he ought to hear it from me."

Well there it was, I thought; a perfectly reasonable explanation.

"I've assigned two of my men to take turns standing guard outside the Brauns' shop," he continued. "I promised Judge Hoffman there would be someone there at all times. Maloney wants a uniformed cop on the premises, too."

"Is that really necessary? I thought we wanted to keep her release as quiet as possible."

"I've arranged to have my man take the post out front, while the uniformed man watches the rear. That's the best I can do. She's still under arrest for murder."

"Yes, of course. I understand." As I could think of nothing else to say, I bid him good day and we went our separate ways.

Yes, it had been a perfectly reasonable explanation, I thought again as I continued to Attorney Harlan's office. And proof that I was letting my overwrought nerves get the best of me. It wouldn't do for me to keep second guessing Simon at every turn. It was time to forget about the past, and my father's dire warnings, and to let myself trust him once again.

CHAPTER SEVENTEEN

I braced myself as the egg cracked over my head, anticipating the plop of yolk on my scalp, then gradually relaxed as Fleurette's strong fingers worked it into my hair. I gave myself over to the rhythmic pressure of her hands, feeling the knots loosen in my neck, drawing a full breath for what seemed the first time in days.

Things had not improved since I saw Eliza off in the carriage on Thursday afternoon. To my great disappointment, Attorney Harlan had told me sympathetically but emphatically that he could not proceed on a case without a defendant's explicit authorization. I had intended to bring the issue up again with Mrs. Braun when I saw her in the shop, but when I arrived she was in a swivet about the men who'd been assigned to keep surveillance over the premises. Knowledge of her daughter's arrest had apparently not yet spread through the local community; for while the shop customers recognized Eliza by sight, few knew her by her married name, and those that did apparently either hadn't seen that name in the newspapers or hadn't matched it to the woman at the register. Mrs. Braun was concerned that the men's presence would arouse her customers' curiosity, and that they would take their business elsewhere if they discovered her daughter was a suspected murderer. She calmed down only slightly when I assured her that the uniformed man would stay out of sight in the rear yard, muttering darkly that if he tried to come through the shop during business hours, she'd chase him out with a pushbroom.

Then, when I went upstairs to examine Eliza, Mrs. Braun had insisted on going with me, standing at the foot of her daughter's bed and pelting me with disapproving glances. It was hardly an atmosphere conducive to confidential exchange with my patient. Eliza, looking drawn and fatigued in an unbecoming gray flannel nightdress, had answered my questions in a clipped monotone, glancing frequently at her mother. Though she consented reluctantly to an examination, she seemed uncomfortable at my touch, and anxious to get the visit over with. On Friday afternoon I returned, determined to speak with her in private—but she was asleep when I arrived. According to her mother she'd gone into her bedroom after lunch, and never reemerged. She looked so dead out when I looked in on her that I decided she must need her rest and let her be, although I knew I wouldn't be able to come again until Sunday, what with all the preparations for the Fiskes' ball. Finally, to top everything off, there'd been a parcel from Professor Bogard waiting for me when I returned home, containing several more journals and instructions to incorporate their findings on time distortion in hysterics into our research paper. I'd spent the entire evening trying to integrate the new material, but my brain had been so preoccupied with Eliza, Simon and the upcoming ball that I barely recalled what I had done.

"So, Mademoiselle, tonight is the big night!" Fleurette said in her heavy French accent, kneading her fingers over the base of my skull. "Miss Fiske will at last announce her engagement to the Earl."

"Not necessarily," I reminded her, wincing as her fingers hit a snag. "It's not officially an engagement ball." Society watchers across the city, including, apparently, our hairdresser Fleurette, had been anxiously awaiting an announcement ever since the Earl began courting Olivia in earnest in December. To be sure, the scale of the ball—which was to include not only the usual dancing and late supper after, but a formal dinner before as well—suggested that the Fiskes' expectations also lay in this direction. According to my father's confreres at the Union Club, Branard's solicitors had in fact arrived from London the previous week to begin negotiating a marriage settlement. It was rumored that in exchange for the title and debt-encumbered estate the Earl would bring to the union, Mr. Fiske had offered one and a half million dollars worth of stock in his street railway companies, with a guaranteed minimum annual yield of 4%; enough, I thought sourly, to keep the Earl's mistress in roses for some time. "She might still hold out for someone better," I said, with more hope than conviction, as Fleurette tilted my head forward over the washbowl.

Her hands paused on my temples. "Better than an Earl?"

"He's nearly twice her age," I muttered into the bowl. "I'd hardly call it a perfect match."

"There's nothing wrong with an older man!" she said, dumping a pitcherful of water over my head. "I think she is the luckiest girl in the world."

I could appreciate why Fleurette, whose hands were raw from scrubbing other people's hair, and to whom the height of leisure was a trip to Coney Island, would consider Olivia's future an enviable one. And perhaps if there had only been the matter of the Earl's mistress, I might have agreed. Not all American heiresses who'd married impoverished aristocrats over the last two decades had ended up as badly as Ella Haggin, whose yachtsman husband was rumored to have marooned her on a cannibal island. Some, even without their husbands' love, had managed to lead satisfying and productive lives.

But what if Hauptfuhrer was right, and Olivia did have Huntington's Chorea? Though I still thought it unlikely, the possibility cast the disadvantages of a loveless marriage into harsh relief. If Olivia became seriously ill, what comfort would a title and a European address afford her? Would people still think she was the luckiest girl in the world if her husband abandoned her to take refuge in the arms of another woman?

Fleurette was rubbing a block of soap against my hair, working it into a toffee-colored lather. "I brought something for you."

I opened one eye, turning my head to squint up at her. "What?"

She wagged her eyebrows. "It's a surprise. I'll show you later, when I am finished with your Mamma."

After she'd rinsed and towel-dried my hair she took her implements up to my mother's room, while I forced myself back to my desk and the professor's paper. Once again, however, my mind refused to cooperate. I was drawing little circles in the paper's margin, wondering how I was going to ferret out Charles Fiske's whereabouts on the morning of the murder, when I heard my father calling down to Katie for his opera pumps.

I put down my pen. Father had stayed late at the office the evening before, and I hadn't had a chance to confront him about what Simon had told me. I got up and went to the door, and saw him standing at the top of the stairs. "Father? Do you have a minute?" I called, then withdrew into my room and took up position before my desk, turning to face him squarely.

"Shouldn't you be getting ready for the ball?" he asked when he appeared in the doorway a moment later, eying my damp hair and ink-stained hands.

"I will soon." I braced myself against the desk. "I need to ask you a question first."

"Ask away," he said.

"It's about Mrs. Shaw."

He stiffened. "What about her?"

"Did she leave your employ voluntarily? Or did you let her go?"

Though his face hadn't changed, I could tell from the sudden stillness of his shoulders that his breathing had come to a halt. "What difference does it make?"

"It's true, then," I said, sinking back against the desk.

"I didn't have any choice, after what happened."

"You told me she left us for a better position."

"I thought it kindest not to tell you."

"You thought it was kind to lie to me?"

He clasped his hands behind his back. "You had formed an attachment to the son. It was best for you to believe that he'd left of his own free will. Which he should have, had he a shred of decency."

"Maybe you thought I'd try to make you reconsider, if I knew the truth."

"Nothing you could have said or done would have changed the outcome. Of that you may be certain."

"Why is that?" I asked him. "Why were you so intent on getting rid of Simon? Was it really because you thought he'd acted improperly with me—or was it simply because he was a servant, and dared to have feelings for me at all?"

"Are you suggesting it should make a difference?"

"Mrs. Shaw was a loyal employee! I don't see how you could just turn her out onto the street."

"I imagine there are many things you can't understand, having never been a parent yourself."

"I think I can recognize the difference between right and wrong."

He shook his head. "You're a very clever girl, Genevieve. But you're also extremely naïve, as you continue to demonstrate with comments like that. What I did, I did in your best interest, taking all the circumstances into account. That's all you need to understand."

"What if the circumstances weren't as they appeared?"

"I must say, I find your renewed interest in this subject alarming. From the tenor of your questioning I can see that my concerns about Mr. Shaw's reappearance here are well founded. It's obvious that he's trying to reinsinuate himself into your affections."

"He's doing no such thing! I found out what you'd done by accident. I also discovered that the 'circumstances,' as you call them, were not at all what they appeared. The kitchen maid lied about Simon boasting, because she had a grievance against him. He never said a word to anyone about our . . . relationship."

"I don't care what he said," he snapped. "No daughter of mine is going to be mauled by a common stable boy!"

I flushed with anger and embarrassment. "I was the one who went down to the stable that night," I reminded him, determined to put the blame where it was due.

"That's something that has always troubled me. But you're older now, and hopefully wiser. I can only trust that you'll have the good sense not to disgrace yourself a second time."

Mary knocked softly on the door and pushed it open. "Excuse me, sir; Maurice is calling from the carriage house, to ask if you'd like him to put the new headlamps on the motorcar."

"All right, Mary, I'll be right down." Shooting me a look that brooked no argument, he added, "I believe we're finished here." He started to leave, then stopped. "I almost forgot—a telegram came for you." He pulled it from his pocket and handed it to me.

I stared down at the Western Union envelope. "It's probably just more instructions, from the professor," I said, lowering it to my side.

Katie now appeared at the door, carrying Father's polished black pumps. "Here they are, Sir," she panted, holding them out to him. "I put a touch of tallow around the soles, too, to keep out the damp."

As he was taking them from her I slowly swung shut the door, effectively sweeping them both out; then I raced back to the desk and slit the telegram open. As I'd suspected, it was from Dr. Huntington, informing me that he was arriving in town on Wednesday for a four-day visit, and would be happy to examine Eliza during his stay. He asked me to leave a message for him at the Fifth Avenue Hotel, suggesting a time and place for us to meet.

The telegram set my stomach to fluttering. Dr. Huntington's verdict would be final. Although I expected him to give Eliza a clean bill of health, I couldn't be sure of it. If he declared that Eliza had the disease, my chances of persuading the authorities to consider any other suspect would be next to nil, short of producing a signed confession.

I was sitting at my desk, still pondering the telegram, when Fleurette returned to finish my hair. She put down her basket, lit the kerosene lamp on the vanity and laid the curling tongs inside it to heat. "Are you ready for your surprise?"

I slipped the telegram under the desk blotter. "Ready," I said, joining her at the vanity.

She rummaged in her basket and pulled out a jar with a flourish.

"What is it?" I asked, squinting at the contents, which looked suspiciously like marmalade.

"A very special pomade, from the best salon in Paris." She unscrewed the lid and held the jar under my nose.

I sniffed. "It smells like heliotrope."

"You have an excellent nose, Mademoiselle!"

"You're going to put that into my hair?"

"Just watch." She scooped some out with her finger and dabbed it onto my bangs. Handing me the jar, she reached into the basket again and extracted a rat made of fine wire netting. She laid the rat on top of my head, curved my jellied bangs over it, and secured the ends with a clip. Dividing the rest of my hair into sections, she crisscrossed them over and behind the rat. "And there you are!"

I stared at my reflection in the mirror. "I can't wear a pompadour."

"Yes, you can! You see? This way the short hair in front blends right in!"

I frowned at her. "But you can see the scar."

"What scar?"

She knew perfectly well what scar, I thought, pointing over my right eye.

She bent closer. "You mean that tiny white line?"

I pulled out the rat and flattened my bangs against my forehead.

"But Mademoiselle," she wailed, "you can hardly see it!"

I handed her the jar without a word.

After my brother's accident it was some time before anyone noticed the gash in my head, from the nail in the workmen's ladder. My parents had retreated to Mamma's bedroom, and the servants were busy arranging the funeral, leaving me largely to my own devices. It was two days before I found the nerve to tip-toe in behind the maid when she brought my parents their lunch tray. Nothing in the bedroom was as it should have been. The shades were still drawn, casting the normally cheerful gold and white room into perpetual gloom. My mother lay motionless under the bed canopy, her hair matted on the pillow and her eyes puffed shut; while father sat in a chair beside her with an unopened book on his lap, holding her limp hand. Father didn't look up when the maid removed the untouched tray from breakfast and replaced it with the fresh one. He didn't look up when I climbed quietly into Mamma's reading chair, or when I scuffed my feet against the fabric, or even when I coughed—softly at first, and then more loudly. I watched him for what seemed hours, waiting for him to change back into someone I recognized. When the book slipped off his lap and landed with a thud on the rug I rushed over to retrieve it; but although he allowed me to slide it back under his hand, he didn't look at me, even then.

It was Katie who finally noticed my wound. She clucked over it and cleaned it and sprinkled it with sugar, but by then it had already turned an angry red. I'd spent the morning of the funeral in front of the mirror, combing and re-combing my bangs over my forehead with a mixture of water and salt to make sure they would stay in place. Though the length and style of the rest of my hair had changed over the years, I'd been wearing bangs ever since.

"Are you sure?" Fleurette coaxed, lifting my hair back up again and shaping it with her hands. "It would bring out your beautiful cheekbones."

"I'm sure."

She released my hair with a sigh. "Very well," she said, reaching for the curling iron. "We'll do Marcel waves again, like last time."

AT PRECISELY HALF past six, after being coiffed, manicured, perfumed and levered into my blue-sequined dress, I descended to the sitting room. I stopped on the threshold to stare at my mother, who was sipping a glass of sherry in front of the fireplace. She was dressed in a new gown of dark green Liberty satin, wearing a sparkling emerald necklace and tiara that hadn't been out of the safe in years. Her hair was arranged in an elegant French twist, and her cheeks, if I was not mistaken, had been brightened with a touch of rouge.

"Mamma! You look beautiful!" I said, crossing to kiss her cheek.

"I thought it was time for something new," she replied with a self-conscious smile. "I didn't want to put you two to shame."

My father was standing beside her, crisp and handsome in his white tie and black tailcoat. "You're looking lovely yourself, Genevieve," he said. "I must say that tonight, Monsieur Henri has earned his fee."

Katie brought our coats and slipper bags and we walked out to the curb, where Maurice was waiting with the motorcar. He helped me and Mamma into the back and arranged our lap rugs, while Father took his usual seat in the front, from which he could comment on Maurice's fledgling driving skills at will. Fortunately the engine had been left running and we were able to depart immediately, without the usual fussing over the hand crank. This was of course important, as Lucille Fiske was famous for turning away any guest who arrived more than fifteen minutes late.

Maurice drove around the block on the one-way streets and turned left down Fifth Avenue, grinding the gears as he accelerated cautiously from a snail's pace to a turtle's crawl, drawing catcalls from passing vehicles as he continued in fits and starts down the roadway. Pulling the lap rug up to my neck, I squirreled lower in my seat and watched ornate rooftops alternate with empty sky along the relatively undeveloped northern stretch of the Avenue, while I tried to come up with a strategy for the evening. As my education had failed to include training in espionage, however, I was unable to come up with any brilliant ideas; and by the time the rooftops had merged into an unbroken line, I'd decided to just keep my eyes and ears open.

I sat up as the motorcar ground to a stop. The Fiske mansion rose up ahead on our left, a massive French Renaissance re-creation that took up half the block. A long line of carriages was waiting to unload in front of it, backing up traffic in both directions. The jam was made worse by cordons of mounted police stretching along both sides of the Avenue, there to hold back the crowds who'd come to watch the cream of society alight.

As we drew closer I could see footmen in brilliant scarlet livery standing at both ends of a red carpet on the sidewalk, holding flaming torches aloft. Guests in lush furs and gleaming top hats streamed two-by-two across the carpet toward the open double doors, their jewels and gold-tipped walking sticks flashing in the flickering torchlight. As we waited our turn I glanced toward the police line, and glimpsed three young boys standing just beyond the quivering horseflesh, hopping from foot to foot and blowing into their bare hands. One, I saw, was wearing boots with no toes, while another's pants were held up by a string. The contrast between the shivering boys in their tattered coats, and the opulently attired guests passing through the Fiske's marble pilasters, struck me hard in my solar plexus.

Maurice started inching the motorcar forward again, then slammed on the brakes as the four-in-hand in front of us came to a sudden stop. Sticking my head out over the car door, I saw that the tallest boy, the one with the string for a belt, had run out in front of the four-in-hand and seized the lead horses by the reins. The coachman shouted, apparently calling to the footman in the rear for help; but before the latter could descend from his platform, one of the other boys ran up to the carriage window and raised a battered tin cup toward its occupants.

The cup hadn't cleared the ornate crest on the door before a police whistle shrieked and two of the mounted officers broke out of line. One headed for the boy at the reins, while the other swooped toward the one with the cup, his nightstick raised over his head.

I jumped up in my seat, banging my head on the motorcar's canopy. "No!" I cried.

Father swiveled toward me. "Genevieve, sit down."

"He's going to hit that little boy!"

"Those boys shouldn't be out in the middle of the street. They'll get far worse than the butt of a stick if they don't move out of the way."

From the way the first officer was backing and filling between the carriage horses, I deduced that the boy in front had taken cover under the harness. The boy with the cup, however, had nowhere to hide. I watched in horror as the second officer leaned over and delivered a vicious crack to the back of his knees, dropping him in a heap into the slush.

I pushed open the car door and jumped out, getting twisted up in my skirts and nearly falling to the ground before I managed to yank them free. I had just started toward the fallen boy when the other lad, who'd apparently been flushed from the tackle, came careening around the side of the carriage and dashed past with an officer in hot pursuit. Without stopping to think, I stepped into the horse's path, holding up my arms. The horse snorted and reared as the officer pulled back on the reins, skidding toward me in the slush.

A hand grabbed the back of my jacket. I twisted around to see my father behind me, with one hand on my jacket and the other on the escaping boy's collar. He pulled us both back from the flailing hooves as the officer cursed and struggled with the reins.

The horse dropped to all fours and danced nervously over the ground, snorting steam clouds into my face. "You want to be more careful, Miss," growled the officer, patting the animal's neck. "You could have been hurt, rushing in like that."

"I'm terribly sorry, Officer," said my father, still gripping my jacket. "Maurice, please help Miss Summerford into the car." He waited until the chauffeur had me firmly in hand before releasing me. Dragging the boy by his collar, he stalked to the curb and propelled him unceremoniously onto the sidewalk. Then he returned to the injured boy and, hoisting him by the back of his coat, deposited him likewise onto the curb. To my great relief the boy rose immediately to his feet and limped after his friend into the crowd.

Maurice handed me into the back seat.

"Are you all right?" my mother asked, her face pale.

"I'm fine," I said, although my legs were shaking.

"Oh, Genna; look at your dress."

Looking down I saw that the bottom of my gown was soaked through. "It's not so bad," I muttered, swatting at a ridge of slush. "The fabric's so dark no one will notice."

My father climbed into the car and pulled the door shut. No one spoke as the footman's horn blared up ahead and the four-in-hand rolled forward. My father's shoulders were so rigid that I could have balanced tea cups on them. I dabbed at my hem with my handkerchief and waited for him to say something. As Maurice ground the motorcar into gear, he finally turned to face me. "What on earth do you think you were doing?"

"Trying to protect that little boy."

"It was none of your affair. You should have left it to the authorities."

I gave up on the hem, crumpling the soaked handkerchief in my hand. "Did you see how hard he hit him? He could have crippled that boy for life."

"Nonsense. The boy was fine, just a little bruised. The police know how to use their clubs to make a point. All you accomplish by interfering is to undermine their authority, not to mention make a spectacle of yourself."

"They weren't hurting anyone," I said, cupping my knees in my hands to try to stop them from shaking. "There was no need to hit them."

"If you start bending the rules you produce nothing but chaos," he insisted. "All of us, those boys included, benefit from living in an orderly society. Surely you can see that."

We had arrived at the Fiskes' door. I remained silent as I pulled off my street shoes and slid on my satin slippers. A week earlier, I might have conceded the point. But my faith in 'authority' had been slipping over the past few days. I was no longer sure just who the rules were made for. For the life of me, I couldn't see what benefits our orderly society had conferred on those three, gaunt-faced little boys.

Maurice helped my mother and me out of the car and Father escorted us up the steps into the house. More footmen stood inside the enormous entrance hall, their scarlet livery dazzling against the screens of white carnations that rose from floor to ceiling along every wall. In the center of the floor, a marble urn held an enormous arrangement of pure white orchids.

"Emprere albas," gasped my mother, bending to smell the blooms. Before she could straighten a cloud of servants was upon us, whisking away our coats and hats and holding up a mirror for Mamma to check the cant of her tiara.

Music was drifting down from the floor above. We started toward it up the circular staircase, climbing past more footmen standing like tin soldiers in the recesses of the stairwell: all blonde, all well-built, and since footmen were paid by the inch and the Fiskes could afford the best, all very, very tall; and took our place at the end of the receiving line, Mother and I panting slightly in our boned gowns.

Charles, Lucille and Olivia Fiske stood beneath an imposing Goya near the ballroom entrance. My attention went first to Olivia. She was wearing an empire dress of apricot silk voile, with a pearl dog collar around her long neck and a spray of white flowers in her dark hair. Shifting from side to side in the line to keep her in view, I watched her greet her guests. Olivia and I were not strangers, by any means; I could remember passing her in her pram on Fifth Avenue when she was an infant with a nurse and bodyguard in tow, and in the years since our paths had crossed regularly at social events. But while her face was not new to me, tonight I saw it with fresh eyes. Tonight, when I looked at Olivia, I saw Eliza.

There were differences, certainly. Olivia's eyes were brown and she had a dimple in her chin, and her voice, which I could hear only indistinctly from where I stood, was lower and more measured than her mother's. But one only had to look for the resemblance to see it. Whatever lingering doubts I might have had about Olivia's true parentage dissolved as I shuffled toward her. Under the glittering light of the hall chandeliers, supposition had taken on flesh and blood.

CHAPTER EIGHTEEN

The receiving line moved slowly forward until only old Mrs. Fenton and her son stood between us and Charles Fiske. Charles was looking very modern in one of the tail-less dinner jackets—the "tuxedo", they were calling it—that King Edward and his Marlborough set had made fashionable. Though he stood only a few inches taller than his wife, his broad chest and clean-shaven, square-cut features exuded strength and solidity. He struck me as very much at ease, attentive and yet somehow detached at the same time, seeming to draw out his guests while keeping his own thoughts close to the vest.

The footman announced us, and we stepped forward. Charles greeted my parents, shaking their hands in turn, then turned to look at me.

"You remember our daughter, Genevieve?" Father said.

"Of course I do," he said to me, taking my hand in his firm one. "Although it seems to me we haven't seen as much of you these last few years."

"She's been away at medical school," Father explained.

Charles assessed me with new interest. "So you're a doctor," he said.

"Yes, I'm a medical psychologist."

His eyes were intelligent and unblinking. "Intriguing field, psychology. I take an interest in it myself."

"Do you really?" I said in surprise.

"I've always believed that there's more to a man than what's on the surface. I like to try to find out what's underneath—especially when his interests are at odds with mine."

As his direct gaze bore into me, I had the absurd but nonetheless uncomfortable sensation that he was reading my mind, and knew I had come to spy on him. "Do you really?" I said again, realizing too late I was repeating myself.

"Take that man over there, for instance," he said, nodding at a man by the spittoon near the top of the stairs. "He's been trying to interest me in a business opportunity for over a year. It's in a growing industry, and the figures look good, but I'm not going to bite. You know why?"

I shook my head.

"Because every time he talks about the risks, he does this." He tugged on his upper lip with his thumb and forefinger.

I stared at him, uncomprehending.

"Do you play poker, Dr. Summerford?"

"Not very well."

"Nine times out of ten, when a player touches his lip it means he's hiding something."

"How very interesting," I said, keeping my own hands locked against my sides.

"Keep it in mind." He winked. "I guarantee it will improve your game." He turned back to my father. "Hugh, I've had a chance to look over those drawings you gave me. I've got some questions for your engineer, but if he can answer them to my satisfaction you can count me in."

"Why, that's wonderful!" Father said, looking stunned. "I'm glad to hear it; very glad indeed!"

"Why don't you have your engineer call my secretary, Mr. Combs, to set up a meeting. I'd appreciate it if you came, too."

"Of course I'll come; I wouldn't miss it for the world!" Father pumped Charles hand, and we moved on down the line.

"You never mentioned that Mr. Fiske was going to finance the lung," I whispered to my father, as we were awaiting our turn with Lucille.

"I didn't know if he'd go for it," he murmured back. "I knew he'd invested in other medical projects, but I had no idea if he'd be interested in our work."

"How much did you ask him for?"

His mustache twitched. "$100,000."

He must have seen my surprise, for he added, "I thought if I was going to ask, I might as well aim high."

"Do you think he'll give you the whole amount?"

"I don't know. It's not a good time, what with all the uncertainty in the stock market. But it is possible. And if he agrees . . ." His mustache twitched again.

If Charles agreed, the artificial lung that Father had been working so long and hard on might finally become a reality. "Well he certainly sounded interested to me," I said encouragingly. Inwardly, however, I was thinking that if I were to actually discover something tonight that supported Simon's theory, and Mr. Fiske was accused of murder because of me, funding was the last thing Charles would want to give my father.

"Evelyn, you look stunning!" Lucille exclaimed, turning to greet my mother. "You should wear green more often." She herself wore a drop-shouldered, ivory velvet dress that set off her heart-shaped face and porcelain skin to perfection. She leaned forward to embrace my mother, holding her head carefully erect under the weight of her famous diamond tiara, which had been designed to resemble an English crown. "And here's Genevieve," she said, pressing her gloved hands over mine. "I'm so glad you could come; I want the house to be full of young people tonight!" She glanced at Olivia, who was bending down to listen to old Mrs. Fenton. "After all, we have to show the Earl that our American beauties can vie with anything Europe has to offer."

"I can't imagine he needs much convincing," I said, "having already made Olivia's acquaintance."

Lucille eyed me approvingly. "You'll forgive a proud mother for agreeing with you."

As my father took his turn with Lucille, I moved on to Olivia, taking her offered hand and saying, "Olivia, you're a vision."

She smiled. "You're very kind."

"Just truthful," I assured her.

Father drew up alongside me. "Well Olivia," he said jovially, "where's this Earl I've heard so much about?"

She glanced toward the grand staircase, her cheeks coloring. "I don't believe he's arrived yet, but I expect he'll be here soon."

I thought she looked more agitated than pleased by the prospect. "I understand your family's been showing him around New York," I said. "You must find his maturity and world view refreshing, after our homegrown boys."

Her eyes flicked again toward the staircase. "I am sure the Earl is most agreeable," she said, slowly and carefully, like a child reciting a lesson.

I thought it an odd response. I would have liked to pursue the subject further; but the line was pressing us from behind and we were forced to continue into the ballroom.

This was a vast space, perhaps some sixty feet deep and two stories high, made larger still by countless gilded mirrors hanging on the wood-paneled walls. I paused inside the doorway, dazzled by what appeared to be an endless sea of jewel-colored gowns and glossy black lapels shimmering under an infinite number of crystal chandeliers. A low stage illuminated by torches at its four corners occupied the far end of the room, under a mysterious array of ropes and wires that hung from the high, coffered ceiling. Four empty, throne-sized chairs faced the center of the stage. More seats had been lined up behind them, many of these already occupied by elderly guests. To the right of the stage, partially hidden by a wall screen covered top to bottom with potted red azaleas, a large orchestra was churning out a familiar ragtime tune.

I saw Emily waving at me through the throng and left my parents to go say hello. Halfway across the floor I hesitated as I saw the two women she was standing with. Louisa Legget and Clara Borden inhabited an exalted inner circle to which I had never belonged. Elegant, well-traveled and self-assured, they were adept at the sort of social banter that always left me feeling flat-footed and one beat behind. Reminding myself that they had never dissected a cadaver, I curved my lips into a smile and continued over to join them.

Emily stepped forward and took my arm. "Genna, you're missing all the gossip. Louisa was just telling us that Olivia doesn't want to marry the Earl at all, but that her parents are forcing her into it."

"What makes you say that?" I asked Louisa.

"Our maid is friendly with the Fiskes' cook," Louisa divulged. "She says they never let her go out without a chaperone for fear she'll try to post a letter or a telegram. They've practically got her under lock and key."

"A letter to whom?" I asked.

"Her secret beau," Emily answered in a stage whisper. "Rumor has it she met him in Newport last summer. Not someone from our set, mind you."

"I understand he's a tennis instructor," said Louisa.

"I heard he was a mechanic who worked on her father's motorcar," Clara chimed in.

Emily smiled at me. "As you can see we're a little foggy on the details. But everyone agrees she's smitten, and not with the Earl."

Though I normally didn't put much faith in gossip, I knew that if Clara or Louisa was the source, it was apt to be at least half true. "Does that mean the engagement is off?"

They looked at me as if there were corncobs sticking out of my head.

"Well they can't force her to go through with the marriage if she doesn't want to," I said testily.

"Perhaps not," Louisa replied, "but they can make her life miserable if she won't."

"Cut her off without a penny," Clara agreed with a nod.

"Is she even putting up a fight?" I asked.

Clara shrugged. "What would be the point? It's not as though she could marry the other boy. I can't imagine Olivia Fiske living on bread and beans."

"Besides, Lucille would never permit it," Louisa said. "I hate to think what she'd do if Olivia tried to defy her."

"Is she really that formidable?" I asked.

Louisa and Clara exchanged glances.

"Genna's been out of town a great deal," Emily said, patting my arm.

"Why, did I miss something?" I asked.

"Nothing much," Louisa airily replied. "Only a social revolution."

I might have been socially backward, but I wasn't completely oblivious. "If you're referring to Mrs. Fiske's ascension," I said, "I was aware of it." Caroline Astor, the reigning queen of New York society for most of my life, had been forced to give up the position two years earlier, after a fall left her too frail to entertain. This had created a gaping hole in the social framework, most noticeable in the second week of January, when Mrs. Astor's annual ball had traditionally marked the climax of the season. Many had tried to assume Mrs. Astor's title, including such heavyweights as Alva Belmont, Mamie Stuyvesant Fish and Tessie Oelrichs; but it was Lucille Fiske, a relative newcomer, whose ball now held pride of place on the January calendars of best society.

Emily leaned toward me, raising her eyebrows theatrically. "But do you know how she accomplished it?"

"Let me guess," I said; "she outspent the competition?"

"That was part of it, of course. But it took a certain genius as well. All last season, they were vying to outdo each other with their entertainments."

"It was all really quite vulgar," Louisa sniffed.

"I don't know," Clara said wistfully; "I rather liked the cloud of butterflies at Alva Belmont's Winter Ball."

Louisa eyed her with misgiving. "Did you really? I must say, I prefer my soup without dead bugs in it."

"That wasn't her fault," Clara protested; "she couldn't know they'd fly too close to the chandeliers."

"In any event," Emily continued, "Mrs. Belmont suddenly jumped the pack by moving the date of her annual Winter Ball from early December to the second Saturday in January. She sent out the invitation weeks ahead. It seemed there was nothing the others could do."

"But then Lucille sent out invitations for her own Ice Ball to take place on the exact same night," Clara continued. "On purpose. Of course, no one was going to go. Everyone said she was done for."

"Until—" Emily held up a finger. "—she let it be known that a Russian Prince would be her guest of honor."

"And all Mrs. Belmont had was an Italian duke," added Clara. "I wish I could have seen her face when she found out."

"So everyone went to the Ice Ball after all," I concluded.

They nodded, fluttering their fans.

One of the scarlet-clad footmen stopped beside our little circle and offered us a tray of punch. He was strikingly handsome, even by footman standards—with clean-cut Germanic features, and standing well over six feet tall.

"Thank you, Heins," said Louisa as she took a glass.

"Isn't that your man?" Clara asked her when he had moved on.

Louisa nodded, sipping her punch. "Lucille's borrowing him for the evening. Her first footman left town unexpectedly, and there was no time for her to train a replacement."

"Are you mad?" Clara asked her. "You know Lucille's penchant for stealing good servants."

Louisa shrugged. "Mother had no choice. Lucille came to the house during visiting hours on Tuesday, and said she wouldn't leave until Mother agreed. Of course she was laughing when she said it, but we both believed her."

"Well, I'm afraid you've seen the last of him," Clara said with a sigh.

"Don't be silly," Louisa retorted. "Heins would be a fool to jump ship. Lucille keeps the men packed in her basement like sardines. Besides, she assured Mother she was holding the position open for her own man, when he returns."

"That's awfully civil of her," Clara said skeptically. "I should think she'd be livid, after he left her in the lurch like that."

"Apparently it wasn't his fault," said Louisa with a. shrug. "It seems his mother suddenly took ill, back in 'the old country', and there's no other family there to care for her. Anyway, he's always been one of Lucille's favorites. He was the one who used to lead us on pony rides in the back garden, at Olivia's birthday parties. You remember— she was always calling, 'Hagan do this', and 'Hagan do that'."

I sipped my punch, listening with keen interest. Although I still found it hard to think of Charles Fiske as a murderer, it did strike me as a rather strange coincidence that one of his most trusted servants had left town right around the time Dr. Hauptfuhrer was slain. Simon and I had never discussed the possibility that Charles might have hired someone else to kill the doctor; in our hypothetical scenario he'd been acting in haste, and therefore presumably on his own. But while it might have been difficult for Charles to find a professional murderer-for-hire on two days notice, if he'd looked among his loyal staff for a hired gun, he might have had better luck. "How soon before the ball did you say he left?" I asked Louisa.

"It was just the day before she came to visit. Which means Lucille had less than a week to replace him."

Louisa had said her mother's visiting hours were on Tuesday, which meant that the footman must have left on Monday. The very day that Dr. Hauptfuhrer was killed. I took a gulp of my punch and nearly choked on the fizzy concoction, spraying drops down my dress front. Emily pounded on my back as I tried to wave her off.

"Oooh—there he is!" Clara cried, looking toward the ballroom entrance. "The Earl of Branard!"

We all turned to see a slender man with an upturned moustache joining the Fiskes at the door. Unlike his host, he wore a traditional cutaway tail-coat, with a row of miniature medals on his left lapel and a large gold medallion hanging from his watch fob. He bowed to the ladies, speaking to each in turn, then took up position beside Olivia, clasping his hands behind his back as he archly surveyed the room. Olivia stood with her gaze fixed straight ahead and her lips clamped shut, looking as stiff as the marble door pilasters that framed her. As word of the Earl's arrival spread, heads around them began to turn, until the entire congregation seemed to be staring in their direction. Suddenly, the orchestra stopped what it was playing to break into a bouncing rendition of "I Love a Lassie". I cringed, imagining that Olivia cringed too.

"He's got a castle in Ireland, you know," Clara said. "The real thing, not just an old pile of rocks with a flag on top."

"With real drafts too, no doubt," said Louisa, "and no plumbing to speak of."

"Nothing a hefty dowry can't fix," murmured Emily.

"Do you think Olivia might invite us to visit?" Clara asked with a sigh.

"Do you suppose he ever smiles?" wondered Louisa, staring at the Earl.

"You don't really think they'd force her to marry him if she didn't want to, do you?" I blurted out. "A title can't be that important."

Clara turned to me, eyebrows raised. "Of course it's important," she answered. "It's the only thing they haven't got."

I watched the Fiske entourage cross the room toward the refreshment table, parting the sea of ball gowns. Lucille led with Charles, nodding regally to her right and left, while Olivia followed on the Earl's arm, hesitating slightly before each step, her face fixed in something between a grimace and a smile. I found it an oddly disturbing scene. I'd gone along with Simon's theory about Charles more out of desperation than conviction, hoping all along that a more palatable murder suspect might turn up. But the hard satisfaction I saw now on Charles' face chilled me to the bone.

Excusing myself from the others, I made my way to the powder room at the end of the entrance hall, which I was relieved to find unoccupied. Locking the door, I moistened one of the hand towels stacked on the marble basin and sat down on the closed commode, dabbing at the punch stain as I tried to digest what I'd seen and heard. If Charles wanted a title in the family badly enough to force his daughter into marriage, it didn't seem such a stretch to think he might resort to murder, as well. Prominent citizen or not, my father's potential investor or not, Charles Fiske had both the motive and the resources to kill Dr. Hauptfuhrer. And like it or not, it was up to me to look for proof connecting him to the crime.

The logical starting place, I supposed, was with Hagan, the Fiskes' recently departed first footman. Perhaps I could locate his room, slip inside, and search for incriminating evidence. My stomach started clenching just at the idea of it. How would I know which room was his? And what would happen if I was discovered? Glancing down at my bodice I saw there was now a large wet circle where the small, sticky spots had been. I dabbed at this for a few more minutes with a dry corner of the towel before I gave up with a curse and started back to the ballroom, still undecided what my next move should be.

I was padding down the carpeted stairhall, and had nearly reached the top of the stairs, when I heard a woman on the landing below demand, "What are these?"

I stopped, recognizing Lucille's voice.

"They're cigars, Ma'am," came the quavering reply.

Peering cautiously over the banister, I saw Lucille huddled with a cringing maid on the landing, holding up a box of cigars.

"Mr. Fiske does not smoke Belinda cigars," Lucille spat out. "He smokes El Rey del Mundos."

"I know Ma'am," the maid said, "but they didn't have any at the tobacconist."

"Didn't have any?" Lucille repeated, her voice silky with threat. "Did you tell them who they were for?"

There was a long pause, filled only by the beating of my own heart, before the maid miserably replied, "No, Ma'am. I . . . I didn't think it would make any difference."

Lucille's free hand darted out and slapped the girl across the face.

I pulled back from the rail, stifling a gasp. I knew I should go, before I was found eavesdropping—but my fascination with the unfolding household drama temporarily trumped my instinct for self-preservation. I stayed where I was, holding my breath, just out of sight of the pair below.

When Lucille spoke again, her voice was as cold and hard as an iceman's hook. "I want you to go back there this instant and tell the shopkeeper who they're for."

"But Ma'am," the maid whimpered, "the shop will be closed . . ."

I heard a second slap, louder than the first. "Then find the proprietor and wake him up," Lucille demanded. "Tell him who the cigars are for. I don't care if he has to go to every other tobacconist in town, he will find El Rey del Mundos, and you will not return without them. Do you understand me?"

"Yes, Ma'am," whispered the maid.

I heard the shuffling of feet, and then the rhythmic thump of someone climbing the stairs. Horrified that Lucille would see me and deduce that I'd witnessed the scene, I turned and fled back into the powder room.

I leaned against the door and let out my breath, deeply disturbed by what I'd seen. I found it shocking that someone as outwardly cultured and beautiful as Lucille could treat a servant so badly. My own mother had never raised a hand in anger toward anyone on our staff. Such behavior was more than a breach of etiquette; it was an abuse of power, a power that if not self-regulated, would not be regulated at all.

Louisa's words suddenly struck me with new significance: Hagan, she'd said, was one of Mrs. Fiske's favorites. Not Mr. Fiske's, but his wife's. I sank back down on the commode, reexamining everything I knew personally or had ever heard about Lucille. By the time I left the powder room, I was wondering if I might have been after the wrong Fiske, all along.

CHAPTER NINETEEN

By the time I reentered the ballroom Lucille was seated in one of the throne-like chairs in front of the stage, gazing up in rapt attention at an aerialist in a sequined leotard who tottered across the high-wire over the platform. I watched in amazement as she oohhed and aahhed along with the crowd, clapping gleefully at each suspenseful dip and recovery. I would never have guessed that she'd just been battering her maid.

The perfection of her attitude after such an unpleasant altercation, and the ease with which she projected it, only added to my suspicions. I found myself replaying Simon's hypothetical scenario, putting Lucille in the murderer's role. We knew that Dr. Hauptfuhrer had met with Lucille in his office on the Friday before the murder, presumably to convey his concern that Olivia might have inherited Huntington's Chorea, and to insist that the Earl be informed. The doctor had likely contacted Lucille again on Sunday, after Eliza phoned him to say she'd be coming to his office the next day. Lucille would have seen the scimitar on Hauptfuhrer's desk during her office visit; she might have thought of it again on Sunday night, while plotting ways to silence him. For after what I'd heard and seen tonight, I had little doubt she'd have wanted to silence him. She had invested too much in Olivia's marriage to let the doctor stand in her way. The decision to kill him would have been easier if she'd known she wouldn't have to bloody her own hands to do it. She could simply recruit her favorite manservant, paying him enough to stay away until the dust cleared, or even to live out a comfortable retirement in the Old Country.

The high-wire act ended to the patter of gloved applause. Lucille introduced the next entertainer, the opera diva Johanna Gadski—who, she proudly informed the assembly, was taking a break from rehearsals at the Metropolitan Opera to entertain us. Miss Gadski clearly took her performance for the Fiskes as seriously as any before the Diamond Horseshoe, rendering Donna Elvira's pain with a moving, piercing intensity; but it was Lucille's more subtle performance that continued to absorb me as the entertainment progressed. Indeed, I was so engrossed that I jumped when someone tapped my shoulder. I turned to see Bartie Mattheson standing beside me, holding a plump red rose.

"Hello, beautiful," he greeted me.

I raised a cautioning finger to my lips, nodding toward the singer.

"Mother said she saw you come in," he whispered loudly. He handed me the rose. "This is for you."

I eyed it dubiously. "Where did you get it?" I whispered back. "From the refreshment table?"

"Coat room, actually." He shrugged. "It wasn't doing anyone any good in there."

"I'm flattered."

A jack-o-lantern smile lit up his angular face. "Excellent! Just the effect I was after."

I smiled too, for what felt the first time in days. After all I'd been through, Bartie's familiar presence felt as comforting as a hot bath after a long day's ride. When the entertainment concluded, he gave me his arm and guided me toward the refreshment table.

"So," I asked him, "what do you think of the Event of the Season so far?"

With his free arm he made a sweeping gesture encompassing the scene before us. "The ladies are all lovely, the champagne is Cliquot, and the entertainment is above par. What more could anyone ask?"

"Spoken like a gentleman," I said, which of course, he was. Indeed Bartie's only defect, as far as society matrons were concerned, was his uncompromising dread of the altar. He fell in love as often as most men changed handkerchiefs, and fell out of it just as quickly. He got away with this disappointing behavior because, while he lasted, he was a generous and devoted suitor; and when the infatuation was over he always made it look as though he was the one who'd been turned out. "Speaking of lovely ladies," I asked him, "who's the lucky one tonight?"

"I beg your pardon?"

I had known him too long to be thwarted by his evasive tactics. "The apple of your eye, the target of your affections, the Eve to your Adam, the desire of your loins . . ."

"All right!" he cried, throwing up a hand; "I get your point."

"You're not still courting Marjorie Fuller, are you?"

"History, I'm afraid. She couldn't tolerate my taste in neckties."

More likely he had discovered her penchant for gratuitous backstabbing, I thought, but didn't say so. We were passing by the front of the stage, where a bevy of young women had gravitated toward the Earl like iron filings to a magnet. "What about Cora Richardson?" I suggested, nodding toward the most striking of the group. "I've always thought you two would make a lovely couple. Why don't you go take her off the Earl's hands?"

"I'd rather stay here with you."

"That's my gallant Bartie."

"I quite mean it," he said, sounding suddenly awkward. "I'd far rather hear the latest on germ research than what they're wearing in Paris."

I eyed him suspiciously. "You haven't been listening to them, have you?"

"Listening to whom?"

"Our parents. They seem to have hit on the idea of joining us in connubial bliss."

"Now that you mention it, I had gotten wind of it, yes."

"Well you needn't worry," I said, patting his arm. "I have no intention of marrying you, so you're off the hook."

"I don't know; I thought it was rather a nice idea," he said, looking put out. "If I have to settle down, I'd just as soon it be with someone I can stand."

"You'd be miserable with me, and you know it! You didn't call me Miss Bossy Boots all those years for nothing."

"You've changed."

"I haven't. And neither have you, I'm glad to say."

He scratched his head. "You don't think we ought to at least give it a try, for the parents' sake?" He glanced toward his mother and father, who were standing a few yards away.

"Dearest Bartie, I won't let you throw your life away on me," I said lightly. "But I will let you get me something to drink." I tucked my hand over his elbow, and we started again toward the refreshment table.

One would never have guessed, seeing the heaping plates of finger foods laid out there, that we would soon be eating a six-course dinner, followed by breakfast after the dancing. Although I found I had no appetite, I did accept a glass of Roman Punch, for it gave me a reason to linger by the table and observe Olivia, the Earl and their new circle of admirers, now standing just a few yards away.

"Have you spoken with the Earl yet?" I asked Bartie, glancing toward the guest of honor.

"More times than I care to recount," he replied, waving a crabmeat canapé dolefully in the air. "He's everywhere I go these days."

"Don't you like him?"

"I suppose I'm just jealous. It's hard work competing with an Earl, where the ladies are concerned."

"Don't tell me you've taken a fancy to Olivia!" I teased. "And here I thought you'd set your cap for me."

"Olivia? Good God, no."

His vehemence surprised me. "Why not?" I asked, peering at him.

"Oh, well," he said quickly, "I just meant that—I don't think I'd be her cup of tea."

"That's not what you meant at all."

He squirmed under my gaze, ratcheting up my curiosity several notches.

"Out with it, Bartie."

"You're right, you are still a bully."

I crossed my arms, and waited.

He sighed. "It's just that there's been . . . talk. Totally unfounded, I'm sure."

"About what?"

His big blue eyes beseeched me; Bartie would rather sleep on nails than disparage a lady behind her back.

"You know I won't repeat it," I said patiently. "Now tell me; what did you hear?"

"Well if you must know. . ." Lowering his voice, he continued, "it's been suggested that all this marrying-the-Earl business has affected Olivia's nerves."

"How do you mean?"

"As I recall, the talk started after the Harriman's Thanksgiving ball. After that incident with Cato Armstrong."

I looked at him blankly.

"Oh I forgot; you weren't there. Olivia was dancing with Cato when suddenly, for no apparent reason, she fell. Of course at first we all assumed it was on account of Cato's three feet—but later he told Harvey Lipton that she'd been wobbly as a carriage with a broken wheel the entire time they were on the floor."

"Was she hurt?"

"Apparently not. There was a doctor on the premises—as a matter of fact, it was that doctor who was murdered a few days ago. He was Mandy Maidlaw's cousin, you know. Anyway, he looked her over and pronounced no harm done. But then just a week later, at one of the cotillions, she shattered a glass of punch. I saw it myself; the glass just dropped from her hand onto the marble floor."

"Perhaps she was simply over-tired," I said, trying to ignore the alarm sounding in my head.

"I expect you're right," he agreed, far too quickly.

"All right, what aren't you telling me?"

"I beg your pardon?"

"There's something else, isn't there."

He sighed. "Just the grumbling of a discharged lady's maid. And you know you can't put any stock in that."

"Olivia's maid? What is she saying?"

Grimacing, he bent closer to confide, "She claims that Olivia throws tantrums. More specifically, that she tossed a bust of Ophelia off the second floor balcony when the maid took too long bringing her ice cream. And that she refuses to leave the house without changing her gloves at least half a dozen times."

I stared at him. "She threw it off the balcony?"

He nodded. "It was a Woolner, too, if I remember correctly. Damn shame if it's true."

"Over a bowl of ice cream?"

"Yes, well, as I say, it's only talk." He glanced at Olivia. "All the same, I have no great urge to be in the Earl's shoes."

I gripped my punch glass with both hands. Falling, dropping things, fits of temper; they could all be signs of Huntington's Chorea. Even compulsive behaviors like the alleged glove-changing fit the profile. And Dr. Hauptfuhrer had been there, when Olivia fell. Perhaps he'd observed her at other functions, as well. I knew he had treated her grandfather, when he fell and broke his arm; perhaps some similarity in their behaviors had made him suspect an inherited disease, causing him to take a closer look at Eliza, and to eventually voice his concerns to Mrs. Fiske.

I watched Lucille rejoin the earl's entourage, twining her arm around Olivia's and drawing her close. To all appearances, it was an affectionate maternal embrace. But what if it was really something else? What if Lucille was trying to hide the fact that her daughter was ill—trying to hold her together, as it were, while also partially shielding her from view?

It struck me as entirely plausible, considering Lucille's determination to make her daughter a countess—except for one important fact. While Olivia may have been acting clumsily and having tantrums, I hadn't seen her exhibit any of the classic, choreic, twisting-type movements most closely associated with the disease. I stared now at her free arm, extended tautly at her side, searching for the slightest tremor or involuntary movement; but it was stiff and still as a wooden Indian's. If it was Huntington's Chorea that was causing Olivia's strange behaviors, surely she should have been experiencing at least some degree of chorea. I forced my shoulders to relax and sipped my punch. There had to be some other explanation.

Charles came over to claim the Earl and lead him toward another group of guests, leaving Lucille, Olivia and three young women I knew only by sight to chat among themselves. I sidled closer to listen in, drawing Bartie with me, nodding occasionally as he related a long story about a sledding party that had gone awry; while from the corner of my eye I watched Lucille deftly fill the gap created by the Earl's departure. She'd always been an animated speaker, given to dispensing colorful opinions and witty nuggets of advice—but tonight as she flitted from one topic to another, punctuating her comments with flutters and jabs of her enameled fan, I imagined I detected a shrill note to her chatter that hinted at an underlying unease.

"I'm sick to death of cotillions and waltzes," she was saying, waving her fan dismissively in the air. "I've told the orchestra I want nothing but popular music tonight. It will be good for Branard to try something American for a change." Her mouth tightened for just an instant, as her eyes flicked toward the Earl. The next second her eyes were sparkling once more, as she launched into a story about seeing "Tum-Tum" dance the Cakewalk at Biarritz, tossing off King Edward's nickname like so many pennies to the poor. She was, I thought, a born performer, with a performer's instinctive ability to use voice and gesture for calculated effect. And yet, as I watched, I became gradually aware that her attention was never far from her husband. Time and again I saw her eyes seek him out as he moved among the guests, lingering for a moment on the side of his face or his broad back, watching him with an expression that took me completely by surprise; for what I saw in her face was hunger: a hunger so raw and naked, it made me feel I should avert my eyes.

Instead, I stared in fascination, wondering for the first time about the nature of the Fiskes' private relationship, and whether it might have somehow played into their murderous scheme. I was still staring when Lucille suddenly glanced in my direction, and our eyes met. She cocked her head, raising her eyebrows with a smile. Mumbling excuses to Bartie, I stepped over to join her.

"I was just admiring your tiara," I told her. "I've never seen anything like it."

"Thank you; I designed it myself," she said, raising her hand to the diamond-encrusted headpiece. "Although lately I've been thinking of trying something new. Something a little simpler, perhaps, in plain gold and silver, without all these heavy stones."

"Something to complement Olivia's coronet, when she marries the Earl!" the young woman beside me eagerly offered.

Olivia flushed and looked down at the floor, as an awkward silence dropped over the group.

"I mean, if he asks her to marry him," the young women amended, her own cheeks turning red. "That is, if they should wish to marry . . ." she trailed off.

"I was thinking of something a bit more modern," Lucille said tartly, suggesting that the Earl's delay in proposing to Olivia was indeed becoming something of a sore point.

"I haven't had a chance to speak with the Earl," I chimed in. "Is he enjoying his stay in New York?"

"I believe he's quite taken with it," Lucille replied.

"I hope he wasn't upset by that dreadful murder. I'd hate to think he felt he had to worry about his safety, while he was here."

"My dear, murder is hardly unique to New York," Lucille said, with a flutter of her fan. "I'm sure the Earl feels as safe here as he would in Belgrave Square."

"Besides," said the woman standing beside Olivia, "I understand they've already caught the murderer, so there's no need to fear it could happen again."

"Of course, you're right," I said, still watching Lucille. She hadn't appeared particularly disturbed by my mention of the murder, but I had too much respect for her skills at deception to take her reaction at face value. "I suppose it's just that I myself was so shaken by it. To think that something like that could happen right in our own back yard."

"It was an unfortunate event, but an isolated one," Lucille said firmly, as if to bring the subject to an end.

"Did you know the doctor?" I asked her.

"Remotely. He served on the Metropolitan board, with his sister."

"But he's not your physician."

"Oh no, we've used Dr. Hartness forever."

Then what, I wondered silently, was she doing in his office the Friday before his murder? Emboldened by catching her out in what seemed at least a lie by omission, I went on, "It seems he was something of a jack-of-all-trades. He was known for his work with blood disorders, but he had other interests as well." I hesitated, gathering my nerve, then added, "Delivering babies, for example."

Lucille's fan paused in mid-flutter. "Is that right?"

"Yes, apparently he's been doing it for years, for a discreet clientele." I glanced toward Olivia. "Twenty years, at least."

I would have had to be blind not to see that I had struck a nerve. Lucille's expression was suddenly so frosty that my heart skipped a beat in response.

"You seem very well informed," she said. "Were you involved with the doctor professionally?"

I licked my lips. It was not a pleasant experience, I was finding, to be on the receiving end of Lucille's scrutiny. I hadn't really intended to go head to head with her—but now that I'd gone this far, I couldn't turn back. "No, I learned about it from a patient of mine. A woman from the German district. He delivered her baby, years ago."

"How very . . . extraordinary." Her eyes glittered, reminding me of a snake that's been stepped on in its lair.

"I thought so."

Her butler approached and stood expectantly at her shoulder. She turned her cheek toward him, but her eyes remained on me as he murmured into her ear. "Very well," she told him, "tell the orchestra it's time." She slipped her fan lead over her wrist. "If you'll excuse us, ladies, we have to go find the guest of honor. Dinner is about to be served." She grasped Olivia's elbow and steered her out across the floor.

I watched them go, shaken by our exchange and not sure what, if anything, I had achieved. Lucille was now aware that I suspected Olivia's origins and her own connection to Dr. Hauptfuhrer, while I had gained nothing but her doubtless formidable enmity. I jumped, as with a musical flourish from the orchestra, the doors to the adjacent room were flung open. Lucille crossed the threshold first on the Earl's arm, followed by Charles and Olivia. I found my escort and queued up with the other guests, filing into the dining room behind them.

This room was nearly as large as the ballroom, filled from one end to the other with round, damask-covered tables. Gilt monograms sparkled on the white china plates, aligning precisely with vases of red Gloire de Paris roses at the center of each table. My escort, a Harvard student who, I soon learned, was taking a leave of absence to market some novel greeting cards of his design, led me toward a table in the middle of the room. Lucille, the Earl and Olivia were sitting at the far left end of the room, while Charles commanded a table on the far right. From my spot in middle Siberia I could only watch my suspects from afar, and then only when the guests at the intervening tables obliged me by leaning in the right direction.

I resigned myself to learning more than I would ever need to know about the growing pains of the greeting card industry, smiling and nodding and picking at my food as a parade of footmen set one course after another in front of me. It was a feast worthy of society's reigning queen: plump oysters served with a dry sauterne; consomme with custard squares and sherry; sole, shrimp and mussels in a fines herbes sauce, with a very cold champagne; a ham mousse; mutton and roast potatoes with an aromatic claret; cold artichokes; frozen punch; and a chaudfroid of quails. Though I did my best, I could eat only a quarter of what I was served, and by the time the cheese arrived I was nearly stuporous from excess. Sitting back in defeat, I glanced to my left, trying to catch another glimpse of Lucille's party. The occupants of the intervening tables had conveniently aligned so as to give me a reasonably good view, and by stretching my neck I could see the Earl, just lifting his glass to make a toast. I craned my neck a little further, trying to read his lips, wondering if a marriage deal had finally been reached.

Olivia sat very erect beside the Earl. Although the other guests at her table were already raising their glasses in response, she appeared to be a beat or two behind. I watched her reach slowly, stiffly for her glass. It was nearly in her grasp when, for no apparent reason, her hand jerked forward and knocked it onto its side.

Before the Earl could look down—before the ruby liquid had even soaked into the cloth—Lucille reached toward the fan near the top of her own plate, pushing her finger bowl over in the process. The bowl rolled across the table and collided with the overturned glass. Lucille made a great a to-do, shaking her head and clapping her hand to her chest as if to say, "how clumsy of me", as a footman swooped in to remove the glassware and lay a fresh napkin over the stain.

It was an amazing performance. A casual observer might easily have concluded that the whole accident was of Lucille's doing. I might have doubted my own eyes, if it weren't for the irritation I saw flash across her face when she looked at Olivia, once the toast had resumed, and the way Olivia thrust her hands under the table and hung her head in shame. The Earl finished his toast and sat down, eliciting only a lukewarm "here, here"—hardly the celebratory response an announcement would have provoked.

I turned back to my own table, trying to make sense of what I'd seen. The tension in Olivia's arm as she reached for her glass had been decidedly abnormal, the abrupt, twisting hand motion that knocked the glass over very similar to what the literature on Huntington's Chorea described. Neither could be attributed to simple fatigue. Considering what my own eyes had just witnessed, along with Bartie's earlier revelations, I was forced to concede that Olivia might have the disease after all. Which, if it were true, meant that Eliza must have it as well.

I took a swig of port, trying to ease the tightening knot in my stomach. The possibility made it more imperative than ever that I uncover the real murderer before Eliza went to trial. And the evidence pointed increasingly to Lucille. She had been prepared when Olivia spilled her wine, suggesting this was not the first such episode. She clearly knew there was something wrong with Olivia, and was trying to hide it. I found myself wondering if she had even concocted

Olivia's 'secret beau', spreading rumors of his existence so that she'd have an excuse to keep Olivia indoors and out of sight while the marriage negotiations were underway.

I sipped my port dispiritedly, only pretending to listen as the fish-breathed old man on my left let loose a long tirade concerning the dire effects of unscrupulous copper speculators and the San Francisco earthquake on the current financial markets. I came to full attention, however, when a man with a walrus mustache three chairs down quipped, "I'm sure Charles will keep the country's interests in mind when he finalizes his daughter's marriage settlement."

"Do you mean you see a connection between the health of our economy and Olivia Fiske's marriage?" asked orange-haired Mrs. Selby, selecting a piece of cheese.

"A very direct connection," the man replied. "Considering that the Earl is on the board of the Bank of England."

"What does the Bank of England have to do with our economy?" queried Mrs. Selby, waving the cheese aloft.

"Too damn much," muttered the fish-breathed man on my left.

"British fire insurance companies had to pay out millions in claims after the San Francisco quake," the mustachioed man explained. "When the outflow of capital threatened to destabilize the pound, the Bank of England decided to raise its exchange rate, refusing to rediscount American trade notes."

"Blatant discrimination," grumbled the old man. "Doubled our indebtedness in a matter of months."

"Well that doesn't seem fair," said Mrs. Selby, biting into her cheese.

Dropping his voice a notch, the younger man continued, "With the Earl's personal fortune so depleted, people are hoping that Charles will see the marriage settlement as an opportunity to make him more sympathetic to our plight."

I lowered the biscuit I'd been nibbling on. "Do you mean they're hoping he'll bribe the Earl to persuade the board to lower the rates?" I asked in astonishment.

He winced. "I'd prefer to say, they see an opportunity to promote overseas friendship with an example of American generosity."

A piece of biscuit seemed to have lodged halfway down my throat. "What if there is no marriage?" I choked out, knowing that if Lucille Fiske was charged with murder, the engagement would surely fall through.

The old man beside me snorted and shook his head. "Then we're going to have a contracture the likes of which we haven't seen in years."

The footman had just finished refilling my port glass. I grasped the stem and downed the contents in two gulps. It was bad enough being responsible for what happened to Eliza and Olivia; I didn't think I was up to shouldering the national economy, as well. I sank back in my chair, caught up in despondent thoughts, as the discussion moved on to Harry Thaw's murder trial.

"Genevieve, have you ever heard of this 'Dementia Americana?'"

I dragged my attention back to the conversation. "I beg your pardon?"

Emily's mother, Mrs. Clark, was addressing me from the other side of the table. "The defense they're claiming in the Thaw trial; they say it's a kind of insanity brought on in a man whose wife's purity has been violated. Did you ever come across it in your studies?"

"It sounds like a toothpaste to me," opined Mrs. Selby, burping into her hand.

"I've heard of similar arguments," I replied, "though never by that name."

"Well I think the lawyers have a point," remarked Mrs. Clark's balding neighbor. "A man has a right to protect his wife's purity, after all."

"But his wife's affair with Mr. White was over when he married her!" Mrs. Clark objected.

"All the same . . ." He shook his head. "If someone had been trespassing on my wife, I'd want to take a shot at him."

"They say Thaw beat her, even before he found out about her affair with Stanford White," the man with the walrus mustache volunteered.

"That's a husband's right as well," the balding law and order man pronounced. "How else is he supposed to preserve order and propriety in his own home?"

"It seems to me that a man's right to wave his fist ought to end where his wife's body begins," Mrs. Clark protested.

"Even if she's driving him mad by attracting attention from other men?" the law and order man retorted.

"What do you think, Genevieve?" asked Mrs. Clark. "Should a man be excused for murdering out of love?"

I thought again of how a jury would respond if Eliza's lawyer tried to argue that love for her child had caused her to murder Dr. Hauptfuhrer. "That strikes me as more of a moral than a medical question," I answered. "But I do think that if we grant a husband the right to shoot his wife's lover, we ought to grant the wife the right to shoot her husband if he beats her, as well." I turned to the law and order man. "In the name of protecting her purity, that is."

"Here, here!" cried Mrs. Clark.

"Two different things entirely," muttered her balding neighbor.

Fortunately the baba au rhum arrived just then, interrupting our conversation before it could take a nasty turn. The others applied themselves with gusto, despite the copious amounts already consumed. I, however, had no appetite for dessert, preoccupied by the challenge in front of me. I had to find proof that Lucille was involved in Hauptfuhrer's murder; and if the proof was here in the Fiskes' house, I had to find it tonight. I very much doubted, now that Lucille knew of my suspicions, that she'd be inviting me back anytime soon. I shook my head at a footman's offer of candied fruit and hothouse strawberries, wondering if I dared try to locate Hagan's room after all. But I wasn't even sure what I'd be looking for. The murder weapon had already been found at the crime scene, after all, and the chances were slim that the footman had left any bloody clothes lying around.

Glancing around the room in frustration, I watched a footman lower a box of cigars onto Charles' table. Although I couldn't see the brand name on the cigar box, I had no doubt it contained El Rey del Mundos. Charles took a cigar, clipped it, and lit it with a match from a gold dispenser. Holding the cigar aloft in one hand, he used the other to select a chocolate-glazed petit four from a platter at his elbow, jabbing the little cake in the air for emphasis as he responded to a question. I found myself waiting somewhat anxiously for him to eat the little cake before the chocolate could melt all over his hand. It was when he finally popped it into his mouth and reached for a napkin to wipe his fingers, that inspiration struck.

Fingerprints. The prints on the murder weapon had never been identified. If Hagan was the murderer, there was a good chance they belonged to him. All I had to do was find something he'd handled and give it to the police, and they could compare his prints to those on the sword. I jumped to my feet, to the surprise of the greeting card salesman, who was in the midst of describing his unique pop-up mechanism. "Utterly fascinating," I said, pumping his hand; "I wish you the best of luck." Pushing back my chair, I turned and hurried as directly as my wine-infused limbs would allow to the door.

CHAPTER TWENTY

I trotted down the empty hall and pushed through the swinging door at the end of it, into the servants' stairwell. Despite the supposed sedative effects of alcohol, my heart was hammering under my stays as I crept down the two flights to the basement. Emerging through the door at the bottom, I found myself standing at one end of a dimly-lit, white-tiled hallway that cut straight through the center of the basement. I took a few tentative steps forward. The clank and clatter of plates being unloaded from a dumbwaiter indicated that the kitchen was at the far end of the hall. To my immediate left I could see an open store-room, with nets of fruit hanging over shelves of earthenware crocks. Past that was the wine cellar, and beyond that a closed door that I presumed led to the servants' dining hall.

Taking a deep breath to dispel the fog of liquor from my brain, I turned and eyed the four evenly spaced doors on the right side of the hall. Normally in a household this size, the butler and valet would be housed on the upper floors and the coachmen and lower house staff in the stable, leaving the basement rooms for the highest-ranking footmen. Which meant that one of the four rooms across from me should have belonged to Hagan. I didn't dare approach the one by the coal bins, at the farthest end of the hall, for it was almost directly across from the busy kitchen. But it might be possible to take a quick look into the others without being seen. And now would be a good time to attempt it, while all the rooms' occupants were off tending to their ball duties.

The third door from the stairs was already open a crack. I tiptoed over and nudged it open a few inches more. Peering in, I saw a narrow room hardly larger than Eliza's prison cell. Pale yellow light from an areaway window in the back wall illuminated a bed, a wardrobe, a washstand and a small desk. A pair of trousers were thrown over the desk chair, while the sheets lay in a tangled pile on the bed. Hagan might have left in a hurry, but no well-trained first footman would leave such disorder behind. I concluded that this room was still being lived in, and pulled the door shut.

Glancing up and down the hall, I moved quickly to the next door and eased it open. This room was furnished identically to the first. A light had been left burning in one corner, however, and a copy of the daily newspaper lay on the bedcover. A pair of shoes poking out from under the bed confirmed that the space was still occupied. This wasn't Hagan's room, either.

I froze, hearing voices moving toward me from the kitchen. I ducked into the room and closed the door, pressing my ear against it. The voices grew louder, then continued past to the stairwell. I let out my breath. The wine's effects were rapidly evaporating, and I was beginning to wish I'd never started on what felt increasingly like a wild goose chase. But I'd already come this far, and there was only one more room left to search . . . .

Steeling myself for a final attempt, I slipped back out into the hall and continued to the last door, which was closest to the stairs. First footman in rank, first room from the stairs, I wondered hopefully? I pushed the door open and stepped in. Here the bed was stripped, and the floor beneath it bare. I hurried over to the desk and pulled open the single drawer, looking for some identification, but found only a pen and a half-empty inkwell. I crossed to the wardrobe—and hit paydirt. A first footman's morning dress ensemble and formal livery were hanging inside. Folded into the pocket of the waistcoat I found a coarse linen handkerchief with the letters JH embroidered on the corner. I'd done it, I thought giddily. I'd found Hagan's room.

Now all I needed were some fingerprints. I unhooked my silk evening bag from my waist. Whatever I took had to be small enough to fit inside it. I returned to the desk drawer and stared down at the pen and inkwell in indecision. Both had likely been frequently handled; either would serve my purposes well. I finally scooped them both up in a handkerchief and stuffed them into the bag.

A few minutes later I was back in the ballroom, watching the guests on the dance floor bounce to a syncopated ragtime beat. My heart was beating to its own, staccato rhythm as I thought about the bounty in my bag. With this one fell swoop, Eliza might be cleared. And if I handled things well, the Fiskes needn't even know I was involved. I couldn't wait to tell Simon.

My elation dimmed a notch when I glanced to my left and saw my mother and Lucille alone at the edge of the dance floor. Lucille stood with her back to the dancers and her hand on my mother's arm, suggesting a private tete-a-tete. I hastened over to join them, my scalp prickling at the sight.

"Genevieve," my mother said, "you'll never guess what Mrs. Fiske has proposed." Her cheeks were flushed, and her eyes sparkling with excitement.

I looked at Lucille.

"I want your mother to design a garden for me," she said. "I've been thinking about doing something for the children of this city for some time, and I've just decided that a garden would be the perfect thing."

"It's going to be a teaching garden," Mother gushed, "with an allée of fruit trees to provide shade for picnics, and winding perennial paths with little sculptures hidden along the way . . ."

"It has to be not only beautiful, but hardy enough for a city climate," Lucille said. "Which is why I thought of your mother. I need someone with her horticultural expertise."

"But she's never designed a public garden," I observed.

Lucille entwined her hand more securely around Mother's forearm. "Exactly. I'm looking for a fresh approach. I can't wait to see what your mother comes up with."

This sudden interest in my mother made me more than a little uneasy. I was trying to think how I might gracefully talk my mother out of it, when Lucille suddenly threw up her hands and cried, "Oh listen; it's the Maxixe!"

The orchestra had started playing a dramatic piece featuring an accordion, violins, pianos and a guitar. "Evelyn, where's that handsome husband of yours?" Lucille asked, scanning the crowd. "Oh there he is; Amy Parker's got him in a corner. Hugh! Hugh!" Father turned, and she gestured to him to come over.

"Quick," she said the moment he arrived, placing Mother's hand in his; "I need you two to get out there and dance."

My parents blinked at each other. "Dance?" my mother repeated.

"Yes, dance." Lucille frowned at the guests bobbing awkwardly about the floor. "Somebody has to show them how it's meant to look. And you always were the best dancers in the room."

"It's been a long time," said Father, still looking at Mamma.

"Then you shouldn't waste another minute, should you?" coaxed Lucille.

"What do you think, Ev," Father asked; "should we give it a try?"

"Oh, I couldn't," she said, looking stricken. "I wouldn't know how."

Lucille clucked impatiently. "Nonsense. It's nothing but a tango with a little two-step thrown in. There isn't any one way to do it; that's the fun of it. You're allowed to make it up as you go along."

I watched, fascinated by the struggle taking place on my mother's face.

Father smiled crookedly at her. "I suppose we might still have a dance or two left in us."

My mother's eyes locked onto his, as if seeking strength there. Then she swallowed, and nodded her assent.

He led her out onto the floor. They faced each other—heads erect, Father's arm encircling my mother's slender waist—and just listened for a moment, as if giving themselves over to the music. I had vague memories of my parents cavorting around the piano when I was very young, memories involving billowing skirts and twirling feet and girlish laughter. But I was not prepared for what came next. As they started to dance, my parents became different people. Gone was my suffering, distracted mother, replaced by a woman of extraordinary grace and pride. Gone my stern, conscientious father, transformed into a figure of passion and finesse. The music was strong and expressive, and they matched it note for note. Arms outstretched, bodies rising and sinking in perfect synchrony, they advanced across the floor. They seemed to respond instinctively to the music, changing their steps to complement the complex rhythm, reflecting the change of mood with their bodies as it slipped from major to minor key. They reached the far end of the dance floor and started back, deepening their lunges, turning from side to side in such sharp, perfect unison it seemed they must be joined at the hip, and controlled by a single mind. When they sailed past me they were smiling: smiling with pure joy.

I stared after them in astonishment. What could account for it? The music? The flowers? The free-flowing champagne? I didn't know—but I wished it could go on forever. I found myself dreaming of things I'd stopped dreaming about long ago. Of life going back to the way it once was, and my parents being happy again . . . .

"They look happy, don't they?" Lucille said, echoing my thoughts. She tapped her folded fan thoughtfully against her cheek as we watched my parents glide across the floor. "Your mother's been through a very difficult time. It's good to see her come out of her shell. The garden commission is just what she needs. She'll be meeting new people, exercising her talents. Building a future instead of living in the past."

"It was kind of you to think of her," I said stiffly.

"Not kind, my dear. Expedient." Her face turned toward mine. "I want you to see just how generous I can be."

With a shock, I realized she was trying to bribe me; to befriend my mother in an attempt to keep me silent about what I'd learned. I blinked at her, dumbfounded by this apparent admission. What could it mean, except that she was guilty? I could imagine no clearer proof that my suspicions were correct.

"It really is beautiful to see," she said with a sigh, gazing out again across the floor.

I stared at her serene profile. Did she really think it was that simple? That by having the doctor murdered, and now buying my silence, she could keep Olivia's ill health a secret from the Earl and the rest of the world? "I haven't seen Olivia on the dance floor," I said pointedly.

"Olivia isn't dancing this evening. She injured her ankle earlier today, while dismounting from her horse."

So that was her plan; she was simply going to keep Olivia off the dance floor until the engagement was sealed—as if that could make the problem go away. "I never would have guessed. She seems to be walking on it just fine."

"Oh it's all right to walk on. But the doctor says she should refrain from dancing for a few weeks, to give it a chance to mend. Of course she wanted to dance anyway, but we insisted."

"That's a mother's job, isn't it?" I said sharply. "To protect her child even when that child doesn't know she needs protecting? To think of her long term interests, and put everything else aside?"

She drew back slightly, regarding me through narrowed eyes. "Yes, you're quite right," she said slowly. "Everything I do, I do with Olivia's interests in mind."

Either she was frighteningly cynical, I thought, or it had never occurred to her that Olivia's interests might be different than her own.

"But let's talk about you," she said suddenly, snapping open her fan. "Your mother tells me you graduated near the top of your class. That's an impressive accomplishment for a woman."

I didn't reply.

"I'm always looking for opportunities to advance the feminine cause," she went on. "I contribute to the suffragist movement, of course, but I also like to take a more direct approach, by supporting individuals I believe show special promise in their fields." She smiled thinly. "You, Doctor, are obviously a woman of unusual depths. Practical as well, it would seem. I understand you're experimenting with a new kind of mental therapy. What would you say to your own clinic? A place where you can test out all your ideas, and work with any one you wish?"

I gaped at her, marveling again at her willingness to so openly display her hand. My questions about Dr. Hauptfuhrer must have unnerved her even more than I had realized.

"Just tell me where and what," she continued, "and you'll have it. You needn't concern yourself with the financial details. I can offer you income for life, with no distractions from your calling."

For the briefest moment I imagined it: my own ground-breaking clinic; a warm, inviting, enveloping space, where patients from all walks of life could come to find relief from their suffering, guided by me and my devoted trainees. She was offering the one thing that might tempt me, in exchange for my silence. But accepting would mean turning my back on Eliza, and that wasn't something I could do. "I'm happy with my current arrangements, thank you."

She pursed her lips, studying me with clear green eyes. "Something else then," she said with a shrug. "I understand your father has asked my husband to invest a considerable amount of money in an invention of his. A mechanical lung, if I'm not mistaken. What if I were to persuade Charles to give him the full amount? Of course I can't make promises, but I do have a certain amount of influence."

Keep your influence to yourself, I wanted to shout, and leave my parents alone. "I believe my father and Mr. Fiske already have an understanding, of sorts. And in any event, the machine speaks for itself. It's sure to turn a substantial profit once it goes into production. Those with the vision to invest in it will get their money back in spades. It's only a matter of finding them."

"But that will take time," she mused. "And it isn't just about profit for your father, is it? I suspect his interest in saving life is much more personal than that. The sooner he can heal others, the sooner he himself can be healed, wouldn't you agree?"

I didn't answer, more disturbed than I would let on by the perceptiveness of her comment. My parents whirled past us again, joyful as tethered birds just set free.

"So full of life, after all these years," sighed Lucille. "Be sure that you don't take it for granted, Miss Summerford. Happiness is such a fragile thing. You must handle it with care."

The threat couldn't have been clearer if it was stitched across her bodice. For her, I supposed, it would be child's play: drawing my parents out of their isolation, luring them into a sense of false security—and then crushing them without a moment's hesitation. We both knew they would never get up again. Somehow, in just a few days, Lucille had managed to take my parents' tender, vulnerable psyches into her perfectly manicured little hands. The thought made me almost physically ill.

"Ah! Here comes an admirer," Lucille said, smiling at someone over my shoulder.

"Do you mind if I borrow Genevieve for this dance?" asked Bartie, appearing at my elbow.

"Of course not." Lucille turned her glittering smile on me. "I enjoyed our little chat, Miss Summerford. I'm sure we'll be speaking again soon."

I went with Bartie willingly, eager to distance myself from Lucille. At the dance floor's edge, however, I balked.

"Come on," Bartie protested; "we've got to make a stand for the younger generation. Your parents are putting us all to shame."

"I don't feel much like dancing."

"Then I'll do all the work," he said, tugging me forward, "and you just come along for the ride."

I followed reluctantly, and we started to dance. To my relief the Maxixe ended almost as soon as we had begun, and was followed by a simple two-step that allowed me to entertain my thoughts without landing too frequently on Bartie's toes. The more I reviewed my conversation with Lucille, the more concerned I became. If Lucille was already responsible for one murder, as I was now convinced was the case, there was no reason to think she wouldn't murder again to keep her secret safe. Which meant that every day she remained at large, I was in danger.

I could go to Detective Maloney and tell him everything I'd learned. But my euphoria over securing potential evidence had diminished since my chat with Lucille. Too much hinged on Hagan's prints being identified on the sword. If they weren't, my revelations to Maloney could come back to haunt Eliza. Once the detective knew that Dr. Hauptfuhrer had taken her baby, he could argue that she'd had a motive to murder him. Without incontrovertible evidence implicating Lucille, I couldn't trust him to go after her instead.

The music ended and Bartie, having exhausted the two-dance-per-partner limit, handed me over to Timothy Drummond, who'd been waiting in the wings. Timothy was just the partner I needed at the moment, so happy with the sound of his own voice that he failed to notice my complete lack of attention. If I could just put off going to the police until I met with Dr. Huntington, I thought as we bobbed through an awkward Chicken Reel, I might have something more than fingerprints to rely on. Not just a clean bill of health for Eliza—which I was still fervently hoping for—but information connecting the Fiskes to Hauptfuhrer's death, as well. It was possible that Dr. Hauptfuhrer had had further contact with Dr. Huntington, and told him he was planning to convey his concerns about Olivia's health to the Fiskes before her betrothal to the Earl could take place. That, combined with the "LF" notation in Hauptfuhrer's appointment book, might be enough to convince the authorities that Lucille had a motive for murder, with or without the supporting evidence of Hagan's fingerprints.

Then again, it might not. My brain kept churning as I humped through a Camel Walk with Edgar Bruce and flapped through a Turkey Trot with Addie Graham, balancing the risks against the benefits of disclosure. Unfortunately there were too many unknowns to make a purely rational decision, and I was beginning to feel like nothing so much as a Cooked Goose when the orchestra finally took a break. I would go to the police after my meeting with Dr. Huntington, I decided at last, threading my way alone off the dance floor.

I heard my mother call my name, and turned to see her cutting toward me through the crowd, pulling my father behind her. They drew up flushed and smiling before me.

"You were amazing out there," I said.

To my surprise, my mother leaned forward to give me a hug. "It was fun," she said breathlessly. "But I'm afraid it's worn us out." She smiled up at my father. "We're going to go home."

"I'll come too," I told her. Though it was still early by ball standards, it had already been a very long night for me as well. I didn't see what more I could accomplish by staying, and the idea of stripping off my torture chamber of a dress and consigning my feverish brain to sleep was suddenly very appealing. "I'll just say good night to Emily, and meet you downstairs."

Before I could go, Bartie returned carrying two foaming glasses of champagne punch. "I thought you might need this," he said, holding one out to me. "I'd hate to have you pass out from lack of nourishment."

"Thanks, but we were just leaving."

"What? You can't leave yet! What if they announce the engagement after you go? You'll never forgive yourself."

"There's no need for you to leave, Genna," Mother said, "just because we are."

"That's right," said Bartie. "Besides, you know how I hate to drink alone."

I caught the look that passed between my parents, and stifled a groan. "Why don't you share a glass with Claire Kimball over there?" I asked him.

He frowned, eying the cluster of men vying for Miss Kimball's attention. "I suspect she's fairly bloated already."

"Now look, Genna," my father broke in, "just because we're old and boring doesn't mean you have to cut your evening short. You stay here and enjoy yourself, and we'll send Maurice back for you later. Come along, Ev."

Belatedly it occurred to me that they might prefer to be alone. And so I stayed, and made the rounds with Bartie, sipping on punch and making small talk while my mind continued to churn with the evening's revelations. After what seemed an eternity we finally went in to breakfast, where I kept my mouth full of chipped beef and slivered eggs and listened to the others gossip about Anna Gould's divorce from Count Boniface de Castellane-Novejean—"Boni" to his friends, who as one wag put it, had turned out to be more "good for nothing" than "good". At last the party broke up and I headed downstairs, too tired and bleary-eyed to argue when Bartie insisted on accompanying me.

We stood on the red carpet as a footman went to find my driver, I in my short velvet paletot, Bartie shivering stoically in his tailcoat. Clusters of coachmen and chauffeurs were huddled along the sidewalk, the red tips of their cigarettes glowing in the dark. More snow had fallen during the evening and a soft white carpet lay over the street, glistening like spun sugar in the yellow lamplight. I shut my eyes and drew a deep breath of crystalline air.

Almost immediately I opened them again, feeling warm lips close over mine. "What on earth are you doing?" I asked, pulling back.

"Kissing you good night," Bartie said. "Do you mind?"

I didn't answer right away. I understood that he was making me an offer, which deserved more than a moment's consideration. I liked Bartie—he was funny, kind, not bad looking, and he didn't try to tell me what to do. Despite my earlier assertion to the contrary, we had always gotten along. I should feel flattered, perhaps even grateful, for his offer; after all, there wasn't a long line of suitors queued up behind him. Although I didn't feel ready for marriage, I didn't want to end up old and alone, either, with only a houseful of cats for company. And yet . . . I couldn't help wishing for something more. "I just—I just don't think—"

"That we're right for each other?" he said with a smile, making it easy for me.

I shook my head. "I'm sorry."

"Well I can't say you didn't warn me. But I thought it was worth another try."

I reached for his hand. "Please don't hate me."

"I couldn't. You know that."

"Promise?"

He crossed his heart. "And hope to die."

Maurice was accelerating fitfully down the avenue in the motorcar, trying to pass a caravan of snow-filled sanitation carts on their way to the river. "You'd better go in before you catch pneumonia," I said, squeezing Bartie's hand.

With a solemn bow, he turned on his heel and strode, stiff-shouldered, through the door. The picture of a dejected suitor, I thought, smiling just a little at the performance. It wasn't that I thought him insincere; but Bartie was a creature of mercurial emotions, and I doubted his disappointment would outlast the night. I myself felt a brief pang of loss—but it was followed by a much greater sense of relief. I couldn't marry someone just to have a body across from me at the breakfast table, even if it did mean consigning myself to the company of felines. I drew another deep breath, let it go, and started down the carpeted steps toward the sidewalk.

I was on the last step when, from the corner of my eye, I noticed a man break away from a group of coachmen and move toward me. He wasn't dressed in bright livery like the others, but wore a dark coat that made him hard to make out in the murky light. It was clear from his deliberate stride, however, that he was coming straight for me. I tightened my grip on my evening bag.

Moving into the light from the doorway, he drew to a stop in front of me. "Just your type," he said, jerking his head toward the spot where Bartie had been a moment before.

"Simon! What are you doing here?"

He shrugged, thrusting his hands into his pockets. "I was in the neighborhood, so I thought I'd drop by to see what you'd learned." His dark hair was disheveled, and he smelled unmistakably of beer.

"'In the neighborhood?' It must be five o'clock in the morning!"

"I was at a wake," he said, by way of explanation.

"You were drinking at a funeral?"

"I didn't say a funeral," he carefully corrected; "I said a wake. It's a celebration of a man's life. And Jimmy Fitzpatrick's life, God bless him, was worth celebrating." He looked up the steps toward the Fiskes' door. "Unlike the sorry spectacle that passes for a life in some parts."

The motorcar heaved to a stop at the curb and Maurice jumped out, clasping his cap securely to his graying head. "Is everything all right, Miss?" he wheezed.

"Yes, Maurice, it's all right. I've just run into an old acquaintance." Simon would have to watch himself now, I thought; he might get away with being rude and insulting to me, but Maurice wouldn't think twice about putting him in his place.

Simon turned toward the car. "Maurice? Is that you?"

The old man squinted at him uncertainly.

"I never thought you'd give up the whip," Simon chortled. "How's that elbow you broke when you fell off Semper Fidelis? Still ache when it snows?"

"Simon?" Maurice straightened, breaking into a grin. "Simon Shaw! Well aren't you a sight for sore eyes!" He stepped forward and grasped his hand. "Grown up some since I seen you last, haven't you?"

"I need some fresh air," I said irritably. "Maurice, I'm going to walk for a way with Mr. Shaw. You can follow us in the motorcar."

Maurice tipped his cap to me, nodded and smiled again at Simon, and climbed back into the vehicle.

I started up the snow-covered sidewalk.

"What's the matter," Simon asked, falling in beside me; "afraid I'm going to molest you?"

I didn't like the way he was slurring his words. I was used to him being unpleasant, but this was different. I could feel his agitation circling me like a restless swarm of bees. "I can't very well walk unchaperoned at this hour, now can I?"

"Not with the likes of me, you mean."

"Not with anyone, as you well know. Are you drunk?"

A discarded cigar lay smoldering in the snow ahead of us. Simon swung back his leg, took careful aim and launched it at a nearby fire hydrant. "I suppose it would be all right for you to walk alone with Billy Long Legs back there."

"You mean Bartie? Don't be ridiculous. Bartie would know better than to even try."

He snorted. "Then he's as gutless as the rest of them."

"The rest of whom?" I asked, losing patience.

"All of 'em," he said, sweeping his arm vaguely through the air. "All covered in satin and jewels, but not a beating heart among 'em. You should have seen their servants chasing the lads from the steps; they'd rather throw the food away, than give the boys a piece from the scrap heap."

"I'm not going to argue with you," I said, trying to walk in a trail of footprints that someone else had left in the snow. I'd forgotten to change out of my slippers, and frozen granules were already sifting down around my heels and melting through my stockings. "Just remember that I didn't go there tonight to enjoy myself. I went to find out where Charles Fiske was on the morning of the murder."

"So where was he?"

"I don't know. But it doesn't matter."

"Why not?"

"Because he's not the one who did it." I related everything I had observed during the course of the evening, happy to share my suspicions, and my fears, after the nerve-stretching intensity of the last several hours. It wasn't only relief I felt, however, as we continued up the snow-blanketed sidewalk. I was acutely aware of the inches of space between us, widening or narrowing as I struggled to maintain my footing, closing to nothing as my silk-sheathed hip brushed against his wool coat. It was the briefest of contact—but my entire awareness was drawn to it. I couldn't help wondering if he was aware of it, too.

"So are you going to tell the police, about this Hagan character?" he asked when I was done.

"Not just yet."

"Why not?"

Maurice rolled through the intersection behind us with an awful grinding of gears. "Because if I let the cat out of the bag about the adoption before I have irrefutable evidence implicating Lucille, Eliza will be in an even worse position than before. And she's not the only one. Once I go to the police it will become public knowledge that Olivia is illegitimate. She's going to have enough to deal with, coming to terms with her illness. I don't want to mark her as a bastard as well. Not unless it's absolutely necessary."

"Why should the girl care what other people think? She may be a bastard, but she's a rich one."

I frowned at him. "Do you really think that makes a difference?"

"Of course it does. Money always makes a difference."

"It can't protect her from being treated badly by people who feel they're morally superior. And the worst of it is, it wouldn't even be because of anything she's done. She'd be paying for her parents' sins.

He snorted. "Well now, if people like you didn't think sex was such a sin, there wouldn't be a problem, would there?"

"People like me? Meaning people like you think it's fine to impregnate a girl and then abandon her?"

He shrugged. "I'd say the sin was in the abandoning, not the sex. If two people have a mind to pleasure each other, I don't see why God or anyone else should take offense."

"A woman doesn't engage in the sexual act for pleasure," I retorted. "She only consents to satisfy a man's needs because she believes it will bind him to her."

"There's more to it than that," he scoffed.

"Really? Such as?"

"You don't understand the things that go on between a man and a woman."

I turned to face him, irked at his tone. "I'm not as innocent as you presume."

He cackled with amusement. "A kiss from Billy Long Legs there hardly qualifies you as an expert."

"What does, then?"

He bent to leer in my face. "I'm talking about *sexual intercourse,* Doctor; the whole kit and caboodle."

"Well then, as I said, I'm not as innocent as you presume."

His smirk faded. "I don't believe it," he said, straightening.

I shrugged, enjoying a moment of smug satisfaction.

"Not with him?" he groaned, jerking his head toward the Fiskes'.

"No," I said tartly, "not that it's any of your business. My point is, I know from personal experience that the sexual act, absent the production of a child, offers nothing of interest to a woman."

"Nothing of interest." He stared at me. "I can't believe you're saying that. Not you."

This reference to my past conduct all too predictably set my face on fire. "I said it and I meant it," I insisted.

He shook his head. "Then you can't have tried it with the right man."

I turned and continued briskly up the sidewalk.

"You can't shut down that part of yourself," he said, loping along beside me. "Sweet Jesus, don't let them take that away from you, too!"

I stopped again, swiveling toward him. "'Them'? I really have no idea what you're talking about."

His eyes glittered in the lamplight. "No, you don't, do you? You don't even realize that your parents are still running your life, sucking all the joy and possibility right out of it."

"That's absurd."

"Why haven't you told your father how deep you're involved in this murder case?"

"I told you before, I don't want him to worry about me."

He shook his head. "That isn't it. You're afraid he'd be disappointed in you, if he knew what you'd been up to."

Well yes, that was part of the reason. But I didn't see how that gave Simon the right to feel the contempt I saw in his eyes. "I don't want to hurt him again. I owe him that much."

He leaned closer. "You don't owe him anything. Not a God-blessed thing! Come on, Genna, you're not a little girl any more. When are you going to start thinking for yourself?"

"I wouldn't expect you to understand," I said, stung by his response. "You've never had a father whose opinion you could care about."

My words hit their mark. I saw his mouth tighten, contracting all the little muscles along his jaw. "Maybe not," he growled, "but from what I saw yours put you through, I'm glad of it."

"My father has always had my best interests in mind."

"I was there, remember? I saw what happened after your brother died. The way they made you suffer."

My parents, make me suffer? I opened my mouth to say he must be drunker than I thought—but before I could utter the words, a visceral memory of pain and loneliness welled up inside me, swamping any protest. I shook my head, more in dismay than denial.

"You can't undo what happened back then," he said gruffly. "You can spend your whole life trying to please your father and everyone else, trying not to make another mistake, but it won't do you a bit of good. Your brother's gone, forever. And one day you'll be gone, too. So for God's sake, don't waste the rest of your life apologizing! It's high time you cut loose and started walking on your own two feet." He straightened, pushing his fingers through his hair. "I'm not saying it'll be easy, but I guarantee you'll gain more than you lose. You just have to take it one step at a time."

His words reverberated inside me, the way true words do. Of course I had always understood, deep down, that nothing I ever did would be good enough. I had nevertheless felt compelled to try. I looked up the avenue, where dawn was turning the limestone facades the color of a baby's cheek. A few blocks east I could hear the rumble of the Third Avenue Elevated on its first morning run. Daybreak in the city was a magical time: a promise of birth and transformation on a grand scale. I felt a sudden longing to be part of that great transformation—to let go of my painful past, and sail into that pink dawn. But I didn't know how. I didn't even know where to begin.

The motorcar had crept up behind us and was rattling at the curb. Simon sighed, and shook his head. "You'd better get home before your father sends out a search party."

He was right. I should go. But I was suddenly loathe to leave him. It occurred to me that I had felt more myself in the last twenty minutes than I had at any time during the ball. Why this should be was a mystery. Simon and I had nothing in common, except old memories, many of them unpleasant. He clearly despised my world, and I felt uncomfortable in his. Be that as it may, I couldn't deny that when he'd materialized before me on the Fiskes' sidewalk I'd felt the same leap in my chest that I'd experienced as an adolescent, when he came to fetch me for our rides in the park.

He pulled open the motorcar's rear door and I reluctantly climbed in, pulling my damp skirts behind me. "Can I offer you a lift?" I asked.

A flash of impatience crossed his eyes. "What would your father say?"

"I don't see why he needs to know," I said with a conspiratorial little smile.

He stiffened as if I'd hurled an obscenity at him. "I don't hide from any man," he snarled. "Especially your father." He slammed the door shut.

I sank back in my seat as the car started up the avenue. Simon's hatred for my father radiated from him like heat from an over-stoked stove. It seemed to always be there, just beneath the surface, as much a part of him as blood or bone. What did hatred like that do to a person over time? Had it changed Simon—was it changing him still—in ways I couldn't comprehend? I turned to look out the rear of the motorcar, needing reassurance that the loathing I'd heard in his voice didn't extend to me. But he had already turned down the side street, and his face was hidden from view.

CHAPTER TWENTY-ONE

Although I was exhausted from days of nervous tension and nights with too little sleep, I slept only fitfully upon my return home. After a few hours of tossing and turning I finally gave up and dragged myself out of bed. In the silent dining room I poured myself a cup of tea from a pot waiting on the warmer and carried it with the freshly ironed paper to the table. Dr. Hauptfuhrer's death was now five days old, and with no new developments pointing either toward or against an indictment of the accused murderer at the grand jury trial, it had been moved to a back page. There was a brief paragraph about the doctor's funeral service, followed by a sentence noting that detectives were planning to go through the doctor's records with his daughter in hopes of finding a motive for the vicious attack. No date was given for the grand jury trial, leading me to conclude that none had yet been set.

"I didn't expect to see you up so early," Katie said, coming in from the pantry with a basket of fresh scones and a bowl of orange butter. "There's a ham in the oven and porridge on the stove, but they won't be ready for a while yet."

"A scone will be plenty," I said, reaching for the basket. "I ate enough at the ball to last me until summer."

"Was it as grand as everyone said, then?" she asked, putting the basket on the sideboard and returning with the teapot.

"Oh yes, it was very grand," I told her, spreading orange butter on the scone. I took a bite and groaned in appreciation. My exertions of the evening before must have distended my stomach, for I was suddenly ravenous for more.

"Did you see the Earl?"

"He was hard to miss," I answered between mouthfuls.

She hovered beside me, cradling the teapot in both hands. "Well? What was he like?" she demanded, starry-eyed as the greenest chambermaid.

"I think it's safe to say he puts his pants on one leg at a time, just like everyone else."

"Oh, Miss Genna," she clucked, shaking her head as she refilled my cup.

I was sick to death of all the fawning over the Earl; you'd think after everything our country had gone through to establish a democracy, we wouldn't be so quick to grovel before any odd duck with a title. "Are mother and father sleeping in?" I asked, changing the subject.

"Your father is. Your mother's been out in the conservatory for hours."

I looked up in alarm. My parents had built the conservatory soon after Conrad's death, fitting it between the back of the house and the old chestnut tree. It had quickly become my mother's private refuge, the place she disappeared into during her sad spells, often for hours at a time.

"Don't worry," Katie said with a reassuring smile; "I brought her some tea when I saw the kerosene lamps were on, and she was as flushed and sparkly as a young girl. Something to do with a new garden project, and deciding what plants she was going to use. I can't remember when I've seen her so excited."

I smiled back uncertainly. While it was thrilling to think that my mother's zest for life might finally be returning, it was more than a little disturbing to think that we owed it to Lucille. "But she couldn't have gotten more than two or three hours of sleep," I said. "Do you think I should try to make her come in?"

Katie's big hand landed gently on my shoulder. "I think your mother has slept enough these past years, don't you? Why don't we let her enjoy being really awake, for a change?"

I nodded silently, taking another bite of my scone. But my appetite seemed to have vanished, and the pastry now tasted like powder in my mouth.

A HALF HOUR later I was descending the steps to the Holy Trinity parish hall basement, where my second class was scheduled to begin. I had arrived a few minutes early to hang some curtains I'd asked Mary to sew for the door and window, which I was hoping would add a bit of cheer to the room. Unfortunately the splashes of red toile only seemed to magnify the vast expanse of gray wall and ceiling. Lucille's 'modern clinic' flashed through my mind, causing me a pang of regret. I pushed it firmly aside, remembering the stark hospital room where I'd spent my practicum. I'd seen astonishing things in that plain little room: morose, prostrate consumptives crying with relief during a post-lecture discussion; speechless boys from the Cuban battlefields—boys who'd been labeled "unreachable"—springing back to life. As Cassell had made clear, it was the power of the doctor's authority—not the color of the walls—that made the difference.

Curiously, not even Dr. Cassell could explain why the class approach worked as well as it did. Conventional thinking held that the distractions in a group setting—the patients' tendency, in particular, to try to discuss their problems among themselves—would be counterproductive, undermining the doctor's authority, and therefore his effectiveness, and resulting in slower cure rates than individual therapies. In practice, though, this had not been found to occur. Despite the blows to my self-confidence in recent days, my belief in the technique remained steadfast; and I was as determined as ever to put it to good use.

I sat at the little desk reviewing my outline, keeping my ears tuned for early arrivals. I heard the floorboards creak in the office above me, and the distant rumble of voices, but no sound from the other side of the partition. Strolling to the kitchen, I fetched a glass of water and brought it back to my seat. I took a sip, staring at the partition, straining constantly now for the sound of footsteps. The church bell chimed eleven o'clock, and still no one had appeared.

Not one? I hadn't reached a single one of them? I lifted the water glass, sipping mechanically while several more minutes ticked by. Finally, I put the glass down. That was that, then. I collected my notes and shoved them numbly back inside my bag, not caring that some of the pages caught and tore. It seemed I wouldn't be needing them any more.

I was getting up from my chair when I heard it: the clunk of boot heels on the basement stairs. Cocking my head, I caught the lilt of a female voice, followed by a familiar laugh. Other voices joined in as the footsteps moved across the floor toward the partition. I had just sat back down when Anna swept around the edge of the partition, followed closely by Margaret, Florence, and Wilhelmina.

Anna was wearing a black derby and carrying a lizard-head cane. "Sorry we're late," she said. "I bumped into these three while I was posting a letter for the Reverend, and asked them to wait." She drew to a stop in front of me, looking me up and down. "You look like hell, Doctor. You ought to get more sleep."

I laughed. "Why, thank you, Anna. You look rather fetching yourself."

She scowled in reply, but it seemed to me there was a new bounce in her step as she continued past me to her chair. The others followed and they all took their seats, stowing their belongings beneath them and settling back expectantly. I pulled my notes back out of my bag, unable to keep a smile from my face. When I looked up, they were smiling too.

"Well, I'm glad that almost everyone made it today," I said, waiting to see if this provoked a reaction. But if anyone was aware of what had happened to the fifth member of our class, it didn't register in their faces. I turned to my notes in relief, glad not to have to offer an explanation.

Today's topic concerned the importance of recognizing feelings of guilt and blame. It was a subject that touched close to home for all of them, and one I hoped would be sufficiently compelling to both engage their interest and discourage interruptions. Things did indeed go well at first—until I suggested that feeling anger toward someone who had died was a natural human reaction.

"I was angry, all right, when my Willie died," Florence broke in. "So angry . . ." She glanced sheepishly at the others. ". . . that I cut up all his clothes."

Anna crowed with delight. "That's brilliant! I wish I'd thought of it."

"But what if their death was an accident?" Margaret broke in.

"Ladies, please," I said, mindful of Cassell's policy toward interruptions. "If you would just save your questions and comments until the end, we could . . ."

"But how can you be angry at someone for something they couldn't help?" Margaret insisted. "How can that be right?"

I sat back. It didn't feel right to ignore her question when she was trying so hard to understand. Perhaps it wouldn't hurt to relax the rules just a little. "It doesn't have to be 'right' in the logical sense," I explained to her. "Emotions aren't right or wrong. What I'm saying is that it's a normal human reaction, for which you shouldn't take yourself to task."

There were several more interruptions and personal revelations by the women as the lecture progressed. And yet, despite Cassell's warnings, when the class finally drew to a close I sensed a new optimism and energy in the group—achieved, it seemed, *because* of, rather than despite, the patients' participation.

I continued to mull this over as I started down Second Avenue toward the Brauns' flat, where I was hoping to speak with Eliza before her mother returned from church. It had been four days since Eliza's release from prison, and I'd still had no opportunity to speak with her in private. I was determined that today would be the day. It wasn't only her chilly reception outside of the Tombs that I was anxious to discuss; I also had to persuade her to let Dr. Huntington examine her. This task might require some delicacy, since I had no intention of revealing the more frightening aspects of her suspected disease unless and until Dr. Huntington confirmed that she had it. Despite all the evidence in front of me—Dr. Hauptfuhrer's letter,

Olivia's odd behavior, Lucille's flagrant bribes and barely veiled threat—I still couldn't see any clear symptoms of Huntington's Chorea in Eliza. If Dr. Huntington pronounced her affected, however, I would accept his verdict absolutely. Then, and only then, would I reveal to Eliza the exact nature of the disease.

As I approached the Brauns' building I noticed a new man sitting on the stoop across the street, reading a newspaper. From his shabby clothes and sunken face I guessed he was another of Simon's rescued petty offenders, put to work standing watch over the shop. I nodded as he looked up, and he tipped his cap.

I entered through the private building entrance that flanked the door to the shop and climbed the narrow stairs to the second floor flat. To my dismay, Mrs. Braun answered my knock. She grimaced on sight of me, and it was all I could do not to grimace back. "We're expecting Reverend Palmers at any minute," she informed me. "He's coming to visit Eliza after the last service. You'll have to come back another time."

"I really do need to examine her today," I said, determined not to be put off. "I promise it won't take long."

When it became clear I wasn't going to leave she grudgingly stepped aside and let me enter. The flat was in the shape of a narrow rectangle with a sitting room on the front end, a kitchen in the back, and two small bedrooms off the hallway in the middle. I had come in on the kitchen end of the hallway. I could see a soup pot simmering on the stove, and through the steamy window beyond it, frozen laundry hanging stiffly from a line in the back yard.

Mrs. Braun led me wordlessly down the hall to one of the bedroom doors. Eliza was propped up on the bed inside, dressed in a pretty pink nightgown and robe and drawing in a sketchbook. She clapped the sketchbook shut and laid it on the bedside table. "Dr. Summerford! I'm so glad you've come!"

"Well, I don't even have to ask how you're feeling," I said, immeasurably relieved by her warm welcome. "I can see that you're doing much better."

"Yes I am, thanks to you."

I sat on the bed beside her and opened my medical bag. "It's Mr. Shaw you should thank," I reminded her, although I was inwardly pleased by her response. "He's the one who convinced the judge to let you out." Whatever the reason for her previous coolness to me, it was apparently a thing of the past. Perhaps it had just been due to the shock of her arrest and temporary illness, after all.

Once again Mrs. Braun stood behind me as I began my examination, uttering grunts of disapproval when she wasn't answering the questions I put to Eliza. She tersely informed me that Eliza had had another bad headache the evening before, along with more stomach pains, but that both were gone when she awoke in the morning. Indeed, except for a slightly elevated pulse, a light flush and the dark shadows under her eyes, I could find nothing wrong with my patient, and she herself reported, when finally given the chance, that she was feeling ready to get out of bed.

"You should rest a little longer, all the same," I told her. "You don't want to overdo." I wasn't about to call her cured yet; not when doing so would send her straight back to the Tombs.

"I could use her down in the shop, now that she's feeling better," her mother said. "I've been sorely shorthanded."

"Do you feel up to it?" I asked Eliza.

"I'd rather work than sit in bed all day," she answered cheerfully.

"Why don't you give it a try, then. But just for an hour or two, and you must promise to go right back to bed if the pains return." I looked up at her mother, determined to shake her loose for at least a few minutes before the Reverend arrived. "I am a bit worried about her color, though; that flush could mean she's dehydrated. Do you think you might fix her a pot of tea?"

"What, now?" Mrs. Braun said.

"If you wouldn't mind."

She didn't look particularly happy at this request, but left to do as I asked.

I smiled at Eliza. "Alone at last," I said, closing my medical bag.

She smiled back, her eyes shining with their old softness. "You're awfully good to come here and check up on me."

"I'm just glad to see you smiling again. I must say, I was afraid I might have offended you somehow. You didn't seem very happy to see me, outside the prison."

She looked astonished. "Offend me? But you've been nothing but kind!" Her eyes clouded. "If it wasn't for you, I'd still be in that horrible place."

"Yes, well, you shouldn't have been in there in the first place."

"Is it over, then? Are they done with me?"

"Why, no," I said, sitting back, "you've only been temporarily released, until your grand jury trial. Didn't your mother explain when she came to get you?"

She slumped against the pillows. "They still think I killed the doctor, then."

Her emotions were as transparent as a child's, I thought, watching despair reclaim her. I hated to see her slip into another funk. I was tempted to tell her everything I'd discovered, about Joy and the Fiskes and Hagan, just to give her hope.

But how much comfort would it bring her to hear that I'd identified a possible murder suspect, when even if the charges against Eliza were dropped, the death sentence of chorea could still be hanging over her? Or to discover that her daughter had been located, only to learn that she, too, might be suffering from a fatal disease? I would save her from that roller coaster ride, if I could. Better to wait a few more days, until Dr. Huntington had had a chance to examine her. "They still have to prove their case," I reminded her. "Which brings me to the second reason for my visit: do you remember the letter I told you about in Dr. Hauptfuhrer's files, suggesting you'd inherited an illness from your father?"

She nodded. "The sickness that makes people violent," she said gravely.

"Yes. I think we ought to have you examined by an expert, who can prove once and for all that Dr. Hauptfuhrer was wrong."

"But you can tell that I'm not violent, can't you?" she asked, watching my face intently.

"The court will want an expert opinion," I explained. "And it's in your interest to provide it. The prosecution doesn't understand this disease; in fact, very few people do. Dr. Huntington is the leading expert. If he examines you and says you don't have it, no one will be able to argue otherwise."

"But you don't think I have it, do you?" she persisted.

I hesitated. "I haven't seen you exhibit any of the symptoms," I said truthfully. "But we have to make sure, all the same."

She let out her breath. "All right, then. I'll see this expert if you want me to."

"Excellent. I'll have to bring him here to the flat, hopefully at a time when your mother is otherwise engaged. I think it would be best if she wasn't present for the examination."

She thought a moment. "Mother goes to the abattoir every Thursday morning to buy meat, before the shop opens. She's usually gone from seven to nine. You could bring him then."

"Perfect. That should give us plenty of time." I paused, checking her face for signs of unease. "Are you worried she'll be angry with you if she finds out? She doesn't seem to like my interference."

"She won't find out," she said with a shrug. "It will be our secret."

Her apparent lack of concern surprised me, since I still assumed that fear of her mother's opinions had been at least partially responsible for her earlier distance from me. I was about to address the issue more directly, when I heard a knock and looked up to see Reverend Palmers standing at the door.

"Good morning, Reverend,' I said, rising to greet him.

"Dr. Summerford! What a pleasant surprise."

Mrs. Braun entered the room behind him, carrying a loaded tea tray. "The doctor was just leaving," she told him, setting the tray on the bedside table.

Eliza sat up to tighten her robe, bumping her elbow into the tea tray in the process. The tray bumped in turn against her sketchbook, knocking it onto the floor and dislodging some loose pages.

I stooped to retrieve it. I had gathered up the pages and was sticking them back between the covers when I froze in a half-crouch, arrested by one of the drawings. Unlike all the others, which were in pastel chalks, this one had been drawn in charcoal. It was of a lone female figure, rendered in smudged and broken lines, positioned on the lower left side of the page. The figure's nondescript clothes were crudely shaded, while its limbs terminated in shapeless stumps. The small mouth was half rubbed out, and the eyes omitted the pupil entirely, creating an impression of blindness, or perhaps emotional vacuity. What seized my attention most forcibly, however, was the heavy line that had been drawn across the neck, essentially severing the head from the body.

"Let me help you with that," said the Reverend, reaching for the book.

"No! That's all right, I've got it." I closed the book and stood up, sliding it gingerly onto the table.

The Reverend straightened, glancing from me to Eliza. "I hope I'm not interrupting. If you like I could come back another time."

"That won't be necessary," said Mrs. Braun. "As I said, Dr. Summerford was just leaving. Weren't you, Doctor?"

I glanced back at the sketchbook. A corner of the disturbing sketch was still jutting out the side, but not enough to reveal any of the figure. I didn't need to see it, however, to recall the bizarre details. Why would Eliza draw such a thing?

I realized they were all looking at me. "I beg your pardon?"

"I said, I'll see you out," Mrs. Braun replied.

"You needn't bother; I can see myself out." Collecting my gloves and medical bag from the foot of the bed, I turned back to Eliza with an effort. "Goodbye, Eliza. I'll . . . I'll come again soon."

"Goodbye," she said, her soft eyes as innocent as ever. She smiled. "And thank you again. For everything."

CHAPTER TWENTY-TWO

I was still thinking about the disturbing sketch the next morning at breakfast, as my father railed on about the latest blackballing at his social club. Now that he believed my ill-advised experiment had come to an end, he was content to turn his critical eye to other matters. First in line this morning was a split in the club's membership between those willing to accept the crude but coffer-swelling nouveaux riche, and those against it. Since he had strong opinions on the subject, I was able to sip my tea and nurse my thoughts in silence.

All night I'd been struggling to come to grips with what I'd seen, trying to put the sketch into perspective. It was just a picture, after all. It was possible that Eliza had drawn it after her arrest, as a sort of cathartic exercise, to defuse the horror of discovering the doctor's body. Or it might have been inspired by a vivid nightmare. It was a woman's figure, not a man's, so it couldn't be taken as a literal depiction of the doctor's murder. The fact was that I couldn't know its meaning until I'd had a chance to ask Eliza, and I told myself to put my apprehensions aside until then.

Katie handed me a telegram on my way out of the dining room. It was from Professor Bogard, letting me know he'd be back on Friday and asking if we might meet to go over the completed paper sometime that afternoon. The professor and his paper undulated hazily in my mind's eye, occupants of a world that seemed a thousand miles away. Since I hoped to return to that world one day, however, I had no choice but to finish the paper, despite everything else going on. I had given the professor my word. Returning upstairs to my desk, I dipped my pen in the inkwell and, trying to shut out the frightful clamoring in my mind, set to work on the final draft.

It was about two hours later when the call came. Working on the paper had allowed me to forget my current circumstances, for a time at least, and to imagine I was back in the relatively safe and predictable world of academia, where the greatest threat was to one's pride. So effective was this illusion that I felt no foreboding when Mary told me I had a telephone call, but trotted unsuspecting down to the 'phone closet with thoughts of Janet's theory on the narrowing field of consciousness in hysterics still percolating through my mind. I shut the closet door behind me and picked up the dangling handset. "This is Genevieve."

Simon's voice came over the wire, sounding strangely hollow. "When was the last time you saw Mrs. Miner?" he asked without preamble.

I thought back. "Yesterday, around noon."

"Do you know if anyone's seen her since?"

I frowned at the receiver. "Why? Has something happened?"

"Just answer the question." He sounded more rattled than I'd ever heard him.

"Reverend Palmers was with her yesterday, when I left. And of course her mother will have seen her since then."

I waited for an explanation, but heard only ragged breathing on the other end of the line.

"You'd better get down here," he said finally.

Something in his voice was causing the hairs on the back of my neck to stand on end. "Down where?"

"Dr. Hauptfuhrer's office. I'll be inside."

Before I could ask what in the world he was doing back at Hauptfuhrer's office, the line went dead.

Twenty anxious minutes later I stepped out of a hansom cab in front of Hauptfuhrer's building and stared at the scene out front. A black ambulance was parked a little ways down the street, in front of two police cars. I stood paralyzed on the sidewalk, experiencing a sickening déjà vu. Then the building door opened and I saw Simon standing in the vestibule. I hurried toward him. "Simon, what's going on?"

His face was chalk-pale. "You'd better come in and see for yourself."

I looked past him into the empty hall, my throat stopped up with dread. Every cell in my body was telling me not to go in.

Simon stepped aside, motioning for me to precede him. I put one foot into the small entry—then stopped as a photographer's flash spilled out of the waiting room. "What in God's name . . . ?"

"Go on," Simon said hoarsely.

I forced myself through the entry, across the hallway and into the waiting room. Three policemen stood in a solid line with their backs to me, facing the row of chairs that lined the back wall. A photographer stood off to one side, inserting a fresh plate into his camera, while an ambulance surgeon and two attendants waited at the other end of the room, speaking in hushed tones. As two of the policemen turned to look at me I saw through a gap between them, to the chair beyond.

I stared at the thing that was sitting on it, uncertain at first what it was. A person but not a person, was my first thought. It appeared to be a mannequin, wearing a high-collared, dark blue dress and holding a piece of paper in its lap. It was the size and shape of a young woman, life-like in every detail—except for the fact that it was missing a head.

A second later my lagging brain registered the fleshy red stump rising just above the collar, and the blood-spattered wallpaper behind it. My gaze dropped reflexively to the floor, searching for the missing piece, locating it near the foot of the chair. Miss Hauptfuhrer's startled brown eyes stared up at me from her decapitated head, under a neatly-pinned pile of blood-soaked hair.

My legs buckled beneath me. I felt Simon catch hold of me, and heard him say, "All right, you've seen it; now let's get out of here." He half-led, half-carried me to the front door.

I stumbled out into the sunlight and propped myself against the side of the building with both arms, feeling my stomach rise. I waited until the urge to retch had passed, then lifted my head to ask, "Why didn't you warn me?"

"I thought you needed to get the full effect, to be clear on what this killer is capable of."

I straightened, swallowing down bile. "You think Eliza did this?"

"Who else?"

I remembered the drawing in Eliza's sketchbook: the figure had clearly been female, the line slashed unequivocally across her neck. My quivering legs suddenly gave up their struggle to support me and I sank down to the ground, resting my back against the wall. But it couldn't have been Eliza, a piece of my brain protested; whoever did that to Miss Hauptfuhrer was an animal, a fiend. I looked up at Simon. "You spoke with her at the prison. You must have gotten some sense of what she's made of. Do you really believe she could have done something so vicious?"

He blew out his breath, shaking his head in agitation. "I don't know," he said finally. "I was willing to believe you might be right about her. But we can't blame this murder on Lucille Fiske. She didn't have any reason to kill the daughter."

"Maybe the two crimes are unrelated," I said dully.

"The method is the same. The killer was just a little more thorough this time."

"Not exactly the same. The scimitar is in police custody."

"Different blade, same result. Any knife large enough to hold with two hands would do, according to the ambulance surgeon. He says it probably took two or three strikes to finish the job. The first must have been deep enough to sever the brain from the spinal cord, since there doesn't appear to have been a struggle."

I felt my gorge rising again at the thought of Eliza—the same Eliza who'd held my hands and smiled so sweetly into my eyes—hacking away at Miss Hauptfuhrer's neck. But Eliza had had no reason to kill the doctor's daughter either, I reminded myself; her quarrel, if she'd had one, was with Dr. Hauptfuhrer. "What was that piece of paper in her hand?"

"Passages from the Bible. 'Life's breath returning to God who gave it,' that sort of thing. It was written out in block letters on a piece of plain stationery."

I tried to make sense of this, but my dazed brain was unable to draw any connections. I glanced over my shoulder at the front window as another powder flash lit up the sidewalk. "How did you find out what had happened?"

"I was at the police station when the call came in. I asked the boys to let me tag along."

"And she was just . . . sitting there like that, when you arrived?"

He nodded. "The maid found the body on her way upstairs to get the dirty linens, a little after ten o'clock. It hadn't been there when she lit the fires at 7:30."

"Do they know how the murderer got in?"

"Right through the front door, apparently. There was no sign of a forced entry, which suggests Miss Hauptfuhrer let her killer in willingly."

And then sat down and read some scripture, apparently, while her visitor started swinging at her with a knife. I shook my head. "I can't imagine that Miss Hauptfuhrer would have invited Eliza inside, if she found her standing at her door."

"She might have opened the door to talk to her, if she was desperate enough."

"Desperate, for what?"

He shrugged. "For answers, about her father's murder. Sometimes people left behind are so desperate to understand the motive that they lose sight of everything else."

"It seems far more likely to me that she would have slammed the door in Eliza's face and run to call the police." Something in his words, however, was tickling at my memory. The next minute, I had it. "Wait a minute—" I sat up. "Lucille did have a reason to kill Miss Hauptfuhrer! In the newspaper yesterday, it said that detectives were planning to go through Dr. Hauptfuhrer's records with his daughter, to search for a motive for his murder. Lucille might have seen it and been worried they'd discover something in his files about Olivia having a degenerative disease!"

He shook his head. "They searched the whole house and nothing else was disturbed. What good would it do to kill the daughter, without destroying the files?"

"Apparently the doctor kept his records in a kind of shorthand. That's why the detectives needed Miss Hauptfuhrer's help; she was the only one who could make sense of them. Without her, the files couldn't reveal anything."

"You can't assume that Lucille Fiske would know that."

"Perhaps not—but she would expect the doctor to keep the adoption files in a protected place. She might have worried—quite rightfully, I should think—that Miss Hauptfuhrer would stumble upon them in her search. If she did, Olivia's true parentage, and Dr. Hauptfuhrer's concerns about her health, might have come to light."

"I thought you said Lucille's henchman had already left the country. Are you suggesting Lucille killed the daughter herself?"

I couldn't frankly imagine Lucille performing the ghastly execution on her own, despite the violent streak I'd glimpsed on the stairwell. "Maybe she found someone else. Or maybe the story about Hagan going back to Ireland wasn't true. For all we know he's been here all the time, lying low until Eliza's trial is over and it's safe to come out. Not so low, though, that Lucille wouldn't know where to reach him if she needed him for another errand." I watched him mull this over.

"All right," he conceded after a moment; "so it's theoretically possible that Mrs. Fiske had a reason to kill again, and someone to do it for her. But once again, you've got no proof. What we do have is a prisoner who's already been accused of murder, out on the loose, within striking distance of the victim."

"But Eliza's not out on the loose," I reminded him. "She's under house arrest. There have been guards watching her around the clock. They would have seen her if she went out."

"Maybe they did," he said.

"Has anyone questioned them yet?"

"Maloney left a little while ago, just before you arrived."

"Maloney's at the Brauns?" I got clumsily to my feet.

"Where do you think you're going?"

"I need to know what he finds out."

"We have to talk about how we're going to handle this, first. The police want to keep a lid on it for now, to avoid a panic. No one knows about it yet except the maid, and I've arranged to send her on holiday upstate with her family. But Maloney, you won't be surprised to hear, is convinced that this was Mrs. Miner's doing. For now, he's confining her to her flat and posting another man outside the door, but you can bet someone from the D.A.'s office will be in court in the morning, trying to get her release order rescinded."

"Can he do it?"

"Technically, as long as the police can't show that Mrs. Miner violated the terms of her house arrest—which is to say, that she ever left her own building—the prosecution has no grounds to request that the release order be rescinded. I can probably exert enough pressure on Judge Hoffman to hold steady, so long as there's no public outcry. But it seems to me the real question is whether you still want to keep her out."

His implication was clear: if Eliza had in fact perpetrated this atrocity on Miss Hauptfuhrer then I, as the one who had argued for her release, was directly responsible—and would be for any future harm she inflicted, if she wasn't returned to formal custody immediately.

My first reaction was that we had to send her back to the Tombs immediately, just to be on the safe side. But with my next breath I realized that doing so would have devastating consequences for Eliza if she was innocent. Not only would it be seen as an admission by her doctor that she was a danger to society, it would also take any pressure off the police to look for another suspect in Miss Hauptfuhrer's murder. If Eliza remained under house arrest, Maloney would have to look for proof associating Eliza with the crime, to support a request to rescind her release. In the process he might uncover the real culprit, thereby vindicating Eliza in both murders.

Simon was waiting for my answer. As I struggled to reach a decision, I felt again the visceral belief in Eliza's innocence that had taken root in me from the start—a belief that had insisted on thriving despite any evidence to the contrary, like a flower blooming in a rain of ash. I couldn't be absolutely certain, one way or the other. I would just have to listen to the silent voice inside me, and pray that it was right.

"Yes," I told him. "I still want to keep her out. The fact that this murder occurred while Eliza was under house arrest proves that there's another killer at large."

He was watching me closely, his own eyes inscrutable. I waited with bated breath for his response, realizing that everything now lay in his hands. A hansom cab had stopped to discharge a passenger halfway up the street. I started slowly backing toward it, my head cocked in question.

"All right," he said finally, "I'll talk to Judge Hoffman, and try to make him see it that way."

"Thank you," I breathed, feeling my indebtedness to him multiply tenfold. I turned and ran toward the cab, shouting for the driver to wait. "Eighty-third Street and Third Avenue," I told him as I climbed in; "and hurry, please!"

FROM THE CAB'S interior I could see Maloney standing on the sidewalk in front of the Brauns' building, huddled with the scruffy watchman I'd seen on the stoop the day before, and a taller man in police uniform. I instructed the cabbie to drive past them to the end of the block. Having learned not to expect full disclosure from Detective Maloney, I thought it might be best to try to glean covertly whatever information he'd discovered, before attempting a more direct approach.

I paid the driver through the hatch in the roof and waited to get out until a wood merchant I'd seen walking up the block drew abreast of the cab. I stepped out and fell in behind him, pulling my hat down low and taking cover behind the sack of kindling over his shoulder, as we approached Maloney's trio from their blind side.

"Nah, she didn't go out the back either," I heard the uniformed policeman say as we drew near. "I was out there all night, and nobody came out the door or the windows."

Maloney said something I couldn't make out, and they all turned to look up at the roof.

"She'd have to be a monkey," the scruffy watchman remarked.

As the wood merchant moved to the left to avoid Maloney and the others, I cut to the right to stay behind them, squinting up as I did so at the jagged roofline. The Brauns' brick tenement stood between two other buildings of identical height. If Eliza had climbed the stairwell to the top of her building and tried to escape by that route, she could have easily walked east or west across the immediately adjacent rooftops. But continuing any farther would, as the man said, have required either the climbing skills of a monkey, or a formidable array of ropes and tackle. Going west, she would have had to drop three stories down a flat, windowless wall onto the top of a two-story townhouse, then scale six stories back up the sheer party wall of the adjoining tenement. Traveling east would have been no easier, requiring her to scale buildings of similarly divergent heights. Even if she'd had the strength and equipment to manage this extraordinary feat, she would have been clearly visible the entire time to the watchmen below.

The uniformed cop was still looking up as I walked past. "I suppose she could have come back down through one of the buildings next-door, and walked right out the front door," he suggested. He shot a scornful look at Simon's man. "He might have missed her, if he wasn't looking for her there."

"I didn't miss nobody," the scruffy little man retorted. "Maybe you're the one who missed her, coming out the back."

"All right, knock it off," Maloney said. "I talked to the owners of the adjacent buildings as soon as I found out she'd been released from the Tombs. They both told me they keep their door to the roof locked, and the only key in their possession."

Once past them I crossed the sidewalk and stood in front of the bakery next to the Brauns' shop, pretending to peruse the glazed buns in the window.

"Have you seen her yet this morning?" I heard the detective ask.

"She came down to fill the register, about fifteen minutes before the store opened," Simon's man replied.

"You're sure it was her?"

"Sure I'm sure. I could see her through the window, plain as day."

"And you didn't see her go in or out of the building anytime before that."

"I told you, no one went in or out until the old lady came out to sweep the sidewalk, just before nine."

"What about last night? When was the last time you saw her then?"

"I didn't. My shift doesn't come on until midnight. The place was quiet by then."

"Well who was on before you, and where can I find him?" Maloney asked irritably.

"Joseph Kearny." The watchman glanced down the street. "He oughta be here any minute for his shift."

"I'll wait," said Maloney. "Fallon, call the station and tell them I want another man posted upstairs, right outside the flat."

"Starting when?" the officer asked.

"Starting yesterday. The prisoner is confined to her private quarters from now on."

The frustration in the detective's voice was music to my ears. My confidence in Eliza's innocence, it seemed, had been well founded. I was still anxious to talk to her, however. Keeping my head low, I started toward the private entrance of the Brauns' building.

"Dr. Summerford," Maloney called out, spotting me before I was halfway to the door. He strode toward me, his expression even more sour than ususal. "Where might you be going?"

"I have an appointment with Mrs. Miner."

"I guess you didn't hear. Dr. Hauptfuhrer's daughter was murdered this morning."

"I did hear. Mr. Shaw telephoned me with the news. I was shocked to learn of it."

"Shocked? I don't know why. I told you Elizabeth Miner was dangerous. And now she's gone and killed someone else. How does that make you feel?"

His cold conviction was unnerving. "Eliza was under 24-hour guard," I reminded him. "If anything, this murder proves that the real killer is still at large."

His hard eyes were unmoved. "How many deaths is it going to take before you stop singing that tune?"

"All right, then, Detective, you tell me: how did she get out and back in again without being seen? Or are you suggesting she was in two places at once?"

"I don't know how she did it yet, but I'm going to find out. And the minute I do, she's going straight back to the Tombs. For good, this time."

"I'm afraid you're going to have a very long wait. But how you choose to spend your time is your affair. Now please, step aside and let me pass so I can tend to my patient. I'm responsible for her medical care while she's under house arrest."

"You and me both know there's nothing wrong with Mrs. Miner, except in her head," he scowled.

"If you have a complaint about the terms of her release, Detective, I'm afraid you'll have to take it up with the judge."

"Unfortunately I don't have the pull with Tammany judges that some people do," he spat out, "so instead I get to go around cleaning up after their mistakes."

"Well I'll let you get back to your job," I said coolly, "and I'll get back to mine." I started to walk past.

He threw out an arm to block me. "No way, no how. No one talks to the prisoner until I've had a chance to question her."

"But the judge said—"

"I don't give a rat's ass what the judge said," he hissed. "You take one more step and I'm putting you under arrest."

I felt my face flush. I had no doubt he'd carry out his threat. Though I was anxious to speak with Eliza, it seemed I was going to have to wait. "Very well," I said stiffly, "I'll come back another time." I turned and made an ignominious retreat down 83rd Street.

BACK HOME THE aftershocks of the morning's ghastly discovery began to make themselves felt on my battered psyche, bringing my anxiety to a whole new level. Although I kept reminding myself that neither Eliza nor I was culpable, the possibility that I was in some way connected to Miss Hauptfuhrer's demise gnawed away at me. Further work on Professor Bogard's paper was out of the question. Instead, I spent the rest of the day with my mother in the conservatory, trying to block out the memory of Miss Hauptfuhrer's mutilated body with eyefuls of lush greenery and the sound of my mother's unusually cheerful voice as she chatted about her garden design.

I managed to keep up a normal patter with my parents over dinner, even joining them afterward by the fire for a game of Round the World with Nellie Bly before I retired for the evening. The effort of keeping the day's horror at bay took its toll, however, and I could barely keep my eyes open as I brushed my teeth, shook out my hair and pulled on my nightgown. The instant my head touched my pillow I fell into a heavy slumber that was unperturbed by any dreams I could later recall.

Still, some nervous agitation must have persisted, even in my exhausted state; for at some point in the night I awoke abruptly, my senses on full alert. I stared up at the dim ceiling, wondering what had awakened me, for I could hear no sounds from the sleeping house. My eyelids began to grow heavy again, and I had almost drifted back to sleep when I heard it: a distinct thud against my window.

I turned and looked across the room. In the faint glow from the Fifth Avenue street lamps I could see a roughly circular shape, backlit at the bottom of the window. I pushed up on one elbow, straining to distinguish the dark blob from its paler background. Perhaps it was a pigeon, I thought. The blob moved, accompanied by another thumping noise, followed by a sharp strike against the window sill.

Now fully awake, I rose from my bed and crept slowly toward the window. But by the time I got there the shape was gone. Stepping cautiously up to the panes, I peered down at the street two stories below, and the visible part of the sidewalk. Both were deserted. I watched for several more moments, shivering in the draft, but neither heard nor saw anything more. I concluded that it must indeed have been a bird, pecking at the sill, and scrambled back under the covers.

The next time I opened my eyes the sky was bright outside the window. I came slowly to consciousness, sensing the heaviness of the past days' events before full memory returned. With all my being, I wished that those events had been a dream. But reality refused to budge. I forced myself out of bed, washed and dressed, and walked down the hall to the top of the stairs. There I paused, hearing an unfamiliar male voice down below. Peering over the banister, I saw the domed cap and uniformed shoulders of a police officer. I stepped back, stifling a gasp.

They couldn't be coming after me at this late date for breaking into the doctor's office—could they? I inched forward for another look. My parents, Katie and Mary were in the hallway with the officer, conversing in grim tones. I had an urge to run back to my room—but of course, that would only delay the inevitable. I straightened my shoulders, and went downstairs to join them.

They all turned to look at my approach. I immediately recognized the policeman as affable old Officer Boyce, who directed traffic at the 85th Street intersection. "Good morning," I said with a weak smile, trying to read my father's face. "What's going on?"

"Come into the drawing room, will you Genevieve?" Father said.

I trudged after him into the front room, followed by Officer Boyce and the others, steeling myself for whatever reprimand was to come. Instead of ordering me to sit down, however, my father pointed to the window, saying, "Mary discovered it when she came down this morning."

I looked blankly at the window. It was partially ajar, but there was nothing unusual in that; Mary always opened the downstairs windows for twenty minutes before breakfast, to allow the rooms to air.

He took me by the arm and drew me closer, pointing to the windowsill. "There."

Following his finger, I saw that the wood on the exterior side of the sill was chipped and splintered in places, as if it had been struck by a chisel.

"Someone tried to break in," he spelled out for me, when I still failed to respond.

"If your father hadn't installed those new window catches," my mother added, "they would have made away with all the silver."

I looked back at the mutilated sill, remembering Father's insistence on retooling the windows after a rash of burglaries a few years before, at the same time he'd purchased a pocket pistol for self-protection.

"Your normal burglar's tumbler won't work on a catch like that," Officer Boyce agreed, nodding in admiration. "It'll open 'er up, all right, but it can't get past the chain."

Suddenly I recalled the noises I'd heard at my own window during the night. I was about to announce that the burglar had tried to break in through my window as well, when an awful thought occurred to me. "Were any other houses burgled last night?" I asked the officer abruptly.

"None from around here. But the car barn hooligans have been pushing farther west lately. Could be they wandered over to your neighborhood."

The Irish rowdies who congregated in front of the streetcar barn at 96th and Second had become enough of a menace over the past year to earn the moniker, "The Car Barn Gang". Although previously their activities had been confined to snatching goods from delivery wagons or passengers on the trolleys, recently they'd become bolder, engaging in armed robbery and openly defying the police. Just two weeks ago they'd posted a "dead line" notice on the gashouse wall stating: "No Cops Allowed to Pass Below 98th Street, By Order of the Committee." That same night, two officers were beaten with their own clubs on 97th Street by a group of mixed-sex gang members. Since then the police had taken to patrolling the area in groups of four or six, but that couldn't protect them from the bullets and bricks that rained down on them from the tenement rooftops.

"Have you ever known the gang to strike this far west?" I asked Officer Boyce.

"Can't say that I have. But if it wasn't one of theirs, it was probably just a squatter from the vacant lots up north of here."

I told myself to stay calm—that of course it had only been a burglar, not someone trying to do me harm. Perhaps the dark shape at my window had only been the shadow of the man below, cast up by passing headlamps along with the sounds from the man's tools. After all, it would have been impossible for the intruder to reach my second floor window, unless he'd brought a ladder with him. This thought reassured me momentarily—until I realized it would have been just as difficult to reach the ground floor window I was looking at, since the recessed areaway was located directly beneath it. "How did he get up to the window?" I asked out loud. "He couldn't reach it from the bottom of the areaway."

"Yes, how did he, do you suppose?" Father asked, looking at Officer Boyce.

"Easy as pie," the policeman replied. "Come on outside, and I'll show you." We all trooped outside and formed a shivering semicircle on the sidewalk. The officer pointed to one of the flat-topped, shoulder-high concrete posts that anchored the areaway railing. "All he had to do was climb up on that."

From the top of the square post it was only a step up to the ledge that ran beneath the drawing room window. And from there, I saw with a sinking heart, a reasonably agile person could just as easily have climbed to the ledge under my own window on the next floor, using the deep decorative trim for hand and footholds. The thuds and scrapes I'd heard could have been the sounds of someone struggling to work the tumbler and jimmy together, while balancing on the narrow ledge; someone who'd chosen my window for a reason, and who, when that window proved too difficult, had tried to get to me by coming through the drawing room window, instead . . . .

I must have made a noise, because the officer said, "Now don't you worry, Miss; the patrol will be making extra rounds on your block in the days ahead. But I don't think the burglar will be back. There are too many easier houses to break into."

I looked up at my window again, searching for outward signs of disturbance, but could detect none from the sidewalk. I shivered and rubbed my arms.

"Why don't we all go back inside before we freeze to death," my father said. "I for one could use a good, strong cup of coffee."

Katie hurried down to the kitchen to get the coffee and reheat our breakfast, while Mother went with Mary to shut the drawing room window and Father closeted himself with Officer Bryce to make out a report. I used the opportunity to run up to my bedroom. Crossing to the window, I released the complicated catch and pushed up the groaning sash. With a sinking heart I saw that the exterior sill was deeply gouged and splintered, worse even than on the window below. I stared at it for several shallow breaths, then slammed the window shut and double-locked the catch.

I backed away, feeling my stomach clench as Miss Hauptfuhrer's headless corpse flashed across my mind. I dropped onto my bed, staring at the window, aghast at how close the intruder had come. I'd always felt secure in my home before; but now I felt frightfully exposed, as if I were living in one of those half-demolished houses one sometimes passed on the sidewalk, with the front wall missing and the plumbing and fireplaces all open to view. If it was me he was after, could a fancy lock or extra patrols really keep me safe? I didn't know how I was ever going to sleep in this room again.

I jumped at a tap on my bedroom door. "Breakfast is being served, Miss Genna," Mary called.

Tearing my gaze from the window, I rose shakily from the bed and followed her back downstairs.

CHAPTER TWENTY-THREE

I nursed a cup of tea and tried not to gag on my oatmeal as my parents rehashed the morning's discovery and discussed arrangements for the window's repair. I was sorely tempted to tell them about the attempt on my own window—to tell them everything, in fact, in the hope that they might somehow protect me. But of course, they could do nothing but worry along with me until I was ready to convey my suspicions to the police. And with Dr. Huntington's visit only two days away, I was loathe to deviate from my original plan. So I sipped my tea in silence, and struggled alone with my fears.

After breakfast, Father called the locksmith and arranged to have him come immediately to install yet another layer of protection on our windows. Since Father was needed at the lab, and my mother had a horticultural society lecture to attend, I was elected to supervise the installation effort. Around noontime I telephoned the Brauns' shop to be sure Maloney hadn't dragged Eliza back to prison in handcuffs. Mrs. Braun assured me that her daughter was still at home and in tolerable spirits, although chafing at being confined to the flat.

By four o'clock, all the windows in the house—my own included—were sporting the latest in home security innovation, and I was feeling a little calmer. I was just returning from a snack of cornbread and raspberry jam in the kitchen, having finally regained my appetite, when Mary stopped me in the hallway and handed me an envelope.

"This came for you by messenger, Miss, while you were downstairs."

"*Dr. Summerford*" was written in cursive lettering across the front. I turned it over. The back was blank. "Thank you, Mary." I carried it up to my bedroom and slit it open. Inside I found a single piece of paper containing three handwritten sentences:

> *Please come to the shop tonight at midnight. It's urgent that I speak*
> *with you. The door will be open.*
>
> *Elizabeth*

I sank into my desk chair. What could possibly be so important as to require a midnight rendezvous? I wondered if something had happened during Maloney's visit that Eliza was anxious to tell me about. Or perhaps it concerned Dr. Huntington's examination on Thursday. That would explain the midnight assignation; presumably her mother would be asleep by that hour, making it possible for us to speak in private.

Although I certainly wanted to speak with her, I balked at the idea of going out alone in the middle of the night. It would be a dangerous proposition under the best of circumstances; but now that I suspected someone wanted to do me harm, it struck me as downright foolhardy. Besides, I doubted Maloney's new guard would let Eliza come down to the shop at midnight. I would go see her first thing in the morning instead, I decided, slipping the letter under my blotter.

As I straightened up the papers on my desk, however, the letter continued to nag at me. Eliza had called the matter urgent. I doubted she would have made such a request lightly. What if something had happened that required my immediate attention? I worried, too, that despite a lack of evidence, Maloney might be planning to drag her back to police court at any moment to slap her with a second murder charge. If that were to happen, I might never have another chance to speak with her.

I pulled the letter out again. If Lucille really had sent someone to kill me, he would likely wait for the police to stop making extra patrols around my house before he tried again. He wouldn't, in any event, expect to find me out on the streets at midnight. And if I went, I needn't be defenseless; I could take Father's pocket pistol with me.

But it wasn't only Lucille's henchman I was afraid of, I admitted to myself. A small part of me worried that I might be wrong about Eliza; that it was in fact she who had murdered Miss Hauptfuhrer, and she who'd been chiseling away at my window the night before. Though I could think of no rational reason for her to want to kill me, a private midnight meeting would give her a perfect opportunity to do so.

Still, I didn't see how in good conscience I could let fear of Eliza keep me from going. As both Simon and Maloney had reminded me, I was the one who'd gotten her out of prison, insisting that she posed no threat. Just yesterday I'd told Simon it was safe to keep her out. How, then, could I justify cowering at home? If I believed she was dangerous, I should tell the authorities so immediately, and help them put her back behind bars before she could harm someone else.

But I didn't believe she was dangerous; not really. I crossed to the window and gazed down at the empty street. I had made the decision to stand by Eliza, and stand by her I must. I would go to the rendezvous, and find out what she needed to tell me.

So IT WAS that at twenty minutes to midnight, a few moments after I'd seen the patrolman stroll past the drawing room window, I slipped out the front door and started down the street behind him. The lights were extinguished in the houses along the block, blurring the familiar facades and creating shadows in every corner. I hurried down the sidewalk at a half-trot, nervous as a rabbit out of its burrow, glancing behind me every few seconds to be sure I wasn't being followed.

My book bag hung over my shoulder, heavy with the weight of Father's pocket pistol. I'd found the gun nestled in its case in the top drawer of his bedstand, next to a thin cartridge already filled with round-nosed bullets. I had never used a gun before, but the cartridge was obviously designed to fit into the cavity in the handle, and slid in with a satisfying click. The pistol was a pleasingly compact thing, no longer than my hand, with straight, modern lines and an engraving of a rearing colt on its rubber grip. It had a hidden hammer that would keep it from firing if I dropped it, and a large safety hook that I trusted would prevent me from shooting myself in the foot. Although I didn't expect to have to use it, knowing it was in my bag made all the difference in the world.

Up ahead of me, the officer had reached the intersection and was turning left on Madison to continue his patrol around the block. I arrived at the corner a few moments later and turned in the opposite direction. As an additional safeguard, I had decided to forego my usual route across 92nd Street and take Madison down to 86th instead, which was likely to be more populated at this hour. Although the blocks along Madison were largely residential, enough people were trudging up from the streetcar terminus at 86th Street to provide at least a modicum of company, keeping my nerves in check. I walked quickly with my ears cocked and my hand pressed over the lump in my bag, and arrived a few minutes later at 86th Street.

As I'd hoped, the thoroughfare was still humming with late-night traffic. Further east I could see the glowing heart of the German commercial district, lit up by thousands of tiny incandescent bulbs on the shop signs. As I drew closer the sidewalks began to fill with couples on their way home from the theater, and brewery workers coming off their shifts. Although the old eel seller was gone from the steps of the Yorkville Casino, I could hear a brass band playing inside as I went by, and see dancers wheeling past the upstairs windows.

It was with some reluctance that I turned right onto Third Avenue, leaving the theater lights and music behind. Here under the elevated tracks the sidewalks were empty, the barber shops and bookstores and singing clubs all locked up for the night. Even the tenements looked unusually forlorn, shorn of their daytime bustle. A cluster of milk bottles stood forgotten on a stoop, their caps popped off by frozen cream. Darkened windows stared blankly at me from both sides of the street, blind to my passing.

It didn't help my nerves when, a few minutes later, a freezing rain began to fall, flying sideways under my hat brim and bouncing off the pavement against my ankles. I turned up the collar of the plain cloth coat I'd worn to discourage robbers, wishing now that I'd worn something more substantial. Although a few headlamps were making their way up the avenue from downtown, I couldn't see another soul out on foot. I wondered if I should turn back. But I'd already come this far, and it was only two more blocks to Eliza's street. I slipped my hand inside my bag, feeling the reassuring shape of the gun.

I had just crossed the 84th Street intersection when the freezing rain stopped as quickly as it had begun. I looked up to see black storm clouds breaking up overhead, combining with smoke from the electric generating plant to turn the sky a bruised, purplish-yellow. After the steady clatter of the sleet, the street now seemed preternaturally quiet. As I continued quickly onward I could hear nothing but the sound of my own footsteps, clicking against the wet pavement and echoing off the building walls.

Suddenly, I became aware that the echo had broken out of synchrony. Was that someone behind me? I swiveled around to look, but there was no one there. I started again toward the next intersection. I was halfway there when my twitching ears picked up the faint sucking noise of flat soles leaving wet pavement, perhaps twenty feet back. I picked up my pace, tightening my grip on the pistol. To my horror, the other steps quickened in response.

Without turning for another look, I leaped off the curb and ran diagonally across the avenue, pulling the pistol from my bag. The sighting nub caught on the inside of the bag, resisting my tug. I jerked it free, too forcefully in my haste, causing the gun to bobble in my hand. I struggled to secure a grip but couldn't quite hold on. The gun dropped from my hand, landing with a clatter on the paving stones.

I stooped in mid-stride and peered down at the street, trying to make out the blue-black pistol against the wet paving stones. I thought I spotted it a few feet ahead, and lunged toward it. As I did so my left foot kicked something small and hard. I caught a glimpse of gleaming metal as the pistol skidded the rest of the way across the street and slid through the sewer opening in the curb, landing with a faint splash in the catch basin. Groaning in frustration, I pulled myself upright and followed it across to the opposite curb, jumping onto the sidewalk and running across the north side of 83rd Street toward the shop. Simon's man should be keeping watching on the stoop, up ahead. I searched for his figure in the darkness as I drew closer, ready to cry out for help; but the stoop was empty.

I hesitated, heart hammering, not sure whether to run across to the Brauns' shop or to continue on in search of help. Just then the door to the bakery opened on the other side of the street, and two men stepped onto the sidewalk carrying sacks of old bread. I nearly cried out in relief. One of the men turned to lock the door as the other put down his sacks to light up a cigarette. Emboldened by their presence, I spun around to confront my pursuer.

The wet sidewalk glistened, silent and empty, behind me. Scanning it from one end to the other, I thought I saw something move near the entrance to an alleyway, some fifteen yards back. I cautiously retraced my steps. But the alleyway, too, was empty when I arrived. I peered down it toward the dark yard at the other end, straining to hear over the pounding of my heart. I could see indentations in the slush, but it was impossible to tell if they were fresh, or even footprints. I had no intention of following them in to find out.

Glancing behind me, I saw that the bakers had picked up their sacks and were moving away down the sidewalk. I crossed the street and hurried back in their wake to the Brauns' shop. A light was burning somewhere in the back. When I tried the door, it swung open. I stepped inside and closed the door behind me, watching from inside for any sign of a pursuer. When none appeared after several minutes, I began to wonder if it might have been just a petty criminal hoping to snatch my bag. Or then again, I thought with chagrin, the whole thing might have been just a figment of my imagination, which admittedly had been working overtime since I'd seen the jimmy marks on my window.

I checked the time on my pendant watch and saw that it was just three minutes before midnight. "Eliza?" I called quietly, turning toward the back room. "Eliza, are you there?"

There was no response. Seeing that the counter hatch had been left open, I passed through it into the back room. Everything there was as clean and tidy as the last time I'd seen it, except that the door to the meat locker stood ajar. The light appeared to be coming from inside it. I stepped around the door and looked in.

The locker was about ten feet wide by fourteen feet long, filled with slabs of waxen-looking beef that hung from iron hooks along either side. Blocks of ice behind the meat dripped through a wood slat grid onto the brick floor below. The light came from a gas ceiling lamp that hung above the narrow, central aisle. "Hello?" I said, although the aisle was empty, and there was no other place for a person to stand. The air from inside was damp and cold and held the scent of decaying flesh. I started to back away.

Suddenly a tremendous blow against the middle of my back threw me forward onto the floor. I landed on my knees on the rough wooden slats, gasping for breath as the locker door slammed shut behind me. I scrambled to my feet and turned around, ignoring the pain in my back as mindless fear overtook me. I saw a lever handle inside the door. I grabbed it and yanked it upward.

It didn't budge. I tried again with both hands, using all of my strength, but still the handle wouldn't move. Whoever had pushed me in must have locked it from the outside. "Let me out of here," I cried, banging on the door with my fists. "Let me out!"

I pressed my ear to the door, but heard nothing from the other side. I straightened. Had someone been behind me on the street after all? Had he followed me into the store and pushed me in? I didn't see how it was possible; even if someone had been hiding in the alley, it would have taken him time to reach the shop and sneak in behind me—longer than the few seconds it took me to walk from the front room to the back. Had it been Eliza, then? Had she lured me here, just to push me in? I put my ear back to the door. "Eliza?" I called hoarsely. "Are you there?" I heard no sound but the steady dripping of the ice blocks.

I looked around for something to wedge under the door handle to force it open. The drainage slats were thin enough, but looked too soft and brittle for the job. I glanced up at the iron hooks—but they were welded onto the iron racks, which were bolted in turn to the ceiling. My gaze dropped to an overturned crate in the middle of the aisle. A box of matches on top suggested it was used as a step for lighting the overhead lamp. Perhaps it would be sturdy enough to use as a bludgeon. I carried it to the door and whacked it up against the handle from below—but only succeeded in breaking it into pieces.

I dropped the dangling pieces to the floor. "Help!" I shouted at the top of my lungs. "Someone help me, please! I'm locked inside!" I held my breath, praying for some response. But the outside world slumbered on, as oblivious to my predicament as the insensible meat all around me.

I sank onto the floor and sat back against the door, hugging my scraped knees. Who had done this, and why? Were they hoping to kill me? It was cold in the locker; cold enough, I supposed, to produce symptoms of exposure if I was left in here long enough. I took a quick inventory. Though my legs and torso were mostly dry, the rain that had fallen on me on my way to the shop had soaked through to my head and shoulders, and I could already feel a chill seeping through the sleeves of my thin coat. It would be seven or eight hours before Mrs. Braun came down to open the shop, and found me inside. Long enough, conceivably, for the cold and damp to take their toll . . . .

I squeezed my knees more tightly against my chest, tamping down rising panic. If I were to die in the cooler, who would benefit? The more I thought about it, the less inclined I was to suspect Eliza. Even assuming she could have persuaded the guard to let her come down alone at midnight, if I turned up dead on the premises, she would be the obvious suspect. I doubted she would willingly back herself into such a corner. Besides, she would gain nothing from my death, and would lose her staunchest supporter.

Lucille Fiske, on the other hand, would accomplish two things at once: she would get rid of me and my suspicions; and she would lay another body at Eliza's door, clinching the presumption of Eliza's mental instability and assuring that she was convicted for the murder of both Hauptfuhrers. I had let her know, at the ball, that Eliza was my patient. Considering her interest in the case, and her ample resources, she probably also knew that Eliza had been released. It would have been simple enough for her to sign a letter in Eliza's name asking me to go to the shop, then send a henchman to push me into the locker when I arrived. I didn't know how her man had managed to open the shop door, but I supposed he could have found a way. The more I thought about it, the more I felt it had to have been her. As far as she was concerned, I wouldn't even have to die, so long as I was found in the locker, the apparent target of a woman whose sanity was already in doubt. It was a simple yet cunning strategy—exactly what I would expect from Lucille.

A shiver rattled through me, raising goose bumps all over my body. I found myself reviewing the progressive symptoms of exposure: first the shivering, as the brain attempted to raise body heat; then the foggy thinking and loss of body functions; followed by gradual paralysis as body temperature continued to drop; leading finally to death. I had a vivid image of my body sprawled out on the slats in the morning, stiff as one of the carcasses hanging above me. It wasn't going to come to that, I thought angrily, pushing myself to my feet.

With a fresh burst of zeal I sidled behind the hanging meat, trying not to touch the greasy ribs as I searched for some hidden means of egress. But there was no window, no chute, no opening of any kind save for a small vent in the ceiling for lamp fumes, and a sink-sized drain in the floor. I tried shouting again, keeping it up for several minutes in case someone was trying to follow the sound of my voice, but no rescuer arrived at the door. A more violent shiver wracked through me.

I kicked the crate pieces aside and started doing scissor jumps in the aisle, swinging my arms up and down as best I could in the narrow space. I continued until I'd warmed up, then stopped to rest, starting up again when I felt another chill coming on. This worked well, but was more tiring than I'd expected, and I soon switched to a high-stepping march to save energy. After doing this for what seemed an eternity, I checked my pendant watch and found that only a single hour had elapsed.

When the shivers came back I reluctantly started up again, trying to pace myself as conservatively as possible and still stave off the chills. But it was becoming harder and harder to maintain the necessary level of activity, and soon, despite my best efforts, I was shivering pretty much constantly. The next time I checked my watch, my fingers were so stiff it was hard to work the latch. It was now just a little past three o'clock; I had four more hours still to go.

I decided to take a short rest. I slid onto the floor slats and leaned back against the door, trembling from head to toe. I really should cover my head, I thought dully, to slow the loss of body heat. It was several seconds before I recalled that I was already wearing a hat. I noted this mental lapse with a strange sense of detachment. At some point I felt my head falling toward my chest and jerked it back up, unable to remember the last few minutes. My teeth were chattering now and my shoulders were locked up under my ears. My body seemed to have taken on a life of its own, contracting in violent spasms that were impervious to my efforts to resist. I found myself thinking of how Nanny used to bathe me and Conrad in the big laundry tubs in the kitchen, and then bundle our shivering bodies in thick towels and plunk us in front of the stove to dry. The shimmering heat would roll off the cast iron stove in waves, vaporizing the water on our skin and hair, turning Conrad's cheeks a cherry red. He looked just like an angel then, I thought dreamily, with his silky hair and bright blue eyes. Sometimes he'd climb into my lap and I'd rock him from side to side with my chin on his head, stealing the warmth from his solid little body, tickling him now and then just to hear his belly laugh. I could almost hear his laugh now, and his voice, calling to me. Calling my name . . . .

My eyes opened, and I returned to the present with a start. With what felt like an enormous effort, I forced myself to sit up. I had to do something to stop the shivering. I looked at the sputtering gas lamp, wishing now I hadn't broken the crate, for I could have stood on it to warm my hands, at least. Suddenly, I remembered the box of matches that had been lying on top of it. Dropping forward onto my hands and knees I crawled down the damp, rank aisle until I found it under one of the hanging carcasses at the far end. I slid the box open with a stiff thumb. It was more than a quarter full. Digging out one of the little wooden sticks, I struck it clumsily against the flint strip and watched it burst into life.

I'd never seen anything so beautiful. Now all I needed was something to burn. Dropping the spent match, I broke apart the smashed crate with the heel of my boot and piled half the pieces on a damp section of the wood-grid floor. I tried to pull up one of the drier wood slats as well, but it wouldn't budge. The crate would have to do for now. I dug some pages of research notes from my bag and wadded them up, arranging them under the wood. Now all I had to do was light it.

This, however, was easier said than done. My fingers were so numb I couldn't manage to pluck another matchstick from the box, and had to shake one into my hand. When I tried to light it, it dropped out of my senseless fingers in mid-strike. I paused, trying to remember how I'd managed it the last time. I shook out another match and tried locking it in the crook of my thumb and forefinger, but it, too, fell lifeless to the ground. I stopped to rest, worn out by my exertions, feeling tears of frustration well in my eyes. Did I need to preserve body moisture? I couldn't remember. Trying to hold back the tears just in case, I shook out yet another match and pulled it listlessly across the strip.

This time, perhaps because I wasn't really trying, it flared into flame, surprising me so much that I almost dropped it. I lowered it carefully to the wadded paper and watched it take, holding my breath as the boards' splintered edges caught along with it. I was so thrilled that I didn't realize the match flame had reached my thumb until I smelled burning flesh. Dropping the matchstick, I leaned toward the fire and let the heat caress my face. The little pile of wood generated a surprisingly generous amount of warmth. Although smoke gradually filled the room, the ceiling vent kept it from becoming suffocating, and by adding the remaining pieces of crate one at a time I was able to keep the fire alive and the smoke at a tolerable level for more than an hour. By the time it went out, sensation had returned to my hands and face, although I was feeling utterly exhausted. I slumped back against the door, too tired to think, and allowed my eyes to close for just a minute . . . .

"WHAT IN THE world . . . ?"

I opened my eyes and looked up into Mrs. Braun's astonished face. Turning my head, I discovered I was lying on my back half in and half out of the meat locker. I must have fallen out when she opened the door. I tried to push up on my elbows, but couldn't find them beneath me.

"Wait a minute," Mrs. Braun instructed, kneeling behind my head.

I felt her arms slide under my shoulders.

"All right; try now."

With me pushing and her pulling I got onto my feet and shuffled over to the table. I dropped heavily into a chair, feeling as though I'd just climbed Mt. Everest. My head throbbed and I was shivering so badly that I could hardly stay on the seat.

"What in the world . . ." she began again, leaning over to peer into my face. She broke off, straightening, as a violent shudder nearly bucked me off my chair. "The kettle's on upstairs; I'll bring you some tea."

She went out the side door into the hall and up the stairs to her flat, while I made a determined effort to control my shaking. By the time she returned a few minutes later with a heavy wool blanket and a steaming mug, I'd managed to reduce it to a sporadic shudder. She handed me the tea and draped the blanket over my shoulders. My hands were trembling too badly, however, to tip the mug's contents into my mouth. After watching me spill some down my coat front, she put her own hands on the mug and raised it to my lips. The tea was strong and sweet and blissfully hot. I drank it eagerly, not stopping until I'd finished the last drop.

"Thank you," I said, handing her the cup, meaning for more than the tea. "I don't know what would have happened if you hadn't found me in time."

"What were you doing in there in the first place?" she finally managed to ask me.

"I received a letter with Eliza's name on it, asking me to come to the shop. I went into the back looking for her when I arrived, and someone pushed me into the locker."

"Good Lord!" She sank onto the chair beside me, clasping her hand to her chest. "Why would anyone do such a thing? And how did they get into the shop?"

I shook my head, loosing a fireball of pain behind my eyes. My back was sore, my knees were stiff and my tongue felt as though there were cotton balls sticking to it. "I'm not really sure."

"You don't think . . ." Her gaze flicked toward the ceiling.

"No," I said quickly. "I don't. Eliza has no reason to harm me." Although she didn't refute this, I could see the doubt in her eyes. "You didn't hear anything last night from your flat?" I asked. "Anything to suggest a break in?"

"No, nothing," she answered, shaking her head. "I didn't hear anything from the stairwell either, when I went down to the furnace to shake the ashes. You could ask the guard outside our flat, though; he might have heard something."

"I think we're going to have to keep the police out of this," I said reluctantly, although I would have sorely liked to ask for some protection. "They're going to assume Eliza did it, even if they can't prove it. You might take a look around, though, to see if anything's been disturbed. If it has, you could at least report a break-in."

She quickly scanned the room. "Everything looks all right in here. I'd better go check out front."

As she went out to investigate I huddled under the blanket, feeling the sting of returning blood in my fingers and toes, trying to reconcile myself to what had happened. Hard though it was to accept, someone had targeted me—not once, but twice—and might quite possibly do so again. Much as I wished it were otherwise, nothing stood between me and a third attempt but my own ability to identify, and outsmart, my attacker. This bald truth pumped a fresh cascade of adrenaline through my exhausted body. I dropped the blanket from my shoulders and got cautiously to my feet. My legs were shaky, but they did what I asked. If I couldn't yet say for sure who the attacker was, I could at least try to confirm who it wasn't. Retrieving my bag from the locker, I made my way stiffly through the side door and up the stairs to Eliza's flat.

CHAPTER TWENTY-FOUR

Maloney's guard was sitting in a rickety chair in the narrow hallway, directly across from the Brauns' door. His eyes were bleary and there was rust-colored stubble on his chin and cheeks. I'd been concerned he might be able to guess from my appearance that I'd been through some sort of ordeal; but he barely looked at me when I told him I was Mrs. Miner's doctor, waving me toward the door without a word.

"Did she have a restful night, do you know?"

"How should I know?" he answered. "I ain't a nurse."

Eight hours of sitting alone in an uncomfortable chair apparently hadn't left him in a very jolly mood. I felt like telling him it could have been worse. "So you haven't seen her."

"Nah, I haven't seen her."

"Then . . . how do you know she's in there, if you don't mind my asking?"

His eyes narrowed. "Because she was in there when I came on shift, and she hasn't come out," he said, with more than a touch of belligerence.

Deciding that further questioning would be unproductive, I opened the unlocked door and, leaving it slightly ajar behind me, walked down the silent hall to Eliza's bedroom. She was sleeping peacefully under the patchwork coverlet, with one arm draped loosely over her head. I crossed to the foot of the bed and stood watching her for several minutes, noting the occasional twitch of her delicate fingers, and the movement of her eyes beneath their translucent lids. She looked as innocent and unguarded as a child. I moved closer and nudged her arm.

She stirred, opening her eyes.

"Good morning, Eliza," I said, sitting on the foot of the bed.

"Dr. Summerford . . ." The dreamy fog gradually cleared from her eyes. She pushed herself up on her elbows, glancing at the beside clock. "What is it? Has something happened?"

"I need to talk with you. I'm sorry to wake you, but it's important."

She sat up, pushing the hair from her face. "No, it's all right; I'm glad you've come. I've been wanting to talk to you, too. That detective came here to the shop, to ask me about Miss. Hauptfuhrer. Did you hear what happened to her?"

I nodded.

"He was just dreadful, acting as if I had something to do with it. I don't know why he hates me so."

"What did you say to him?"

"I told him I didn't know anything about it, of course. He kept asking me how I got out of the building without being seen. I told him, I never left. I was here, in the flat, all that night and morning, until I went down to fill the register."

"Could your mother confirm that you were here?"

"She told him she saw me go in to bed, and then saw me again in the morning when I came down to the shop."

"You didn't have breakfast together?"

"Why, no, she went down to cut the meat before I woke up. Normally I would have gotten up sooner, to take the deposit to the bank after filling the register—but now that I can't go out, mother has to make a night deposit."

Her alibi wasn't airtight, then. I pinched the bridge of my nose. My headache had been growing steadily worse, and now felt like an iron band around my skull.

"Are you all right?" she asked.

I dropped my hand to my lap. "Eliza, I need to ask you about the sketch."

She frowned at me. "What sketch?"

Her drawing tablet was still lying on the bedside table. I pointed at it. "May I?"

She nodded, without any visible hesitation.

I opened it on my lap and flipped through the loose pages. Between colorful drawings of flapping laundry and roosting pigeons and brightly decorated Christmas trees I found the sketch I was looking for. It had grown no less alarming with time. "This one," I said, handing it to her.

She held it gingerly between her hands. "Where on earth did this come from?"

"What do you mean, where did it come from? You just saw me take it out of your book."

She handed it back to me. "Well it's not mine. I've never seen it before."

"Eliza," I said sharply, "you have to be honest with me."

She shrank back against the headboard, looking stung. "I swear to you, I've never seen it before!"

"Then how did it get into your sketchbook?"

"I don't know."

"These other pictures are all yours, aren't they?" I asked, fanning them across my lap.

"Yes."

"Then how do you explain it?"

"You're upset," she said anxiously.

"I need to understand. Where could this picture have come from, if you didn't draw it?"

She shook her head. "Maybe someone put it in my book by mistake."

I rubbed my aching temples. "Do you take the sketchbook out very often?"

"Why, yes; after Church on Sunday, if it's a nice day, I usually go to the park or the pier to draw. I don't go out as much in the cold weather, of course, although I did sketch some children skating, around Christmas time."

Sketchbooks were a common enough sight in the parks and other public areas of the city. I supposed it was possible that someone had confused Eliza's book with their own, or that some idle prankster had inserted the picture deliberately. But the subject matter was just too coincidental . . . .

"You think I killed Miss Hauptfuhrer, and drew that picture, don't you," she said in a small voice.

I didn't know what to say. Despite the improbability of someone inserting the picture into her book, my intuition told me she wasn't lying. And yet, something was off. I'd sensed it before, on various occasions—something I could never quite put my finger on, like a bead of mercury slipping constantly out of reach. "What about this," I said, digging the letter I'd received the previous afternoon from my bag. I handed it to her, moving slowly so as not to aggravate the throbbing under my skull.

"I didn't write this," she said.

"It has your signature on it."

"I know, but that's not my writing. My writing's nothing like that." She glanced around the room, as if looking for something. "Wait; I'll show you." Jumping out of bed, she crossed to the closet and reached behind a stack of petticoats to retrieve a small key. Coming back to the bed she dropped to her hands and knees and pulled out a shallow, battered chest from beneath the frame. She unlocked it and propped it open, disappearing behind the lid.

"What's in there?" I asked, craning to see over the top.

Her face popped back into view. "Things I'm saving for Joy." She held up a shapeless pink garment with knitting needles stuck through it. "I'm making her a sweater. It'll be finished soon, and then I'll start on the hat. Do you think she'll like it?"

I tried to imagine Olivia Fiske wearing such a crude thing. Then I thought of all the hours Eliza must have spent on it, dreaming of their happy reunion, and it almost broke my heart. Suddenly, my doubts about her seemed absurd. This was no calculating, cold-hearted murderer kneeling before me. This woman could no more hack off someone's head or toss someone into a meat locker to die than I could.

She rummaged in the chest and popped back up again, holding a small, fabric-covered book. She opened it and held it out to me. "This is what my writing looks like."

I leafed through a few of the pages. They were covered with neat, round letters that slanted evenly to the right, very different from the peaked, backward-slanting writing on the letter. I looked up. "What is this?"

"It's the journal I'm keeping for Joy. Do you see the difference?"

"Yes, I do." I closed the book, and handed it back to her.

"You believe me, then?"

"I do believe you, Eliza."

She smiled, a grateful smile that contained both relief and forgiveness. She put away the book and key and came back to sit beside me. "But... if I didn't send it, who did? Why would somebody send you a letter pretending to be me?"

"I suppose because they knew I'd come if you asked," I said, returning the letter to my purse.

"Come here? But why?" she persisted, with no trace of guile.

"Someone was waiting for me when I got here. They pushed me into the meat cooler and locked me in."

"Good Lord!" she said, looking genuinely shocked. "How did you get out?"

"I didn't, not right away. I'm afraid your Mother got a nasty surprise when she opened up this morning. Fortunately she found me before any real harm was done."

"But I don't understand; why would anyone want to harm you?"

"My best guess is because the killer is worried I'm on to him."

Her eyes widened. "What do you mean? Have you found something?"

"I may have," I said, unsure how much to tell her. "I came across a list in Dr. Hauptfuhrer's files, which suggests that he arranged a number of adoptions besides your daughter's. I think the real murderer might be on it."

"You've found a list!" She grabbed my hands. "Is Joy on it? Do you know where she is?"

The yearning in her voice was so affecting that I found myself longing to tell her the truth, just to savor her reaction. Once again, however, prudence cautioned me to wait. "The list doesn't actually name names," I told her. "It's in a kind of code. I've been working on matching the letters on the list to names in local birth announcements."

"Maybe I could help," she said, gripping my hands in excitement.

"I don't think so," I said quickly; "not from here. But don't worry, I've already got some leads. And judging by what happened last night, I'd say I'm on the right track."

"I can't believe it," she said, fairly bouncing on the bed with glee; "I was beginning to think I'd never find her!" Her face suddenly fell. "But I didn't mean to put you in any danger." She looked me up and down with concern. "Shouldn't we call a doctor, to make sure you're all right?"

"I am a doctor," I reminded her. "And I'll be fine. I just need a little sleep."

"What about the police? Have you told them what happened?"

"I'm not sure that would be a good idea. They might assume that you did it."

"Me! But I was up here in the flat! How could they accuse me?"

I sighed. "I know, it's not fair, but I'm afraid that's what they'd do, all the same."

"I suppose you're right," she said bitterly. "Just like they've accused me of everything else. Still, I feel awful that you had to suffer on my account."

"Fortunately I'm no worse for wear," I said, with more bravado than I felt. "I'll just have to be a bit more careful in the future."

"I wish there was something I could do to make it up to you." Her face brightened. "Are you hungry? I could make you some breakfast, at least."

I was touched by her concern, hard-pressed now to see how I ever could have doubted her. But all I really wanted was to go home and sleep for a week, so I declined her offer and took my leave, assuring her I would let her know if I learned anything more.

IT WAS NEARLY 7:30 when I stepped back out onto the street. The bakery next door was already busy with people picking up their daily breads and pastries, while all along the block people were sweeping off their stoops or hurrying toward the Elevated trains. I took a deep breath, grateful to be alive. At just that moment, my gaze alighted on Simon's man, sitting on the stoop across the street with a newspaper spread over his knees. My contentment melted before a flame of righteous anger, fueled by the memory of my terrified flight down the street the night before.

"You, there!" I called, stalking across the street as best I could on my still unsteady legs. I noticed the man hadn't changed his clothes since I'd seen him last, and was sporting at least two days' growth of beard. I came to a halt in front of him. "My name is Genevieve Summerford. I'm Mrs. Miner's physician."

"Sure, I know who you are," he said, laying his newspaper down. "I didn't know you were inside, though. Mr. Shaw was here a while ago, looking for you. I told him I hadn't seen you."

"Mr. Shaw was here?" I asked, momentarily diverted by the news. "What did he want?"

"Beats me," he answered with a gap-toothed grin. "I just work here."

"Speaking of which," I retorted, my anger returning, "where were you last night? There was no one on watch at midnight, when I arrived."

"Say, now, that ain't true!" he said, losing the grin. "I was here at midnight on the dot."

I remembered now that it had actually been a few minutes before midnight when I arrived. "Well, then, where was the man who should have been on duty before you?" I demanded, seeking a new target for my anger.

"I guess he might have left a few minutes early," he said, dropping his gaze.

Just my luck, I thought; the one time Simon's watchman might have been of some use, he'd been off somewhere getting drunk or playing faro. "I don't think Mr. Shaw will be very pleased to hear it."

His gaze swung back to me. "Aw now, listen lady, you don't want to go telling Mr. Shaw that Joey took off early."

"Don't I? There's supposed to be someone out here watching the premises at all times. Mr. Shaw promised the judge."

"Now look," he pleaded, "Joey's my little brother. He don't mean to mess things up; he just ain't used to working a regular job. Mr. Shaw's been real good to us; I don't want to let him down. Please don't say anything. I swear to you, it won't happen again."

"I'll think about it," I muttered, finding it difficult to remain angry in the face of his frank appeal. "In the meantime, you'd better be sure that there's someone here at all times."

"I will Miss, I promise."

"What's your name, anyway?"

"Donald, Miss. Donald Kearny."

"Tell me, Mr. Kearny, did you see anyone go in or out of the shop last night, after you got here?"

"No, Miss, I didn't see a soul all night. It was quiet as a tomb."

"Quiet as a tomb, eh?" I repeated, remembering my desperate cries. "I don't suppose you might have shut your eyes for just a minute?"

His bristled chin jerked upward. "No Miss I did not," he answered fiercely.

I waved a conciliatory hand, too spent to wrangle with him any further. "All right, I was just asking. Good day, Mr. Kearny."

"Quiet as a tomb!" he called after me, as I turned and trudged up the street.

I was nearly at the intersection before I thought to wonder why Simon would have come looking for me at the crack of dawn. I hadn't told him I was going to Eliza's; I hadn't even had a chance to tell him about the letter. He couldn't have known I was coming, unless . . . .

I stopped short. Could Simon have written the letter, and pushed me into the locker? I remembered what my father had suggested, about Simon offering District Attorney Jerome some sort of carrot in exchange for the Saratoga gambling concern. Jerome—the same man who was prosecuting Eliza's case; the man who, according to Father, was thinking of running for Senate, and would want a quick conviction to assuage the voting public. I'd already had cause to question Simon's relationship with Maloney. Could they all be in this together somehow, using me as their pawn, trying, if not to kill me, then at least to scare me into turning on Eliza?

I tried to tell myself I was becoming delusional, but it didn't help; I was consumed by the devastating possibility that Simon might really hate me that much. A hansom cab rolled to a stop at the corner. I lunged toward it, calling to the cabbie to hold up. He opened the door and I threw myself inside, feeling as if the whole world had turned against me.

TO MY RELIEF Mary was the only one up and about when I got home, sweeping out the floor in the dining room. I tiptoed silently to the stairs and dragged myself up to my room, where I peeled off my damp coat and hat and collapsed onto the mattress. Never had a bed so engulfed me. I fell into a coma-like sleep, only to be awakened what seemed minutes later by an incessant pounding. I dragged the pillow over my head to try to shut out the noise.

"It's eleven o'clock, Miss," Mary called through the door. "Your mother says to ask if you're going to go with her today."

I heard her as if from the bottom of a deep well. "What?" I mumbled through the pillow.

"She says if you want to go, you'll need to be ready in half an hour."

I pulled the pillow off my head. "Go where?"

"Calling on Mrs. Fiske."

Dragging my mind back from the depths, I struggled to make sense of her words. It must be Lucille's receiving day; the day when guests from the ball would call on her, to thank her and congratulate her on her success.

"Miss?" queried Mary. "Did you hear?"

I sat up. Though my headache was gone, my limbs felt weak and my mind seemed incapable of sustained thought. Amid the buzz of half-formed beliefs and blurry suspicions that were whirling around in my brain, however, one thing stood out with relative clarity: Lucille Fiske had the most to gain from the Hauptfuhrers' deaths. Calling on her with my mother would give me an opportunity to question her again, and perhaps to determine if she had masterminded my recent ordeal. "Yes, Mary," I called back, "tell her I'll be right down. And Mary? Ask Katie to make me a pot of coffee, will you? Tell her to make it extra strong."

An hour later my mother and I were being shown into the Fiskes' sumptuous drawing room. Lucille rose from the sofa and floated over to kiss my mother's cheek. "Evelyn, how lovely to see you again. And Genevieve," she added with a nod. If she was surprised to see me alive, she didn't show it. "Do have a seat, won't you?"

We lowered ourselves onto two stiff-backed gondola chairs as Lucille settled back onto the deeply cushioned sofa. A polar bear hide stretched across the floor between us, head intact, eyes regarding me balefully. A full-length Sargent portrait on the wall behind Lucille captured our hostess in her famous tiara, wearing an enigmatic smile. She was wearing the same smile now, I realized, as we waited for the maids to finish refreshing the teapot and lay more logs on the fire.

"It's been too long since you paid me a visit," she said to Mamma when the maids were gone, leaning to pour the tea.

"I don't do much visiting anymore," my mother admitted.

"I hope that's going to change. You have a great deal to offer, Evelyn, and I for one would like to see much more of you." Her voice was perfectly modulated, her posture impeccable as she tipped the tea into three, gilt-edged cups. In her snug ribboned bodice and full Oriental sleeves, she looked like a delicate Chinese doll.

"Did you enjoy yourself at the ball?" she asked my mother, passing her one of the cups.

"Oh my goodness, yes," Mamma replied. "Immensely. I can't imagine how it could have been any finer. The flowers alone . . ." She shook her head. "I've never seen anything like it."

"And you, Genevieve?" Lucille said, handing me a cup. "Did you find the evening satisfactory?"

"It was indeed unique, in every way," I said, taking the tea.

Her smooth brow crinkled slightly. "Are you feeling all right, my dear? You look a little pale."

My mother turned to peer at me. "Oh no, I hope you're not coming down with something."

"I'm just a little tired." I looked back at Lucille. "I didn't sleep very well last night."

"Thinking about your patients, no doubt," she said, pouring some cream for Mamma. "Young women today are extraordinary, aren't they Evelyn? So ambitious, and ready to take on the world." She stirred some cream into her own tea and sat back. "But there's a danger in being overzealous, in Genevieve's line of work, especially."

"What danger is that?" I asked

She shrugged daintily. "Why, the tendency to become overly involved in the affairs of others, at the risk of one's own health."

I nearly choked on my Earl Grey. Though her words were innocuous enough, her eyes were as cold as the ice in Mrs. Braun's meat locker as she uttered them. Was she admitting that she'd locked me in the cooler? If so, it was a bold thing to do—and yet it made perfect sense. She'd want me to know that she had done it, to demonstrate the unhampered reach of her will. After all, if she could lock me in a meat cooler overnight with no one the wiser, what couldn't she do? The message seemed clear: accept her bribes and keep my nose out of her affairs, or suffer the consequences.

I glanced uneasily at the gilded French furniture and frescoed ceiling and grimacing polar bear at my feet. Lucille wanted me to believe that her wealth lifted her above both law and convention. I didn't want to credit it—but it was my own neck on the block. My cup landed noisily on its saucer, spilling tea onto the table.

"Genna!" exclaimed Mother. "Are you sure you're quite all right?"

"Shall I ring for some ice water?" Lucille asked helpfully.

"I'm fine," I said again, dabbing at the tea with a napkin. "I'm just a little clumsy this morning."

"Well, you didn't have any breakfast," Mother said reprovingly.

Lucille held up the pastry tray. "Perhaps a sweet would help."

Lord, she was cool. I'd never met anyone like her: a woman who knew what she wanted and was determined to get it, no matter who or what stood in her way. I didn't underestimate the damage she could do, to me or to my parents. But even as she mocked me with her false concern, I felt a thawing in some icy region of my heart at the growing conviction that neither Eliza nor Simon had been plotting against me.

"Aren't those darling," Mother murmured, leaning forward to examine the miniature cakes, which were decorated with gold leaf.

"Our pastry man thought them up, in honor of the Earl," Lucille said. "You see? It's in the shape of his family crest."

Mother clucked in admiration. "You've certainly treated the Earl handsomely during his stay. He must have been very impressed by the ball."

"We hope that he enjoyed himself," said Lucille, putting down the tray.

"Will he be in New York much longer?"

"Actually, no. He has a hankering to see the far West. The grizzlies and the cowboys, you know; the British can't get enough of them. We've arranged to bring him out in our private train car at the end of the week."

"You're leaving New York?" I blurted out in surprise.

"Why, yes, on Saturday."

"All of you?"

She raised an eyebrow at my ill-mannered inquisition, but replied, "We'll all go as far as Colorado Springs, so that Olivia and the Earl can spend more time together before the Earl goes buffalo hunting with Charles." She smiled at Mamma. "I understand the Antlers Hotel has become so popular with our overseas friends that they've dubbed it 'Little London'. Just seeing it is reason enough to make the trip."

But not the only reason, I was sure. It must have been extremely frustrating for Lucille to have her ball come and go, with no engagement announcement to show for it. No doubt she'd do everything she could to rectify that omission during their western sojourn.

"The Earl seemed very attentive to Olivia at the ball," Mother said, as though having the same thought. "Didn't you think so, Genevieve?"

"He struck me as very . . . courtly." I replied. "As one might expect of a man his age."

"Heavens, you make him sound positively rusty," Lucille said, with a tinkling little laugh.

"He is old enough to be her father."

"Old enough to make a mature and devoted husband, should Olivia choose to marry him," my mother said, arching an eyebrow at me in warning.

"Do you believe happiness is reserved for the young?" Lucille asked me.

"Of course not. But an older man is accustomed to living life as he pleases, and with whom he pleases. My concern is whether the Earl, after so many years of bachelorhood, would be capable of giving Olivia the understanding and support she needs—now, and in the future."

"My dear Miss Summerford," said Lucille, putting down her cup, "a husband is not a girlfriend or a priest. Olivia has her friends and family to confide in. A distinguished man like Branard can give her other things: a title, an estate, a prominence in short that she could never achieve in a common marriage."

Whether it was Huntington's Chorea, or some other ailment afflicting Olivia, I'd heard and seen enough to know that she wasn't well. Was it possible Lucille hadn't considered the possibility that her daughter would soon be too ill to enjoy whatever shallow pleasures a title would confer? Or did she simply choose to live in a world of make-believe, convincing herself that Olivia was going to be all right? "Don't you think that given Olivia's . . . delicate constitution, something more may be required?"

She eased back against the sofa. "You're a romantic, I see."

"I'd call myself more of a realist," I said shortly. "Reality may not always be pleasant, but I believe it should be confronted head on."

"Genevieve!" my mother admonished.

"Oh, I don't mind," said Lucille with a little wave of her hand. "The young are entitled to strong opinions. They have plenty of time to change them."

"You're very understanding," my mother said, setting my teeth on edge. I couldn't bear the ease with which Lucille had taken her in thrall.

"Speaking of the young, Evelyn dear, I have a favor to ask you," Lucille went on, deftly changing the subject. "Sally Courtlandt is having her annual skating party on Friday night. It's gotten more difficult for her to manage, what with her rheumatism, and she's asked me to help round up some chaperones. I thought if you weren't busy, you might like to come. It should be an entertaining crowd—I understand Louise Bouchard is in town with her daughter and will be stopping by. You used to hunt with her at her place in Millbrook, didn't you? I've even got a spare pair of skates, if you'd like to take a turn on the ice."

My mother's hand fluttered to her throat. I waited for her to refuse, as she always did on the rare occasions when people still sought to include her.

"I can't remember the last time I was on skates," she said.

"Good! Then I won't be the only one making a fool of myself," Lucille said with a smile. "Just tell me you'll come, and my job will be done."

"All right, I'll come," said Mother, smiling back at her. "But won't it be too much for you to go, when you're leaving town the very next day?"

Lucille's lips twitched. "To tell you the truth, I wasn't planning on attending. We're all a bit wrung out, from so much entertaining. Olivia, especially, is feeling the strain, as you might imagine. But the Earl is eager to attend. It seems he's never been on ice skates before."

"That will make three of us, then, sitting on the ice," Mother said with a laugh.

Lucille glanced toward the front window as an elegant four-in-hand rolled up to the door. "There's Minerva Penniman," she said, clapping her hands expectantly. "I was hoping she'd come; I'm not going to let her leave until she's told me how much she's paying her new chef." She winked at Mamma. "I intend to steal him for my next party."

Mother rose to her feet with a smile. "We'll leave you to it, then."

Lucille rose as well and, slipping her arm around my mother's elbow, walked us to the door. "I was hoping you might prepare a preliminary design for the new garden while I'm away," she suggested to Mamma. "That way we can meet with the landscapers as soon as I get back."

"I've already come up with a few ideas," Mamma confessed. "I hope you'll like them."

"I'm sure I will. Oh, by the way—I put in a word with Charles about your husband's mechanical lung. I wouldn't be surprised if he decides to fully fund the project."

To my amazement, my mother seized her in a heartfelt embrace. "Thank you, Lucille. You've done so much, for all of us. I don't know how we can ever repay you."

"Don't be silly," Lucille said. Her eyes met mine over my mother's shoulder. "Helping each other is what friends do."

CHAPTER TWENTY-FIVE

The sidewalk in front of the Fifth Avenue Hotel was empty the next morning when my electric auto-cab rolled up to the curb, except for a bespectacled gentleman standing just outside the hotel entrance. The man had a pointy white mustache and trim goatee, and was holding a medical bag. I guessed from the way he huddled near the door, clasping his hat to his head, that the wind was whipping up past the prow of the Flatiron Building with its usual ferocity, buffeting everything in its path.

I opened the cab door and leaned out. "Dr. Huntington?"

He came toward me, lifting his hat from a head of fine white hair. "Dr. Summerford, I presume."

I shook his hand. Though his grip was firm, he looked frail to me, as though he'd recently been ill. "Do come up and get out of the cold."

He stepped up into the vehicle and eased himself onto the worn leather seat beside me. His movements were calm and unhurried, suggesting someone who'd seen too much of life to give the next minute any more importance than the present one.

"I apologize for getting you up at such an early hour," I said, "but it was the only time I could arrange to have you see Mrs. Miner in private."

"It's quite all right; I'm accustomed to waking early. I don't like the day to go to waste."

I smiled, liking him already. "I can't thank you enough for agreeing to see her. It's extremely important that we get a reliable diagnosis. The outcome of Mrs. Miner's trial could depend on it."

He steadied his medical bag on his lap as the snub-nosed cab pulled out into the light morning traffic. I noticed that his ungloved fingers were long and fine, the sort of fingers one would expect to see on a surgeon, rather than on a country doctor.

"Perhaps you could tell me a little more about your patient, and the accusations against her," he said.

I explained why Eliza had been referred to my class, and told him the details of her arrest, and that the prosecution was claiming she was suffering dementia caused by Huntington's Chorea. "Although I don't believe she's showing the symptoms you describe in your monograph, I can't be absolutely sure," I explained. "That's why I've been so anxious to meet with you."

"I understand. I'm sorry I couldn't come sooner, but I had just returned home when your telegram arrived. I've been in North Carolina, recuperating from a lung condition, and I had to take care of some business before I could leave home again. Let me ask you this: what was it that led the prosecution to suspect Huntington's Chorea in the first place?"

"The police found a copy of the letter Dr. Hauptfuhrer sent to you, asking you to confirm his diagnosis of Mrs. Miner. I assume you received the original?"

"Not soon enough to be of any assistance, I'm afraid. It was forwarded to me in North Carolina, but didn't reach me until after the doctor's death."

"You never talked to him about Mrs. Miner, then, or made any tentative diagnosis based on his observations?"

"I never had the opportunity."

So if Hauptfuhrer had conveyed his suspicions about Olivia to Lucille Fiske, I concluded with relief, he'd done it without any encouragement from Dr. Huntington. "Unfortunately the detective on the case, a man named Maloney, has convinced himself not only that Mrs. Miner is suffering the mental impairment that Dr.

Hauptfuhrer referred to in his letter, but that it caused her to commit the murder. I'm hoping that your examination will change his mind."

He nodded. "Detective Maloney came to my home, while I was gone. According to my housekeeper he was very keen on questioning me about Dr. Hauptfuhrer's patient. I contacted him after I received your telegram, to let him know I'd be coming to the city to examine her. He's asked me to meet with him this afternoon to discuss the results."

I supposed I should have known the detective would catch up with the doctor eventually. I reminded myself that if everything turned out as I expected, the meeting could only go in Eliza's favor. "You should know that there's been another murder since then," I informed him. "Dr. Hauptfuhrer's daughter was decapitated in her home, four days ago."

"Good God!"

"Mrs. Miner was under house arrest at the time, with guards standing watch over the premises around the clock. They've found nothing at all to connect her to the second crime. But the detective is determined to pin that one on her as well. He's fully expecting you to confirm not only that she has the disease, but that she likely killed both Hauptfuhrers because of it."

He sighed, and shook his head. "It never ceases to amaze me how intolerant people are of what they don't understand. There is no reason to assume that a victim of Huntington's Chorea, especially in the early stages, is any more likely to commit a crime than the next person. These people need our help, not our suspicion."

"So you don't think the disease could drive a person with no previous criminal inclination to commit a murder?"

He turned to look at me. His clear gray eyes were penetrating, but not unkind. "Murderers, Dr. Summerford, come in all shapes and sizes. If a murderer was short, we would not conclude that all short people are murderers. If he had a limp, we would not say that the limp caused the murder. Nor would this disease, I believe, of itself create a murderous tendency in someone who did not already possess it."

"Have you ever personally known a victim of this type of chorea who did commit a murder? Or any other violent crime?"

"No, I don't believe I have. Which is not to say they can't become physically aggressive in the advanced stages of the disease. I've seen patients push or strike their family members when they're upset. They're like children, you see; they want everything now, and are apt to react with a tantrum if they don't get it. But for an otherwise moral and law abiding citizen to be so transformed by the disease as to intentionally kill another human being?" He shook his head. "It strikes me as extremely unlikely." He paused to cough into his hand.

I thought of all the people with this disease he must have tended to over the years, and of the suffering he must have witnessed. "I can't imagine what it must be like," I murmured.

"To have the disorder, you mean? That's what they call it, you know, 'the disorder'. Whole families of them, affected generation after generation. I'll never forget the first time I saw it. I was just a young boy, driving with my father on his rounds, when we passed two women walking on the Amagansett road. They were thin as cadavers, bowing and twisting in the most unnatural way. I couldn't stop staring when my father slowed the carriage to bid them good day. I was horrified when he told me later there was nothing he could do for them. I determined then and there to dedicate my life to conquering the disease." He sighed, shaking his head. "Unfortunately, it has proved to be a more stubborn adversary than I anticipated."

We arrived at the Brauns' building a little after seven o'clock, to find Eliza waiting for us alone inside the flat. I introduced her to the doctor and we each took a seat at the small kitchen table. Eliza looked apprehensively from me to the doctor.

"Don't worry," the doctor told her; "none of the tests I'm going to perform are the least bit painful or intrusive, I promise." Pointing to his medical bag he added with a smile, "This is just for show." He stowed the bag under his seat, then asked, "I wonder, Mrs. Miner, if you might bring me a glass of water before we start."

"Of course." She fetched a glass from the cupboard, then filled it and carried it back to him. I noticed he was watching her closely the entire time.

"Thank you," he said, taking a sip. "And now, since you're already up, why don't we begin by having you walk back over to the door there, touching your heel to your toe with each step."

She did as he asked, evidencing no difficulty with the maneuver. "Like that?" she asked over her shoulder.

"Like that exactly. Now if you would just stand there for a moment, with your eyes closed and your heels together. Excellent. All right, you can come sit down."

When she was seated he asked her to recite the months of the year, then instructed her to tap her thumbs and forefingers together. He stuck his tongue rapidly in and out, eliciting laughter from his subject, and asked her to do the same. Raising his hat high above his head, he told her to look from his nose to the hat, then spread his empty hands apart and had her look from thumb to thumb. I couldn't see anything unusual in any of her responses—but then, I didn't know what to look for.

Finally he smiled and sat back. "There. That wasn't so bad, was it?"

"You mean we're finished?" she asked.

"We're finished."

I sat up straighter in my chair.

"Well, am I . . . am I all right?" Eliza asked.

"I wish I were in as good health."

"You mean she doesn't have it?" I asked.

"She shows none of the usual indicators."

I turned to Eliza, and saw my own relief magnified in her eyes. I reached out impulsively and gave her a hug.

"Does this mean that the detective will have to leave me alone?" Eliza asked breathlessly when I had released her.

"Knowing Maloney, I wouldn't count on it," I said. "But it should certainly take some steam out of the prosecution's case."

Dr. Huntington rose and put on his hat. "I'll convey the results of my exam to the detective personally, when I see him this afternoon. Of course, I'm only one doctor, but I don't think he'll find anyone to controvert my opinion."

"I should say not," I agreed, rising alongside him. Not even Maloney would be foolish enough to insist Eliza had Huntington's Chorea, if Dr. Huntington himself declared that she didn't.

The doctor retrieved his bag from under his chair and we all walked to the front door. "Goodbye, Mrs. Miner," he said. "Please tell your attorney that I'd be happy to testify on your behalf, if he thinks it would help."

"Thank you, I will."

"I'll walk you out," I told him. I gave Eliza another hug, telling her I'd be back soon, then accompanied the doctor out of the building. I practically skipped out onto the sidewalk, so happy I even smiled and nodded at Simon's man, on the stoop. He nodded back, tipping his cap.

The doctor offered me his elbow and I fell into step beside him, moving at a much more dignified pace than I could have managed just then on my own. "Are you absolutely certain?" I asked him.

"As certain as it's possible to be."

"How can you tell? What exactly were you looking for in there?"

"Over the years I've noticed a number of indicators that crop up in the early and middle stages of the disease. They may not all be present in a particular case, but I always see at least some."

"What are they, exactly?"

"The most obvious, of course, would be any choreic movements of the hands and feet, along with the typical gait abnormalities, and slurring of speech. But if those aren't present I have to look for more subtle signs. A very low body weight can be a clue, although it's not always present initially. To look for early interference with voluntary muscle movement and balance, I'll ask the patient to walk heel-to-toe across the room, as you saw, or manipulate her tongue and fingers."

"Why did you ask her to recite the months of the year?"

"If you listen to the speech of a person with this type of chorea, you'll notice that they have difficulty sustaining their vowels. The names of the months include all of the vowel sounds, so I use them for convenience. Recently I've observed that many of my patients have unusual eye movements, as well. Their eyes seem to travel more slowly than is normal between objects, making little stops along the way, especially when they're looking up. They also tend to blink excessively, and to move their head along with their eyes when they're tracking something. But Mrs. Miner had no difficulty looking from my nose to my hat, or fixing her gaze on an object for an extended period of time."

"I had no idea there were so many clear signs," I said, shaking my head, "and I thought I'd covered all the literature. You must think me terribly uninformed."

"Nonsense, my dear. It's not in the literature. This disease isn't widely recognized, let alone well documented. It's my fault, I suppose. I've always meant to publish more, and to share what I've observed. But . . ." he finished with a shrug, ". . . life has a way of intruding on one's plans."

"What about the hand motions and facial grimacing I read about in the reports?" I said, wanting to be sure we'd left no stone unturned. "I have seen Mrs. Miner wring her hands, on occasion. And her lips twitch at times, especially when she's upset."

"I'd suspect those are more signs of a nervous disposition, possibly a compulsion, than symptoms of this disease. In the early stages of chorea you're more apt to notice a general clumsiness of the hands and feet, and only minimal involvement of the facial muscles. The writhing and grimacing come a bit later, when the muscle contractions are too severe for the patient to suppress by voluntary action."

I nodded, delighted to cross another concern off my list. "Her mother says she's also prone to forgetfulness and changes of mood," I added, in the interests of full disclosure, "although I can't believe that those things alone would support a diagnosis."

"I'm afraid that the mental aspects of the disease are even less well documented than the physical ones," he told me. "It does appear that the range and progression of symptoms vary considerably among patients. But it's a far cry from a lapse of memory, to the mental derangement that would induce a person to commit murder. Absent any physical signs, I'd have to assign Mrs. Miner's psychical symptoms to another cause."

I was trying hard to remain objective, although by now I felt I was floating several feet above the ground. "Of course, she is only thirty-five," I cautioned, releasing his arm as we reached the intersection. "I suppose it's possible that she could start showing symptoms later on."

He turned to face me. "It's highly unlikely that she'd be completely symptom-free at this point if she had the disease. Especially if her father is the suspected carrier, as you've mentioned. Three generations of my family have administered to these afflicted souls, Doctor, and our combined case records have yielded some very interesting statistics. One curious thing I've discovered is that when the disease is passed by the father, the offspring show the symptoms at an earlier age than when they receive it on the maternal side. I was inclined to dismiss this as coincidence at first, but recently other researchers—Hoffman and Curschman, to name just two—have remarked on it as well. Now the more I look for it, the more I see it. Not only does the disease appear earlier with paternal transmission, but it progresses more rapidly and with more severe symptoms. Hoffman noticed something else, which my own records support: if the disease is passed by males in successive generations, the onset will occur progressively earlier."

"You mean, the victims will be younger and younger, in each generation?"

"Precisely."

"Why should that be?"

He shook his head. "I wish I knew. Like so many other things about this disease, it leaves me baffled."

"But—based on your understanding, if Eliza had inherited the disease from her father, she would definitely be showing symptoms by now?"

"That is my considered opinion, yes."

If only Dr. Hauptfuhrer had waited to hear these same words! Instead he had panicked, and run to Lucille with his worst fears, costing him and his daughter their lives. "I never really believed that she had it," I gushed, riding a fresh wave of relief. "It was just that Olivia seemed so clumsy at the ball, and then there was that story about her falling, and it was all just so odd and unexplained that I started to think it must be related in some way . . ."

"I'm sorry; I don't remember you mentioning anyone named Olivia."

I realized that if he'd never communicated with Dr. Hauptfuhrer, he couldn't know about Eliza's daughter. "She's Mrs. Miner's illegitimate daughter—although I'll have to ask you to keep that in confidence, as it isn't generally known. Dr. Hauptfuhrer attended Olivia's birth, and arranged for her to be adopted. I think he came to believe that the daughter had inherited Huntington's Chorea, and intended to warn her once you'd confirmed that her mother was ill."

"I see," the doctor said. "And how old is the child now?"

"She just turned twenty."

"And you say she's been acting clumsily?"

I told him what I'd personally witnessed on the night of the ball, along with what Bartie had related. "But of course she's far too young to be manifesting the signs of chorea. And her movements are stiff, rather than rolling or writhing. Stiff and slow. Almost forced."

"You say her hand seemed to jerk toward the glass when she knocked it over," he repeated, stroking his goatee.

"Yes, I saw it quite clearly."

"What about her speech? Do the vowels seem to fall short?"

"Well, I didn't speak to her at any length. I do remember thinking she sounded a little . . . flat, but I assume she was just feeling a bit downcast, because of her situation. She's being courted by a titled foreigner, you see, and everyone around her has been holding their breath, waiting for him to propose."

"Curious. I'd love to have a look at her sometime, if I could."

"But she can't be affected," I said in surprise. "You said yourself, the disease never skips a generation."

"It never has, to my knowledge. I'd be interested in taking a look, all the same."

"I'm afraid that would be difficult to arrange. She doesn't have any idea of Dr. Hauptfuhrer's suspicions. Although I suppose, if you wanted to observe her from afar, you could go by the lake in Central Park tomorrow evening. Olivia will be attending a skating party there;

I believe it starts at six o'clock. You could watch her from the bank, and no one would be the wiser."

"Perhaps I will, if I'm not otherwise engaged." He smiled ruefully. "That's one of the privileges of getting older: having the time and freedom to satisfy one's idle curiosity."

He looked tired as he said this, despite his smile, and I took it as my cue to say goodbye. "Thank you again for coming, so very, very much," I said, shaking his hand. "You may very well have saved Mrs. Miner's life."

"It's always a pleasure to deliver good news."

I watched him cross Third Avenue, feeling the weight on my shoulders lighten by half. He was clearly a man of integrity, and I was hopeful that he'd be able to make Maloney accept the truth, no matter how little the detective wanted to hear it. I would go see Maloney myself after they had met, and see if he was ready to consider another suspect. With Lucille planning to leave the city on Saturday, and Eliza's grand jury trial apt to be called at any moment, I couldn't afford to wait any longer. It was time to lay everything I had learned—along with Hagan's pen and ink jar—on the table.

CHAPTER TWENTY-SIX

The 23rd Precinct station house on East 88th Street was a plain brick building with bars across the lower windows and a mixed fleet of bicycles, motorcycles and patrol wagons parked out front. I followed the doorman through the bustling booking area, nervous as a hen in a fox's den, keenly aware that the information I was about to divulge could be used against Eliza if the detective saw fit. I could only hope that his earlier meeting with Dr. Huntington had cracked his mind open to new possibilities.

The doorman led me into a room in the back, where a half-dozen clerks were clacking away on typewriters. The wall behind them was covered nearly end to end with photographs of what I assumed were wanted and convicted felons. Through open doors in the hallway on my right I could see uniformed men hunched over piles of files and official looking forms. The doorman led me in the opposite direction, past the washrooms and a janitorial closet, around the corner into a truncated hall. A single door opened off of this. The doorman rapped on it and announced, "You've got a visitor," then retreated back down the hall, leaving me standing in the doorway.

Peering around the frame, I saw Detective Maloney seated at a small desk under an unshaded electric light.

"Well, well, look who's here," he said, sitting back in his chair.

"Good afternoon, Detective." I glanced around the room. The desk, two chairs, and some hard-used file drawers were the only furnishings. There were no framed clippings on the walls, commemorating promotions or notable arrests; no plaques honoring years of service or involvement in charitable activities. The only item on the walls at all, aside from a calendar advertising Pope Military Bicycles, was a faded photograph of a man in an old-fashioned, double-breasted police uniform. The subject was an older, fleshier version of Maloney, with the same humorless mouth, and eyes that seemed to be challenging the camera. I guessed he was Maloney's father, the man Simon suggested had been murdered by his own peers because of his refusal to participate in graft.

"If you're here to gloat, you can just turn right around," the detective said.

"I'm not here to gloat," I said, crossing the few feet to his desk. "I'm here to give you evidence."

Surprise flared in his sunken eyes.

"That's what you wanted from me, wasn't it?" I asked, settling onto the chair across from him. "Evidence to help you convict the murderer? Well, I'm here to give it to you." There were stacks of file folders and arrest reports and Bertillon cards piled on both sides of the small desk. Taking Dr. Hauptfuhrer's list from my bag, I laid it in the narrow space between them and slid it toward him. "Starting with this."

He picked it up, frowning at me with suspicion, and flipped through the pages. "This don't look like psychological records to me."

"It's not. It's a list of babies that Dr. Hauptfuhrer delivered in secret, over a period of twenty-three years."

He cocked a rust-colored eyebrow. "Hauptfuhrer delivered babies?"

"In secret," I said again. "Apparently, he took them from mothers who didn't want them or were told they couldn't keep them, and sold them to barren women of means."

He flipped back to the beginning and scanned the pages more slowly. "Where'd you get this?"

"From the doctor's filing cabinet. I went back to his office, after the murder."

His head snapped up. "You're telling me you stole this from the crime scene?"

I shrugged. "Somebody had to try to find out the truth," I replied, with more nonchalance than I was feeling.

"Do you realize I can have you thrown into jail for—"

"Yes, yes, I know, Detective," I broke in with a sigh, "but why don't you at least let me tell you what I've discovered, before you throw another innocent person into jail?"

He scowled at me, tossing the list onto the desktop. "All right, let's hear it. But this better be good."

I explained first how the list worked, leaning across the desk to point to the various columns. Next I told him about the birth announcements I'd located in the newspapers, identifying some of the prominent families who were on it.

"So what about it?" he asked when I was done. "Are you saying this had something to do with the doctor's murder?"

"Come now, Detective, you're an intelligent man," I said, sitting back. "Surely you can figure it out."

"Why don't you spell it out for me," he drawled.

"Every person on that list had a secret that Dr. Hauptfuhrer could have revealed, which means that every one of them had a potential motive to kill him. Now that you know Eliza doesn't have Huntington's Chorea, you have no grounds to assert that she killed the doctor in some sort of irrational fit. That being the case, I respectfully suggest you consider the possibility that someone else committed the crime."

He looked down at the list, tapping his pencil against the desktop. "And you're suggesting I question everybody on this list?"

I sat up straighter, sensing a breach in his resistance. "That won't be necessary; I've already narrowed down the field for you." Taking a deep breath, I told him everything: that Lucille had adopted Eliza's illegitimate daughter, and was set on her marrying an Earl; and that Hauptfuhrer had believed the girl had an incurable disease and had been planning to tell the potential bridegroom. I told him about

Lucille's threatening behavior toward me after I quizzed her on her relationship with Dr. Hauptfuhrer, and about Hagan's suspicious departure. I even told him about being thrown into the meat locker, and Lucille's veiled admission to me afterward. He listened without interruption, his chin propped on one fist, his eyes darting over his knuckles with each new revelation.

"You realize you just gave Mrs. Miner a reason to kill the doctor," he said when I was done. "If he took her baby, she would have had it in for him."

"I gave you a lot more than that," I retorted. "Even if you could explain why Eliza would kill the only person who could help her locate her daughter—not to mention why she'd wait twenty years to do it—she had no reason to kill Miss Hauptfuhrer, or to try to kill me. Lucille, on the other hand, would need to silence all three of us to ensure that her secret remained safe."

He mulled this over, his pencil tapping more rapidly on the desktop.

"There's more," I said. I extracted the bundle from my purse and placed it before him, unfolding the handkerchief corners to reveal the pen and inkwell inside. "I took these from Hagan's desk."

He bent for a closer look. The light from the overhead fixture threw his eye sockets into shadow, accentuating the gauntness of his face. For the first time I noticed the lines of fatigue that ran down the sides of his nose, and the hair that straggled over his ears, badly in need of a cut. Detective Maloney, it struck me, did not lead an easy life. As he reached for the handkerchief I saw that his nails were bitten to the quick, and that he wore no wedding ring. Seeing him in this barren little cubicle, set apart from his fellow officers, with nothing but piles of files to keep him company, I had a sudden, visceral understanding of the lonely life he'd carved out for himself after his father's death.

He pulled the items toward him by a corner of the handkerchief. "Did you touch them?"

I shook my head.

He contemplated the nest of potential evidence, rubbing his chin. "Why would Hauptfuhrer tell Mrs. Fiske her daughter was sick, if he never got confirmation?"

"I expect he thought a wedding announcement was imminent. He was probably hoping she'd postpone it until a definite diagnosis could be made. Whatever you might think of Hauptfuhrer's illicit activities, he seems to have been a man of some conscience. He understood that the disease was hereditary, and believed that if Olivia was afflicted the Earl should be informed."

I waited while he mulled this over.

"The Fiskes are leaving town on Saturday," I prompted, when several more moments had passed. "If you're going to question them you'll need to do it soon."

He continued to frown down at the list in silence, still rubbing his chin. I felt a fresh wave of anxiety. He *had* to agree to investigate the Fiskes. There was no other way to prove Eliza's innocence. Catching a glimpse of the photograph over his shoulder, I had a sudden inspiration. "I understood that the Maloneys were men of honor," I said.

He looked up sharply, as if suspecting my words held a hidden taunt.

I nodded toward the picture on the wall. "It's what he'd tell you to do, isn't it? Make sure that no stone is left unturned?" He looked at the picture in surprise, then back at me. From the expression on his face, I could tell I'd hit a bulls-eye. "If I'm right," I went on, "and you don't investigate, an innocent woman could go to the electric chair." I held his gaze, willing him to concede, knowing that if this didn't work I had nothing left in my bag of tricks.

He let out his breath in a slow hiss. "All right," he said finally, "I'll have them dusted for prints."

Relief sapped my limbs. "Can you do it today?"

He flipped open his watch. "I suppose I could get them there in time."

"What about comparing the prints to the ones on the sword?" I pressed. "Can that be done today, as well?"

He grimaced. "We got a little thing called procedure, for evidence in custody," he said sourly. "But I should probably have an answer by late tomorrow."

I stood up, hardly able to contain my excitement. "Could you let me know as soon as you find out? You can telephone me at my home." I wrote the number on a scrap of paper and handed it to him. He pocketed it without a word.

I impulsively held out my hand. "Thank you."

He didn't take it. "Don't get me wrong. My money's still on Mrs. Miner."

I let my arm drop. "Don't worry, Detective. I wasn't about to accuse you of having a heart."

I RETRACED MY steps down the maze of corridors and out of the building, feeling as though I had just moved a mountain. With the lab checking the fingerprints, and the police investigating the Fiskes' activities, Eliza's vindication might only be a few days away. After everything I'd been through, I felt I finally had some cause for celebration, and I was eager to share my news.

But not just with anyone, I admitted to myself as I drew up at the end of the block. I wanted to share it with Simon. I looked down the avenue, toward his saloon. My fear that he might have pushed me into the meat locker had been banished by Lucille's behavior during my visit with Mamma, and I felt badly, once again, for having doubted him. I longed to tell him about Eliza's clean bill of health, and let him see I'd been right to believe in her.

As if of their own accord, my feet turned south toward the Isle of Plenty. After all, Simon deserved to know what had happened, after everything he'd done to help keep Eliza out of prison. I owed it to him to keep him informed. While I was at it, I could ask him why he'd been asking for me on the morning of my captivity, and put that little mystery to rest.

When I arrived at the saloon a few minutes later, however, Simon wasn't there. A man eating fried potatoes at the counter told me he was at a "relo" on 95th Street, by the river. As I had no pressing

engagements—and as by now my heart was quite set on seeing him—
I decided to look for him there. I left the saloon and turned in the
direction the man had indicated, unsure of my precise destination. As
it turned out, I needn't have worried; I saw Simon the moment I
stepped onto the block in question, sitting on a heap of furniture and
bric-a-brac stacked in the middle of the sidewalk.

I stopped, transfixed by the sight. He was leaning back over a
faded carpet that had been thrown on top of the haphazard pile, his
knees bent over a battered bureau underneath, popping peanuts into
his mouth as he chatted with a man in a woolen cap who was
standing on the sidewalk beside him. A stout woman in a red
headkerchief sat on an overturned bucket at the man's feet, clutching
a small box to her chest and watching three little boys pitch pennies
against the nearby stoop.

A *relocation*; that's what the man in the saloon had meant. These
people were being evicted. One saw it every now and then: a family
turned out onto the street with all their possessions, regardless of the
season or time of day. I hesitated, wondering if I should wait to speak
with him another time, when he looked up and saw me. Straightening
my hat, I continued to the foot of the pile.

"What are you doing here?" he asked when I was within earshot.

It was hardly the warm greeting I'd been secretly hoping for. I
smiled up at him uncertainly. "I heard you were looking for me."

"Who told you that?"

"Your man, Donald Kearney. He told me you came looking for
me at Eliza's yesterday morning."

There was no mistaking the surprise that flashed across his eyes.
He hesitated for a full two beats before saying, "You must have
misunderstood him. I did stop by, but only to ask if he'd seen anyone
go in or out during the night."

He was lying; I was sure of it. I stared at him in dismay, not
wanting to believe what my eyes and ears were telling me. I'd been
convinced, after my last chat with Lucille, that it was she who'd
arranged my ordeal in the meat locker. But if that was true, why
wouldn't Simon want me to know that he'd been asking for me at the
shop? The only reason I could think of was that he'd gone there to

determine whether I'd escaped from my imprisonment during the night. "Do you make a habit of stopping by the Braun's shop at the crack of dawn?"

He must have heard the edge in my question, because his own tone was terse as he replied, "A woman had her head chopped off a few days ago, and the possible perpetrator is out of prison because of me. It seems to me the least I can do is check on her whereabouts, now and then."

How I wanted to believe him. If he'd just admitted that he'd been asking for me, and given some plausible explanation, I would happily have done so. But Kearney had no reason to lie to me, while Simon . . . I bit my lip, trying to see past the boy I'd known, into the mind of the man before me, and divine his true intentions.

"All right," he said gruffly, glancing across the street, "I told you I haven't been looking for you, so you can be on your way."

I wasn't going anywhere, I decided. Not until I knew what he was playing at. "We need to talk."

"Now's not a good time," he said, looking back across the street. "I'm busy."

Following his gaze, I saw a handful of men chatting idly on the opposite sidewalk. Except for the men, and a boy riding his bicycle at the end of the street, the block was empty. "Oh yes, I can see how busy you are," I retorted.

"Why don't you wait for me at the saloon," he said, with ill-concealed impatience. "I'll come back as soon as I'm finished here."

Why was he so eager to get rid of me? "I think I'll just wait here," I said, crossing my arms.

If looks could kill, I would have been lying face-down on the sidewalk. "If you won't leave," he muttered, "you'd better come up here, where you'll be out of the way."

I looked around the empty street in amazement. "Out of the way? Of what?"

"Just come or go," he snapped.

"Fine." Lifting my skirt with one hand, I climbed up a rolled mattress at the back of the pile and picked my way over a lamp and a protruding pair of table legs to sit beside him. "My, isn't this comfy," I said, patting something hard and lumpy beneath me.

"You can leave anytime."

I glared at him. "What are you doing up here, anyway?"

"The Longobardis have been evicted. They're waiting for a cart to pick up their things."

"And you're playing King of the Hill while they wait?"

"I'm keeping the wolves at bay," he said, jerking his head toward the opposite sidewalk.

I looked again at the rag-tag group of men that was assembled there. This time, I noticed the assorted implements that were dangling from the men's hands: a bat; a stick; what looked like pieces of steel pipe. I swallowed. "What do they want?"

"You're sitting on it," he answered, popping another peanut into his mouth.

I stared at him. "Do you mean they think they can just walk over here and take things that don't belong to them?"

He shrugged. "They're hungry. Hunger makes a man mean."

I felt a prickle up the nape of my neck. I wished now I had taken his advice and gone to wait in the saloon. I ran my hands over the edge of the carpet, searching for something underneath with which to defend myself.

"Just sit there and look charming," he said in a low voice. "You don't want them to think you're afraid."

This was not an easy instruction to follow. I did my best however, imitating his relaxed pose, and even forcing a brittle smile. "How long have they been there?" I asked between clenched teeth.

"About ten minutes."

"What do you suppose they're doing?"

"Getting up their nerve."

"What happens when they . . ." I stopped, sensing him stiffen. Looking back across the street, I saw that the men had started toward us, led by a bent-nosed man swinging a short length of pipe.

Simon handed me the bag of peanuts. Peeling off his coat, he stood and straddled the top of the pile. "Gentlemen, you're just in time," he called. "The cart will be here any minute, and we can surely use your help."

"We'll help you, all right," snickered the man with the pipe, as the group formed a ragged half circle around us. "We'll help take this junk off your hands."

Mrs. Longobardi grabbed the boys and pulled them against her as her husband started toward the men, muttering in Italian.

"No, Gianni," Simon said sharply; "stay there." He turned to me. "You too. Don't move unless I tell you to, and keep your trap shut. Understand?"

I nodded emphatically.

He jumped off the pile and landed neatly as a cat on the sidewalk, facing the leader with his legs splayed and his arms hanging loosely at his sides. "I'm afraid I can't let you do that," he said, sounding genuinely sorry. "I promised these people I'd deliver them and their belongings safely to new lodgings."

The ringleader came a step closer, slapping the pipe against his palm. "Maybe you shouldn't make promises you can't keep."

Simon didn't budge. "I never do."

I was too frightened to move, unable to look away from the beating that was about to ensue. Whatever Simon might have done to pay me back for my past transgressions, I didn't want to see him hurt.

The gang leader raised his pipe and lunged forward. I cringed, knowing it would be impossible for Simon to get out of range in time, waiting in horror for the pipe to connect with his skull. Instead of moving back, however, Simon stepped forward, straight into the man's chest. Quick as a snake, his left arm shot up and wound around the man's raised bicep, yanking it down. At the same instant his right elbow came up and slammed into the man's chin. The elbow struck a second time, and then a third, until the pipe fell with a clatter onto the street. Shoving the man back, Simon crouched to retrieve it and came up swinging. The pipe smashed against the man's ear, dropping him like a stone.

Simon straightened, waving the pipe aloft. "Anybody else?" he asked.

The other men shifted on their feet, a few of them backing up a step, none of them willing to meet his gaze.

"All right, then," said Simon, throwing the pipe to the ground. "I still need to move this pile. I'll pay any man that helps a dollar, on the spot."

A murmur rose up from the group. For men like these, I knew, a dollar would cover half a week's rent. They looked from Simon to their fallen leader, loyalty clashing with hunger in their dull eyes.

"You'd better get him out of the street," Simon said. He gestured toward me. "Why don't you bring him up on the sidewalk, where the good doctor here can take a look at him."

Two of them crossed to the downed man and dragged him over by the armpits, as I slid off the pile to tend to him.

Simon turned back to the others. "So how about it, gentlemen? I'll even throw in an extra dollar for your injured comrade there, just so there'll be no hard feelings."

This apparently squared the deal in the men's minds. A bat dropped to the street and rolled over the paving stones, followed in short order by the rest of the makeshift weapons.

Raising his thumb and finger to his mouth, Simon turned and whistled to a cart parked halfway down the block. A young boy was at the reins. He must have arrived during the altercation, and been waiting until it was safe to approach. "All right, Tim, bring her in," Simon called.

The boy steered the cart up alongside the pile.

"You, there," Simon said, pointing to one of the bigger men, "Grab the other end of that rug. We'll start at the top, and work our way down."

The man peeled off his threadbare coat and stepped forward, rolling up his sleeves. Together they lifted the rug off the pile and heaved it into the waiting cart. Two of the others stepped in behind them to hoist up the battered bureau.

While the men worked on moving the pile, I bent over their unconscious leader and tried to assess the extent of his injuries. The skin was broken and bleeding profusely above his ear. I palpated the area around it, feeling a large lump amid a leathery maze of old scars, but no obvious sign of fracture. I was checking inside his ear for possible hemorrhage when he opened his eyes, and blinked up at me. One pupil was noticeably larger than the other. "You have a concussion," I told him pressing my handkerchief against his wound to staunch the bleeding. "Do you understand?" He stared up at me without answering. I used some whiskey from the flask in his pocket to sterilize the wound then wrapped the handkerchief snugly around it.

When next I looked up the men had finished transferring the furniture into the cart and were loading the Longobardis on top, to the delight of the shrieking children. Simon handed a fistful of dollars to the wife. "This should get you through the end of the month." He turned to her husband. "You remember who to ask for at the Building Department?"

"Si," the man said, grasping his hand. "Grazie, signore Shaw; grazie mille!"

Simon signaled to the boy at the reins, and the cart rolled down the street. Turning back to the men, he handed each a dollar and shook his hand. "There's more where that came from, for anyone who's willing to put in a fair day's work. Come to the Isle of Plenty tomorrow morning, on 84th Street, and I'll get you started."

Mumbling and touching their caps, the men pocketed their bills and retrieved their weapons. Two of them hoisted the wounded man to his feet and they all straggled off down the sidewalk. I watched them go, both impressed and disturbed by what I'd seen. I'd known that Simon had a violent streak, and that it had erupted at least twice before: once over an insult to his mother, another time because of an act of cruelty toward a helpless animal. But I hadn't known he was capable of this kind of cold, calculated punishment. He could have stopped before that last, brutal blow with the pipe, but he'd wanted to make his point with the rest of the men. The gang leader would be lucky if he escaped without permanent damage.

This hardened version of Simon not only frightened, but saddened me, for I suspected my betrayal was a root cause. When he and his mother were thrown out of our house without a reference, the die had been cast. On the hardscrabble streets of New York, the sensitive boy

I'd known in my youth couldn't have survived for very long. But there was no use now feeling sorry for him; I had to stop thinking about the person he used to be, and protect myself from the man he had become.

He glanced over as he was pulling on his coat, and caught me looking at him. "What?"

I turned to face him squarely. "Are you working with the District Attorney?"

"What?" he repeated, snapping his sleeves straight.

"Are you trying to help him build a case against Eliza?"

"Have you gone daft?"

"I know he's agreed to let you run a casino the state shut down."

"Oh, you do, do you?"

"A casino in Saratoga. Why would he do that, unless he was getting something in return?"

"In the first place," he said with a frown, "it's not a casino. It's a stable. And in the second place, Jerome didn't give it to me. I bought it fair and square from Richard Canfield."

I stared at him. "But the state shut it down, and confiscated the assets."

"Illegally, as part of Canfield's larger operations. I'd already made the first payment when they closed it down. Jerome's trying to claim my contract is worthless, even though the stable's got nothing to do with the casino."

I moistened my lips, sensing that I was on shaky ground. "How could you afford to buy Richard Canfield's stable?" Canfield's racing thoroughbreds were nearly as famous as his casinos. He should have been able to command top dollar for the Saratoga property.

He planted his fists on his hips, scowling down at me. "We worked out a deal where I would pay him in installments, not that it's any of your business. They'd been raiding him for months, driving him slowly into bankruptcy, and he needed the money."

I had the uncomfortable feeling we had played out this scenario before: me accusing, Simon having an answer for everything. Last time it had ended with me wearing the dunce's cap. But my confidence in Simon had been repeatedly shaken in the last few days, and I couldn't stop the questions from coming. "Why you? Why not August Belmont, or some other millionaire breeder?"

"Because we're friends."

"You and Richard Canfield," I said skeptically.

"That's right," he shot back. "After your father threw me out, my first job was hiding the bank and gambling equipment in his secret vault, whenever Parkhurst's anti-gambling fanatics came around. We got along all right, and he asked me to help him out with other jobs over the years, before I opened my first saloon. He knew I understood horses, and when he decided to start breeding thoroughbreds in Saratoga, he asked me to help him pick out the stock mares."

He had moved within spitting distance. I barely held my ground, seeing the indignation in his eyes but still not quite ready to believe. "And just how do you intend to get Jerome to honor your contract?"

"Not by providing incriminating evidence against Mrs. Miner, if that's what you're thinking," he spat out. "I've got my own methods, and they don't include lying and double-crossing." He straightened, pulling away from me. "And now if I've answered all your questions to your satisfaction, I'll be on my way." He stalked off down the street.

I watched him go in dismay. If I'd been so wrong about the casino, maybe I'd been wrong about what happened the morning after my lock-in as well. Maybe Donald Kearney had gotten it wrong, after all. I started forlornly down the street in his wake, so upset at having falsely accused him once again that it was several minutes before I realized I hadn't even told him the news about Eliza.

CHAPTER TWENTY-SEVEN

I spent Friday in an agony of suspense and regret—suspense over the forthcoming lab results, regret at having pushed my one ally away at such a critical juncture. After roaming aimlessly about the house all morning I had a light lunch with my mother, who was fortunately too busy fretting over what to wear to the skating party to notice my skittishness, then went up to my room to put a few finishing touches on Professor Bogard's paper. By the time I came down again at 5:30, Mother had left for the park and Father to dine at his club. Since the house staff had been given the night off, this left me with only my thoughts for company.

Although the police were still making extra patrols around our block, I found the silence unnerving. At seven o'clock I telephoned the station house to ask for news, only to be told that the detective had been called out on a case and probably wouldn't be back for some time. I hung up the phone, listening to the ticking of the hall clock in the silence. I didn't think I could bear to wait idly for several more hours until the detective's return. I decided to walk across the park to the lake instead, where the skating party would be in full swing. It would provide an hour or two of distraction, and the exercise would help settle my nerves. Maurice was already there with the motorcar, waiting for my mother, so I could ask him for a lift home when I'd had enough.

I pulled on my coat, hat and gloves and set out, locking the door behind me. The night was clear and mild, warmer than it had been in weeks, and carried the scent of freshly exposed earth. Peering up and down the street to be sure no one was lurking in the shadows, I walked to the end of the block, then down Fifth Avenue and into the park, striking south and west along the most heavily-traveled paths. I breathed in deep lungfuls of the moist air, glad to be out and about. It seemed to me there was a festive mood in the air, as if my fellow pedestrians were anticipating the coming weekend; but perhaps it was just the lightening of my own burden I was sensing, at the prospect of Eliza's ordeal coming to an end.

I skirted the reservoir, pausing to watch some children sled down the knoll near the overpass, and then continued toward Hernshead on the west side of the lake, using the distant gables of the Dakota apartments as my guide. The red ball was up over Vista Rock, signalling that the ice was safe for skating. As I drew closer I could make out a curling match underway on one edge of the lake, inside a circle of calcium reflector lights, and beyond it the spectral forms of figure skaters gliding by moonlight. I made my way toward the Ladies Shelter, guessing that the Courtlandt party had assembled there so that the women could don their skates without exposing their calves to public view. A few moments later I spotted them: perhaps thirty guests huddled along the lake's edge, watching another dozen or so who'd ventured out onto the ice and were sliding more or less gracefully over the surface.

From behind a small stand of trees I watched the Earl scissor away from the bank, clinging to the arm of a young woman who looked only slightly more secure on her own blades. I couldn't make out the woman's face, but she was too short to be Olivia. I searched for the latter's tall, willowy figure and found it at lake's edge. She was still in her street shoes, standing with Lucille, my mother, and a woman I didn't recognize, who was holding a little black dog on a leash. Lucille's arm was wrapped around Olivia's waist, but her face was turned toward the Earl.

I'd been watching for a few minutes when I saw Olivia point toward a footman who'd been skating around the guests, carrying cups of what I assumed was cocoa on a tray at his shoulder. Lucille glanced at the footman, shook her head, and returned her attention to the Earl. Even from my remote vantage point I could detect Olivia's irritation. She started to pull away—but Lucille, without turning her head, pulled her back. The footman stopped to hand out two steaming cups and then circled back toward the bank. As he passed in front of Olivia, she broke away from her mother and struck out in his direction.

Though her determination was evident in the forward tilt of her torso, her legs didn't appear to be cooperating. Her gait was oddly stiff and halting—more so, it seemed to me, than the slippery surface warranted. Her mother called after her but she kept on going, her chin thrust stubbornly toward the footman's tray. She was nearly there when the little black dog pulled out of its owner's grasp and charged after her with its gold leash trailing behind. Olivia didn't see him until he was nearly underfoot. He circled around her, drawing the leash around her ankles as he barked and wagged in excitement. She tried to step over him, but once again her legs seemed unnaturally slow to respond. Throwing up her arm in a vain attempt to balance herself, she staggered back and fell hard onto her bottom. She sat on the ice, rubbing her wrist, as the little dog climbed up her chest and licked her face.

Lucille was at her side in under ten seconds. She pulled the dog off by the scruff of its neck and hauled Olivia to her feet. Olivia shuffled without protest toward the bank, her eyes downcast, as the dog's owner rushed out to retrieve it. Waving aside the woman's apologies, Lucille led Olivia back to my mother, then beckoned sharply to the circling footman. She lifted a cup from his tray and passed it to her daughter, waiting for Olivia to take it in both hands before she released it. As the footman skated away the three women stood beside each other in silence, Lucille staring over the ice with a stony smile on her face, my mother gazing anxiously at Olivia, and Olivia staring into her cup.

I wasn't sure what to make of it. Olivia had walked with much the same stiff-legged gait at the ball, I remembered, though not with the same energy or frustrated purpose. There it had been possible to attribute the stilted movements to nerves, or even an assumed hauteur; here in this informal setting, they were harder to account for. If she didn't have Huntington's Chorea, I found myself wondering once again, what on earth did she have?

For some time I'd been aware of a tall, slender man in street shoes moving around the edges of the party on the ice, sliding a walking stick in front of him. Now the man approached Lucille, lifting his hat in greeting. Seeing the white-haired head underneath, I realized with a start that it was Dr. Huntington.

He held up what appeared to be a woman's glove, addressing both Lucille and Olivia. Lucille said something in reply, and shook her head. He turned to Olivia, gesturing with the glove as he spoke, moving it from side to side at eye level. She answered with a sentence or two, then shook her head as well. The doctor doffed his hat and continued past them up onto the bank, tucking the glove into his coat pocket as he started up the path to the West Drive.

I hurried to catch up with him, cutting through the trees to the path. "Dr. Huntington, wait!"

He turned. "Dr. Summerford! I was just on my way to my hotel to telephone you; I've had a chance to observe Miss Fiske at close range."

"Yes I know, I saw you talking—"

"It's all there!" he interrupted. "The pronounced rigidity of her legs as she was trying to avoid the little dog; did you see it? And the speech and eye disturbances—you couldn't miss them! It's the Westphal variant; I've only seen it once in my practice, but I've read of at least six cases in the literature."

"Wait a minute; I don't understand . . ."

"I'm sorry, I'm rattling," he said, visibly reining himself in. "What I'm trying to say, is that Miss Fiske appears to be an example of the relatively rare, early onset case."

"Early onset? Of what?"

"Why, Huntington's Chorea of course."

I stared at him. "But you told me her mother isn't affected! And if Eliza doesn't have it, she can't have passed it on to Olivia."

He shook his head. "I know . . . but the walk is unmistakable. And the glove; when I asked her if she'd dropped it, did you see? Her whole head moved as I passed it in front of her. Her vowels have started to shorten, as well. The effect is subtle still, but detectable to the trained ear."

"It can't be Huntington's Chorea," I insisted. "Olivia is only twenty years old. You said in your monograph you'd never seen the disease manifest before the age of thirty."

"And I haven't, not in its classic form. But the Westphal variant is an entirely different beast. It manifests extremely early, in the second or even the first decade of life. It differs markedly in other respects as well, which is why neither I nor anyone else even recognized until recently that it was the same affliction. In these cases, the predominant aspect is the limb rigidity, with gait abnormality being the usual presenting feature. The choreic movements are either secondary or absent altogether. Hoffman was the first to speculate on the relationship between the two, after he found limb rigidity in the young children of a father with the more typical, choreic symptoms. The Germans are ahead of us here, you know; they've done some very compelling research . . ."

I had stopped listening. I felt as though a giant fist had appeared out of nowhere to slam me in the face. Just when I'd thought we were free of this damned disease, it had ricocheted back to deliver a knock-out punch. "Are you absolutely certain?" I asked when he paused for breath.

"Well of course, I'd like to perform the usual test battery, for further confirmation. But I'm fairly confident of the outcome."

I shook my head in disbelief. I'd only revealed my hand to Maloney because I was certain that Eliza's mental status was no longer in question. "You said Eliza didn't have it," I repeated in a daze. "You said you were sure."

He pursed his lips thoughtfully. "Well of course, it is still possible that she's not affected. What do you know about the girl's father?"

"Her father?" I blinked at him. "Why, nothing much; he was just some boy Eliza had a brief encounter with, when she was fifteen."

"You might try to find out more about him. As I said, in cases of early onset the father is very often the transmitter."

Of course, I thought, grasping at this reprieve; I'd been so busy looking for signs of transmission on Eliza's side that I hadn't thought twice about Olivia's father, the itinerant young man who'd so blithely impregnated Eliza before going on his merry way. My relief was followed almost immediately, however, by the realization that paternal transmission would be difficult to prove. I doubted Eliza had stayed in touch with the man, or even knew where he was. "Are you going to tell Detective Maloney about Olivia?" I asked the doctor.

He eyed me soberly. "I don't see that I have a choice, do you?"

"But you're still willing to testify that Eliza is not affected, aren't you? You did say before that you were certain."

"I said I was as certain as it was possible to be, if you remember. And yes, I do still believe she's asymptomatic. But it's easier to be certain of what does exist than what doesn't—and Miss Fiske is definitely showing symptoms. Which means that unless and until her father is found to be the transmitter, there is a chance that Mrs. Miner could be affected, and will manifest at an unusually late age."

I walked numbly beside him as he started back up the path, my head reeling from his news.

"I'm sorry," he said, glancing over at me. "I know you have a personal interest in this case. I wish it had turned out differently."

The finality of his words was terrifying. Poor Olivia; I could hardly bear to think of the horrors that awaited her. I had developed a deep sympathy for the girl, knowing what I did of her past, watching her cope with the pressures of living in her gilded cage. It grieved me to think of the ugly way her fairy tale life was going to end.

"You ought to tell her," the Doctor said, as if reading my mind. "She should come see me as soon as possible so that we can determine the extent of the disease's progression and begin a therapy program."

"She doesn't even know that she's adopted! How could I possibly explain it?"

"She knows that something's wrong, I can assure you of that."

I imagined Olivia in a drafty castle, far from family and friends, fighting increasing panic as her symptoms not only failed to subside, but worsened over time. Would the Earl's doctors even be familiar with the disease, I wondered? I kicked the snow on the walkway.

"I know," he said quietly. "It isn't fair."

"No, it isn't! No one should have to face this ghastly disease."

He glanced at me. "We are only the messengers, doctor. We don't cause these illnesses to occur. If we're lucky, we can do something to help. That's all we can ask of ourselves."

"And in this case? What can we do to help Olivia?"

"We can ensure that she receives proper exercise and nutrition," he said firmly, "so that she can continue to function as long, and as well, as possible. We can teach her family members not to blame her when she behaves badly, and how to feed her when swallowing becomes difficult, and how to keep her from hurting herself. And when the time comes, we can help place her in a suitable asylum where she'll be treated humanely until the end."

"That's all?"

"There is no cure to date, as you are doubtless aware. Quinine has been found to allay mild choreic movements, but only temporarily, and it's unclear if it would help with this variant. Nor has there been much long-term success with hyoscyamine, despite the initial reports, or with bromides of potassium or arsenic."

We had emerged onto the sidewalk along Central Park West. A long line of chaufferred vehicles was parked along the curb, my own among them. "How long does she have?" I asked.

"In cases of early onset, death typically comes within ten years. Based on Miss Fiske's current condition I would guess she first became symptomatic three or four years ago."

"So she has seven years at best."

"I truly am sorry. I wish I could give you better news."

We stopped and faced each other.

"Shall I accompany you home?" the doctor asked.

"That's not necessary. My driver is already here."

"I'll say good night, then." He shook my hand. "I do hope you'll consider telling her, as soon as possible. In almost every case, my patients have expressed relief at being told the true state of affairs. The distress caused by lack of information and the absence of support, it seems, is even worse than knowing the truth. I'll be in town through Sunday afternoon. If you want to contact me, you can reach me at the hotel."

IT WAS AFTER nine by the time Maurice dropped me back at home. I went directly into the telephone closet and sat down. I stared at the handset, saying a silent prayer. Maloney was going to tell me that Hagan's prints matched those on the sword. They had to match—or Eliza would be in even worse trouble than before.

The operator connected me to the sergeant at the front desk, who asked me to hold while he put me through to the detective. I waited on pins and needles for his voice to come on the line.

"That you, Doc?" he said at last.

"Yes, Detective, it's me."

"I was just about to call you. I've got the results."

My tongue had turned suddenly sluggish in my mouth. "Yes? And?"

"The prints don't match."

No. It couldn't be. He must mean that the prints weren't clear enough to identify. "I suppose I might have smudged them with my handkerchief, when I picked them up—"

"Nah, you did good. We got a nice clean set. They just don't match any of the fingerprints on the sword."

I stared at the receiver. It had to have been Hagan; it had all added up so perfectly. "There must be some mistake."

"Well now you see, that's the beauty of this thing. Every fingerprint is unique, so there's no such thing as mistakes."

"The lab could have mishandled it somehow."

"Proper procedures were followed, I assure you."

I gripped the handset cord, telling myself to breathe. "He must have been wearing gloves then," I said, struggling to keep panic out of my voice. "Either that, or Lucille hired someone else to do the job."

I heard him sigh on the other end. "I'll say one thing for you, Doc. You don't give up."

"None of the underlying facts have changed!" I practically shouted at him. "I still believe Lucille is responsible for both murders."

"Then I respectfully suggest it's time you consider the possibility that you're wrong," he said sourly, echoing my words to him that morning. "By the way, Mrs. Miner's grand jury trial is on the calendar for next week. I'll be meeting with the D.A. on Monday, and passing along what you told me. I wouldn't be surprised if he wants you to take the stand."

"Against my own patient?" I protested in dismay.

"Against the woman who murdered two innocent people," he shot back.

"Detective, please," I said, as my head begin to swim; "if you'll just look in the doctor's appointment book, you'll see that he met with Mrs. Fiske four days before he was murdered. All I'm asking is that you talk to her before she leaves—"

"Give it a rest, Doc." The line went dead.

I slowly placed the handset back on its hook. I hadn't saved Eliza; I'd only helped them dig her grave. Tomorrow Dr. Huntington would tell Maloney that Olivia had Huntington's Chorea, and then Maloney would tell the prosecutor, who would of course argue at trial that Eliza had passed the illness to her daughter and must be suffering its effects herself. Dr. Huntington could testify until he was blue in the face that Eliza wasn't showing any signs of mental degeneration; the possibility would linger in the jurors' minds. It would be the glue holding the case against her together, the putty that filled in all the holes.

I rubbed my face, trying to calm my spinning brain. The only way I could keep that from happening was to establish that Olivia had inherited the disease from her father. If I could do so before Lucille left for Colorado, I might still be able to persuade Maloney to stop her. He had accepted the possibility, however briefly, that Lucille was implicated in the murders. I had to do everything I could to keep that flame alive.

But I couldn't do it without Eliza's help. I glanced at the hall clock. There was no point calling her now at home, when her mother would be hovering in the background. Eliza would never talk to me about the baby or its father in Mrs. Braun's presence. I'd have to wait until the morning, when Mrs. Braun was downstairs in the shop. If I could get Eliza to identify the father, I'd have until the afternoon to locate him, or someone who'd known him, and try to establish that he had Huntington's Chorea. It was a daunting task, with as much likelihood of success, I feared, as paddling up the Niagara River with a teaspoon; but it was the only way I could think of to try to save Eliza.

CHAPTER TWENTY-EIGHT

I placed the call shortly after breakfast the following morning. I would have preferred to speak to Eliza in person about such a sensitive matter, but I couldn't afford to wait. The hall clock read a few minutes after 8:00; assuming the Fiskes' private train car was attached to one of the two overnight westbound Specials, it would be departing around mid-afternoon, which meant I had five or six hours at most to locate Olivia's father.

"Hello?" Eliza said on the other end of the line.

"Eliza, thank God; it's Dr. Summerford. I don't have much time so I'm going to have to get straight to the point: I need you to tell me who Joy's father is. And where he might be living now, if you have any idea."

There was such a long pause on the other end that for a moment I thought we'd been disconnected. "Joy doesn't have a father," she said at last. "She only has me."

I knew that I'd broached a delicate and emotionally complex subject; but there was no time now for tact. "I understand that he hasn't been a real father to her, but they are still biologically related, and that's all that matters right now. I have to find him, Eliza, or someone close to him who's likely to know the state of his health. The outcome of your trial could depend on it."

"What does Joy have to do with my trial?" she asked in surprise.

I drew in my breath; there was so much she still didn't know. "Quite a lot, as it turns out." If telling her the truth was the only way I could get her to reveal the father's name, then I couldn't put it off any longer. "Eliza, I've found your daughter."

I told her the good news first: that Joy had been brought up in the lap of luxury and been well cared for over the past twenty years, enjoying every possible advantage. After giving her a few precious moments to savor this revelation, I went on to explain as gently as possible that her daughter wasn't well; that she was in fact suffering from the same ailment Dr. Huntington had been looking for in Eliza. "And that's why we have to find Joy's father," I finished. "To prove that he's the one who passed it on to her. If we don't, a jury could assume she inherited the disease from you. And if they believe that, they can be persuaded that it caused you to kill the doctor."

"She can't be sick," she said. "She was a perfect little baby. Absolutely perfect!"

"I'm afraid she is, Eliza. Dr. Huntington himself confirmed it. Now I hate to pressure you, but we're running out of time. You have to tell me who her father is. If not for your sake, then for Joy's. She's going to want answers, and we need to be able to give them to her."

"But I told you, she has no father. Joy was a present to me from God."

She'd said the same thing before, I remembered, on the first day I'd met her. This time, however, I had the disturbing sensation she meant it literally. "God doesn't make babies," I said sharply. "Men do."

"I thought you understood," she said, her voice starting to break. "I thought that's why you were helping me find her."

I was momentarily speechless. Was it possible that she was trying to protect him? It was the only rational explanation I could think of. "Eliza, your life is at stake," I reminded her. "You owe this man nothing."

"There is no man!" she cried. "Why won't you believe me?"

Absurd though it was, she sounded utterly convinced of what she was saying. I felt a sinking sensation in my gut. Was this delusional thinking I was hearing, manufactured by a disease-impaired mind? Could she be the disease carrier, after all?

I told myself not to rush to conclusions, but to analyze the situation dispassionately. Her denial, though bizarre, was not accompanied by the paranoia or grandiosity that typically characterized chronic delusion. Nor did it seem to be part of a larger system of false ideas. Indeed, her stated belief that her baby had no father struck me as less a fabrication, than a refusal to remember. I was reminded of something I'd read in Janet's Symptoms of Hysteria just a few days before, while working on the professor's paper. Janet believed that in certain predisposed individuals, real memories, if they were painful enough, could be relegated to the subconscious and replaced by less painful, artificial ones. All people found comfort in telling themselves 'fine stories', according to Janet; but in these susceptible individuals the stories gained the upper hand, becoming fixed illusions that completely replaced the more disturbing reality. The hysterical amnesia that resulted was not a product of a diseased or insane mind. It stemmed, rather, from the weak energy of the subject's personal identity, leaving the intelligence and moral faculties intact.

I knew that Eliza's illegitimate pregnancy had caused her extreme and prolonged psychic distress. Perhaps the combination of her humiliation and her mother's anger had prompted her to bury the initiating sexual event deeply in her unconscious, producing an hysterical amnesia. Considering the very limited and particular scope of her denial, this seemed a more reasonable explanation than dementia for what I'd just heard. Unfortunately, if this was the case, and her unconscious mind was keeping the father's identity from her, I could scold and cajole all day without results. I glanced again at the clock. I'd envisioned many potential obstacles in the search for Olivia's father, but this had not been one of them. I had no back up plan. I was going to have to pry the information out of her some other way.

Hypnosis, I thought, was the logical solution. It had been used more successfully as a cure for hysterical symptoms than for any other purpose, except perhaps the relief of pain during surgery, in the days before anesthetics. What's more, when it was undertaken by a skillful practitioner it could yield results in a single session. With hypnosis it might be possible not only to uncover the identity of Olivia's father, but to shed light into some of the other mysterious corners of Eliza's psyche, as well.

As I'd never had an opportunity to become proficient at inducing the trance state, however, I would need to enlist someone's help to go that route. Someone with ample experience in the technique, who lived here in the city, and whose discretion I could count on. Someone like . . . Professor Bogard. The idea broke over me like a bracing wave. There was no one I trusted more, or who I believed was more up to the task. According to the professor's telegram, moreover, he had returned to the city the previous evening. With any luck I would find him at home, and we could be at Eliza's within the hour.

"I'm sorry if I've upset you," I said to Eliza. "I know this has all come as a terrible shock, and I don't mean to make it any harder. But I also know that you hope to be reunited with Joy one day, and that can't happen if they send you off to prison." I felt cruel saying it, but I feared it was the only way I could gain her cooperation.

"I'm telling you the truth," she said, sounding close to tears. "I don't know what else I can say."

"You know, it's possible that you did have relations with a man, but have locked it away in your memory. People do that sometimes; they forget things from their past, to protect themselves from unpleasant feelings."

"I don't see how I could have forgotten," she sniffed.

"There's a way to find out for sure. We could try hypnosis."

"You mean like at Coney Island," she said doubtfully, "when they tell people to stand on a chair, and bark like a dog?"

"Not like that at all. This would be a scientific undertaking. One of my professors at medical school, Dr. Rudolph Bogard, is a highly trained doctor and hypnotist, very well regarded in his field. I could ask him to assist us."

She was silent for a long moment. "He wouldn't ask me to do anything silly?" she asked finally.

"Progessor Bogard would never do anything to compromise the dignity of his subjects. He'll just put you into a very relaxing trance state, and ask you questions about your past."

"I don't know . . . I really don't see the point."

"For Joy's sake," I urged. "The worst that can happen is you'll have a pleasant rest, and get to say, 'I told you so'." I heard the soft, slow release of her breath.

"All right," she said. "For Joy."

I KNOCKED LOUDLY on the professor's front door. His elderly housekeeper opened it, carrying a broom in one hand and a worn slipper in the other. "Miss Summerford!" she exclaimed. "I didn't know the professor was expecting you."

"He isn't, but something urgent has come up and I need to speak to him right away. Could you tell him I'm here?"

"Why, I don't know if he's even up yet," she said, sounding peeved. "The poor man didn't get in last night until after dinner."

"I'm sorry to disturb him, but the matter really can't wait."

Her lips pursed in disapproval, but she stepped aside to let me in and went muttering down the hall to fetch him.

Ten minutes later the professor rounded the door into the parlor, buttoning up his waistcoat. "Good morning, Doctor! Aren't you out bright and early!"

I nearly swooned at the sight of him. "Oh Professor, I'm so glad to see you . . ."

"And I you, my dear. I commend you on your dedication." He bounced toward me on the balls of his feet, his palm extended. "Let's have a look, then, shall we?"

I stared at his open hand, uncertain at first what he was referring to. "Oh, you mean the paper; of course, but there's something pressing I need to discuss with you first."

He frowned. "Don't tell me it's not finished," he said, his fingertips curling in dismay.

"Oh no, there's no problem with the paper; it's about a patient of mine, the one I told you about just before you left. Her name is Eliza Miner—"

"You brought it with you, then?" he interrupted.

"The paper?" I asked, struggling to keep the exasperation from my voice. "It's right here." I yanked it partway out of my bag to show him.

"Ah, excellent," he sighed, his brow relaxing. "I knew I could count on you." Leaning toward me, he confided with a wink, "I just found out they've made mine the lead address at the conference."

"That's wonderful, Professor, but if you don't mind, this really is quite urgent . . ."

The housekeeper now bustled in, carrying a Wedgewood plate stacked with chocolate-covered pastries.

"Mrs. Whelan, I see you've been to Dean's!" cried the professor, rubbing his hands.

"I knew you'd be missing your profiteroles while you were away," she simpered, lowering the plate onto a table between the parlor chairs. Casting me a reproachful look, she added, "If you can't get a decent night's rest, I can at least be sure you start off your day with a solid breakfast."

"My dear Mrs. Whelan, whatever would I do without you?" said the professor, bending over the plate with relish.

I could have sworn the old woman blushed. "I'll bring the tea the minute it's ready," she told him, scurrying out of the room as fast as her bowed old legs could carry her.

"You have to try one of these, Doctor," the professor said, turning the plate to inspect each cream-filled pastry. "They bake them fresh, three times a day."

"I've already eaten," I replied, nearly choking now on my impatience.

"You don't know what you're missing." He finally selected one and took a bite, sighing in contentment.

"About Mrs. Miner . . ." I began.

"Shall we make ourselves comfortable?" he asked, gesturing toward the parlor chairs. He settled himself into one, pastry in hand, while I dropped onto the seat across from him.

"Now then," he said at long last; "what is it you wanted to tell me?"

I didn't need any further prompting. Answering in what I hoped was a coherent torrent, I filled him in on everything that had happened over the last two weeks. His expression gradually changed from polite interest, to concern, to outright alarm, his enjoyment of the profiterole seeming to decline in direct proportion to the length of my story. "Good heavens," he muttered when I was finished, lowering the unfinished pastry to his knee.

"I realize that as my supervisor you should have been advised of Eliza's arrest right away, but I didn't want to discuss it in front of Professor Mayhew."

"Well now, I don't really think we can call me your supervisor," he said quickly. "After all, we've barely discussed this patient's case until now."

"I know, I'm sorry, I did want to tell you sooner but you left the day after it happened. I've told you everything now, though. And there's still a chance we can turn things around."

"We?" he repeated, eyebrows raised.

I leaned toward him. "I thought you might hypnotize her, so we could find out who Olivia's father is."

"Oh dear," he said, drawing back, "I'm not sure that's a good idea."

"Why not? I know you could do it. Remember that boy in my class who was terrified of geese? You helped him recover a memory of being chased by one as a child, and cured him of his fear."

"I meant that I don't know if it would be wise for me to become involved. Not now, with the conference coming up."

I frowned at him. "I don't understand; what difference does the conference make?"

"A man in my position is expected to adhere to a very high standard of conduct," he answered stiffly. "It wouldn't do to be seen as aiding and abetting a murder suspect."

I felt a chill run down my back, so real I almost turned to see if the front door had blown open. I couldn't believe he'd let fear of public opinion stand between us, not when I so clearly needed his help. "You mean, you don't want to damage your reputation," I said slowly.

"You needn't take that tone with me, Doctor. I should think you'd be concerned about your own reputation. As a woman, people are expecting you to make mistakes. I can't imagine why you'd want to give them fuel for the fire."

"You think I made a mistake with Eliza, is that what you're saying?" I asked, hearing the shrillness in my voice but unable to control it. "You believe that she's guilty, and that I'm somehow responsible?"

He sighed. "From what you've told me, I don't see that anyone really knows what happened. That being the case, I think the wisest course would be for you to remove yourself from the controversy."

"And how am I supposed to do that?"

"You've done your duty, and told the police everything you know. I don't see that anything more is required of you."

"I can't abandon Eliza now."

"She isn't your responsibility."

"She has no one else! Her own mother believes her case is hopeless. Her lawyer hasn't seen fit to meet with her yet except to claim his fee, although her grand jury trial is scheduled for next week. I'm the only one who seems the slightest bit interested in trying to prove her innocence. But I can't do it alone. Please, Professor, I need your help."

His gaze dropped to his pant leg. "There's no guarantee that she would reveal the information you seek under hypnosis," he said, brushing off a crumb. "Besides, I simply don't have the time. Not with the conference coming up. "

"It would only take an hour or two," I pleaded. "We could go right now, and you'd be back before lunch."

He looked up. "I'm sorry," he said flatly, "but I can't."

I thought of all the times at school I'd stayed up late to meet his urgent research deadlines, or set aside my course work to help him with some little crisis he couldn't manage on his own. I'd done it gladly, eager to help, proud to be part of his team. And now, the one time I asked for his help, he refused me. I felt hot tears stinging my eyelids, and blinked them away.

His face brightened. "There is a young doctor I know, however; an experienced hypnotist, just over from France. I believe he trained with Charcot at the Salpetriere. I can give you his name. I'm sure you'll find him quite capable."

"There's no time to get someone else. Besides, how can I ask Eliza to trust someone I don't even know? I don't want some stranger, Professor; I want you!"

"Well, I'm sorry," he said curtly, "but we can't always have what we want, now can we?"

I stared at him in mute dismay. So that was that. He really wasn't going to help. "I should go, then," I mumbled, pushing myself up from the chair in a daze. "I'm sorry to have taken up your time."

"Don't be silly," he said, getting to his own feet. "You know I'm always happy to give you the benefit of my advice." He rocked up on his toes, patting his waistcoat, his good humor restored now that I was leaving and taking my problems with me. "Be sure to keep me abreast of things. And don't worry overly much; I'm sure everything will work out in the end."

His cheap assurances made me want to gag. I lifted my bag over my shoulder and started for the door.

I was nearly through it when he called, "Genevieve, wait!"

I stopped, my heart hitching in my chest. Thank God, he'd come to his senses. Of course he wouldn't abandon me when I needed him most! He'd only needed another moment to consider. I whirled around, ready to forgive him everything.

He held out his hand. "You forgot the paper."

There was a strange rushing noise in my ears, as though all the air were being sucked from the room. I had the odd sensation that I was growing lighter and higher, expanding into space. The professor looked different from this vantage point, as if I were viewing him through the wrong end of a telescope: smaller somehow, and less assured. I noted the slight sheen on his brow, and the uncertain smile on his lips. Suddenly, it dawned on me: the professor needed me. *He* needed *me*. I squeezed my elbow over my book bag, experiencing an unfamiliar frisson of power. I had tried appealing to his heart, and to his conscience, and gotten nowhere. Perhaps it was time for another approach. "Actually," I said slowly, "now that I think about it, the paper isn't quite ready. There are a number of improvements that should still be made."

"I'm sure it will be fine."

"I really couldn't hand it over, in good conscience."

He wiggled his fingers. "Just give me what you've done so far, and I'll make do."

"Make do?" I raised my eyebrows. "That hardly seems good enough, does it Professor? After all, there's your reputation to consider."

He slowly lowered his arm. "What are you up to, Genevieve? Are you telling me you're not going to give it to me?"

"Oh, I'll give it to you. As soon as I've had a chance to give it the proper attention. Right after this other pesky little matter is cleared up."

"It seems I've underestimated you," he said sternly. "I didn't know you were capable of blackmail."

"Neither did I," I replied truthfully. "But then, as you once told me, we never really know what we're capable of, until we're pushed to it." I could smell my bridges burning, but I didn't care. Overcome with a strange but exhilarating giddiness, I added, "Of course, if you absolutely can't wait, I'd be happy to recommend someone else. There's a librarian I know, a very competent researcher. I'm afraid she knows absolutely nothing at all about your topic, but in a pinch . . ." I winked at him. "I'm sure you'll find her very capable."

I caught a gleam of reluctant amusement in his eye. "I take your point, Doctor."

"Do you?"

"If your point is that I can't afford to take you for granted, then yes, I do."

"You'll help me then?"

"I don't appear to have a choice. But if I'm going to become involved in this woman's defense, I must at least insist that you take notes of our session. There may be something in it that I can use for my next paper."

"Fine. As long as you don't reveal Mrs. Miner's identity."

"Agreed. And I have to be back by noon; I have an appointment with my publisher."

"I wouldn't dream of keeping him waiting."

He stepped past me, to the call box. "I'll have Wilson bring the motorcar around."

The housekeeper rushed in with the teapot as we were starting into the hall. "But Professor," she wailed, "your tea!"

"Can't be helped, Mrs. Whelan," he told her with a sigh, glancing wistfully back at the profiteroles.

Hoisting my book bag over my shoulder, I took hold of his arm and led him firmly out the door, leaving the housekeeper gaping in our wake.

CHAPTER TWENTY-NINE

Fifteen minutes later we were standing at the door of Eliza's flat. On the ride up I had explained more fully the details I was hoping to confirm through hypnosis. Although the professor's pride had still been piqued by my heavy-handed persuasion tactics, his natural curiosity—and, I suspected, the prospect of publishing a case analysis of a suspected murderess—had eventually risen to the fore; and by the time we arrived at the shop he'd mapped out a rough strategy for the session. Since the identity of Olivia's father seemed to be the information Eliza least wanted to divulge, the professor had decided to work in reverse chronological order, beginning with the baby's birth and moving back to the time of conception, exploring the issues I had touched on as we progressed.

Eliza opened the door and greeted us nervously. I introduced her to the professor and followed them both into the flat, watching as the professor put his considerable charm to work. Before we'd even reached the front room, he had Eliza eating out of his hand. Just as he'd had me doing all these years, I realized now.

Eliza settled self-consciously on a worn sofa in front of the windows, while I pulled two chairs around to face her. "You needn't be afraid," the professor assured her, his eyes twinkling as warmly as old St. Nick's. "The trance state is simply a place between sleep and wakefulness—not so very different, really, from a daydream. While you're in it you'll have access to memories and feelings that lie outside of your conscious awareness. Your conscious mind will still be present, but it will be watching from the wings, as it were."

"You won't ask me to do anything silly?" she asked, apparently still harboring concerns on this score.

He smiled. "That would be a waste of both of our time, don't you think?"

"Or anything I wouldn't normally do?" she added.

"As I said, your conscious mind will still be watching. It won't permit you to do anything at odds with your values or beliefs."

"So what do you say, Eliza?" I asked encouragingly. "Are you ready?"

She took a deep breath. "I suppose."

"Perhaps you'd like to rest your arms on that pillow," the professor suggested.

She moved a crocheted pillow from the corner of the sofa to her lap and folded her arms on top of it.

"Are you comfortable?"

She nodded.

He turned to me. "Ready, Doctor?"

I centered my writing pad on my lap and placed my inkwell on the sofa table in front of my knees. "Ready."

"Then let's get started." Unclipping his pocket watch, he lifted it by the chain and held it in front of Eliza's face, slightly above eye level. "Mrs. Miner, I want you to keep your eyes on my watch," he said as he started swinging the chain. "Try not to pay attention to anything else but the sound of my voice. Don't worry about any noises you hear from the street, or any thoughts that come into your mind. Just fix your entire attention on my watch as it moves back and forth, back and forth before your eyes . . ."

Eliza sat stiffly upright with her hands clasped on top of the pillow, her eyes moving dutifully to and fro with the watch.

"Remember that you are under no one's control," the professor went on, "but are a willing participant on this journey into the pleasant state of deep trance. You are allowing Dr. Summerford and me to guide you into this state to retrieve helpful information from your past. You may speak or move or interrupt us at will, whenever you desire." His voice was slow and lulling, his body still save for the slight motion of his fingers on the chain.

"Now feel your body begin to relax. Be aware of your breath as it moves in and out . . . deeper and deeper into your lungs, staying in contact with my voice as you follow the watch moving back and forth, back and forth, steady as the beat of your heart." His voice droned on, smooth as melted beeswax. I could see Eliza's face begin to soften, her shoulders droop a little more with each pass of the watch.

"As you follow the watch your eyes may begin to feel heavy," the professor continued. "They may feel so heavy that it's an effort to keep them open, but try to keep them open if you can, enjoying the pleasant sensation of heaviness as you follow the watch, keeping your eyes open even though it feels as though there are weights on your eyelids, pulling them down, making it harder and harder to keep them open . . ." Eliza's eyelids, I noted, were slipping gradually lower as he spoke. "Your eyes are now so tired that it's difficult to see through them," he said, as her eyelids started fluttering. "They're so tired and heavy that you may feel you have to blink. Your eyelids are so heavy that you can no longer hold them open." Her eyes blinked a few more times, and slid shut. "Your eyes are closed."

He lowered the watch to his lap. "Now notice as the heaviness in your eyes seeps down your face, into your nose and your cheeks and along your mouth and jaw, releasing any tightness that lingers there . . ." He went on in this manner for several minutes, moving Eliza's attention gradually down her body, until the rise and fall of her chest was nearly imperceptible. My own eyes were now at half-mast, my breathing as slow as if I'd swallowed half a box of Hoffman's Drops. The world seemed to contain nothing but the professor's voice and the steadily swinging watch.

"I'm going to ask you a question, Eliza, that can only be answered by your subconscious mind," the professor was saying. "For while your conscious mind is like a tiny harbor, shallow and hemmed in, your subconscious is as wide and deep as the ocean. Your conscious mind can guess at how your subconscious will answer my question, but it cannot know. Only your subconscious can give me the answer. The question I am asking is this: Does your subconscious mind think it will go into a trance instantly, or within the next few moments? If the answer is instantly, then the index finger of your right hand will lift from the pillow, *automatically*. If the answer is in the next few moments, then the index finger of your left hand will lift from the pillow, *automatically*. Your subconscious mind can tell my conscious mind what it thinks or understands by simply causing a finger on your right or your left hand to lift. Now be aware of your hands, and see what the answer is. Feel the slight movement in your finger as your subconscious tells it what to do. Feel the finger beginning to move upward, off the pillow, as your subconscious responds to my question."

Eliza's right index finger twitched and rose off the pillow.

"Good. Notice that your finger feels like something separate and distinct, moving under its own will. This is your subconscious mind revealing itself. Now that your subconscious has answered this question, it can answer other questions as well, using your voice just as easily as your finger, as easily as if it were your conscious mind responding. Now let your finger return to the pillow. When your finger touches the pillow, you will be ready to go into an even deeper state of relaxation."

As her finger dropped to the pillow, he continued, "Imagine, now, that you are walking down a long staircase. The staircase leads to a special place deep inside you. This is a very safe place, where only you can go. Imagine walking down the steps, one, two, three, four, staying in contact with my voice as you descend, allowing yourself to go deeper and deeper into this special place. This is the trance state. You don't have to think about it; it just is, like your breathing, or the waves in the ocean. While you are in this deep place a part of you is able to hear me and to answer my questions. Can you describe to me what you are feeling?"

"Heavy," Eliza muttered, her lips hardly moving around the word.

"Tell me where you are, if you can."

"A safe place," she murmured. "A secret place."

"Now that you are in this safe, secret place, I want you to imagine that you are looking at the hands of a clock. Note that the hands are moving in reverse, going backward in time. As the hands of the clock move backward, you will be able to go with them. You can go back a day, or a year, or many years, remembering events now as clearly as you experienced them at the time. Some of these memories will be happy, and some will be sad. Some of them may have been hidden away or forgotten over time. But remember that all of your memories are welcome here.

"Now watch the hands of the clock turning back, through the years, to the time when you were pregnant with your daughter Joy. Try to remember how your body felt when you were pregnant, how round and heavy. Perhaps you can feel a slight pressure in your back or lower abdomen. Perhaps you can even feel the baby moving inside of you . . ."

Eliza's hands slipped off the pillow and cradled her belly.

"Good, you're remembering. Now try to recall all the sights and sounds and smells as vividly as if you were experiencing them for the first time."

Her face tightened. "It hurts," she said, her fingers closing now over her belly.

"Are you having a contraction?"

She grimaced in response. Rousing myself from my stupor, I noted with amazement that her contorted face looked exactly like those of laboring women I'd observed during my internships.

"Can you tell me where you are?" the Professor asked.

"At the hospital," she said breathlessly.

"Why are you having your baby at the hospital, instead of at home?"

"The doctor is here. Mother arranged it."

"Are your mother and the doctor there with you now?"

"Yes."

"Is any one else there?"

"The nurse . . ." She stopped, her face twisting again at another apparent contraction.

I glanced at the professor, wondering if it was a good idea to reenact the entire labor.

As if having the same thought, he instructed, "Now look at the hands on the clock again, Eliza. Notice that they are moving forward in time, to the moment your baby is born. Go with them to that moment. Your baby is here; can you see it?"

"It's a girl!" she said with a smile. "She's so beautiful! They're wrapping her up in a little pink blanket . . ." Seconds passed, and her smile began to fade.

"What's happening now?" the professor asked.

"The nurse won't give her to me; she's taking my baby to the door."

"What do you see?"

"There's someone there, in the hallway outside."

"Who is it?"

"I don't know; a lady, in a black veil." She stiffened. "They're—they're giving her my baby! Mamma, help! Don't let them take my baby!" She made a strangled, gasping noise, shrinking back against the sofa.

"What is it?" asked the professor.

"She . . . she slapped me," she said in a small voice.

"Who did?"

"My mother. She says to be quiet and stop making a fuss. She says I'm lucky someone's willing to take the bastard off my hands."

The color had drained from her face. Though she was apparently describing something from her past, her physical body was undeniably reacting in present time. I glanced at the professor in concern.

"Remember, Eliza, you're in a safe place," he said. "Look at the clock hands, now, and notice that they are moving back in time again, to the spring before your baby was born. It's June and the flowers are just coming into bloom. The park is green again, and the air is soft and warm."

She let out a soft sigh. "I can smell it," she said, lifting her face serenely to an invisible breeze, as if the scene she'd just relived had never occurred.

"Your baby has been growing inside you for many months now."

"Yes," she said, "I feel it moving."

"Where are you, Eliza?"

"On the roof."

"The roof of your building?"

"Ummm."

"What are you doing up there?"

"Just thinking. I moved some boards against the old pigeon coop to make a lean-to, so no one can see me when I'm inside."

"Do you go there often?"

"Whenever I can get the key. Mother doesn't like me to come up here; she keeps the key on her ring in the kitchen. But she wasn't watching today."

"Have you ever taken someone up there with you?"

"No."

"What about the baby's father?"

"Who?"

"The father of the baby you're carrying. Has he ever seen the lean-to?"

"My baby doesn't have a father."

The professor glanced at me. I shrugged.

He thought a moment, then asked, "Eliza, have you ever been kissed by a man?"

"Grandfather kisses me, when he visits at Christmas." She grimaced. "I don't like it, though. I don't like his mustache."

"Has a man ever kissed you on the lips?"

"Oh no. I don't think I should care for that at all."

"Tell me, Eliza; do you know how babies are created?"

"Of course I do."

"Then you know it requires sexual intercourse between a man and a woman?"

She didn't answer.

"Eliza? Can you answer me?"

"That may be true for other babies, but it isn't true for mine."

"It isn't? How do you suppose your baby came to be, then?"

"God gave her to me, for being such a good girl."

"You must be a very good girl, indeed."

"I try to be."

"But you took the key to the roof, against your mother's wishes. That wasn't being very good, was it?"

"That's different. The baby was for being good to Papa, when Mother was mean to him."

The professor cocked his head. "Is your mother mean to your Papa?"

"Sometimes. But I can always make him feel better."

"You're close to your Papa, then."

"Oh, yes. I'm his Little Princess."

"Have you told him about your baby?"

"Mother told him," she said, her voice turning grim. "She wanted him to beat me, but he wouldn't."

"Did you tell him who the baby's father was?"

"Yes, I told them both."

He leaned forward, his palms inching forward on his knees "Tell me what you told them, Eliza."

"That the baby is a gift from God."

The professor sat back in defeat. I gestured to him to let me have a try.

"Eliza," I began, "remember that this is a safe place. No harm or shame can come to you here for remembering. It's all right to see the father's face, Eliza, and to say his name."

She said nothing.

"Your baby is going to want to know who her father is. Do you think you could tell us, for her sake?"

A tear appeared at the corner of her eye and trickled down her cheek.

"I'm sorry to make you cry," I said gently. "But maybe if you tell us, you'll feel better."

"I'm not crying," she said in a matter-of-fact voice.

"I can see a tear on your face."

"That's not my tear."

"It's not?" I couldn't help smiling. "Whose is it, then?"

"It's hers."

"Whose?"

"The sad one's."

"I'm sorry, I don't—" I stopped, as Professor Bogard's hand landed on my arm.

"Why is the sad one crying, Eliza?" he broke in.

"I don't know," she said carelessly. "She's always crying."

"Does the sad one have a name?"

"She's called Bitty."

He turned to me, jabbing his finger toward the writing pad. "Double personality," he rasped in my ear; "one-way cognizant at the very least!"

Turning back to Eliza, he asked, "Do you think Bitty would be willing to talk to us?"

"I don't know . . . she's never talked to anyone before. Lately, though, I think she's wanted to."

"Could we ask her?"

"If you like." Her chin drooped toward her chest, as her breath left her in a soft exhale. Several seconds passed.

"Bitty?" the professor said tentatively.

Eliza's head rose. "Yes?"

My hand froze on the writing tablet.

"Hello, Bitty. My name is Dr. Bogard. My assistant, Dr. Summerford, and I would like to ask you some questions, if you don't mind."

"What do you want to know?"

I couldn't have been more shocked if I was holding the live end of an electric wire. For although it was Eliza's face I was looking at, and Eliza's lips that were uttering the words, the voice that I was hearing belonged to someone else.

CHAPTER THIRTY

The professor wagged his eyebrows urgently toward the writing pad, but I couldn't get my hand to move. This voice was lower, sadder, *emptier* than Eliza's. Her posture had changed as well, her chin and knees drawing toward each other, hunching her over, as if she was warding off potential attack. I was of course familiar with the phenomenon of divided personality; we'd studied it at school, giving particular attention to both Azam's "Felida X" analysis, and the Bourne case reported in Henry James' "Principles of Psychology". But while I'd always accepted the concept in theory, I'd never before been asked to accept that it was sitting on the sofa across from me.

"We're trying to find someone," the professor was saying. "We hoped you might be able to help."

"I know," replied Eliza, or Bitty, or whomever we were speaking with. "I've been listening."

The professor lifted the pen and pad from my lap. 'Successive and mutually cognizant,' he scratched across the paper, underlining it twice before handing it back to me.

The pad lay idle on my knees as I struggled to accept the fact that the woman I'd become so intimately involved with over the past two weeks was actually two personalities in one. Though it was a deeply unnerving idea, I couldn't reject it out of hand. The theory behind divided personality was well established. We knew that the mind was made up of individual neurons that acted together to form organizations of increasing complexity. Some very distinguished thinkers had posited that these complex organizations were in effect subordinate minds, each with its own mental continuity. It was believed that in unstable individuals, a physical or emotional blow could produce a disintegration of the primary, conscious organization, permitting one or more of these alternate, unconscious systems to push through.

"It's very important that we find the father of Eliza's baby and determine his current state of health," the professor said to Bitty. "But Eliza won't tell us who he is."

"She can't," Bitty said. "She doesn't know."

"You mean she doesn't know his name?"

"She doesn't know because she wasn't there."

"I see," the professor said slowly. "But you were there, is that correct?"

She nodded.

"Could you tell us who he is, then?"

"I want to," she said softly, "but I'm afraid."

"What are you afraid of, Bitty?"

She didn't answer.

"Bitty?"

"He . . . he said if I told, he wouldn't let me go to Bridget's house any more. And that he wouldn't buy me a new coat, and I'd have to wear a second-hand one from Rosenbergs, like Eva Hertz."

The professor sat slowly back in his chair. "I see," he said again, with a trace of sadness in his voice.

I looked at him in bewilderment. What did he see? What on earth did the baby's father have to do with second-hand coats?

"It's all right, Bitty; you don't have to tell me," the professor said. "I think I already know. You're talking about your own father, aren't you?"

Her head tipped forward in the barest of nods. I felt a crawling sensation in my stomach.

"It must be very hard to talk about what your father did," the professor said. "But it's safe to tell us, if you wish to."

She hesitated for a long moment, as another tear trickled down her face. "I didn't mind it, at first," she said hoarsely. "He used to tickle me with his whiskers, after he came home late from the saloon, and play Indian Bill on my back. Sometimes he even gave me pennies, for candy . . ." She trailed off.

"But then something changed?"

She nodded.

"What was it that changed, Bitty?"

Her tears were flowing more freely now. "He said he was cold," she said, in hardly more than a whisper, "and needed to come under the covers to warm up."

"Your father came into your bed with you?"

"I didn't want him to; I didn't like the way he talked, or the way he smelled. He kept rubbing up against me, and making funny noises. Sometimes he squeezed me so tight, it made me want to cry . . ."

"Did this happen more than once?"

She nodded. "I tried to give him his pennies back," she said, her voice breaking. "I told him I didn't want them any more."

"But he wouldn't take them."

She shook her head.

"Did you ever tell anybody?"

"I couldn't."

"Because he wouldn't let you see your friend."

"Not just because of that," she said, becoming agitated. "I was afraid he'd be angry if he found out. But it didn't matter. He got angry anyway. The time . . . the time the baby happened."

I didn't want to hear any more; I wanted to tell her to stop right there, as if by staunching the memory I could somehow stop the thing itself from happening. But the professor was already urging her on.

"I want you to go back to that time, Bitty. To the time the baby happened. I want you to try to remember everything you saw and heard and felt as clearly as though it were happening right now." He waited for a moment, then asked, "Is it night time?"

"Yes," she answered thickly.

"What are you doing?"

"Helping Mother with the dishes."

"Where's your father?"

"He's coming up the stairs. I can hear him cursing, and bumping into the walls. Mamma hears him too. She says I should finish the dishes, and that she's going in to bed." She was pushing the words out in short bursts, her breath coming fast and shallow. "But I don't want to stay out here alone! I want to go in with Mamma—" She stopped.

"What is it, Bitty?" asked the Professor.

"The door won't open. She locked the door! Mamma, let me in! I don't want to be alone with Papa!" Suddenly she shrank back, hugging herself.

"What's the matter?"

"Papa heard." Her face blanched. "No, Papa, don't!"

"What's happening?"

"He's grabbing my hair," she wailed. "He's pulling me into my bedroom and calling me names—horrible names . . ." Her head rocked back against the sofa. "No, Papa, don't; get off of me! Papa, that hurts—"

I reached toward her, but the professor stopped me with a quick shake of his head. She writhed and moaned for a few more moments, and then her body went slack. She turned her face against the sofa and sobbed, open-mouthed, into the fabric.

The professor waited until her tears had subsided, then said quietly, "It's all right, Bitty. It's over now."

She drew a deep, shuddering breath.

"You can rest."

Her breath left her in a long, weary sigh as her head dropped toward her chest.

I sank back in my seat. Never in my wildest imaginings had it occurred to me that Eliza's father might also be Olivia's. And yet, it explained everything. Dr. Huntington had been right in suspecting that paternal transmission was the reason for the early onset of Olivia's disease. He could never have guessed, however, that in this case, father and grandfather were one and the same.

"May I speak with Eliza now?" the professor was saying.

Her head rose once more from her chest, and Eliza's cheerful voice asked, "Did she talk to you?"

"Yes, she did," the professor replied. "She was telling us about your father."

"Bitty doesn't like Father very much," she observed.

"Do you know why?"

"I suppose because he favors me over her."

"Ah, yes. You're his little princess, aren't you? Tell me, Eliza, do you love your father?"

"Of course I do."

"Is he kind to you?"

"Oh, yes; he's always giving me treats, and telling me stories."

"Has he ever done anything to hurt you?"

"Goodness, no!"

"He never asks you to do things you don't want to do?"

"I told you, I'm his Princess. Elizabeth is the one who has to do the chores."

"Elizabeth?" The professor cocked his head. "Who's Elizabeth?"

"She's the old one. Dr. Summerford met her, at the church."

"I did?" I asked in astonishment.

"Don't you remember? She was there at the beginning. She didn't want to stay, though; she didn't like what you were saying. But I did. I could tell you knew what it was like to miss someone the way I do, every single day. I thought you could help me find my Joy."

I recalled how sullen and withdrawn Mrs. Miner had seemed at the start of my first class, twisting her hands in apparent distress and protesting that she didn't belong there. It had been a different woman altogether who'd unburdened herself to me after the others were gone. Indeed, I remembered thinking how young and vulnerable that confiding woman seemed, in contrast to the dour persona of before. "Call me Eliza," she had said—not Elizabeth, the name Reverend Palmers and Mrs. Braun called Mrs. Miner by. "I remember," I said, trying to behave as though this was the most normal conversation in the world, although my mind was turning somersaults.

"Then you can understand why Papa doesn't care for her. She really is the most disagreeable thing."

The "old one", she had called her; did that mean that Elizabeth was the "real" Mrs. Miner? I stared at the familiar face in front of me, trying to sort out the parade of personalities that apparently existed behind it. In the Felida X case, the original, or primary, personality had been an introverted, uncommunicative girl who worked hard but took little joy in life—not unlike the somber woman I had glimpsed that first day of class, and perhaps again outside the Tombs, and even on my first visit to Mrs. Miner's home, after her release. Felida experienced frequent pains in her temples, followed by a brief state of deep lethargy from which the secondary personality emerged. This secondary personality was less constrained than the original, more sensitive and open to others—much like the "Eliza" I had come to know.

But if Eliza was a secondary personality, what purpose did she serve? Her love for Joy was unconditional; of that I was certain. Finding her daughter was the be-all and end-all of her existence. But Joy, I now knew, was the result of a paternal rape. Why would a personality be dedicated to remembering such an abomination, let alone trying to find her?

In the next second, the question answered itself: it was precisely because of the impossibility of loving the child with knowledge of its conception that Eliza needed to exist. Unaware of the rape, Eliza had been able to feel love for the child blossoming inside her womb—a love untainted by shame or anger or self-hatred. Eliza was the Loving Mother, the personality allowed to experience both the miracle of Joy's birth, and the pain of her loss. The one who kept Joy's memory alive.

"Tell me about Elizabeth," the professor was saying.

"She really is too tedious to talk about," Eliza replied with a sigh. "Although I'll admit, she's had me worried lately. She seems to have gotten worse and worse since the boy died."

The professor turned to me, one eyebrow cocked.

I'd almost forgotten about Mrs. Miner's second child, conceived during her brief marriage to a dock worker. "You mean the one who died in his crib, a few years ago."

"Yes," she said, "she took it very badly."

"What do you mean when you say she's gotten worse and worse?" the professor asked.

"Just the other day, she tried to cut herself with the box knife. I had to take it away from her."

"Was she trying to kill herself?"

"No, I don't think so. I think she was just punishing herself."

"What for?"

"Oh, I don't know, she's always punishing herself for one thing or another. That's just the way she is."

The professor pondered this for a moment. "Does Elizabeth know about you and Bitty?" he asked.

"Heavens no, she doesn't know anything. Although I think Bitty leaves her little presents sometimes, to try to make her feel better."

The professor glanced briefly at my writing pad, as if trying to work out the appropriate classification. Apparently abandoning the effort for the time being, he turned back to Eliza and asked, "Has she ever managed to actually hurt herself?"

"Well, I can't always be there to stop her. One time when Papa didn't like the way she ironed his shirts, she burned her hand on the flatiron. And once, when he shouted at her from the window for taking too long with his growler, she ran in front of a delivery cart— on purpose. It's just lucky that the driver saw her in time."

"Has she ever hurt anyone else?" I asked.

"I don't think so."

"Are you aware of everything she does?"

"Lord, no! I couldn't stand to watch her all the time. All that praying, and 'yes, Mother,' and 'no, Mother' . . ."

The discovery that Mrs. Miner was a multiple personality explained many things that had perplexed me. But it also raised a frightening possibility. I still believed that the woman I'd come to know and care for, the personality that called herself Eliza, was incapable of murder. But I couldn't vouch for Elizabeth, or Bitty, or whoever else might exist in that crowded mind. I believed Eliza had told me the truth about what she witnessed in Dr. Hauptfuhrer's office on the morning of the murder. But what if she hadn't been there the whole time? What if some other personality had emerged to kill him, returning at a later date to kill his daughter, too?

I told myself it was too fantastic an idea to consider seriously; that none of the reported cases had demonstrated such a radical schism in moral functioning. And yet, I couldn't help thinking of the most familiar double personality of them all: the infamous Dr. Jekyll and Mr. Hyde. There was a case of two minds in one body—and one of them had belonged to a killer. Of course, that was just fiction. Mr. Stevenson had been using the device to examine the dual nature that existed in us all. It couldn't happen in real life—or could it?

Leaning toward the professor, I asked, "Do you think we could get Elizabeth to speak with us?"

He frowned, and shook his head. "If she isn't aware of the others' existence, it could be very confusing for her," he murmured. "Possibly even harmful. Better to wait until a later session, when we've had a chance to lay the groundwork." He turned back to his subject. "Now Eliza, I want you to look at the clock and see that the hands are once again moving forward in time. Go with the hands, moving forward to the present. I'm going to count from ten to one; when I reach one, your eyes will open and you will be fully awake."

She was very tired when she came around, which the professor assured us both was a normal reaction. He confirmed for Eliza, when she asked, that she had achieved the trance state, then gave her a draught of opium and henbane and told her she should sleep for a while, promising that we would review the session with her when she woke up. I helped her off the sofa and guided her into her bedroom down the hall. The windowless chamber looked different to me now—no longer a plain but unremarkable bedroom, but instead a trap for a helpless young girl. Tamping down my revulsion, I turned on the bedside lamp to soften the gloom and folded down Eliza's covers.

She removed her shoes and lay on her side, fully clothed, on the bed. "Mother will be upset if I don't finish adding up the accounts," she said drowsily, tucking an arm under her pillow. "I promised I'd get it done today."

In my mind's eye I saw again the image of Mrs. Braun locking herself into her bedroom, so blinded by self-righteous anger over her husband's drinking that she couldn't see what was happening to her daughter on the other side of the door. "Don't worry," I said to Eliza; "you just get some rest. Leave your mother to me."

CHAPTER THIRTY-ONE

The professor was sitting at the kitchen table, writing on my pad when I emerged. Looking over his shoulder I saw the words, 'Multiple Successive, Partially Mutually Cognizant, One-way Amnestic??' scrawled across the top.

"You believe it, then," I said, dropping into the chair next to him.

"Of course I do. Don't you?"

I sighed. "I suppose I'm just finding it all a little hard to digest."

He laid down his pen. "Which part—the paternal rape, or the existence of a multiple consciousness?"

"Both." I shook my head. "I can't believe a father could use his own daughter so abominably."

"Fathers are just human beings, like the rest of us. And just as capable, unfortunately, of falling prey to their baser instincts."

"It must have been because of the disease," I insisted. "It must have destroyed his moral judgment."

"Possibly, but I wouldn't assume it. Many men without mental defect have been guilty of the same transgression."

I supposed that if Mr. Braun had been sufficiently intact physically to carry out the rape, it was likely he'd also still had enough will power to restrain himself, if he'd been so inclined. I couldn't excuse him so easily.

"It was a tragic breach of trust, to be sure," the professor was saying, "but perhaps we can turn it to some good, by using the case to shed light on the effects of such trauma on the mind. You and I have been given a rare opportunity, Doctor, to contribute a new case analysis to the multiple personality literature."

I was unable to respond with any enthusiasm, still coming to grips with the fact that the woman I'd thought I'd known so well was actually an amalgam of unfamiliar parts.

"I suppose you consider multiple consciousness a freakish event," he said, gazing at me over the tops of his spectacles.

"Isn't it?"

"I believe it's much closer to the norm than people realize. We're all made up of many parts, after all. Our need to get along in society may require our logical, reasoning self to dominate, but there's far more to us than that. We also have our creative selves, our intuitive selves, our dreaming selves. These are the parts that enlarge and enrich us. Who's to say that they're any less valid than the authoritarian Self we regularly present to the world?"

"They may be valid," I protested, "but they don't take on a life of their own. When we have a creative thought, we don't lose contact with our everyday reality."

"Don't we? What about the poet in his moment of inspiration, or the inventor achieving his breakthrough? What about any of us, when we're 'lost' in thought—or just doing one thing while thinking about another? The only difference between you and me and that woman in there, is that our selves are synthesized, while hers have broken apart."

"And you think the rape caused the break?"

"It could have been the rape, or the smaller, repeated assaults that led up to it, or even some earlier trauma from her childhood. You say her mother remarked that she's always been "strange", which suggests the initial split may have occurred when she was younger, with additional personalities emerging to handle the later crisis. As best as we've been able to determine, any physical blow or strong negative emotion can cause the disintegration to occur, if the neural constellations are so predisposed. The effect is similar to the cerebral shock induced in experiments on localization, where the frontal lobes are cut."

"So Eliza was twice cursed," I summed up: "in her father's flawed character, and in the predisposition of her mind."

"Although we could consider the dissociation a blessing in this case, don't you think?" he remarked. "It did, after all, give her a way to cope with unbearable conflict."

To cope perhaps, I thought, but not to conquer. The burden seemed merely to have been split three ways: between poor suffering Bitty, consigned to bear the shame of the rape; and dreamy-eyed Eliza, charged with preserving some shred of filial affection along with her love for Joy; and sour, reclusive Elizabeth, driven to please others even as she tried to destroy herself. I sighed and rubbed my eyes.

"What's troubling you?" the professor asked.

"It's just that—Eliza seems so normal. It's hard not to think of her as the 'real' Mrs. Miner. She's so much more alive than Elizabeth, so tender, and full of feeling."

"You make a good point. It's not uncommon for a new personality to be livelier and more attractive than the original; the original has, after all, lost a large portion of consciousness, leaving it necessarily constricted. But you mustn't forget that the secondary self, while often more appealing in respects, is almost always unsuited to the practical purposes of life."

This led me to a distressing thought. "Does that mean that Eliza will have to be . . . 'eliminated', for Mrs. Miner to be cured?"

He frowned. "First of all, you must understand that achieving a complete cure in these cases is difficult at best. Cures have been reported, of course—Boris Sidis's Hanna case, in particular, comes to mind—but just as often, all that can be achieved is a longer time between alternations, or perhaps elimination of the most troubling symptoms, regardless of the doctor's dedication. Even Professor James, despite his best efforts, was unable to unite the divided selves in the Ansel Bourne case.

"But to answer your question: where a cure has been effected, the selves have been able to merge and achieve a single, continuous memory that includes the experiences of each. This, I think, is what we must strive for in Mrs. Miner's case. Not the dominion of the personality you know as Eliza. Eliza, stripped of the defenses of skepticism and selfishness, would be helpless on her own."

Although I could see the sense in what he was saying, it distressed me to think of losing Eliza as I knew her. It was hard to appreciate, moreover, what qualities the disagreeable Elizabeth would bring to a united identity. "What about the personality of Elizabeth?" I asked him. "Would you consider her helpless, as well?"

He peered at me over his spectacles. "If you're asking me if I think she murdered the doctor and his daughter, I'm afraid I don't have the answer. We're in uncharted territory here. But it is at least theoretically possible that she did, without the others being aware."

"And if so? Would that be grounds for sending them all to prison?"

"It's a fascinating question isn't it? But you're getting ahead of yourself, Doctor. Nothing I've heard so far indicates that any of the personalities is guilty of murder."

Nothing he'd heard, perhaps; but he hadn't seen what I'd seen. "There's something I have to show you," I said. "I'll be right back." I returned to Eliza's bedroom to retrieve the sketchbook from the bedside table and brought it into the kitchen. "These are all Eliza's," I told him, flipping the pages until I came to the charcoal figure. "Except this one. She claims not to know where it came from."

He leaned over it, his eyes darting from one detail to another. "And you're concerned that this implicates Elizabeth in the murders," he said after a moment.

"Well, look at it," I said, thrusting my hand toward the bold line across the figure's neck.

He nodded thoughtfully. "It does strike me as something Elizabeth might have drawn, knowing what we do about her so far. But it doesn't necessarily depict someone else. It could just as well be a self-portrait. Remember, Elizabeth has no memory of what happened to her physical body during the rape, or of the pregnancy afterward. In a sense, her mental and physical lives have been severed. The line across the neck could be a subconscious recognition of that separation."

"What about the eyes? They're completely blind, with no pupils at all. Couldn't that represent a denial of the crimes?"

"It could. Or it could symbolize a more general disconnection from the world. Especially when taken together with the practically absent feet and hands. The figure appears to exist in a vacuum, ungrounded and out of contact with the physical reality that surrounds her."

I fervently hoped that he was right; but I didn't think we should count on it. "I suppose I ought to inform the police, if there's even a chance that Elizabeth is dangerous."

"You ought to do nothing of the kind!" he said quickly. "The only way to get to the truth is to keep her here, where we can work with her."

I couldn't help wondering if his eagerness to take advantage of a rare scientific opportunity might be clouding his judgment. As long as Mrs. Miner remained under 24-hour watch, however, with a guard right outside her door, I supposed it wouldn't hurt to remain silent just a little longer. "Do you really think we can? Get to the truth, I mean."

"I think we stand an excellent chance. But we'll have to work more intensively than usual, in light of the circumstances. I'd suggest we meet back here this afternoon, after the sedative has worn off, to set up a schedule. We might even attempt another session then, if she's amenable."

"So soon?"

"Seize the day, Doctor!" he exclaimed, with all the zeal of Teddy Roosevelt on the charge up Kettle Hill. He tore his notes off the pad and folded them into his pocket. "I can't wait to give my publisher the news; there hasn't been anything like this since Prince's analysis of the Beauchamp case! We're going to be famous, Doctor! Why don't you join Mr. Altman and me for lunch, and we can go over our terms?"

"Thank you, but no, I'm going to stay here. I'd like a word with Mrs. Braun."

"As you wish. I'll see you back here later then," he said, starting for the door. "Shall we say, 4:00? I gave her a strong draught; I doubt we'll be able to rouse her before then. And remember, Doctor—" He pressed an index finger to his lips. "Mum's the word!"

I let him out and closed the door behind him, listening to his cheerful whistle move down the stairs and out of the building. Then I returned to the front room and sat down, watching the hands on the cuckoo clock over the sofa and waiting for noon to arrive.

As soon as the clock announced the hour, I descended the stairs to the street and walked around to the shop entrance. Mrs. Braun was just hanging the "*CLOSED FOR LUNCH*" sign on the door. I gestured to her to let me in.

She cracked the door open. Her apron was heavily soiled, and her face drawn with fatigue. "What is it?"

"I need to talk to you."

"I was just about to have my lunch."

"I'm sorry, but this can't wait."

"Why," she asked wearily, "what's the matter now?"

"I need to talk to you about Eliza's illegitimate baby."

She stiffened. "There's nothing to talk about. All that's in the past, and best forgotten."

"I disagree. I've just been upstairs with Eliza and a colleague of mine, hypnotizing Eliza."

"Hypnotizing her! What gives you the right to—"

"We discovered something very disturbing," I continued, "that I think you ought to know about."

She closed her mouth, searching my face as if trying to guess what new calamity I was about to heap on her. Finally she stepped back and pulled the door open.

Once I'd entered she locked the door and led me through the counter hatch into the back. I took a seat at the table while she closed the back room door, hung her apron on the back, and sat down across from me.

"Have you ever wondered what became of the child?" I asked her.

"No," she answered flatly. "I put it from my mind the day we were rid of it, and I told Elizabeth to do the same."

"Yes, she told me you said that. Did it never occur to you that she could use a little sympathy?"

"Sympathy! The girl had the devil in her, getting pregnant at fifteen. She put us all to shame."

"The devil had nothing to do with it."

"I raised her to be a decent, God-fearing girl—and the minute my back was turned, she let a good-for-nothing delivery boy take advantage of her."

"Eliza didn't have time for secret trysts with delivery boys. She was too busy helping you mind the shop."

"Well she managed it, didn't she."

I leaned toward her over the table. "That isn't what happened. If you hadn't been so self-absorbed you might have seen what was really going on. Maybe you could even have prevented it."

"What are you talking about?"

"Elizabeth didn't become pregnant as the result of some adolescent tryst. She was raped. By her own father. By your *husband*, Mrs. Braun."

She stared at me, her body completely still.

"He used to go into her room after coming home late from the saloon, and get into bed with her. And one night, when you had locked him out and were holed up feeling sorry for yourself, he raped her." I didn't care if I caused her pain; in fact I wanted to cause her pain. I wanted her to be the one to suffer, for a change. "Your husband is the father of Elizabeth's illegitimate child."

I waited for her gasp of horror, the blanching of her flaccid cheeks. But her stony gaze didn't flicker.

I sank back in my chair. "Oh my God . . ." I said slowly. "You knew."

The corners of her mouth twitched.

"You knew what he was doing and you didn't stop him!"

"There was nothing I could do," she muttered.

"You could have reported him to the authorities!" I said, fairly gasping for air.

"What would they have done? No one tells a man how to act in his own home."

"Well you could have at least left him, and taken Elizabeth with you."

"Really? And how would we have survived? I put all my savings into the shop when we married. I had no money to start over."

I gaped at her, chilled by her dry-eyed resignation. "So you just stood by and let it happen?"

"She liked the attention," she said sullenly. "She was always playing up to him, looking for favors, getting him to interfere when I tried to discipline her."

"She wanted love and affection! She didn't ask to be raped!"

"It wasn't my fault he couldn't keep his filthy hands off of her."

"She was your child; it was your duty to take care of her."

"What about me?" she hissed. "Who was taking care of *me*? I had to do everything—he couldn't even lift the meat off the hooks without my help. My clothes stank of beef fat no matter how much soda I put in the wash. He was useless! And still he expected me to treat him like a king, when he couldn't even tie his own shoes."

"He couldn't help the clumsiness, at least; it was because he was ill—"

"He disgusted me! I couldn't stand him pawing at me, breathing on me with his liquor breath."

"So you locked him out, and let Elizabeth suffer the consequences."

Her eyes narrowed. "I was a good wife, so long as he held up his end of the bargain. And he did, at first. But after Elizabeth was born, things started to change. He didn't care about the business anymore. I was working myself to the bone while he went from saloon to saloon, spending the money I'd earned. And still, he always wanted it when he got home. He wouldn't take no for an answer. I had no choice but to lock him out."

"Leaving Elizabeth to fend for herself. And then when she bore his child, you acted as though it had never happened—as if you could make it all just disappear!"

"I did make it disappear. Everything was fine, until you showed up."

"Nothing disappeared," I said between clenched teeth. "You only made things worse for Elizabeth, by making her believe it was her fault. And it didn't stop there. Her daughter is carrying the same disorder that killed your husband. She doesn't know it yet, but she's going to have to be told."

"No," she said quickly. "No one must know."

"If she isn't told, she may bear children of her own who will suffer the same fate."

"No one must know," she said more firmly.

I shook my head. "It's not up to you anymore."

She regarded me for several long moments with an inscrutable expression. Getting up from the table without a word, she walked to the door and took the dirty apron back down from its peg. She tied it on, locked the door with a key she took from the top of the moulding, and slipped the key into her apron pocket.

"What," I scoffed, "do you think you can keep me locked in here forever?"

Smiling grimly, she reached for a long, narrow canvas bag that was hanging with the mops and brooms near the door. Loosening the drawstring at the top, she reached in and pulled out the largest butcher knife I'd ever seen. She turned to face me, letting the bag drop to the floor. "I told you to leave us alone. I tried to scare you away. I did everything I could, but you wouldn't stop poking your nose into our affairs. You just . . . wouldn't . . . stop."

I stood up, knocking back my chair. The blade was longer than her forearm, with a finely-honed edge that glinted under the ceiling light; but it was the glazed look in her eyes that was making my blood run cold. "Mrs. Braun, please, put down the knife. I know you're upset, but I'm sure we can talk about this rationally . . ."

"I should have just left you in there, and let you freeze to death."

I looked up from the blade as her meaning struck home; she was talking about the meat locker. My mind raced back to the morning she'd "discovered" me, remembering how uncharacteristically solicitous she'd been, wrapping me in blankets and bringing me tea. "You pushed me in!" I said aloud, as the pieces fell together. "You wanted me to think it was Eliza, that she was crazy enough to commit murder. . ."

"If you were smart you would have walked away. But instead you stayed, and caused even more trouble. All you've done since you met Elizabeth is cause us trouble. I knew something was wrong the minute she got back from church that day; I could tell from the way she was acting. And then the Doctor called that afternoon to tell me she had contacted him, asking about her baby. Thank God I knew to follow her the next morning. He was going to show her the child's records. I heard him say so, through the door."

"It was you," I breathed. "You went into the doctor's office, while Eliza was waiting in the examining room."

"He promised me when he took the baby that he'd never tell a soul. He swore there would be no records. But he lied."

The emptiness in her eyes was making my skin crawl. Could she really have killed Dr. Hauptfuhrer? It hardly seemed possible; she was just a gray-haired old woman, while the doctor had been a man in his prime. Then again, I thought, looking back at the knife, she was an old woman who'd spent the better part of her life butchering meat, and was no doubt extremely proficient with a blade . . . .

I had to get out of there. But she was standing between me and the locked door, and the key was in her pocket.

"She would have found the child," she was saying, "and told her everything, and soon the whole world would have known. She didn't care who found out what she'd done. She'd flaunt her sin for everyone to see."

There was no point in telling her that "Eliza" herself didn't know her daughter's true origins; she'd never believe me, even if she did give me the time to explain. "What if people did find out?" I said instead, edging behind the chair. "What happened wasn't her fault."

"Do you think that matters?" she sneered. "Do you think people would keep coming to the shop, giving us their business, if they knew what had gone on here?"

"So you murdered him."

"I'm not afraid to do the Lord's work when he calls. I've done it before, and I'll do it again."

I froze with my hands on the chair back. "What do you mean, you've done it before?"

She nodded slyly. "You think I'm a bad mother. But I was the one who stopped it, in the end. When I heard him coming up the stairs that night, bellowing like a bull in rut, I prayed with all my might. I told the Lord I couldn't stand it anymore, not for one more day, not for one more minute; and the Lord heard me and told me what to do. The Lord gave me the strength of five men so I could make sure he'd never lay his shame on anyone again."

I could picture it all too clearly: Mr. Braun climbing unsteadily to the top of the stairs, his legs rendered clumsy by drink and chorea, and Mrs. Braun greeting him at the top with a determined, dry-eyed push . . . .

"The sins of the father were cleansed by the blood of the father," she was saying, staring through me with glassy eyes. "And when the Lord called on me to keep the doctor from revealing what should remain hidden, I didn't hesitate to answer. The door to his office was unlocked, and the sword was waiting on his desk. With the Lord's help, I did what I had to do."

"And the doctor's daughter?" I asked hoarsely. "Did the Lord tell you to kill her too?"

"I had no choice. She was going to give the doctor's old records to the police. I didn't know how much her father had guessed. But I was merciful. I told her I'd found a letter that her father had written to my daughter, that made it clear why Elizabeth had killed him. She was soft, like you, and trusting. She let me right in. She was so eager to read what I'd brought her she didn't even see the knife coming."

I knew how unmoored Miss Hauptfuhrer had been by her father's senseless death. She'd been desperate for answers, just as Simon had said. I wasn't surprised she'd let the old woman in. I could imagine her rushing into the waiting room and dropping into the nearest chair, unfolding the letter in trembling anticipation—while Mrs. Braun followed with her canvas bag concealed in the folds of her skirt. "But how did you get out of your building, without being seen?"

"I kept a set of keys when we were forced to sell the building next door." She smiled bitterly. "A memento of happier times. All I had to do was wait for the bakery to open, then come down from the roof and in through the side door in the hall, wearing an old coat and hat, and slip out with the early customers." Her face hardened. "It should have ended there. But you wouldn't let it, would you?" She pushed back her sleeves, revealing forearms that were sinewy from years of hoisting carcasses and hacking through bone. "Which is why now, I have to kill you, too." Gripping the knife handle in both hands, she lifted the blade over her shoulder like a baseball bat and started around the table toward me.

I lifted the chair and shuffled backward, holding it up between us, wondering if the side door to the hallway was unlocked and if I could reach it before she caught up to me. I was still paralyzed with indecision when she sprang toward me, lighter and faster on her feet than I would have thought possible. I jerked back as the blade swung toward my neck, feeling a breeze as it missed my throat by inches. An image of Miss Hauptfuhrer's severed head flashed through my mind, unleashing a flood of adrenaline. As she swung again I pushed the chair up and out from my chest, stiffening my arms to block the blow. The tip of the blade caught in one of the chair legs, sticking for a moment before she managed to yank it free.

We froze, breathing hard, each waiting for the other's next move. "Eliza's asleep, sedated. If you kill me, they'll know it was you," I panted.

She shook her head. "No they won't. Not if they don't find your body." Tightening her grip on the knife handle, she lunged toward me with a guttural cry.

This time as she swung the knife, I hurled the chair right at it. It hit her hands—hard enough to make her grunt, but not enough to make her drop the knife. I now stood defenseless before her. I looked frantically around for something to use as a weapon, and spotted a broom hanging near the door. I started toward it, rushing up one side of the table as Mrs. Braun ran up the other with her breath rattling in her throat, arriving an instant before she did. I pulled the broom from its peg and whirled around just as she was readying the knife for another swing. I leveled the broom handle, drew it back and jabbed it squarely into her stomach.

She keeled forward with a little popping sound, her mouth pumping like a fish, clutching her stomach with her forearms. The knife was still in her hand. Changing my grip on the broomstick, I pulled it around and swung at the side of her head, striking her hard on the temple. She sank to the floor, dropping the knife as she fell.

I scooped the knife up and stepped back, brandishing it in front of me; but the fight seemed to have gone out of her. Keeping her in my sights, I grabbed a spool of heavy twine from the shelf above the chopping block. She offered no resistance as I bound her hands and feet, or when I removed the key from her pocket. When I tried to lift her up from the floor onto one of the chairs, however, she suddenly raised her bound wrists and raked my face with her nails. "You!" she hissed, livid with rage, spraying spittle into the air. "Why did you have to come along and ruin everything?"

I rocked back, pressing my hand against my forehead where her nails had dug the deepest. "I didn't ruin anything," I said, knowing at last that it was true.

I left her on the floor, using the last of the twine to tie her hands to the radiator, then went out the side door to summon the guard upstairs. I only made it up half a flight before my legs collapsed and I sank onto a stair tread, thinking of what Mrs. Braun had planned to do to me. I wanted to hate her, pure and simple, for all the harm she'd caused. And yet I knew that in her twisted mind, she'd believed she had no choice. With no one to turn to and nowhere to go for help, she'd taken the only path she thought open to her. Her desperate actions had left a trail of innocent victims in their wake; but I supposed that she, too, had been a victim in a way.

Pushing myself to my feet, I climbed to the top of the stairs and shouted to the officer in the hall. He followed me back down to the shop, where Mrs. Braun was now slumped against the radiator, staring blindly ahead of her. When I'd told the officer everything I intended to tell him, he used the shop phone to call for a patrol wagon, while I went upstairs to check on Eliza.

She was sleeping peacefully, with her mouth ajar and her hand tucked under her cheek. I leaned against the door frame, watching the covers rise and fall with her breath. The nightmare was over. Against all odds, and my own self-doubts, I'd managed to get to the truth. Eliza would go free.

I crossed to the bed and sat down beside her. There would be trials ahead, to be sure; but at least she wouldn't be alone in her suffering any longer. I didn't know how or when I'd reveal to her the full extent of her daughter's illness. But I believed that, when the time came, she would be able to cope with it. Because Olivia wasn't the "Joy" Eliza had yearned for. Joy was an idea fixed in time, a symbol embodying an event in Elizabeth's past, just as Conrad embodied an event in mine. Joy and Conrad had been real; they had had real places in our lives. But that place was behind us. It was time for us both to let them go, and move on.

I gently stroked back a strand of hair that had fallen across her eyes. I had helped Eliza, by listening to her as no one had listened before, and allowing her to reveal her terrible secret. But she had helped me, as well—by trusting me, and forcing me to trust myself. I might be imperfect, and a woman, but I'd never again let someone else tell me what to believe, about myself or anyone else. I lifted my head, inhaling the scent of baking bread from the building next door. For the first time in weeks, it felt good to be alive.

I heard the gong of a police wagon making its way down the avenue in our direction. I waited until I could hear policemen's voices in the stairwell, then tucked the coverlet more securely around Elizabeth's shoulders and went downstairs to join them.

CHAPTER THIRTY-TWO

A half hour later I was on the sidewalk outside the shop beside Detective Maloney, watching two officers load Mrs. Braun into the wagon.

"So it looks like we were both wrong," the detective remarked. He had arrived right behind the patrolmen, and had heard enough from Mrs. Braun during questioning to arrest her for the murder of both Hauptfuhrers.

"We were both right, too," I said, "about some things."

He turned to me with a frown. "What made you so sure Mrs. Miner didn't do it?"

"I wasn't sure, not absolutely," I confessed. "But sometimes you just have to trust your intuition."

He snorted. "That's a hell of a way to operate."

"It's better than the alternative," I replied.

The officers closed the rear door of the patrol wagon and climbed into the front.

"I still don't get why she did it," Maloney said, gazing pensively at the wagon's rear window. "If I hadn't seen the knife and the traces of blood and hair inside the bag, I wouldn't have believed it, confession or no."

I murmured noncommittally as the wagon pulled away from the curb.

"I'm guessing it had something to do with that list you showed me," he went on, "and wanting to keep the illegitimate granddaughter a secret. But something's missing. Plenty of people have babies out of wedlock. It's not worth killing over."

Still I said nothing, watching the wagon disappear through the intersection.

"You aren't going to tell me, are you," he said finally.

I turned to him. "You got the murderer, Detective. That's all you care about, isn't it?"

He grimaced—a bit ruefully, I thought.

"Two cases closed in one day," I said, shaking my head in admiration. "Maybe you should take a holiday, to celebrate."

"There are plenty more files where those came from," he said.

"And I'll sleep sounder knowing they're in your capable hands." I smiled at him. "I mean that."

Two pink dots bloomed in his gaunt cheeks. Stuffing his memorandum book into his coat pocket, he strode to the front of the police car and resolutely turned the crank until the engine sputtered to life.

"You take care, now, Detective," I called as he climbed into the driver's seat. "And if I can ever help you with anything else, don't hesitate to call!"

It might have been just a trick of the light; but I could have sworn I saw his lips twitch in the faintest of smiles. Then the car jerked into gear, and with a cloud of exhaust, he was gone.

I glanced up at the sky, leaden now with snow clouds, realizing for the first time how truly bone-weary I was. My stomach was empty, my arms ached, and the scratches on my forehead were throbbing. I decided to go home for a meal and quick nap. Eliza had been in a very deep sleep when I last checked in on her, and according to the professor, wasn't likely to awaken until late afternoon. Detective Maloney had left an officer behind to guard the premises, until a team could arrive in the morning to conduct a thorough search. I'd asked him not to tell Eliza about her mother's arrest, on the off chance she awoke before my return, and had left her a note saying I'd be back at 4:00 to explain everything.

I pulled up my collar, and had just started down the block when I heard a shout. I turned to see Simon's man trotting toward me from the other side of the street.

"Say, Miss, what was all that about?" he asked, gesturing toward the departed vehicles.

"I'm afraid Mr. Shaw is going to have to find you another job," I told him. "Mrs. Miner is innocent. They just arrested the real murderer."

"You mean the old lady?" he asked in disbelief. "That's why they took her away?"

"She's confessed to both murders. Do you think you could find Mr. Shaw and let him know?"

He whistled. "I'll go straightaway. Is there anything else you want me to tell him?"

Was there anything else I'd like to tell Simon? My mind suddenly swam with answers. I'd like to tell him thank you, so very, very much; and that I was sorry for mistrusting him, yet again. Only now that I knew for certain that my suspicions had been unfounded, could I fully appreciate how generous he'd been with his influence and his time, how gracious for agreeing to help me despite my mistreatment of him in the past. But how many times could I expect him to forgive me? And what, after all, was the point in trying to fix things? Now that Eliza was exonerated, there was no need for Simon and me to have any further contact. I doubted he'd want to continue seeing me on a purely social basis; he'd made it very clear that he respected neither me nor the world I represented. And even if he did, it wouldn't work. I fit into his world as awkwardly as he fit into mine. The thought of never seeing him again was as deflating as a piece of glass in one of Papa's tires—but that was the only outcome I could reasonably forsee.

"Just . . . tell him goodbye for me, will you?" I said finally.

"Will do, Miss."

I started wearily down the street.

"Say, Miss!" he called after me.

I turned.

"Did those boys come to see you about the window?"

"What boys?"

He muttered something under his breath. "Mr. Shaw won't be happy; they were supposed to take care of it right away."

"Take care of what?"

"He had a few of his lads keeping an eye on you. Seems they didn't see you come home the other night, and thought something might have been amiss. Or one of the boys thought he saw you, but the others disagreed. I didn't get the whole story; all I know is they took it into their heads to settle the matter by looking into your bedroom window, to see if you were there."

I slowly let out my breath.

"When they couldn't make anything out in the dark, they decided to sneak inside for a closer look, only they couldn't manage the locks. Mr. Shaw got suspicious when he heard about an attempted break-in on your street; seems the older boy has some experience with a jimmy. Anyway, when they finally confessed he told them they'd have to pay for the damage they'd caused out of the money they'd earned at the bakery. That was yesterday. He won't be happy to hear they haven't been to see you."

I remembered the three young boys who'd left the courthouse with Simon on the day of Eliza's arraignment, 'sentenced' to work in a bakery. "Do you mean to say the boys have been following me around all this time?"

He scratched his head. "Mr. Shaw had to do something with them, I guess. There wasn't enough steady work at the bakery."

"You wouldn't happen to know if they were following me the night I was locked in the—that is, the night your brother left his watch early, would you?"

"Why yes, Miss, that's why Mr. Shaw came by the next morning, looking for you. He said the boys told him you'd gone in the night before and never come out."

So that's why Simon wouldn't admit he'd been asking for me that morning; he hadn't wanted me to know he was having me followed—at least not until the boys' overzealousness had made disclosure necessary. I felt a warm flush at the realization he'd been concerned about my safety, followed by an even stronger pang of guilt for having doubted him. "Please tell Mr. Shaw to forget about the window," I told Mr. Kearney. "I'd rather the boys spent their money on something else."

The watchman shook his head doubtfully. "If I know him, he won't let it rest until they've made things right. But I'll tell him what you said."

I thanked him, and wished him well, then turned and continued unsteadily down the street toward home.

"GOOD LORD, WHAT happened to you!" Katie cried, staring at my forehead, as I hung my coat on the rack.

"Is it that bad?" I gingerly touched the scratches.

She put down the tea tray she was carrying and pulled me into the sitting room. "Let's have a look," she said, lowering me into a chair.

I winced as she pulled away my bangs, which seemed to be stuck to my skin.

"I'll get the iodine," she said tersely.

I dropped my head back on the overstuffed chair, listening to the tick of the hall clock and the soft hiss of the radiator, feeling as secure as a silkworm in its cocoon. The nightmare was over. My patient was innocent, my career unscathed. Life could return to normal. There was only one last thing that needed to be addressed. One dark cloud left, on an otherwise clear horizon. The question of Olivia Fiske.

I sighed, rolling my head against the chairback. Was it really the best thing to tell her about her disease, and by extension, about her true parentage? I'd felt compelled to reveal this information before, to establish that Lucille had a motive for murder; but now that I knew Lucille was innocent, the case for disclosure wasn't so clear. Despite Dr. Huntington's urging, it was hard for me to see how in Olivia's case, putting a name to her affliction would be better than leaving her in the dark. Would such knowledge be worth the revelation, at this late date, that she was adopted? And what if she were to learn that she was the product of an incestuous rape? How would that improve the quality of the time she had left?

The repercussions of disclosure for me and my family could still be substantial. Lucille might not have murdered the doctor; but she'd probably been delighted to learn that somebody else had. She'd been willing to go to other extremes, including threats and bribes, to keep Olivia's condition a secret. For that's what she'd been trying to hide all the time, I realized now; not that she'd committed a murder, but that her daughter was ill. I had no doubt that revealing Olivia's condition now could still unleash a storm of reprisals.

If I just kept my discoveries to myself, on the other hand, Olivia could have her grand wedding, and a chance to experience life as a married woman, free of her parents' control. Lucille and Charles would get the title for their daughter they so coveted, while the Earl would receive the millions he needed to restore his family seat—and in appreciation, might even help improve terms for American trade. It was entirely possible, I told myself, that I'd underestimated the Earl's affection for Olivia; for all I knew, he and his family might be more supportive than Olivia's own parents, once Olivia's condition worsened and the Fiskes started viewing their daughter as "damaged goods". Of course there was still the issue of offspring—but at the rate things were going with the Earl, it might be a year or more before he finally proposed and the Fiskes could organize the wedding of the century. By then Olivia's symptoms would be so evident, at least to her, that she would likely decide on her own to delay a pregnancy, until such time as they improved.

I was tired of swimming against the tide; I didn't want to be the bearer of tragic news, or to upset the order of things. Besides, there were my parents to consider. If I stayed silent relations between them and the Fiskes could remain cordial. Father would get his funding, while Mother could continue to bask in the warmth of Lucille's patronage. Was it fair to put their interests in jeopardy, when I couldn't even be sure that Olivia would want to know what I had intended to force upon her?

Katie rustled back into the room with the iodine and blotting papers. "Keep your head back," she said, unscrewing the cap.

I closed my eyes as she dabbed the applicator over the cuts.

"Are you going to tell me what happened?" she asked.

I opened my eyes to see her frowning down at me in concern.

"You know I won't tell your father," she added.

Dear, dear Katie; I would have kissed her big rough hand, if I hadn't known it would embarrass her. As long as I could remember, she'd been ready to help and protect me, even when it meant hiding things I was too afraid to reveal. And there had been plenty of those. But I was done hiding things from my father. "Thank you, Katie. But I'm going to tell him myself."

"You are?" she asked in surprise, pausing in her ministrations.

"Just as soon as you finish fixing me up. I don't want to shock him any more than I have to."

She studied my face for a moment. "Well, good for you," she said finally. The annunciator box buzzed in the pantry. She straightened abruptly. "Dear Lord, your mother's tea! I forgot all about it." She scooped up the iodine and crumpled blotting papers and hurried out of the room.

I got up and crossed to the mirror over the fireplace to examine my wounds. My bangs had dried to one side, exposing three new stripes just below my old scar, tinted yellow by the iodine. I gazed curiously at my reflection, rather liking the way my face looked without a fringe of hair obscuring it, even with the stripes. Perhaps it was only in contrast to the brightness of the wounds, but the old scar hardly seemed noticeable. On a whim I pulled up my bangs and side tresses as Fleurette had done, and liked the effect even more. Perhaps later, when the scratches had healed, I'd try wearing it that way. I released the bangs and started pulling them across my forehead to hide the scratches from Father, but caught myself. I dropped my hand, letting the bangs stay where they fell.

As usual, the door to Father's study was closed. I knocked and pushed it open, not waiting for him to respond.

He was sitting at his desk, surrounded by scattered type-written pages. "Oh, it's you," he said, glancing up. "I thought it was Mary." He ran a harried hand through his hair. "Buzz her again for me, will you?" He returned his attention to the papers.

I stepped inside the door and pressed the annunciator button for the kitchen. I'd never felt comfortable in Father's study. The light from the lamp on the desk didn't reach the dark green walls, leaving the windowless room in perpetual gloom. Furnished for neither comfort nor conversation, it contained nothing but a desk and some free-standing bookshelves at one end, and a reading chaise with a small table at the other. The items on this table never changed: a whiskey bottle and single glass, three worn volumes of poetry, and a shell from some unidentified beach that had been there for as long as I could remember.

"I need to speak with you," I said, closing the door behind me.

"Not right now," he replied, without lifting his head; "I've got to get this contract ready for Charles' signature before he leaves on the afternoon train."

"I'm afraid it can't wait."

He looked up. "What happened to your forehead?" he asked, putting down his pen.

I needed to sit. I crossed to the reading chaise and perched on it sideways to face him. "Father," I said, clasping my hands in my lap, "I haven't been entirely honest with you."

I told him all of it, the good and the bad, hoping that despite his certain anger he'd be able to appreciate what I'd managed to accomplish. For although I no longer needed his approval, I would have liked to have his respect. He listened in silence, an increasing ruddiness of complexion the only clue to his feelings.

"You've been hiding all this from your mother and me?" he said, when I was done.

"I was afraid you wouldn't allow me to help Eliza if I told you."

"Help her! As far as I can see, all you did was endanger everyone involved, including yourself."

I silently released my breath, abandoning further hope. I was ready to accept, once and for all, that nothing I ever did or said would change the way he felt about me. It made me sad—but it also set me free. "I'm sorry I've been a disappointment to you," I said, in all sincerity. "I've tried to make it up to you. Conrad's death, I mean. But of course I never could."

"What are you talking about?" he said. "Don't be absurd."

"I don't blame you for loving him more, Papa. He was your only son. Your hope for the future."

His eyes flared in surprise. "You can't believe I loved your brother more than you."

"It's all right, truly. I understand."

He stared at me for a moment, his cheek muscles twitching. Then he dropped his head into his hands with a sigh.

"Papa? Are you all right?"

When he lifted his head again, his eyes were bright with pain. "If I had a favorite, God help me, it was you."

I stared at him, uncomprehending. "But you wouldn't even talk to me after it happened; you were so angry . . ."

"Not with you! I was angry at myself, for letting it happen." He ran his hand through his hair. "After the accident all I could think of was what I would do if something happened to you, too. I couldn't have stood it, you see. Losing both of you."

I shook my head. "It was my fault he climbed up the tree."

"Don't be ridiculous; you were just a child. I was the one who told the workers to leave the ladder out, so that we could string up the electric lights for the party. Those damned lights! Your mother was worried they'd damage the tree, but I insisted on having them. I was determined to show them off."

My mind was spinning, trying to mesh what he was saying with my own memory of events. I could never forget the way he had looked at me as he staggered toward me from Conrad's still body, or his painful grip on my arms. "You asked me what he was doing in the tree," I said hoarsely. "You shook me, and asked me why he was up there."

"I was in shock. I couldn't understand what had happened. I wasn't angry at you."

I thought of the days after the accident, long days running into nights when I'd wandered about the house like a ghost, unseen and unheard. "Then why wouldn't you talk to me?"

His hands dropped limply into his lap. "I was . . ." He hesitated, searching for the right word. ". . . afraid."

"Of what?"

He shook his head in frustration. "Afraid to love you. Afraid that I'd fail you, as I had failed Conrad. All I could think about from that day on was something terrible happening to you. I was determined to do everything in my power to keep you safe. That's all I've ever wanted, really. For you to be safe."

Maybe it was true, I thought, remembering the times he'd been angriest—when I'd gotten lost in the Ramble, and the park police had had to come looking for me; or when he'd caught me sliding down the second floor banister; or, for that matter, when he'd found out about me and Simon. Maybe anger could be the expression of a crippled sort of love. But that didn't make it any less painful.

I'd always assumed my father knew best. But as poor Bitty had learned, and as I was beginning to understand, fathers were no more perfect than the rest of us, and no more deserving of unquestioning trust. My father had never assaulted me; but he had failed me in his own way, by letting his fears blind him to my pain, and causing me to lose trust in myself. "You can't keep someone completely safe," I said. "You only keep them from living, if you try."

He laughed weakly. "That's just what your Aunt Margaret said. That Christmas Eve in Tuxedo Park, when she gave you a new sled, do you remember? You were determined to ride it down Slaughterhouse Hill the next day with the older children. Margaret caught me trying to pry off the runner, when everyone else had gone to bed."

"You didn't," I said in disbelief.

"She said I couldn't keep you safe from everything, and that I'd only drive us both crazy. She said I was trying to play God. I remember asking her, why not? God hadn't done such a good job of things, after all."

"But the sled was fine; I did go down Slaughterhouse Hill, on Christmas day."

"I know. I realized she was right, and left the sled alone. I did try, you see. To let you take your lumps and learn for yourself. But you were always following your nose into places it didn't belong. I admired that about you, but I feared it, too. I feared where it might lead you. That's why I had to let the Shaw boy go, when I realized you'd grown attached to him. I couldn't stand by and watch you ruin your life with a single bad decision."

"So you saved me, by turning two blameless people out on the street? That wasn't right."

"Life isn't always right or fair," he said sharply. "You do what you have to do to get to the end of the day, and then you start over again, day after day, until you die." He drew in a breath, then added, "Besides, he deserved it."

"But he didn't. I told you, the kitchen maid lied about his boasting. He never talked about me to anyone."

"He should have known better than to encourage you, all the same."

"You mean because he was poor Irish, and that made him less worthy than me."

"Don't be simple. It has nothing to do with worth. It has to do with sharing the same values, and wanting the same things from life."

"And what is it that I want from life? Tell me, Father. Because I don't remember you ever asking."

His eyes narrowed. "I was only looking out for your best interests."

I supposed he believed that. But I saw now that his real motivation had been fear—fear of losing me, fear of losing control. "Don't you think I should have had some say in the matter? I wasn't exactly a child anymore."

He grimaced, as though I was being deliberately obtuse. "Say what you will, I still believe I did the right thing."

Of course he did. Because it was easier that way, easier than admitting that he'd let fear run his life, and mine. I was about to say as much, when I suddenly realized that I'd been guilty of exactly the same thing, when I'd tried to talk myself out of telling Olivia she had Huntington's Chorea. I'd told myself that I would be acting in her best interest, when it was really fear that was persuading me—fear of what might happen to me and mine, should her long-sought engagement be called off.

If I forced myself to look beyond my fear, the truth was obvious. I had no right to withhold the facts from Olivia. She needed to know the nature of her illness, so that she could make sense of what was happening to her, and plan what remained of her life. It wasn't for me to decide what was best for another human being—just as it wasn't for my father to decide for me. The truth was hard, but it belonged to Olivia, to do with as she chose. I glanced at the whiskey bottle on the table, and the well-used glass beside it. Perhaps Father would never be able to escape his fears. But that was his life. I had my own life to live. "Which train is the Fiskes' car coupled to?" I asked.

"The Twentieth Century Limited. Why?"

"What times does it leave?"

"Two forty-five," he said, opening his watch case. "Good God; I have to be there in forty minutes. Where the devil is Mary? I need her to tell Maurice to bring the car around."

I stood. "I'm going with you to the station."

"What for?" he asked, gathering his documents.

"I have to tell Olivia about her illness."

His head jerked up. "You'll do no such thing."

"She needs to know," I said, "before she gets locked into an engagement that she'll find difficult to break."

"Then let her own physicians advise her. It's none of your concern."

"Lucille won't give them a chance. She's managed to convince even Olivia that her symptoms are the product of nervous exhaustion. By the time her illness becomes too pronounced to ignore, it will be too late."

"Too late for what? The Earl isn't going to abandon her once they're married. He's a man of honor. He'll do his duty by her."

"What if he doesn't find out until they've had a child, and the child inherits the disease? Can you guarantee that he'll love and care for that child? Because Olivia may not be around to do it."

"Of course I can't guarantee it."

"Exactly. Neither of us can know what's going to happen. That's why Olivia has to be the one to decide. Her parents are doing everything in their power to force her into this marriage. She deserves to know how much it might cost her. If she still wants to go through with the wedding once she's aware of the risks, I'll be the first to congratulate her."

He leaned toward me over the desk. "The Fiskes are not people to trifle with."

"I'm sorry about your funding, Father. Really I am."

"I'm not talking about the funding!" he cried. "I'm talking about what will happen to you and your mother if you interfere with this wedding! You'll be shunned, socially and professionally."

"Believe me, if there were any way I could avoid it in good conscience, I would."

"Just stay quiet then, and let them go! No one will fault you for it."

I gazed at his stricken face, a face I knew better than my own, after years of tracking it for every nuance of emotion. It would only take a few words from me to smooth the creases from that forehead, and ease the tightness from that jaw. Just a few words, and equilibrium could be restored. "I'm sorry," I said, "but I can't."

For the first time I could remember, my father was at a loss for words. "Well, if you've made up your mind," he finally muttered, "I suppose I can't stop you."

"No," I assured him, "you can't."

"But that doesn't mean I have to help you. I'm leaving for the station now, and I'm not taking you with me."

"Oh for heaven's sake, Father, don't be childish."

He stood. "I'm not going to help you destroy your future."

"You know I'll just call for a cab."

"It's snowing outside, in case you hadn't noticed. You'll be waiting for hours."

"I'll take the El, then."

"You and every one else in the city who's trying to get somewhere in this storm."

"Then take me with you! Please, Father; you must know in your heart that I'm doing the right thing."

"I don't know any such thing," he said, stuffing the papers into his document case. "You're clearly distraught. You ought to be resting, not racing about town. I'm sure that once you've had time to think about it, you'll come to your senses."

I planted myself in front of his desk. "I am not distraught. I'm thinking more clearly than I ever have."

He stepped around me, starting for the door. "I'm going to tell Katie to keep an eye on you until I get back. I trust you won't do anything to upset her." He reached the door and pulled it open. Katie and Mary were on the other side, with their ears lowered to the keyhole. They straightened, looking sheepish.

"Well," Father said acidly, "as you two have no doubt heard, Mrs. Summerford and I are going down to the Grand Central Station to see the Fiskes off. Mary, go tell Maurice to bring the car around at once." She dashed off down the hall. "Katie, please call Dr. Mason and ask him to come look at Genevieve's wound while we're gone. And Katie—I'll ask you to see that she stays in bed until he gets here. She doesn't seem to appreciate the condition she's in."

My mother was waiting in the downstairs hallway. "All set?" she asked Father as we came down the stairs.

"All set," he answered, starting for the coat rack.

She gasped when she spotted me behind him. "Genna, what happened to your head?"

"She walked into a street lamp," Father answered as he pulled on his coat.

"I was attacked," I told her, "but fortunately I wasn't really hurt. It's just a scratch."

"Attacked!" she cried, hurrying toward me. "By whom? When did this happen?"

"Come along, Evelyn," my father said, taking her arm. "She told you, it's nothing serious. She can give you all the details when we get back. We have to go now, or we'll miss the Fiskes."

"But . . . shouldn't we call the doctor?"

"Katie's taking care of it," Father said. "If we leave now, we may even be back before he arrives."

"I don't need a doctor," I told my mother. "What I need is a ride to the station."

"But your head . . ." she looked from me to my father in bewilderment.

"*I'm* a doctor," I reminded her, "And I'm telling you my head is fine."

"But don't you want to rest?"

"Of course she does," Father said, tugging on my mother's arm. "Now really, dear; Lucille will be terribly disappointed if you're not there to see her off."

"You're sure you'll be all right?" Mother asked me, as he dragged her toward the door.

"Yes Mother, I'll be fine," I said with a sigh of defeat. "You go on with Papa."

I watched from the open door as they descended the snow-covered steps and climbed into the waiting motorcar. Father sat in the passenger seat, staring straight ahead, refusing to look my way. Maurice revved the engine and with a grinding of gears the car pulled away from the curb.

CHAPTER THIRTY-THREE

Damn!" I said, slapping the doorframe as the motorcar zigzagged down the slippery street. I climbed down the steps and squinted after it, shielding my eyes with my hand. The snow already lay several inches deep. I watched a delivery wagon spin its wheels at the intersection, considering my limited options. Traffic would be a mess everywhere. The subway would be fastest, but the nearest station was all the way across the park, on Broadway. The Elevated, I decided, was my best bet.

I ran back inside for my hat and coat—and found Katie standing by the coat rack, clutching my coat against her chest.

I came to a halt, seeing the muscles working beneath her soft cheeks. "Katie," I said slowly, "I have to do this, whether Father wants me to or not."

She thrust the coat toward me. "And I'd be disappointed if you didn't."

I grabbed both her and the coat in a tight hug. "Thank you, Katie; I promise I won't let Father blame you for this."

"Now don't you worry about me. The day I can't manage your father will be the day I'm ready to meet my Maker. You just get down to that station, and do what you have to do."

I pulled on my coat and hat, yanked the front door open, and stopped short. Simon was climbing the front steps, his bare head covered with snow and his breath making steam clouds in the frigid air. "What are you doing here?" I blurted out, wishing my heart wouldn't jump so at the sight of him. "Didn't you get my message?"

"Oh I got it, all right," he said with a scowl, coming to a stop a hand's breadth away.

I stepped back involuntarily into the entry.

He stamped his feet and came through after me, planting himself on the entry tiles. "Your patient's off the hook, so you've no more need of me. Is that about right?"

"I thought you'd be glad to hear that the case had been solved," I said, flustered by his reaction.

"Don't you think you could have told me in person?"

I felt my face heating up. "I wasn't sure you'd want to see me, after . . . after what I accused you of last time."

"A simple apology never occurred to you, I suppose."

I bit my lip. What excuse could I possibly have given him for failing to trust him a second time? Except, perhaps, that not being able to trust myself, I hadn't known when it was safe to trust someone else . . . .

He sighed and shook his head, loosing a sprinkle of melted snow. "You know, I'm really not as complicated as you seem to think. I say what I mean, I keep a promise, and I don't hold a grudge. Maybe if you could get that through your thick skull, we could stop having these little misunderstandings."

"That would be nice,' I said hoarsely.

"That's settled, then." He smiled—the same, crooked smile that used to make me go weak in the knees. It still had that effect, I was discovering.

Katie nudged my arm. I ignored her.

"So, tell me now," he said.

"Tell you what?" I asked, for my mind seemed to have suddenly gone blank.

"About Mrs. Braun. Donnie wasn't very clear on the details."

"Oh yes, of course; well I'm afraid it's a rather long and complicated story."

"I've got time."

Katie yanked on my arm.

"*What?*" I asked, turning to her in exasperation.

"The train," she urged, jerking her head toward the door.

"Oh my Lord;" I swiveled back toward Simon. "I'm sorry, I can't—I just—" I shrugged helplessly. "I have to go." I lunged around him, out the door and down the steps, my leather soles slipping over the tamped snow. He must surely think me the rudest, most ungrateful person alive I thought miserably, as I started running toward the El. I could only hope that someday, somewhere, I'd have a chance to make it up to him . . . .

"What train?"

I nearly tripped over my own feet as Simon materialized on the sidewalk beside me. Struggling to regain my footing, I answered, "Olivia's train. I have to talk to her before she goes."

He loped along beside me, taking one stride for every two of mine. "You mean you're going to tell her?"

"If I can get there in time."

"What about your father?"

"I just talked to him, and told him everything," I panted.

"What did he say?"

We had arrived at the intersection. I bent to catch my breath, propping my hands on my knees as I waited for a break in the traffic. "It doesn't matter what he said," I gasped.

He bent beside me to look into my face. "It doesn't?"

I shook my head.

He slowly straightened. "Well I'll be damned."

The policeman who should have been directing traffic was untangling two teams halfway up the block, leaving the intersection jammed with jockeying vehicles and making it impossible to cross.

"What time does the train leave?" Simon asked.

"Two forty-five," I said, peering across the street in frustration.

He checked his watch. "You're not going to make it."

"Maybe not, but I have to try."

He looked past me, up the Avenue. "I've got an idea." He started backing up the sidewalk. "You wait here, all right? I'll be back in a minute."

I squinted in the direction he was headed, wondering what on earth he had in mind. Barring a dirigible, I couldn't imagine anything he might bring back that could get me to the station on time.

"All right?" he asked again, still backing over the sidewalk.

"All right," I finally agreed.

He turned and sprinted up the avenue, disappearing through a curtain of snow.

I was still standing on the corner several minutes later, chastising myself for ever agreeing to wait, when he suddenly reappeared—riding a large gray horse down the middle of the two-way street, drawing a cacophony of horn blasts from the vehicles scrambling to avoid him. As he drew closer I realized that the horse was my mother's mare, Cleo. Simon threaded her between a cab and a coal truck and pulled up in front of me.

"Oliver let you take Cleo?" I asked in astonishment. I would have thought our persnickety new groom would be immune to Simon's charms.

"Oliver didn't have a choice," he said, extending his hand.

I grabbed it, and he pulled me up behind him. There were of course no pommels on the back of the saddle for a female passenger, so I had no choice but to throw my leg across. I hadn't ridden astride since I was a child. I'd forgotten how good it felt.

Simon turned the mare toward the Park, nearly losing me as he swerved to avoid two women stepping off the curb. "You'd better hold on," he called over his shoulder. I clasped my arms around his waist. The horse had been a brilliant idea; by traveling most of the way through the park, we would have a good chance of making it to the station on time.

As we trotted down Fifth Avenue to the park entrance I felt the peace that comes from clarity of purpose, along with a heightening of all my senses. I was acutely aware of Simon's sturdy body beneath his cashmere coat, and the intricate workings of his muscles as he maneuvered the mare. I breathed in deeply, inhaling damp wool and horse sweat and gasoline exhaust. I'd never felt more alive. After entering the park we hugged the wall for a few blocks before veering right to follow the East Drive behind the museum. As I lifted my chin to look up ahead the wind caught my hat and lifted it into the air. I grabbed for it but was too slow. I turned and watched it tumble through the air behind me, letting it go, welcoming the sting of snow against my face.

Except for an occasional sleigh the park was empty, eerily silent under the densely falling snow. I rested my head against Simon's back, lulled by the muffled thud of hooves on crystalline powder, watching trees and lampposts sail past in a gossamer blur. We cantered quietly uphill, past the mysterious hieroglyphs on the Egyptian Obelisk, now half filled with snow, and back down the opposite slope. Familiar paths and rocks and benches had all disappeared, swallowed up by the storm, leaving nothing but the steady beat of Simon's heart beneath my cheek to anchor me.

A few minutes later the twin peaks of the Childrens' Dairy came into view. I opened my coat to check my watch. "It's almost two-thirty," I shouted. "Do you think we can ask her to go any faster?"

He bent forward and murmured into Cleo's twitching ears. "Hold on!" he cried.

Shortening the reins, he rose up in the saddle and let out a blood-curdling whoop. To my astonishment, Cleo responded like a Belmont Park thoroughbred. If Simon hadn't warned me I would have landed in the snow; as it was, it took every thigh muscle I had to keep my seat as she galloped the last quarter mile past the frozen pond and shot out of the Park's southeast corner.

A slow but steady stream of vehicles was moving in both directions along Fifth Avenue. I closed my eyes as Simon threaded Cleo through the gaps between them and continued crosstown, weaving crazily through the slithering traffic before turning sharply right a few moments later. When I dared open my eyes again we were riding along the rim of a vast depression, which I recognized as the excavation for New York Central's new electrified train yard. As if on cue a steam engine shot out of the Park Avenue tunnel behind us and roared up alongside, billowing smoke and steam into the snow-spangled air. It raced us for several minutes, appearing to accelerate as it approached the arch-roofed train shed. Just when a collision seemed imminent, a brakeman appeared at the rear of the engine and released the coupling device. The engine broke away onto a side track while the rest of the cars rolled into the shed with a screech of iron brakes.

We cantered on to the end of the yard and cut hard left toward the terminal. I checked my watch again; we were nearly there, with 13 minutes to spare. I was about to crow into Simon's ear that we'd made it, when we turned onto Vanderbilt Avenue and came to an abrupt halt.

A dense wall of carriages and cabs jammed the avenue all the way to the station entrance. Horses were snorting and police whistles blaring as coachmen and drivers jockeyed for position, trying to get their passengers to the trains on time. Barricades had been set up along the station side to create a reserved lane, making the congestion even worse on the rest of the roadway. As Simon eased Cleo between the wheels of two carriages I saw a policeman pull one of the barricades aside to allow an elegant Victoria into the lane. Simon must have seen it too, for he angled Cleo toward the opening, following in the Victoria's wake.

The policeman saw him coming and waved him away, swinging the barricade back into place. "Hold on," Simon shouted to me over his shoulder. I locked my fingers around his waist and pressed my face against his back, certain I didn't want to see what was coming. Simon shifted higher on Cleo's neck, pulling me with him as the mare surged forward and jumped the barricade, landing cleanly on the other side.

When I opened my eyes the officer was running beside us, hanging onto Simon's leg. Simon shook him off and continued around the Victoria, down the lane, toward the station entrance. The officer blasted on his whistle, attracting the attention of another policeman up ahead.

Simon pulled Cleo up short. "You'd better get off here."

"What about you?"

"Don't worry about me; just get to that train."

I slid to the ground, but hesitated with my hand on Cleo's flank.

"Go on!" he urged.

As the policemen converged on Simon I turned and ran through the army of colored porters unloading luggage in the station's vestibule, into the crowded waiting room. There I stopped to get my bearings. Rows of high-backed benches filled the middle of the spacious room, illuminated by thousands of tiny electric lights that shone down from the beamed ceiling. Beyond the benches, to my left, a series of arched doorways led to the platforms. I hurried across the marble floor, past the ticket booth and through the first door into the train shed.

I emerged onto a narrow concourse that ran perpendicular to the platforms and was separated from them by an ornate iron fence. Watery daylight filtered down from huge glass panels in the vaulted iron roof, landing on the dozen or so trains that were standing on the tracks. Some of these trains were attached to electric locomotives, suggesting they served the shorter suburban routes; while others had no engines at all, having been uncoupled from their dirtier steam locomotives in the yard. But none of them appeared to be outbound. Glancing up at the clock over the concourse, I saw that it was now 2:38. I had exactly seven minutes to find Olivia and deliver my news.

Sprinting to the far end of the concourse, I pushed through the door to the annex—and into another world. Here the air was thick with smoke and cinders and the hiss of escaping steam. Hulking long-haul engines puffed restlessly at the end of each platform, shooting up plumes of flame-riddled steam as they waited for their overnight runs to begin. Passengers and porters and deliverymen were scurrying over the platforms behind them, pouring in from the station and its adjoining cabstand, hauling trunks and boxes and small children into the waiting cars.

I ran along the iron fence, straining to read each destination board as it came into view. Finally, at the last gate, I saw it: the 2:45 train to Chicago, stopping in Harmon and Albany before continuing west to Buffalo, and beyond. The plush red carpet that was rolled out over the platform confirmed that it was the Twentieth Century Limited, famous as much for its style as for its speed. Unlike the rest of the train, which was a dull Pullman green, the last car was painted the scarlet red of the Fiskes' livery. The gold insignia over the rear observation deck conclusively identified it as Charles Fiske's private car. I'd made it, I thought, pausing at the gate to squeeze the stitch in my side.

My relief at locating the train in time was immediately dampened by the sight of what appeared to be a farewell party in progress, directly across from the Fiskes' car. Several dozen well-wishers stood around a table laden with food and flowers, sipping champagne from tulip-shaped glasses. Footmen in scarlet livery tended the table, while a trio of violinists played sedately a few feet away. Leave it to Lucille to turn a simple train departure into an occasion for public display, I thought in dismay.

I started down the platform as I searched for Olivia's face among the assembly, holding my ground with difficulty as a constant stream of porters and valets and florists flowed past me toward cars further up the track. I spotted Charles at one end of the refreshment table, conversing with my parents, and Lucille at the other, surrounded by a coterie of her peers. Olivia, however, was nowhere to be seen.

A train whistle shrieked from the engine end of the platform, startling the company, drawing laughter and light applause. Charles and Lucille glanced at each other across the table. Lucille turned and motioned to the musicians as Charles put down his glass and started toward the car.

One of the violinists rubbed loudly on his strings, as Olivia and the Earl emerged from the rear of the car onto the observation deck. They smiled and waved from the rail while their well-wishers raised their glasses and cried, "Here, here," and "bon voyage". A moment later Charles appeared behind them, laying a hand on each of their shoulders and smiling, close-lipped, at the crowd.

I couldn't imagine a worse time to approach Olivia. But I would have no other opportunity. As the violin launched into a merry jig, I started toward the front end of the car, hoping to slip in undetected and make my way inside to the rear. At just that moment, however, Lucille glanced down the platform and saw me. She put down her champagne glass and hurried over, intercepting me before I was halfway across the platform.

"Miss Summerford," she said, clamping her hand on my arm. "What a surprise to see you here." Her back was to the party, concealing both of our faces from view.

"I've come to see Olivia," I said. "I have to speak to her before she goes."

Her fingers dug into my arm. "Why?" she asked in a rasping whisper. "Why are you doing this?"

"I have to tell her," I said, trying to pull my arm away. "She deserves to know."

"We had an understanding," she hissed. "I've held up my end of the bargain. What more do you want?"

Yanking in earnest, I pulled my arm free and struck out again across the platform.

"Billings!" Lucille shouted toward two footmen carrying a crate of champagne into the front compartment. "Don't let that woman onto the train!"

One of the footmen turned and, dropping his end of the crate in astonishment, started after me. I changed course and ran down the edge of the platform toward the observation deck; but I was no match for the footman's long legs. I was vaguely aware of the violins breaking off their jig as he grabbed the back of my coat and pulled me away from the car. As if it were happening to someone else I heard the gasps of the guests, and saw Olivia and the Earl drawing back from the rail. It flashed across my mind that this moment would forever define me; that the little place I'd occupied in society—that place I'd so often disparaged but which now seemed so achingly simple and familiar—would no longer exist for me after today. I felt a sharp pang of regret—followed by a grim determination that my actions would not be in vain.

CHAPTER THIRTY-FOUR

The footman stopped in the middle of the platform to get a better grip on my coat. The minute I felt him plant his feet, I stepped back and butted the back of my head against his face. He grunted in pain, but didn't let go. I stomped my heel on the top of his foot, but still his grip didn't loosen.

"Take your hands off of her!" my father shouted.

Twisting sideways, I saw two figures in motion among the otherwise paralyzed onlookers—my father, who had launched himself from the refreshment table and was rapidly covering the distance between us; and Simon, who had apparently shed both Cleo and his pursuers, and was now running full tilt from the gate down the platform.

"You, sir," barked my father, reaching me first; "release my daughter this instant!"

The footman looked helplessly toward Lucille, awaiting further instructions. Before she could respond, Simon flew across the platform and hurled himself at the footman's back. "Let her go," he growled, lifting him off the floor in a bear hug that made my own teeth rattle.

"Behind you!" Father called.

Managing to pull partially free, I looked over my shoulder in time to see the second footman run up behind Simon, brandishing a champagne bottle. Simon swiveled around, yanking his captive with him, who was forced to release his hold on me. The man with the bottle swerved to stay behind him. Before he could get close enough to crack the bottle over Simon's head, my father stepped into his path and delivered a solid punch to his nose, then caught him as he slumped to his knees with his nose cupped in his hand.

My father looked up, chest heaving, and met my gaze. He scanned my face, as if recording every detail. "Well, go on," he said finally, tipping his head toward the train car. "We can take care of these two for a while longer."

"That won't be necessary," said Mr. Fiske, striding up beside him. He pointed to the broken champagne crate, sitting in a puddle of bubbles near the front end of the car. "Jeffers, Billings; clean up that mess. Put whatever's left in the kitchen." Simon let go of Billings, as my father lifted Jeffers to his feet. The footmen scuttled off to do as they'd been told.

Charles turned his frown on me. "Now, Dr. Summerford, perhaps you could tell me what's going on."

Drawing a deep breath, I said loudly enough for Olivia to hear, "I have something extremely important to discuss with your daughter before she leaves."

Charles looked quizzically at Lucille, then back at me. "In that case, I'd suggest we all go on board where we can have some privacy."

"But Charles, there's no time!" Lucille protested.

"We'll make time," he said. My mother had crossed the platform sometime during the melee and was now standing beside my father. Charles turned to them both. "Evelyn? Hugh? Would you care to join us?"

"But the train's about to leave!" Lucille cried, clutching his arm.

He turned to her, searching her face. "Then we'll tell the conductor to wait," he said firmly.

She colored, and dropped her hand. Charles gestured us all toward the train.

I followed my parents up the steps, across the observation deck and into the lounge, where Olivia and the Earl were waiting. We all stood in strained silence as Charles strode to the porters' box to call up ahead and ask that the train be delayed. This struck me as an impossible request; the daily race to Chicago between the Twentieth Century Limited and the Pennsylvania Special was legendary, and I couldn't imagine any New York Central conductor worth his salt allowing his train to depart a second off schedule. But when Charles returned he said, "All right, we've got ten minutes. Why don't we all sit down."

This feat—even more than the stained glass and sumptuous velvets and inlaid woods that appointed the luxurious car—drove home to me what a powerful family I'd chosen to meddle with. But I couldn't turn back now. "I'd prefer to speak with Olivia alone," I said.

Everyone turned toward Olivia. She quickly shook her head, looking beseechingly at her father.

"It seems that Olivia would like you to share what you have to say with all of us," Charles said. "So please, everyone, take a seat. We don't have much time."

Olivia and the Earl sank stiffly onto a blue velvet settee in front of the fireplace. Charles guided Lucille toward the two tufted seats across from them, while my parents claimed two carved chairs on either side. I pulled a low stool from beside the fireplace and positioned it in front of Olivia, not so close as to crowd her, but near enough to create at least an illusion of privacy.

I sat down and gazed into her wide eyes, trying to shut everything else out of awareness. "I'm sorry, Olivia, I never meant to cause such a stir. But there's something you need to know, before you make any plans for your future."

"Why are you doing this?" Lucille demanded from behind me, her voice vibrating with frustration. "What on earth do you hope to gain?"

"I'm telling you this, Olivia," I continued without turning, "because I would want someone to tell me, if I were in your shoes."

Olivia looked from her mother to me uncertainly. "What is it you want me to know?"

Lucille jumped to her feet before I could answer. "I'm sorry," she said, stepping around me, "but I simply cannot allow this to continue. Miss Summerford, I must insist that you leave immediately."

"I'd like to hear what she has to say, if you don't mind," Charles interrupted.

"She doesn't have anything to say! It's all lies; she's been trying to blackmail me! I've gone along with it, to keep her from causing us trouble while the Earl is here, but now she's gone too far."

I gaped at her in astonishment.

"Is this true?" Charles asked me.

"No! Mrs. Fiske, you know it isn't! All I'm trying to do is tell Olivia what Dr. Hauptfuhrer wanted you to tell her."

"Hauptfuhrer?" Charles broke in. "What's he got to do with this?"

The question appeared to be entirely sincere. I could only conclude that Lucille had told him nothing about Hauptfuhrer's suspicions concerning Olivia's disease. As I'd suspected, she had taken matters entirely into her own hands.

"Lucille?" Charles prompted.

She didn't answer.

The train whistle shrieked again. "Olivia," I continued, turning back to her, "you have a disorder called Huntington's Chorea. That's what Dr. Hauptfuhrer told your mother. He believed that you, and the Earl, should know."

"What? That's absurd!" said Lucille, managing to sound shocked.

"The disorder can affect speech and coordination," I pressed on, hating to blurt it out this way, but having no other choice. "That's why you've been having trouble with things like dancing and skating, and holding onto things. The symptoms come on gradually and slowly progress."

I thought I saw recognition flit through her eyes. She looked up at her mother. "Is it true?"

"Of course it's not; you mustn't listen to her. Charles, really . . ."

"Dr. Summerford," Charles said, "if you have any basis for making these claims, I want to hear it now."

"Olivia," I said, "do you remember the gentleman at the skating party, who asked if you'd lost your glove?"

Her doe eyes grew even wider in surprise. "Yes, I do."

"That was Dr. George Huntington. The disorder is named after him. He knows more about it than anyone. And he's nearly certain that you have it."

"*Nearly* certain," Charles repeated.

"He'd like to administer some tests," I went on, "to confirm its existence absolutely and determine the extent of its progression; but based on what he saw that night, and his own considerable experience, he's confident of the diagnosis."

"Don't you think you should have talked to us about arranging these tests," Charles asked grimly, "instead of rushing in here and alarming my daughter prematurely?"

I hesitated, glancing at the Earl. "I couldn't."

"Why not?"

From the corner of my eye I saw my father squirm in his chair. "Because if she does have it, there's a strong chance that she'll pass it on to her children."

There was dead silence in the car, as the meaning of my words sank in.

"This is preposterous!" Lucille cried. "There's nothing wrong with my daughter but a little fatigue." She swept her arm toward Olivia. "Look at her; she's perfect!"

Olivia cringed back against the settee as we all turned to stare at her. With her cheeks faintly flushed and her dark hair framing the smooth oval of her face, she did indeed look very beautiful. I felt a rush of anger toward Lucille for putting her through this unnecessary charade. "You don't help her by denying it," I said. "What she needs now is your understanding and support."

"Just a minute, Dr. Summerford," Charles broke in, looking like a lawyer who'd just spied a loophole. "I believe you've missed one very important point. You've suggested that this disease is passed from parent to child. But I can assure you that neither Lucille nor I have suffered any of the symptoms that you describe."

I was astonished to hear him say it. Though I'd been compelled to reveal the disease's hereditary nature, I doubted that either Olivia or anyone else in the room had grasped the full implications. I could think of no reason for Charles to highlight them now. I should have thought that he and Lucille would prefer to inform Olivia that she was adopted in private.

Perhaps he'd misunderstood, believing I'd meant that the disease was "passed" by a germ. "I meant that the illness is passed in the parents' genes," I said, elaborating as delicately as possible. "Olivia didn't 'catch' this disorder; she was born with it."

"I understand. But it's not in our genes, so we couldn't have passed it to her," Charles insisted.

It seemed he was going to force me to make blatantly clear what I had tried to leave implicit. "It's not in your genes," I said slowly, glancing at Olivia, "but it was, apparently, in the genes of her natural father."

"Her 'natural father'?" he repeated with a frown. "What the devil are you talking about?"

The breath suddenly stopped in my throat, as understanding dawned. Charles didn't know. His wife had never told him that his daughter was adopted. He turned to Lucille in bewilderment.

Her eyes were huge in her chalk white face. "I had to give you a child," she whispered. "I couldn't have one of my own; they told me after the last miscarriage it would kill me if I got pregnant again. So I found another way."

"What are you saying?" Charles demanded. "You did get pregnant again; you were pregnant with Olivia."

Her gaze dropped to the floor. "I wasn't. I only pretended to be, until the baby was ready."

He stared at her bowed head, clearly at a loss for words.

She looked up. "Dr. Hauptfuhrer found her for me," she went on, her eyes clinging to him as though he might disappear at any moment. "I told him it had to be a little girl; a little dark-haired girl, just like you'd always wanted . . ."

"You adopted a child," he said slowly, "and didn't tell me?"

"What difference does it make?" she asked, her voice growing shrill. "You're her father! You raised her! She's a Fiske, through and through."

He closed his eyes, releasing a long breath.

"There was nothing wrong with the parents," she insisted, glaring at me. "She's making it all up! You mustn't believe her!"

"There's no point in denying it," I said. "I can prove that you went to see Dr. Hauptfuhrer four days before his death; your name was written in his appointment book. Why would he ask to see you, if it wasn't to warn you that your daughter might be afflicted?"

"*I* asked to see *him*, because the Earl's barristers were pestering me for a copy of Olivia's birth certificate!" she retorted, her eyes ablaze. "I had to be sure that the original records had been properly prepared. He never said anything about any disease!"

Her response was too quick and plausible to be a fabrication. I stared at her in stunned silence, as the puzzle pieces in my mind broke apart and started reassembling into a brand new picture. When Dr. Hauptfuhrer hadn't been able to get confirmation from Dr. Huntington that Eliza had chorea, he must have lost his nerve. He'd never told Lucille he suspected her daughter was afflicted. The secret that Lucille had been holding so close—a secret that, I realized now, would be even worse in her mind than a daughter's fatal illness—was that she'd been unable to bear Charles a child. No wonder she'd thought I was blackmailing her; when I'd found out that Olivia was adopted, I'd unwittingly uncovered her Achilles' heel.

The Earl was getting to his feet. "Are you saying you gave my agents a false certificate?" he demanded of Lucille.

She threw him a withering look. "What do you care? Our money is real enough. That's all that's ever mattered to you, isn't it?"

He thrust out his narrow chest. "I understand that you are distraught, Madam, and apt to say things you don't mean. I cannot, however, overlook the significance of this disturbing information. The Branard line is a venerable one; each generation has a duty to ensure that those who follow are of sound body and mind. Under the circumstances—and despite the deep distress it causes me—I must regretfully decline to pursue a union with your daughter. I'm sure I need not remind you that, in light of the false documentation you submitted, any oral understanding to the contrary would never hold up in a court of law."

He turned and bowed to Olivia. "My sincerest regrets, my dear. Please be assured that you may count on my complete discretion. If I can be of any assistance to you in the future, I hope you won't hesitate to let me know." He glanced in my direction. For a ghastly moment, I thought he was going to thank me; but he only tipped his head and, donning his derby, started for the forward compartments.

"Where do you think you're going?" Lucille snapped.

He paused, turning back to her. "I am instructing my valet to remove my luggage from the train."

"Get back here this instant!" she demanded. "Nothing has changed."

My mother stood and crossed over to her. "Lucille, no," she said quietly, laying a hand on her arm. "This isn't the way."

Lucille's eyes ranged over her face. She opened her mouth as if to protest—but something in my mother's expression seemed to stop her. Her shoulders drooped, and she sagged against my mother's bracing arm.

With a curt bow, the Earl was gone. Mother guided Lucille toward a divan beneath one of the windows, which left Olivia by herself on the settee. The girl was clearly in a state of shock. Father and I glanced at each other; but it wasn't our place to offer comfort. Just when I thought I could stand it no longer, an audible whimper escaped her, breaking Charles from his trance.

He got up from his chair and went over to sit beside her. "Forget about him," he said, awkwardly patting her knee. "You're better off without him, if you ask me. I never could stand the man."

"I don't care about the Earl," she said, shaking her head; "but . . . what's going to become of me? Oh, Father, I—" She stopped, looking stricken.

He wrapped an arm around her and pulled her against him. "I have always been your father, Olivia, and I always will be. That's one thing you need never question." He looked up at me. "All right, Doctor," he said, already taking charge; "tell me how we're going to beat this thing. Money, as I'm sure you're aware, is no object."

"Well, there are things we can do to ameliorate her symptoms," I said slowly, "and to make her more comfortable as the condition progresses. But—there is no cure, as of yet."

Olivia's hand rose to her throat.

"Then I'll find one," Charles said, squeezing her shoulders more tightly, barely missing a beat. "Hugh," he asked my father, "what's the name of that fellow you think so much of, at the medical lab?"

"Tim Murdoch?" Father replied.

"That's the one." Charles turned toward the forward compartments. "Billings!" he shouted, "Tell them to uncouple the car; we're staying here!" He turned back to Father. "Call Murdoch and tell him to meet us first thing tomorrow at the lab. We'll need to get hold of this Huntington fellow too; Genevieve, do you know where he can be reached?"

"He's in town right now, staying at the Fifth Avenue Hotel." I wasn't about to discourage him. Perhaps science alone hadn't yet been able to come up with a cure; but science, money and love together? It was a powerful combination.

I stayed for a few more minutes, listening to my mother croon to Lucille on the divan, and Father and Charles lay out their plan of attack. My part here, however, was done. If anyone had more questions for me later, I would answer them. But I thought we'd all had enough truth for one day.

Leaving the car as I had come in, I found the guests still clustered on the platform, no doubt hoping for more grist for the gossip mill. Their eager buzz of conversation came to a stop as I climbed down the steps from the observation deck. I paused at the bottom, chilled by their predatory stares.

Suddenly Simon materialized beside me, offering his elbow. "It's a little stuffy in here, don't you think?" he murmured. "Why don't we get some fresh air."

I laid my hand gratefully on his arm and he escorted me across the platform. The gawking guests fell away at our approach—some of the younger women, I observed, regarding Simon with considerable interest. "Careful," I muttered under my breath, "they don't see too many like you."

The corner of his mouth twitched, but I noticed he wasn't looking back.

We continued through the gate, out of the annex and into the waiting room, stopping only when we had reached a quiet spot away from the streaming foot traffic. "So, how did she take it?" he finally asked me.

"You know, it's strange," I told him, "but I think she already knew, in a way. Just as Dr. Huntington suggested. Now at least she has a clearer idea of what it is she's up against. And I think her parents are going to stand by her."

He cocked his head, studying me. "And what about you?" he asked. "Are you all right?"

I considered his question carefully, putting it not only to my logical self, but to my other selves as well. "Yes," I answered, "I believe I am." Whatever came of my actions today, I had no regrets. I had done what my heart told me to—and that, I knew now, was the only authority that mattered.

Merging again with the flow of pedestrians we returned to the entrance at the far side of the room. "Where's Cleo?" I asked, peering through the open double doors of the entryway.

"Don't worry, she's fine. Paddy and Mike are watching out for her."

"Paddy and Mike?" I remembered the two red-faced policemen who'd been trying to dismount him just a short while ago. "You're on a first name basis already?"

He shrugged. "It turns out Mike has a cousin in need of a job—"

"—and you just happen to know of one that needs filling," I finished for him.

He smiled wryly. "Something like that."

We looked at each other in silence, neither of us seeming to know what else to say.

"Well, I suppose I ought to get Cleo back to the stable before Oliver pops a cork," he said finally.

"Yes, I suppose you should," I agreed, although I didn't want him to go. I had a terrible feeling that if we said goodbye now, it might be for the last time.

"Can we offer you a lift?"

I laughed. "I think this time I'll take the El. I have to be at Eliza's by 4:00."

He nodded. "How is she faring?"

"She's been through a lot," I said simply. "But I think she's going to be all right."

He nodded again, and the awkward silence returned.

I reluctantly extended my hand. "Thank you, Simon. For everything."

He hesitated. Although he'd gotten better at concealing his emotions over the years, I thought I glimpsed something in his eyes that I recognized from long ago. "Goodbye, Genna," he said at last, shaking my hand. "You take care of yourself." He turned and started out through the vestibule.

I watched him go, feeling as if all the air in the room was leaving with him. So that was that. He would return to his life now, and I would return to mine. Which was exactly as it should be. All the reasons I'd told myself we shouldn't be together still held true.

And yet, as I watched him walk away, those reasons seemed to dissolve and float into the ether. I couldn't do it. I didn't care if it made sense, or what anyone else might think; I wasn't going to let him go a second time. "Simon, wait!"

He turned.

Running up to him, I grasped his face between both hands and kissed him full on the lips.

He pulled my hands away. "What are you doing?" he asked gruffly.

His lips were surprisingly, deliciously familiar. "Kissing you," I answered with my eyes still shut, savoring the taste of him.

"I got that part. But why?"

I opened my eyes reluctantly. It was a good question. Though I had no doubts at all about my feelings for Simon, I wasn't quite sure yet what I meant to do with them. It seemed as though I was only beginning to know myself; I didn't want to have to try to change into whatever he, or anyone else, wanted me to be.

"You don't want to start something you can't finish," he said, when I didn't answer.

I felt a moment of panic—but calmed again as I looked into his steady eyes. I didn't know if we could beat the odds, or if we'd only end up hating each other. But I was willing to find out. "I thought—I thought we might just take it one step at a time."

A smile played over his lips, as he recognized the advice he'd given me after the ball. "Well, I don't suppose I can argue with that, now can I?"

"I don't see how," I said, shaking my head.

His face grew serious. "So long as you understand that once I've decided a thing's worth having, I don't generally stop until it's mine."

I saw it for certain then, in his eyes: the same mix of desire and self-restraint that had melted me like caramel that night in the stable, so many moons ago. "Point taken," I said thickly.

He tipped his head. "I guess I'll be seeing you, then." He backed away, holding me in his sights with a fixity of expression that made my whole body flush, before he turned and walked out the door.

Grinning idiotically, I floated back to the east side of the station and out to the street, emerging to find that the storm hadn't abated at all. Snow had been falling faster than people or vehicles could trample it down, painting everything a pristine white. The whole world, I thought, looked brand new. I tilted back my head, letting the fat flakes melt on my skin, feeling the tensions of the past weeks release their hold.

I gazed up at the station's round turrets, which had replaced the original mansard towers only a few years before. Soon the whole building was going to be demolished so that a more modern terminal could replace it. Just as horse-drawn trains had been replaced by steam locomotives, and as electric engines were now replacing them. And it wasn't just the train station; the whole city was in perpetual flux, constantly shedding the old to bring in the new, thereby keeping itself alive.

I was going to do the same, I decided. Wasn't that what we were here for, after all? To reinvent ourselves each waking moment, through the risks we took and the choices we made? I thought of the parts of Elizabeth's fractured self, consigned to play the same limited roles day after day, unable to survive on their own precisely because of their inability to learn and adapt. But I was not so confined; I could choose not to listen to the external voice of authority, or to an echo from my past. It was up to me. This was my game, and I was going to play it from this moment on. I started up the sidewalk, crunching new snow under my shoes. At the intersection I turned to look back. My footprints were the only marks in the snow. Fresh tracks, leading to a new future. Whatever future I chose.

EPILOGUE

Sunday morning one week later I started out early for the church clinic. Four days of blazing sunshine had melted off the record snowfall dropped by the storm, leaving the sidewalks steam-cleaned. I walked east with a light step, enjoying the faint scent of beer that floated in the air, sweet and nutty as a hazelnut crisp. Every now and then I patted the bulge in my book bag where the proceeds from the sale of grandfather's stock were stashed, thinking of the office I was planning to lease. It was in a good location, offered for a reasonable rent, just ten blocks south of my home. I'd happened past the realtor's sign the day before, and had already contacted him by 'phone. We'd arranged to meet after class so that I could take a closer look.

The stock proceeds would be sufficient to cover the rental for quite some time, if necessary, until I had built up a paying clientele. Once that happened I planned to rent one of the residential apartments above the office as well, and set up housekeeping on my own. I hoped this moment would arrive sooner rather than later, as I had a hankering to be out on my own, and suspected that my parents would be too busy in the upcoming months to notice my absence. Father had agreed to oversee a research project for Charles Fiske testing the relative efficacy of chloral hydrate, valerian and belladonna in the treatment of Huntington's Chorea, using volunteers supplied by Dr. Huntington; while Mother would be taking over as head of the garden committee when Lucille traveled to Germany to investigate the merits of the promising antispasmodic, benzene.

Though the chances of discovering a cure in time to help Olivia were admittedly slim, I wasn't above praying for a miracle. And not only for Olivia; Professor Bogard and I could use all the help we could get, weaving a unified personality out of Elizabeth Miner's many selves. Though it was a daunting goal, Eliza was responding well in our sessions, and it was deeply rewarding to see her old wounds starting to heal. On a more mundane level, I was hoping that my work with Eliza would take my mind off of Simon. He'd left for Saratoga yesterday morning, to put things in order at his new stable, and despite the harrowing tenor of our last few encounters I was already longing for his return. I wasn't sure which had been more nerve-wracking: having him to lunch, and watching Father choke with the effort at being civil; or working at the Tammany winter fireworks festival a few days later, where I'd volunteered to serve cider and fried donuts—and where the way he'd kept looking at me from his perch on the fire truck had made me spill more cider than I served.

When I arrived at the parish hall, little Fiala Petrikova was waiting for me in the hallway. "It's finished," she said, holding up a stack of typewritten pages.

"All of it? Already?" I'd persuaded the professor to hire Fiala to type up our research papers, instead of his usual service. With lessons from the Reverend's secretary, and the use of an old church machine, she was quickly becoming a first-rate typist, making up in dedication what she still lacked in speed. In fact, I was having trouble churning out drafts quickly enough. Soon she'd be earning more from typing than she ever had from rolling cigars. I hoped that Milka would eventually follow in her big sister's footsteps, and that both girls could leave the cigar tenements behind.

I gave Fiala another installment, telling her I'd be by soon with more medicine for her mother, and descended the parish hall steps to the basement. I'd given myself ten extra minutes to straighten up the room and review my notes. But as I walked toward the wood partition, I could hear conversation and laughter on the other side. Rounding the partition's edge, I discovered that all of my patients had already arrived.

I shook my watch, holding it up to my ear. "Am I late? Or are you all early?"

"You're not late," said Anna. She was wearing green silk trousers under a wide-sleeved blouse, with a pair of red Chinese slippers. There were knitting needles in her hands, and a ball of yellow yarn at her feet.

"I see you've brought some busywork," I remarked, as I spread my notes across my desk.

"I thought I might as well do something useful, if we're going to have to listen to another of your boring lectures," she replied, drawing a titter from Margaret.

"If you don't like my lectures," I asked her curiously, "why are you here?"

She shrugged, looping the yarn around the tip of her needle. "I heard they were serving Shepherd's Pie for lunch."

This time, Margaret laughed outright. Dr. Cassell's warning against allowing patient alliances rang faintly in my mind. I felt disinclined to do anything about it, however, for I was frankly too pleased to hear Margaret laugh. "I think you might find today's lecture particularly relevant," I told them. "I'm going to talk about techniques for suppressing unhappy thoughts."

"Now there's an unhappy thought," murmured Anna.

I was about to protest that enough was enough, when I realized that all of them were either smiling in agreement, or trying not to. Something was going on here, something I ought to pay attention to. I sat back. "Doesn't anybody want to hear the lecture?"

They glanced at each other. "It's not that I don't want to hear what you have to say," Florence ventured.

"What is it, then?"

"It's just that I'd like a chance to talk about it more. Like what you said last time, about it being normal to feel angry. I've been wanting to ask . . ." She stopped, glancing at the others. "What about feeling glad? Is that all right?"

Before I could respond, Margaret rushed in to confess, "I was glad when my mother passed; I just couldn't help it. I hardly even recognized her, by the end."

Why, I wondered, after being so reticent to discuss their feelings in the past, were they so eager to share them here? Why should they find it easier to reveal to virtual strangers what they hadn't been able to talk about with their families and closest friends? I paused with my hand on my notes, struck by my own question. Perhaps, I thought, because it was only here, among others who'd been through a similar ordeal, that they felt safe enough to talk. I'd experienced it myself, the first time the group assembled, even though I was their leader and of necessity set apart: a sense of finding my level, of belonging here, though I'd hardly set eyes on the others before.

I slowly sat back, intrigued by the implications. I'd been taught that the patients' relentless attempts to communicate, whether in or out of class, were disruptive and should be discouraged; but maybe we doctors had been missing something, in our zeal to impart healing from above. Maybe the empathic response of the group was, in fact, the secret ingredient that made the class therapy work.

I remembered one of Cassell's patients, an "unreachable" veteran of the Cuban war, who'd spoken for the first time in seven years after one of his classmates, another soldier, hummed "A Hot Time in the Old Town Tonight" during their session. Cassell learned later that the tune had been the soldiers' battle song. This simple communication between two survivors had apparently accomplished what no amount of doctor's lecturing or cajoling could do. I was reminded of the billions of cells in a human body, each with its own unique purpose, acting together to make possible the miracle of life— or of the distinct 'parts' of our personalities that, as Professor Bogard had pointed out, when operating in harmony made us the richly complex people we were. Perhaps healing could be a group effort as well. Perhaps, if we worked together, the whole of our understanding could exceed that of our parts.

"Doctor?" said Anna.

I looked up. "Yes?"

"Aren't you going to start your lecture?"

I looked back at my notes. "No," I said slowly, "I don't think I am." I picked up the notes, lifted them over the side of my desk and dropped them into the trash can.

Her eyebrows arched in surprise. "What are we going to do, then?"

I got to my feet. "Well, we could start by moving our chairs into a circle," I said, carrying my chair in front of my desk. Several more eyebrows rose in question; but they all got up and did as I proposed.

"There, that's better." I sat down, and they followed suit. Here in this room, I decided, every woman would have a voice. Here we would learn from each other's insights, and build on each other's strengths. And who knew where that might lead? I suddenly envisioned a whole army of women, helping themselves as they helped each other, lifting each other like seedlings toward the sun.

"Now what?" Margaret asked.

I smiled. "To tell you the truth, I'm not really sure. What do you say we just play it by ear?"

Acknowledgments

Thanks first and foremost to my husband, Larry, whose support and encouragement have always gone far, far beyond the call of duty. Gisela Boelhouwer, Cuyler Holden, Ursula Overholt and Diane Decker were kind enough to read and respond to the work in progress. I am especially grateful to Phil Andryck and Catherine Clark for their valuable suggestions, and to my agent, Joe Veltre, whose belief in the book meant more to me than he knows.

Dr. Tetsuo Ashizawa generously shared his knowledge of early treatments for Huntington's Disease, while Dr. Jack Dunietz shared his library on dissociated personality—although any misrepresentation in the depiction of either illness is, of course, entirely my own. I feel a debt of gratitude as well to countless unsung writers of long ago, novelists and journalists alike, who captured their era in words and made it breathe for me a hundred years later.

Last but not least, I'd like to thank my sons, Chance and Tucker, for not burning the house down while I was otherwise engaged.

About the Author

Cuyler Overholt worked as a litigation attorney and freelance business writer before turning to fiction. Her interest in old New York was fanned by the reminiscences of her grandmother, whose life spanned over a century of the city's history. She lives with her husband, a psychologist, in the hills of Northwestern Connecticut, where she is currently working on her second novel. To contact her or to learn about upcoming books and events, visit her website at: www.cuyleroverholt.com.

Made in the USA
Middletown, DE
18 June 2015